KRISTINA VERBRUGGEN

ANNELISE
AND THE
PENDRAGONS

LIBERATION

Cover Design by Jamie Noble

Copyright © 2026 by Kristina Verbruggen

Library of Congress Control Number 2026908845

ISBN: 979-8-9955804-0-9

To the ones who make their own adventures...

Chapter 1: The Offer

Jimmy **was fidgeting** behind Annelise as she scratched a perfect circle into the ground around the two of them with the base of her staff. He had pulled his hood over his balding head, and his brown eyes flitted up and down the dark alley. He was acting as though he expected a Conciliar Warden to pop out of the stonework any minute. It was making her nervous. She tied off the circle with a draconic rune. The circle glowed bright blue. The air around them shimmered for a moment, then faded. With the ward up, they could now speak freely without fear of being overheard. With a flick of her wrist, her staff retracted, and her hand was empty.

She turned to face Jimmy. "You can relax now, Jimmy. We're warded. Now, will you tell me what this is all about?"

"You're sure you weren't followed?" He tugged at his collar and hood in an effort to conceal just a bit more of his face. This, however, was impossible as both his collar and hood were already stretched out as far as they could manage.

"I wasn't followed. Why did you want to meet?"

Jimmy took a breath and held it for a second. "You know, maybe this wasn't such a good idea." He turned to scamper down the alley.

Annelise grabbed his arm to stop him from slinking off into the city. "Look. You asked me to meet you here. I'm here. Tell me what this is about."

Jimmy peered up and down the alley again. "Someone's been asking about you."

Annelise frowned, the back of her neck starting to prickle. "Who?"

"I don't know, two guys."

"Are they cops?"

"I don't know for sure. They weren't flashing badges or anything, but when I went to get my money from Frankie, I heard them asking him about that missing VanTover painting he fenced for you last month. They were very persistent. They could be undercovers. And..." Jimmy paused. "They were Pendragons."

Annelise swore. "Are you sure?"

Jimmy nodded. "Golden eyes and everything."

They were almost certainly magical law enforcement then. There was hardly a member of the Pendragon clan out there who wasn't some high-ranking member of the government or working for the government in some capacity. And now these two were after her. The walls of the alley seemed much narrower than they were only minutes ago.

She ran a hand through her hair. "Did Frankie tell them anything about the VanTover?"

"I don't know, I don't think so." He glanced over his shoulder. "That's all I know, really," He looked at Annelise. "So what do you plan to do?"

Annelise shook her head. "I'm not sure yet." A car passed by the entrance to the alley. Annelise's eyes flitted in that direction, waiting and watching to see if the car would reappear. It did not.

Jimmy continued. "If you postpone the meeting with this client, you're going to spook him. And I don't know about you, but I could use the money. I couldn't collect from Frankie today." He fretted with his collar.

Annelise frowned. It would be risky to go through with the deal. On the other hand, she had spent months curating the artwork she was creating for this buyer. He was willing to pay a handsome amount for it. She hated to see all the work that went into putting this deal together go to waste, as well as the thousands of dollars they could make from it.

Annelise looked at Jimmy, weighing his words, tone, and body language. He looked genuinely stressed. She knew firsthand what it was to fall on hard times. When she had, Jimmy had offered her a way out. Now it was her chance to repay the favor.

"Let's still go through with the deal tomorrow. Send the buyer confirmation of the meeting. I will just have to do my best to close the deal as quickly and discreetly as possible. Also, maybe ask the buyer if he would consent to me casting a few wards around his house for extra protection."

Jimmy nodded. "I'm sure that can be arranged. Guys like him love any excuse to interact with magic that isn't the standard transportation or medical stuff."

Annelise chuckled. It was very true. She glanced down at the ward line surrounding them. "I'm surprised you chose to meet out in the open."

Jimmy worked primarily in the cyber world. He mistrusted everything and everyone and preferred to hide behind the ones and zeros on the screen. He was a cyber-fence, arranging meetings between potential buyers and sellers of illicit goods. In exchange for facilitating, he would get a cut. Annelise utilized his services when selling imaginary lost relics. Since the real thing didn't exist, nobody would be looking for it, and the risk was lower.

But when she was selling a recreation, like the VanTover, she went through Frankie for an extra layer of distance and security.

"I needed to change up my methods," Jimmy's eyes were wide, and his voice barely above a whisper. "If they're after you, and they're after Frankie, then they'll be after me next. I couldn't risk our usual methods of communicating."

Annelise raised an eyebrow. Jimmy had no usual methods of communicating. He had been known to deliver messages with methods that ranged from digital billboards to a carrier pigeon. She didn't even know anyone used carrier pigeons anymore until some kid showed up on her doorstep with a fat bird and a note for her in his hands.

"You can't trust anyone or anything." Jimmy glanced up and down the alley again. "Besides, you make me too much money to get caught." He flinched as he chuckled at his own joke.

Annelise didn't laugh. "Yeah." Her stomach felt tight. She couldn't stop thinking about the wardens who were on her trail. It was a disaster waiting to happen. "Thanks, Jimmy. I owe you one."

"Yeah, you do." He pulled his jacket straight and made to scuttle down the alley.

"Jimmy?"

He turned to face her, looking a bit agitated, but listening nonetheless.

"You really strapped for cash?"

Jimmy stuffed his hands in his pockets. "Yeah."

Annelise knew little about his personal living situation, but he seemed stressed about this. She suspected that he had dependents, but she could never tell for sure.

She unzipped a pocket that lined the inside of her navy blazer and pulled out the small wad of cash she kept on her. "Here." She handed him the money.

Jimmy looked at her in astonishment.

Annelise stuffed her hands into her pockets. "Like I said, I owe you. Both for having my back now and… you know. Before." 'Before' being when Jimmy managed to single-handedly pull thirteen-year-old Annelise out of the depths of poverty and give her a lifeline in the form of her first job. He had sent work her way ever since. Annelise wouldn't be the woman she was today without Jimmy Sneke.

Understanding and gratitude crossed Jimmy's face. He held up the money. "Thanks." He tucked it into a deep pocket and scurried down the alley into the shadows.

Annelise watched him go, her mind already racing. How had she been found out? And what was she going to do now?

***

The wind on the roof of the parking garage whipped Annelise's chin-length hair across her face. She sat on the railing, looking out over the city of Canol Dinas: The seat of the magical government in North America. The sun had just set beyond the Sierra Nevada Mountains that surrounded the city. The San Joaquin River that had glimmered on the edge of town mere moments ago now turned a resolute blue that darkened by the minute under the deepening California sky.

From her vantage point, she had a decent view of the Drake's Maw: a tunnel cut beneath a mountain to the south of the valley. The mouth of the tunnel was carved into the shape of an enormous dragon head with mouth open, fangs bared, and eyes fierce. In the fading light, the headlights of the cars flowing out of the tunnel's exit looked like fire pouring out of the dragon's mouth. Below her, a steady stream of cars flowed and merged in an intricate dance of traffic.

A few parked cars were scattered across the top-level parking. The fact that there were cars in the North American seat of magic at all was a marvel owed to the efforts of the integration. Now, it was rare that a car burst into flames from magical overexposure.

A few blocks away from her, she could see the line outside of the magical transporter pad facility snaking out of the building and overflowing onto the sidewalk as people waited to enjoy the privilege and ease of instantaneous travel all across the planet. The long lines of security were a small price to pay for this commodity.

"Annelise Windstarter," a deep voice rang out behind her.

Annelise turned and smiled. "Harold."

A large man with dark skin and a rich baritone voice swaggered up to her, smiling. He carried a large black briefcase in one hand, and the other was tucked loosely into his pocket.

"How's it going?" he asked.

"My day has taken a peculiar turn."

He handed her the briefcase. "How so?"

Annelise didn't elaborate, but balanced the briefcase on the railing and pressed a palm against its surface. Lines of blue light flickered across the top of the briefcase, and it unlocked with a click. She lifted the lid and inspected the contents. The briefcase contained several rolls of canvas, arranged in neat rows. Some of them contained paintings, while others were free from paint. The canvases were all yellowed, some more than others. Small tags near the top of each row dated the canvases. The dates ranged from 1750 to 1896. Perfect for her line of work.

Annelise snapped the briefcase shut and pulled a small velvet pouch from her pocket. She handed the pouch to Harold. "I was wondering if you knew anything about the investigation looking into the VanTover," she asked.

Harold inspected one of the golden Dutch Ducats from the pouch. He looked up at Annelise, his grin never fading. "I hear there's a special warden task force that is cracking down on forgeries and other art-related cons," he said. "I'm guessing these two are a part of it. Marcus says that the client tried to get the VanTover displayed in a national gallery. That's probably how it ended up on their radar."

Annelise let out a controlled breath, between nearly pursed lips, trying to untangle the knots that had worked their way into her stomach. "Frankie needs to find better clients. If he keeps selling to idiots who can't keep their mouths shut and their art in vaults, he's going to get us all busted."

Harold chuckled. "What can I say, a paying client is a paying client." He leaned against the railing, crossing his arms. "I'm surprised that you were the one to swipe the VanTover. Acquisition is not normally up your alley."

Annelise looked out over the city. "You're right. It's not. But... sometimes I create replicas. I never deal in the real thing. It's too risky."

"It was a replica?" Harold asked. He looked impressed. "Did Frankie know?"

Annelise shrugged. "Frankie and I have an agreement. He doesn't ask, and I don't tell. If he believes it's the original, he is more convincing in his sales pitch. And if I don't tell him, I have to ensure that my work is flawless. It works out for both of us. So far, no client has ever been the wiser."

Harold gave a low whistle. "You ever think about selling originals? You could go straight?"

Annelise chuckled. "Sure. Maybe in my second career, I'll be a famous artist, and you'll be a door-to-door salesman."

Harold laughed a full-bellied laugh, after which the two fell silent. Tension returned to Annelise's stomach.

She ran a hand through her hair, but the wind sent it back to whipping her face. "I tried to get in touch with Frankie earlier, but his gallery was empty. Any idea where he went?"

"I haven't heard from him since yesterday. But Jimmy says that some wardens were poking their noses into the VanTover that Frankie fenced for you. My guess is he holed up after that encounter."

She chewed the inside of her cheek. "Do you know anything more about these cops?" she asked.

"Not much. But it seems that the VanTover has put them on your scent. They've been asking about some of your other transactions as well."

Annelise's stomach dropped. She tried to calm her racing heartbeat and quell her growing frustration. "Frankie had better keep his head down and his mouth shut, or I'm going to bruise *his* shins with that stupid cane of his for a change."

Harold put a hand on her shoulder. "You'll get through this. Just keep your head low for a while, and this will all blow over."

Annelise let out a breath through puffed cheeks, trying to calm her nerves.

"Are you... already mixed up in something?" Harold asked.

Annelise nodded. "Yeah. I've got something in the works."

Harold shifted his weight and put his hands on his hips. "Well, if you can rearrange it, do. If you can't, then take the loss. It's better to lose out on some money now than be a guest of the state for the next five years."

"Yeah... I'll see what I can do," she mumbled.

Harold gave her a look and then rubbed the back of his neck.

"Look... I don't normally do this. But if you need me to step in for you, I'm willing to do it. Don't think I've forgotten what you did for me with that Aztec deal two years ago. I could make the sale, and you could keep your head down. If they're after the source, they are more likely to be interested in moving past me to find you."

Annelise's stomach roiled at the thought. She knew he was a professional, but she could not afford for this to go wrong. Going herself was risky, but at least she would have control over the variables.

She smiled wanly up at Harold. "Thanks, Harold. I appreciate the offer, really. But I think I'll be okay."

"And there's nothing I can say to convince you to call it off?"

Annelise pressed her lips into a thin line. It wasn't just her future at stake. She owed Jimmy. He needed this.

She shook her head, "No. I'll be okay. Don't you worry about me."

She had spent a lot of time planning for her meeting with this client tomorrow. If she rescheduled now, she was sure she would spook him, and all that work would go to waste. It was a setback she couldn't afford. All she could do was close the deal as quickly as possible and then go to ground.

***

Annelise stepped through the door of her house. She sighed, and for a moment, she leaned on her staff, pressing her forehead against its familiar surface. Her day had been long and unproductive, not in small part due to the fact that she was preoccupied with the notion of the wardens who were on her scent. She had tried to get a better sense of who they were and what they were after, but to no avail. No one knew anything...or no one was talking.

She kicked off her shoes and placed her staff in its nook by the front door. She tapped a rune next to the door, and it glowed with a pale golden light. Several orbs of light around her house came to life, giving off a pleasant glow and illuminating the room. Her living space was small and opened directly into the kitchen. The room was devoid of furniture save a small table with a single chair that sat near the wall, and a more comfortable chair that sat beneath a glowing orb by the window. A bookshelf climbed up the wall behind it. The rest of the wall was covered in artwork.

Annelise made her way towards the side door that led from the living area into the garage. She clutched the handle and stilled, frustration from the day welling inside her.

She had tried to get a message to Frankie, but he was nowhere to be found, and no one seemed to know how to get a hold of him. No doubt the cops had spooked him, and he had gone underground for a while...or he had been arrested.

Annelise pushed away her worried thoughts. There was something tangible here that she needed to work on, and it was time to focus on that instead of chasing fruitless whispers.

She slipped through the side door of her home and into the garage. The garage was brightly lit, warm, and inviting. No matter what time of day it was outside, it always seemed to be late morning on a sunny day in her garage. Shelves upon shelves of paints, parchments, canvases, clays, and various other art tools lined the walls.

She added her newly acquired antique parchments to her collection.

In the center of the room, on her work table, sat her current project: an antique, corroded knife salvaged from some forgotten corner of the world. With a few artistic touches, a bit of storytelling, and just the right buyer, Annelise would transform it into a long-lost magical relic worth tens of thousands. There were only a few final touches she needed to add to make it perfect.

As she settled into the project, her stress drained away, and her mind cleared. While she carved and wove delicate spells around the knife, the concerns about the wardens and Frankie's potential treachery faded into the background. All that mattered was the work in front of her.

***

"Would you like to see the item?" Annelise asked the rather young, rather portly, and rather *very* rich man sitting across from her.

They were sitting in Mr. Aisel's penthouse suite. Bright sunlight streamed through the floor-to-ceiling windows, which offered a stunning view over the city. A sleek black leather couch was mirrored by two matching armchairs with a glass coffee table in the middle. An astonishing collection of priceless odds and ends were scattered throughout the apartment with no eye for cohesion. If it was expensive, this man wanted it, regardless of whether it fit with any of his other decor.

Still, Annelise had to appreciate his enthusiasm. It worked to her advantage. Rich, sourceless men such as himself enjoyed purchasing magical artifacts for the novelty. He might not have any magic of his own, but there was little that money could not buy.

"Yes, please." Mr. Aisel leaned forward, an excited grin plastered across his face.

Annelise pulled a long, narrow, wooden box out of her bag and placed it on the sleek glass coffee table. She turned it towards Mr. Aisel, who was seated in the opposite chair, and opened it.

Mr. Aisel peered inside. His eyes widened in appreciation. "It's very beautiful."

"And it has quite the history." Annelise lifted the corroded yet elegant blade out of its casing. "Given 500 years ago by Emperor Aang as a gift to his most beloved son, it had the power to assure victory over one's enemies. With this blade in his hand, Emperor Aang's son won many battles in his father's name. But tragically, while caught in a storm at sea, he tried to use it against nature itself. As he pushed the blade beyond the limits of its purpose, it backfired and sank the ship. The ship, its treasures, and this blade have been lost until very recently, when some spearfishermen discovered it off the coast of China. Quite the acquisition for an astute collector such as yourself."

She passed the blade over to Mr. Aisel with care, who reached out to accept it with both hands, holding the blade in reverence.

"How did it come to be in your possession?" he asked, looking up from the blade.

Annelise looked him in the eye and smiled her sweetest smile. "Mr. Aisel," she batted her eyelashes at him. "If I gave you my sources, I'd be putting myself out of a job." She leaned into the arm of the couch, dangling her shoe off her toes. "I'm afraid my source is going to have to remain my little secret for the time being."

Mr. Aisel returned her smile and chuckled.

"I suppose." He turned back to the blade.

"Now you're naturally more than welcome to have a curator authenticate it, but... if I may?" She sat up and gestured towards the blade.

"Please!" He passed the blade back to her.

Annelise placed the blade on the table and flicked her wrist to extract her staff. It appeared in her hand as though it had always been there. Mr. Aisel leaned forward in anticipation. She waved her staff over the blade, and the runes in the ancient draconic language that she had etched into the corroded metal glowed a pleasant blue before fading.

"See here? These are characters for strength, power, and victory." Annelise looked at Mr. Aisel, who was gazing at the blade in admiration. "Would you like to call an authenticator?" she asked. The best way to convince someone they didn't need one was to be over-eager to enlist one.

After a moment, "No." He looked up at her. "I think I'm satisfied. Miss Windstarter, you have yourself a deal."

Annelise beamed as she reached out her hand to shake his.

The front door of the penthouse flew open with a crash.

"Freeze!" Two wardens burst into the room, staves brandished. Their black uniforms were emblazoned with the golden High Council insignia on the shoulder, and "Warden" printed in sharp letters that marched across their chests.

Annelise froze mid-reach to her handshake with Mr. Aisel, her mind racing. How did they get past her wards without the alarm going off? She jumped to her feet, her heart pounding. "What is the meaning of this?" She cried, hoping to sound adequately indignant.

"Miss Windstarter, you're under arrest." The warden with dark brown curls seemed almost gleeful as he sauntered forward, brandishing a set of magic-suppressing cuffs. His golden eyes twinkled in amusement.

Annelise bristled as he pulled her hands behind her back and cuffed her, but she did not resist. No one fought with the Conciliar Wardens.

She felt a numbness sweep over her as the cuffs clicked into place.

His blond companion stood in the doorway, barring any hope of escape.

"On what charges?" she asked, still playing the indignant, wronged businesswoman.

"Hmm. Let's see," He picked up the blade that lay on the table. "Let's start with forgery and black market dealing and see where we go from there."

"Umm... What about me?" Mr. Aisel asked.

"Well, sir, did you buy this item?" He waved the fake relic in front of Mr. Aisel's face.

"Uh, no. Not yet."

Annelise wanted to slap her forehead and might have done so if her hands hadn't been bound. The warden gave him a long look that seemed to express what Annelise felt. *How could he be so stupid?* Conspiring to commit a crime was a crime too.

"Well...then I guess we can't charge you with anything. You had better leave."

Mr. Aisel didn't move.

"Now!" The warden reiterated, gesturing towards the door.

Mr. Aisel tripped over his feet in his rush to leave the room, almost knocking over an original antique vase. By some miracle, it teetered back onto its pedestal as Mr. Aisel scampered past the blond warden and out the door.

"We'll be watching you." The blond one called after him as he disappeared down the hall.

Annelise stood silently as she watched her mark disappear around the corner. She wanted to scream. She had lost her mark and was caught red-handed. How was it that he got off scot-free and she was here in handcuffs?

She waited for the wardens to haul her off to prison, fingerprint her, or at least say *something*, but they did none of those things. They just meandered around the room, observing the random assortment of artifacts that were on display and occasionally looking at each other like they were having some sort of silent conversation.

Annelise used the time to observe her captors and weigh her options.

The blond one's golden eyes matched his neat, straight, golden hair that swept across his forehead. His tall frame had to stoop in a graceful curve to observe some of the artifacts more closely.

Annelise could not discern any weapons on his person beyond his staff, but he remained frustratingly close to the door. She filed the door under "Plan B".

She turned her eyes to the other warden. The dark-haired one bore a striking resemblance to the blond one. Perhaps it was because they had the same golden eyes? But the cut of their jaw was the same as well. Perhaps there was a closer family resemblance than being part of the same ancient clan?

The dark-haired one's complexion was more olive, however, and he had dark curls that danced around his face. He moved around the room with the grace of a martial artist, every move and gesture belying hidden strength.

Annelise flicked her eyes past him to the large window that opened up onto the balcony. No. With her hands tied behind her back and the steep drop below, it was more likely to be a death sentence than an escape route.

She turned her eyes back to the front door, analyzing the furniture between her and her exit. Moving as little as possible, she slipped her heels off her feet. She waited for a moment when the blond one seemed particularly engrossed in a piece of decor, and burst into a sprint. She darted around the glass table and went straight over the couch. She leapt off the backrest and landed in a crouch on the other side. With her hands bound behind her back, she almost lost her balance, but she managed to steady herself as she lunged for the door.

A blur of bright blue barreled into her. The air left her lungs as she was knocked off her feet and sent sprawling to the floor. Her shoulder throbbed with the impact.

She groaned and rolled over onto her back. The dark-haired warden's staff was still glowing faintly from the spell he had just knocked her over with. His eyes were still infuriatingly cheerful.

"So…. What now?" she asked, frustration seeping into her voice.

"Now that you know you can't escape, we take the cuffs off." The blond one said. He helped her up and freed her wrists before moving to lean against the door, blocking Annelise's exit.

Annelise's brow furrowed in confusion. A wave of dizziness passed over her as the magic-suppressing cuffs were removed. Like blood rushing into a previously asleep limb, her whole body tingled as magic surged through her again.

Annelise opened and closed her mouth a few times, trying to figure out what was going on and which question to ask first. Finally, she settled on: "I'm confused."

The brown-haired one looked up from a magical trinket he was inspecting, his eyes twinkling with amusement. "Oh, we're not actually here to arrest you today. We just thought it would be more fun this way. Also, we needed to make sure you wouldn't run."

Annelise ground her teeth. "So… you're not actually wardens?"

"No, we are definitely wardens."

What was going on? "Who are you?" she asked.

"Ah, of course," he turned away from the trinket and gave her his full attention. "We haven't introduced ourselves. I'm Michael Pendragon, and Goldilocks over there is Tristan Pendragon, my cousin." His cousin shot him a dirty look, but Michael continued. "We have a mutual friend. A certain James Sneke?"

Annelise's stomach dropped. Had Jimmy snitched on her? The betrayal stung unexpectedly. She tried not to trust people for exactly this reason, but Jimmy... She thought that, after everything they had been through together... She had thought there was some measure of trust between them. Apparently, she had thought wrong. Trust was always a bad choice.

"This isn't a bad job. How did you do it?" Michael picked up the blade lying on the table, oblivious to her emotional turmoil.

"Why, Mr. Pendragon! It's the real artifact, of course." Annelise's voice was smooth, her denial automatic, but her mind was racing.

Michael just smirked and waved his hand over the runes. "Now I'm no historian, but I was given a proper Pendragon education, and there never was an Emperor Aang in all of Asia's magical history. Add to that the fact that there is..." he held his hand over the blade once more, holding it longer this time. A faint trail of delicate runes glowed white along the knife from pommel to tip and down again. He looked at her in admiration. "...a faint perception ward, wound around a small object like this. I've never seen anything like it. It's pure elegance." He turned back to examine the spell. "How cruel of you to take advantage of the poor man. He never stood a chance."

"Pshh. He is many things, but poor he is not. He has more money than he knows what to do with. I'm merely helping him along by taking some of it off his hands. Besides, if one of the sourceless decides he's going to collect magical artifacts, perhaps he should start by learning something about magical history. I'm simply providing him with an incentive to further his education. It's a good cause. I'm like Robin Hood."

"Robin Hood stole from the rich and gave to the poor," Tristan was still leaning against the door. He seemed unamused.

"Yes, well, he's rich, and I'm poor."

"Well then," Tristan stalked over to the black leather couch and sat down. "You'll be pleased to hear that we are about to offer you a lot of money."

Annelise cocked her head as she sat down and leaned forward. "I'm listening."

"My cousin and I need to acquire a particularly secure and highly illegal artifact. It's a three-man job, and we want you to be the third man."

Annelise raised an incredulous eyebrow at the golden-haired man. "You're barking up the wrong tree. I don't do teamwork, and I don't do acquisitions. It's too risky. Besides, I have no experience in infiltration or extrication. I'd be useless to you. You might as well just…let me go."

"No. Michael and I will be doing most of the infiltration and extrication. We will need you on surveillance. But if the item is discovered missing, we won't be able to get away. We need time."

"That's where you come in," Michael jumped in. "We need you to forge a replica so they won't notice that the artifact is gone until well after we've made our escape."

"We also plan to forge some work orders, so that our presence on target will seem legitimate and greatly mitigate the risk. We require your help with that as well," Tristan added.

Annelise narrowed her eyes at them. "How do I know this isn't a trap? I agree to help you and then, bam! You put me back in those cuffs of yours."

Michael beamed at her. "You don't. But we won't. We already have what we need to take you in if we wanted to. What we don't have is a reason to take the cuffs off of you, unless we really need your help."

He was entirely too cheerful for this conversation. Annelise was sure he was laughing at her. She thought for a moment, weighing her options. "What is the artifact?"

The two wardens exchanged a glance.

Michael squirmed a little in his seat.

Tristan turned his gaze back to Annelise. "A key."

Annelise cocked her head. "Any particular key?" she pressed.

"The key to the Subraek."

Annelise stood up in shock. "What exactly do you want with the Subraek?" She struggled to keep her tone measured. If she was dealing with terrorists, she wanted nothing to do with it.

"It's not what you think," Tristan said, exasperated. "We have no desire to unleash the imprisoned monsters and spirits on the world. We *are* actually wardens." He paused. "We believe the last known dragon was captured and imprisoned in the Subraek."

Annelise sank back into the couch. The Dragon? The last dragon disappeared just over one hundred years ago, right before the integration of the magical community into the sourceless community. She had vanished without a trace. Her disappearance had caused a major stir, and the government had instituted the largest search and rescue operation in a millennium to try to find her again. All their efforts had failed. The Dragon Seat on the High Council remained vacant. It was the highest-profile cold case of the last two hundred years, and still, there seemed to be no clues and no leads.

"I thought only the council had the authority to open the Subraek. If the Dragon was imprisoned by the government, why would they make such a fuss about looking for her?" Annelise asked.

"Because she wasn't imprisoned by the government, but by a small, corrupt contingent within the government. We are trying to break her out and expose the whole plot, but if we go through the normal channels, not only will it take years, but they will probably move her before we get the approval to go investigate," Michael said.

Annelise bit her lip. Their reasons didn't seem deranged. Still, to break into the Subraek... It was high treason. If something, anything went wrong, she would be locked away in a hole so deep she would never see the light of day again.

"Please." Tristan leaned forward. His voice held a new note of desperation and longing. "She's been missing for far too long. We can't do this without you. Your work and your talents could be the key to setting her free. She needs us. She needs you, Annelise."

Annelise paled a little. She didn't want anyone needing her, almost as much as she didn't want to need anyone else. She lived alone. She worked alone. As a rule, Annelise didn't pull jobs with other people. There were too many variables, and she found people too unreliable. She was happiest alone.

And then there were the two Pendragons. Annelise didn't trust them. She didn't really trust anyone, but she certainly didn't trust them. What was keeping them from getting what they needed from her and then leaving her holding the bag? It would read very easily as a headline. *Long-time suspected con woman and art forger, arrested for government vault break-in!* She could already imagine the picture on the front page: her face dejected, as some warden snapped magic-suppressing cuffs onto her wrists. She shuddered.

"You mentioned some compensation?" she asked, stalling for time and searching for a smooth exit from the conversation.

"We are offering you two million dollars. If all goes well, the job shouldn't last more than 10 days."

Annelise crossed her arms. "Two million is rather light considering the risks involved."

Tristan leaned back in his chair, his golden eyes leveled at her. "You are, of course, under no obligation to help us." His tone was light, but there was a hard edge to his expression. "We can put those cuffs back on you and book you for forgery and black market dealing right now. It's your choice."

So that was it.

They were blackmailing her into helping them.

And yet, for a moment, she considered the latter offer. The Subraek key would be held in a government vault, heavily guarded, with all kinds of wards and security. It was a choice between definitely going to jail for 5-10 years and very probably going to jail for the rest of her life. And yet... she couldn't bring herself to give up and let herself be carried away to prison just yet. But she didn't like it. Not one bit.

Annelise shifted in her chair, trying to suppress her frustration and fear at her current predicament. "So just to be clear, all you would need is for me to forge a replica of the key, help forge some work orders, and keep an eye on surveillance while you make the switch?"

Tristan nodded. "And of course, you would need to accompany us to the Subraek while we release the Dragon. We can't risk you getting caught and spilling everything to the authorities before we find her. Besides, we might have further use of your skillset as our little adventure progresses," Tristan said blithely.

Annelise paled. Accompany them to the Subraek? The place where every monster from every history book and children's story ended up? And still, Annelise couldn't bring herself to go to prison instead. She wanted to scream.

"Anything else?" she snarled.

Tristan was unbothered by her foul mood. "No! That is all," he sounded as cheery as though they were discussing tea orders.

They asked a lot. Too much, really. She didn't relish the thought of working with these mages. She *hated* working with other people. But Annelise really didn't want to go to jail, so if there was even a small chance that she could still avoid it, she was going to take it.

"So." Tristan stood up and held out his hand. "Do we have a deal?"

Annelise stood up and reached for his hand, but at the last moment, he pulled away. "Don't shake unless you mean it."

"I know how an agreement of honor works," Annelise bit out.

Tristan held out his hand again, and Annelise took it, resisting the urge to try to crush his hand.

The deal was struck.

Chapter 2: The Choice

"Excellent," **Michael said,** shaking her hand as well. He flashed her a big smile.

Annelise smothered her ire at his cheerfulness, and instead tried to project a calm demeanor.

"Now, Miss Windstarter, tell us what you need to create your forgery of the key," Michael said as he settled into the black leather chair that complemented the couch.

Annelise flopped back down onto the couch and crossed her legs. "First, I'm going to need a guardsman who works in the government vault, and a slinky dress."

Michael laughed. "Is that how you plan to get the specs of the key?" he asked. "Sounds like fun! But not necessary. I have already done the recon myself, but you're welcome to get into a slinky dress if you want." His golden eyes glimmered with mirth, and a touch of mischief pulled at the corners of his smile.

Annelise rolled her eyes. "Just show me what you've got."

Michael stood up and retrieved a cylindrical container that he had left just outside the door. He pulled out a rolled-up sheet of paper with a detailed drawing of the key from several angles and placed it on the coffee table.

"This is good work." She looked up at him, impressed. "Did you draw this from memory?"

Michael nodded.

Annelise turned back to the drawings. They were good, but she was going to need a bit more to make a replica. "I'm going to want a look at it myself if that's okay." She motioned towards the couch.

A look of hesitation flitted over Michael's face before he flashed her a brilliant smile. "No problem." He bounded from the chair to the couch.

Annelise scooted herself a bit closer to him. Michael's cheeks were tinged the slightest amount of pink as she reached up and took his face in her hands. She crushed the stray observation that his freckles were artfully splattered across his obnoxiously perfect nose and focused on the task at hand. Looking into his golden eyes, she reached out with her mind to touch his. The memory of Michael's trip to the vaults bombarded her mind with such force that she wondered if he was trying to hide some other memory or thought. Annelise pushed away her own curiosity and focused on the memory in front of her.

Michael was following a guard through the vaults. A seemingly endless row of locked doors lined the long hallway. A strip of glowing light lined the sides of the hall on the floor and ceiling. Finally, the guard stopped and placed his hand on one of the doors while inserting a key into the lock. The door glowed silver and then swung open. There were several objects in the vault. The key was on a pedestal surrounded by the dancing lights of security wards.

In the memory, Michael walked towards an old scroll with runes she did not understand. The yellowed velum was cracked with age, and the scroll was kept behind glass. Michael pretended to investigate the scroll, but he kept glancing in the direction of the key. As he did, Annelise inspected the key.

It was large. From end to end, it was longer than her hand. It looked to be made of copper that had experienced extensive oxidation. The shape was angular but simple, save for the runes that were etched into the handle along the neck and in the teeth of the key.

Annelise spent some time analyzing the key, memorizing the texture, the details on the runes, and how it played in the light. She only withdrew when her temples started to throb. Michael's face was also scrunched against a headache.

"Sorry." She grimaced as she placed a palm to each of her temples and pressed for a small measure of pain relief. "I lost track of time." She got up to get them both some pain medicine before remembering that they were all still in Mr. Aisel's living room.

Michael graciously waved her off. "No worries." He pressed a light hand to his head. "Do you have what you need?"

"Yes."

"Good," Tristan strode back into the room from the direction of the kitchen with two cups of water and some pain medicine. "Miss Windstarter, can you have the replica complete in one week?" He handed her one of the cups.

She bit her lip. It would be tight, but she could get it done. Then again, all the better. The sooner she finished this job, the sooner she could be rid of these Pendragons. She nodded.

"What materials will you need from us?" He asked.

Annelise shook her head and then winced as her head pounded at the motion. "I prefer to source my own materials. Thanks." She knew where to get what she needed, and on such a tight schedule and high-stakes job, she preferred her own sources over any more unknowns.

Michael clapped his hands together. "Wonderful! We will stop by your residence in one week, and fill you in on the details and discuss the matter of the fake work orders we will need then. I trust you will do an exquisite job. We are depending on you."

"Oh, and Miss Windstarter," Tristan said, as Annelise got up to leave. "If you run, we will find you and throw the entire book at you. That's a promise."

***

Annelise fled the apartment as soon as the Pendragons let her go and raced for home. She stepped through the door of her house in a daze. She drifted through her empty home and passed into her garage. Her art space was her sanctuary and usually gave her clarity. She stared at her empty work table. She would have to get materials... and...

The clarity came, but it was not pleasant. Her mind flitted back to the Pendragons, and her stomach turned. She was sure that they would get what they needed from her and leave her hanging. She stumbled forward and gripped the desk for support; her knuckles stood out like ghosts against her flushed skin. She felt trapped—doomed either to live a short, miserable life facing the horrors of the most dangerous sub-realm known to man, or abandoned to a dark hole of a prison where she would never see the light of day again. She was caught in a current of events that was dragging her deeper in, and she could see no way out. Her breath came in gasps, but she couldn't seem to get any air. She sank to the floor.

She couldn't do this. She needed to get away. She needed to run.

Her mind latched onto that idea like a lifeline. And as she did, her breath returned. As she lay on the floor, the wild beating of her heart slowed, and the shaking of her limbs subsided. She had to run. It was the only way.

With a surge of energy fueled by urgency, she pulled herself to her feet and headed back to the door. She reminded herself that she had gotten along just fine so far in life by depending on nobody but herself. She was the one person she knew wouldn't let her down, and these Pendragons... no. It just wouldn't do.

She was going to get herself a nice new identity and disappear. Forever. She had seven days before they were expecting her, and she would make the most of every minute.

She stepped out the door, her mind racing. She wasn't sure how much surveillance the Pendragons had done on her before approaching her, but she had to assume that all her usual contacts were not an option for a new identity. She groaned.

That left only Waylyn.

He happened to hate her guts.

Annelise wasn't too fond of him either. They had been on bad terms ever since they had both tried to sell forgeries of the same piece to the same client. It had been an unfortunate coincidence, but someone had stolen it, and they had both decided to cash in on the opportunity. Waylyn's brushwork was decent, but Annelise's work was flawless, and side by side, Waylyn's was obviously a forgery. It had ruined Waylyn's relationship with the well-paying South African businessman, and Waylyn had never forgiven her for it.

Now, she needed his help. She specialized in art and artifacts. Waylyn was more of a jack of all trades. He could make her a new identity. Whether or not he would was the real question.

She pushed the door open to the dingy pawn shop that was the front for his real business. Year-old window paint letters advertising a sale that ended almost as long ago blocked the meager light fighting its way into the shop. Stacks of things that nobody wanted were piled around various counters, each with a little paper price tag that shuddered when the outside wind burst through the door behind her and raced through the shop. The bell jangled overhead.

Waylyn took one look at her and pointed to the door. "Out."

"Look, I need your help. I'm willing to pay," Annelise pleaded.

He gave her a long look. "You'll pay double—no triple— or it's no deal."

Annelise clenched her jaw but nodded.

He gave a low whistle. "You must be in some kind of trouble. What do you need?"

"I need a new identity. The full works. I need it confidential, untraceable, and I need it within a week."

Waylyn snorted. "You *are* in some kind of trouble. Don't tell me, I don't care. A small part of me wants to turn you out the door and let you meet whatever's coming to you..."

Annelise held her breath.

"But since you're paying triple, I suppose I'll be lenient."

He took her to the back of the shop, got the pictures he needed for the new IDs, and Annelise forked over a hefty amount of cash.

Her gut churned as she turned over the money. The kernels of guilt stirred within her. She had honored her word all her life. And now... This was the first time she had ever gone back on her word.

She ran her hand through her hair, shoving it out of her face. Why couldn't her mind pick a side? It seemed like she had no good options.

She thought about the Dragon, trapped somewhere for all these years. She gave her head a shake and squashed the queasy feeling of guilt away. It was true the Dragon didn't deserve to be trapped, but it wasn't her fault, and it wasn't her place to fix it. Besides, there was no guarantee the Pendragons were right about her being held in the Subraek. They might get down there to find nothing. This could all be for nothing. It was better to get out now before she was in way over her head.

She spotted a small pile of bracelets lying in a heap. They were woven from thread but each one had a small crystal set into it with a draconic rune woven into the pattern of the band. The rune referred to the way a dragon left no trace when it flew through the sky. Annelise picked up a bracelet, and could feel the hum of magic encapsulated in the crystal. She thought it might be useful to have a charm to protect her from a finding spell.

"You really don't want to be found, do you?" Waylyn asked, seeing her holding the traceless charm.

Annelise put the charm on the counter. "How much?" she asked.

Waylyn rubbed his neck. "Yeah, here's the thing. I only sell those bracelets in sets of," he hesitated, "five. So that's going to be five hundred dollars."

He had obviously pulled that number out of thin air. "Waylyn, I just need the one."

"Yeah, sweetheart, I'm afraid I just can't make an exception. Either you buy all five of them, or you don't buy any. Good luck staying in hiding without one."

Annelise shoved a hand into her pocket and slammed the money onto the counter. "Whatever. I'll take all five." She grabbed the charm off the counter, and then snatched up approximately four more out of the pile as she strode out of the shop. If she grabbed more, Waylyn didn't try to stop her.

The sun was getting low as she left Waylyn's shop. She headed back to her home and looked around the small space. The golden light streamed through the window and danced on the surfaces. She looked around the room, taking in her meager furnishings with a pang of regret. It wasn't much, but it had been her home. Her gaze lingered on the wall of paintings that gleamed in the evening light. They always seemed to come alive this time of day.

These were not forgeries or recreations. These were her own creations. Regret and disappointment coursed through her. She wouldn't be able to take them with her. Perhaps one or two, but not all of them.

Dejected, she decided she wasn't in the mood for dinner and opted for a hot shower instead. The water and steam helped soothe her frazzled nerves, but they did not stop her mind from racing instead of resting through the long and lonely watches of the night.

***

The morning was spent packing and repacking a single bag. She managed to stash away two of her smaller paintings. One was a charming family picnic scene, the very epitome of tranquility. The other, by contrast, was a battle—two mages stood back to back, defending each other from the hordes of voracious creatures.

She had always loved those paintings. The picnic scene she loved for its peaceful setting and the familial affection between the figures. The battle scene she loved because of the trust and dependence the mages showed towards each other. Neither could survive alone, but together, they might just overcome. But now that she looked at it again, the two figures in the painting reminded her of the two Pendragons she had encountered. For a moment, she even thought they had golden eyes. She dropped the painting on her bed as though it had burned her. She blinked, and they were back to their normal blue and hazel.

Perhaps she had better not take that one with her. It would forever be reminding her of her betrayal.

She needed to clear her head. She headed out the door for a walk, trying to focus on anything other than the confusion assailing her mind. She didn't pay any attention to where she was going until her feet had led her to the old academy, which lay just over a mile from her house.

A large wooden door was set into a stone wall that surrounded the Academy grounds. Carvings of various dragons from the past lined the door. Each one had blessed the Academy with its presence in its time. Not anymore.

33

In contrast to the carvings framing the door, the center was smooth as paper. Smooth as magic.

She placed her hand on the center of the door and took a deep breath. "Breath is Life and Magic." The smooth surface glowed blue, and the door swung open, revealing the entrance courtyard of the Academy.

The courtyard was currently empty, but between classes would be full of students going from one class to the next. The courtyard was bordered on three sides by three buildings, with covered walkways connecting each. The gap between each building was a passageway deeper onto the campus. Annelise made her way to the gap on her right.

As she passed through the gap and turned the corner, she almost ran headlong into a very old man, but stopped herself just in time. "Professor Finchley!"

Professor Finchley was old with a flowing white beard that tucked into his belt, and ice-blue eyes framed by a pair of glasses. He was the primary spells professor. It was he who guided all the young mages through the year long process of crafting their staff and ensured that their pronunciation in the ancient dragon language used for spellcasting was precise. He stooped a bit when he walked, but she had seen him dodge many a wayward spell in his time with surprising agility.

"Ms. Windstarter, what an unexpected surprise to see you here. How are you doing?"

A brief flash of her inner turmoil passed through her mind, but she pushed it away. She had always preferred to consult him on intellectual problems, never personal ones. The one time she had opened up... He had meant well, sharing his experience of his own father walking out on him to establish common ground, but it had felt forced and awkward.

"I'm doing well. How about you?" she said.

He leaned on his staff and smiled at her. "Very well, very well, thank you."

"How are your students getting along these days?" She forced a smile.

"Well enough, but never as well as you, child. But I'm actually teaching far less these days."

"Oh?" She cocked her head.

Professor Finchley pulled his glasses off and polished them. "I have started dabbling in law and found quite a passion for it. It seems I have embarked on a second career after all. I've been practicing defense law at Bombardier Offices." He produced a business card and handed it to Annelise.

"I would have never believed it if I hadn't heard it from your own mouth," a faint smile tugged at her mouth despite the headache that was coming on. He had been a teacher for as long as anyone remembered. The thought of him moving on from that profession was difficult to accept. She tucked the card away.

She suppressed the thought that her own second career would be as a member of the prison cooking staff.

"So tell me, what insightful questions about magic do you have for me today?" Professor Finchley asked. "I always enjoy our talks, you know. It's inspiring to see the new generation have such an interest in understanding the beautiful nuances of our craft."

"I'm afraid I have no questions for you today, Professor. I was just out for a walk and ended up here."

"Well then, will you walk with me for a bit?" Professor Finchley asked.

Annelise could not refuse him. She followed Professor Finchley through the corridors, stifling her agitation.

They walked in silence for a while. The clash of staff against staff echoed down the hallway towards them. It was the staff combat class that every first year student was required to take. It helped both improve physical capacity, while improving control over the staff which would be vital when they started casting spells.

Professor Finchley led her to a large courtyard made of stone. Pillared and covered walkways lined the outside of the courtyard, while in the middle was a large stone fountain under the steel gray sky.

The waters in this fountain were Dragon Blessed, bubbling up from a spring that welled up from deep inside the earth. They emanated from the top of a large angular rock and pooled in a stone basin that had been constructed around it. Once, before the Dragon had disappeared, the waters would have spouted from the top of the fountain. Today, the stream was barely more than a trickle.

She dipped her fingers into the fountain, feeling the pure, magical source pulsing with energy. This was the fountain that every mage at the academy used to learn their first spells. Before they tapped into their own source of magic, they learned with this. It was safer to make mistakes with this external source than with the magic within.

The fountain also provided a physical representation of the magic inside each mage: A pool of water bubbling up from the depths of the earth from which one could draw. If you drew too much, the pool would be empty, but given time and rest, it would replenish. But if you broke it, it would never fill, and your life could drain away with your magic.

She traced the waterlines that circled the basin. There seemed to be more lines than she remembered from her days at the academy.

She looked at Professor Finchley, her forehead drawn in a frown. "It's lower."

Professor Finchley nodded gravely. "Yes. The waters of the fountain have been waning for many years now. Ever since the Dragon disappeared."

Annelise stilled. "What does it mean?"

The professor sat on the lip of the fountain and smoothed his beard. "It is what follows when dragons are absent. Dragons are catalysts for magic in the world. They allow it to flow freely. Without dragons, magic... stagnates. It dries up. It no longer flows. Both in this pool and in us.

"It's why the sourceless waged war on the dragons centuries ago. If you kill the dragons, you dry up a measure of the magic in the world."

"And... If the Dragon was to return?"

"I believe, as do many others who remember the days before the Dragon disappeared, that if the Dragon returned, magic would once again flow more freely. Or at the very least that the stagnation would be halted." He sighed. "Alas, I do not believe it will happen in my lifetime. Perhaps... never. Truly a great loss."

Annelise's mind reeled with this information as she stared at the water of the fountain. It twinkled in the daylight, casting dancing reflections on the wall of the basin.

She remembered drawing water from this pool every day for a whole year as she coaxed her staff to grow straight and true. Her life was less complicated then; she didn't carry around this monkey's fist in her stomach.

Professor Finchley gave her a penetrating look.

"You can learn a lot about someone, you know, from the way they craft their staff."

Annelise looked up at him, questioning.

He continued. "Some students hope to supercharge their futures by overwatering their plants. These are often the ones with blind ambition. They seek greatness but have no patience or finesse to reach it. Some students, for the life of them, cannot coax their saplings into growing straight. They have the best of intentions, but not the delicate touch to succeed. And sometimes, Annelise, you meet a student who finds the balance in the craft, who can connect with the magic in the tree as it grows, and guide it straight and true. Who is not overeager, because they understand the balance of magic that supports the growth of the tree. Who delights in the art of wielding, for its own sake."

"And what can you tell about a student such as this?" she asked.

"I don't know. I haven't figured her out yet." He gave her a wink.

A bitter bark of laughter escaped her lips. "I've teetered on the edge my entire life. I don't feel particularly balanced."

Professor Finchley patted her shoulder. "You will find that balance. I am sure you will. I have seen its potential in you from the very beginning."

He stood up.

"If you ever need anything from me, don't hesitate to ask. I'm always happy to help former students."

She nodded her thanks at him, and he left her to ponder his words by the pool. She dipped her hand into the cool water again, hoping to connect with the source of the spring, and that it might ease her mind. The water only dripped from her fingers into the basin, disturbing the calm surface. She looked away, dejected.

She got up from the cold stone in a huff and headed off down the halls again. She knew who she should talk to to gain the clarity she so desperately needed. She stopped when she came to a familiar wooden door, carved with images of the past that writhed and changed to depict a variety of key historical moments. In a few short moments, Annelise watched as the building of the Pyramids, the Dragon wars of the Early 300s, the Mongol invasions, the Polynesian migration, and the (re)integration of magical and sourceless societies flashed across the door.

She raised a hand to knock, hesitated, and let it fall.

Maybe she had better not.

She had just turned to leave when she saw a man with dark curly hair walking towards her with a stack of papers in his arms.

"Annelise?" The surprise was evident in his voice. "How is my favorite student doing?" His signature dazzling smile stood out against his brown skin.

Annelise could only offer a halfhearted shrug in return. "Hi, Professor Hale." She wasn't sure what else to say.

"Well, come in, and let's see if we can't solve whatever problem you're having." With a swipe of his hand over the runes on the door frame, he unlocked the door to his office. Annelise followed him through the door into the familiar setting, placing her staff by the door. The walls of the office were one large bookshelf, each shelf packed with books on history, mythology, and legend. A small sofa and a plush chair sat in the center of the room, and beyond that, a polished wooden desk gleamed in the warm office light. The furniture hadn't moved an inch since she had attended the academy years ago, but Professor Hale seemed to have collected a few more knick-knacks since she had last been here.

"Would you like some tea?" Professor Hale offered. Annelise nodded, and Professor Hale set about making tea. He poured some water from a jug into a teapot, and tapped the top with his staff. Runes painted into the glaze of the teapot glowed blue, and soon the water was steaming from the spout. He poured some hot water into a teacup, and handed it to Annelise.

"Now," he said once they were both settled. "What seems to be the problem?"

"What makes you think there's a problem?" Annelise asked.

"Annelise, I've known you for almost half your life. I know when something's eating at you."

Annelise huffed, slumped back in her chair, and stared at the ceiling. "I'm in trouble," she confessed. "Big trouble. The kind where I might not get to come back."

Professor Hale looked at her with concern but said nothing for the moment, allowing her to continue.

"I'm getting roped into this job. I mean… I kind of agreed, but… It's a big job. It's a dangerous job. I don't want to do it. I don't think I can." She paused. "I feel bad going back on my word, but it's the only good option. I have to leave." She took a shaky breath. "I guess… I guess I came to say goodbye. And to say, thank you." She sat up and faced him. "You're the only person in my life who's really been there for me, and… I owe you more than I think I even know, definitely more than I could ever repay. I will miss you." She stood up, but Professor Hale held up a hand.

"Now hold on just one moment." He motioned to the chair. "Sit back down, we're not finished talking. I have some questions. Now, you said you got roped into a job. How so?"

"I agreed under duress," Annelise flopped back into the chair and crossed her arms. "The choice was: agree to do the job, or get arrested for…" she trailed off.

Professor Hale regarded her keenly but, as always, Annelise could not find any judgement in his gaze. She groaned. "Well, they would have arrested me for forgery and black market dealing."

Professor Hale's eyebrows shot up. "Then the people roping you into this job, as you say, are wardens?"

"Yeah,"

"And they have some dirt on you, so they are making you help them or face prison."

Annelise nodded.

"And you chose to help them do something… dangerous."

Annelise let out a shaky laugh. "So dangerous. And illegal. And don't go asking me what it is, because if I tell you, they could throw you in prison, just for knowing this."

"Annelise, if you're going to get someone hurt—" Professor Hale started.

"We're not going to hurt anyone," she stared at a dragon figurine perched on one of Professor Hale's bookshelves. "They *do* have a good reason for doing what they're doing. Or at least, they do if they're telling the truth. If they're telling the truth… If they're telling the truth, it would be a bigger crime not to do the job. Even I can see that. But it's just too much. I'm sorry, but I'm not up for this job."

"And there's no way to accomplish this good without breaking the law?" Professor Hale asked hopefully.

Annelise curled her hand around her teacup. It was scalding hot, but she didn't care. "Not according to the cops who are blackmailing me. And if anyone knew a lawful way to do this, it would be them."

"Hmm." Professor Hale tapped a finger on the armrest of his seat. He leaned forward in his chair. "Well then, are you afraid of this job because of the consequences if it goes sideways, or are you afraid because you know you're going to have to depend on someone other than yourself to see this endeavor succeed?"

Annelise furrowed her brow. "I'm *afraid* of going to prison for the rest of my life…and dying." But then she thought about it for a moment longer, "… and, well, both, I guess. How can I be sure I can trust them? How do I know they won't hang me out to dry or leave me holding the bag? How do I know they won't abandon me as soon as it's convenient? How, Professor Hale? How do I make sure of this?"

Professor Hale frowned. "That's the thing about people. You can't be sure. You can only see how they've conducted themselves in the past and extrapolate the most likely future. Even then, there is always a measure of trust required."

"I don't think I can trust them." She picked at a bit of loose paint on the handle of her teacup.

"Because they are untrustworthy, or because you have a hard time trusting people?"

Annelise shrugged, trying to calm the emotions roiling within. "I don't… I'm going to end up like my mother." The thought had bubbled to the surface so fast that it had left her mouth before she had a chance to process it. With it came a wave of pain, grief, guilt, and fear. She pursed her lips to keep the corners from pulling downward. She swallowed hard. She was not going to cry.

Professor Hale looked at her, his expression filled with compassion. "Annelise," he leaned forward, "I've watched you do everything in your power over the years to make sure that never happens, but there is a long way between trusting someone and ending up like your mother."

"Good." Annelise tried to blink away the tears gathering in her eyes as she struggled to steady her voice. "I want to be as far away from ending up like her as possible."

A long pause stretched between them.

"Okay." Professor Hale leaned back in his chair. "If you think running is the right thing to do, then okay. But I wonder, did you really come all this way, after all this time, just to say goodbye?"

Annelise fidgeted with her sleeve. The storm of guilt raging within her refused to let her agree and move on with her life. It would be a lie. She sighed, flopped her head against the pillowed chair behind her, and sighed again.

"No. I guess, it's because... Even though I agreed under duress, and even though their plan is one hundred percent crazy, and even though I owe them nothing..." she groaned. "I'm feeling irrationally guilty about going back on my word."

Professor Hale did not say anything for a while. The silence stretched between them, and the only sound to be heard was the soft tick tick tick of the grandfather clock on the far wall.

Finally, he said, "You don't want to be in a position of dependence or vulnerability. But I think you're feeling this guilt because you recognize that if you continue down the path you're on, you will end up as someone who is unreliable and untrustworthy."

Heat flooded her cheeks. She knew what he was alluding to. "I'm nothing like my father," Annelise ground through clenched teeth.

She would never ever do to anyone else what he had done to her. She detested what he had done. As much as she found the idea of working with the Pendragons distasteful, inconvenient, and irksome, the guilt she was already feeling from going back on her word, from abandoning them was eating her alive.

And then there was the Dragon to consider. Annelise didn't imagine that the Dragon enjoyed her makeshift prison any more than Annelise would enjoy a cell. She had been cut off from her home and her freedom for far too long. She wasn't sure she could forgive herself for abandoning the quest to save her.

And if what Professor Finchley said was true, that magic would slowly disappear from the world without her presence... She didn't want to live in a world without magic. She didn't want to bear witness to the slow decay of magic and wonder all the days of her life if she hadn't had it in her power to do something about it.

"I don't know what you've gotten yourself into, Annelise, and I don't want you to get into trouble. But I also want to make sure you're making your decisions with a clear head and in a way you can live with. I think you want that too, which is why you came to see me."

Annelise threw an arm across her eyes, trying to block out her frustration with the light. He was right. She had pledged to help the Pendragons try to free the Dragon, and she would never be able to live with herself if she abandoned them now. Anxiety replaced the guilt in her belly as she realized that she would have to go through with the Pendragons' crazy plan.

All the fight seemed to have left her, and she felt drained. She uncovered her face. "Promise me something, will you, Professor Hale?"

He looked at her fondly. "What would you like me to promise you?"

She stared at the arm of her chair. "When I'm in prison, locked away for the rest of my life, will you come visit me once in a while?"

She glanced up at him, a hysterical giggle bubbling up as she finished her sentence.

Professor Hale chuckled. "I will be your most frequent visitor." He lifted his mug. "I'll bring tea." He swung his mug in her direction, and Annelise halfheartedly clinked her cup to his.

"To tea in prison." She brought the cup to her lips, not sure if she was going to burst into laughter or tears.

Chapter 3: The Plan

Six days later, Annelise was in her garage putting the finishing touches on the replica key. She heard the soft chime of the proximity wards she had spelled into the front door. Someone was approaching her home.

She swore. She had hoped to be finished before they arrived. Getting up from her workbench, she went to the front door.

She slid her fingers down a line of runes that lit up as her hand passed over them. The door unlocked. There on the porch stood Tristan and Michael. Their golden eyes were glimmering with excitement.

A small sigh escaped her lips as she stood aside and let them into her home. They looked around as they entered, placing their staves next to hers by the door. Tristan looked perplexed as he took in the small and simple space.

"What were you expecting?" Annelise asked, catching the expression and feeling confrontational. "A mansion?"

"No. Just more chairs," he replied, his eyes still on the room.

"I have another chair in my workroom. I'll go grab it," she mumbled.

"This is amazing," Michael breathed, gliding past her, his eyes drawn to the art on the walls. He walked over to inspect the paintings more closely, lingering at the very painting of the two mages that

Annelise herself cherished so much. "Are these all your own work?" He turned his head to look at her.

Annelise blushed a bit and nodded.

"Originals?" Michael asked.

"Yeah. They're all my own." A bit of pride swelled within her. She turned to Tristan. "I'm just finishing up and will be right back."

"I'd love to watch," Michael said, making to follow her.

Annelise turned and held up a hand. "No. I can't concentrate with people watching. I'm almost done."

She didn't want to deal with their censure about her methods when they saw how she was perfecting her forgery. Annelise slipped into the garage, leaving the Pendragons behind.

Dipping her brush into the small pot that held a few drops of her own blood, she drew the last rune on the base of the key with slow and steady strokes. She started chanting over it. She felt the familiar rush like water pouring over and through her as the magic used her as its conduit. Soon, it was no longer clear if she was chanting the spell or if the spell was chanting Annelise. She was merely a guide for the magic, not its master.

Annelise thought of her mother. Her mother had been the one to teach her the slow, rich power of blood magic and show her the beauty in its versatility. Annelise fed the pain and the beauty of that memory into the spell.

Her head spun as the magic continued to pour through her. She was completely at its mercy until the spell was completed. She continued chanting.

As Annelise chanted, the entire key glowed red before settling back into its rusted copper appearance. The rush of magic flowing through her subsided, leaving Annelise breathless and her head spinning. She rested her head against the cool tabletop for a moment, recovering from the spellwork. It was a simple spell, but it still made the walls warp and the colors spin a bit.

She inspected the key. For a second, even she almost believed that it was the real thing as the magic she had woven around the key tried to nudge her mind into believing it was true.

Annelise smiled. The spell was working beautifully. She took the small jar containing her blood and tucked it out of sight on the shelves in case the Pendragons came into the garage.

She wrapped the key up in a bit of leather. Carrying the key in one hand and her work chair in the other, she made her way back into the house.

Michael and Tristan had rearranged her furniture so that the table now sat in the center of the room. The comfy chair faced it on one end, and the kitchen chair faced it on the other. Tristan stood up and lifted Annelise's chair out of her hands as she came through the door, while Annelise kept the key.

"You received a package while you were finishing up." Michael waved a large brown paper envelope above his head. Annelise realized what it was and blushed furiously.

"I'll take that, thanks." She tried to snatch it from his hand, but Michael gave her a cheeky smile, his golden eyes dancing as he held the parcel out of her reach and felt the package for its contents. By the rumpling of the paper casing, Annelise suspected he had already been investigating its contents and knew what it was: her new identity package.

"Why Annelise, you weren't thinking of running away and abandoning us, were you?" He clutched at his heart with mock hurt.

She flushed even deeper if it was possible, snatched the package out of his hands, and tossed it onto the kitchen counter where it slid into the sink. "Only for a little bit. Now, let's move on."

"Yes," Tristan scooted his chair closer to the table. "I want to see your key."

Annelise placed the wrapped key on the table, and both Tristan and Michael leaned in with anticipation.

Annelise pulled the leather wrapping away from the key, allowing it to gleam in the dim kitchen light.

Michael drew back with a start, his face etched with shock. "How?" he croaked, then shook his head in confusion. "Wait. What?"

Tristan, who had also paled when she first revealed the key, recovered first and grinned broadly. "Annelise, you are a genius."

Michael nodded slowly as he caught on. "Another perception spell."

"More or less," she smirked.

Michael picked up the key and turned it in his hand, inspecting it from all angles. "This spell is different from the last one." He brought the key close to his face, reading the tiny runes she had engraved into the handle. "It's quite potent. I know this is a replica, and still, I can feel it trying to nudge my mind into believing this is the actual key. It's like, I know the truth…but I don't want to." He handed the key to Tristan.

"Let's just say, I was motivated to do good work and increase our chances of staying out of jail." Annelise hoped they did not get nosy about her methods. She did not think the two wardens would approve. Then, again, these cops were planning to steal a dangerous artifact from the government, so maybe they wouldn't be phased.

"It's magnificent." Tristan held the key up to the light. His eyes scanned the piece with appreciation.

Michael stood up from the comfy chair. "You, Miss Windstarter, are magnificent." He caught Annelise's hand and planted a kiss on the back of it.

Annelise pulled her hand away. "Oh, shut up." He was acting ridiculous. But she couldn't help but smile as she turned back to her masterpiece. It was her best work to date, and she was rather proud of it.

***

As the taxi rolled up the gravel driveway to the safehouse where they would make their final preparations, Annelise gaped at the view outside the window in wonder. Most safe houses were small and inconspicuous. The Pendragons, it seemed, had opted for the opposite approach. Row upon row of windows looked out over the front of the property. False pillars decorated the exterior, and a large wooden door with a dragon-headed knocker graced the front of the house.

The two Pendragons ushered her inside and Annelise placed her staff next to theirs in the nook by the door.

She looked around the house, her eyes wide. She knew most Pendragons came from old money, but still, wow. Elegant paintings covered nearly every wall of the grand rooms she saw. The rooms were tastefully decorated—not cluttered to show off wealth, but each detail was attended to so that it lent itself to the overall aesthetic of the house. Sunlight streamed through large windows, landing in pools of liquid gold on the rich rugs and deep hardwood floors.

A man with a dark, receding hairline, wearing spectacles and a sharp suit approached them as they entered the house. "Welcome back, Mr. Pendragon." He handed Tristan a folder full of papers. "Is there anything I can get you? Perhaps tea or coffee?"

"No, thank you, Manny." Tristan flashed him an affectionate smile and Michael also declined. "Annelise, did you need anything?"

Annelise was stunned. "Um, just some water, please."

With a brisk nod of his head and a friendly smile, Manny whisked off to fetch her water. Okay... so these Pendragons were very wealthy.

Tristan led them from the entrance way through a door to the left that opened up into a dining room with a glass chandelier and a large ebony table complete with matching hand-carved chairs.

Annelise stopped in her tracks. There, at the head of the table, mounted on the wall was a familiar painting. It was a Van Tover. It was *the* Van Tover. The very one she had forged so immaculately and sold. With wide eyes, she approached it and inspected the painting. It was not her work. She looked back at Michael.

"This is the original!" she gasped, her mouth hanging open.

Michael smiled. "It is indeed!"

"It was stolen!"

"Alas, it was not. I bought it and then had it reported as stolen. Tristan and I wanted to see what kind of forgeries turned up so we could find the right artist for our job. When we came across yours, well… It was immaculate."

Annelise huffed. "Here you had me doubting my skills. You played dirty."

Michael held up his hands. "What can I say? We wanted the best man for the job, and it's obvious that we found her. Once we started looking into your other work, we knew that you would be perfect."

"What other work, exactly, did you look into?" Annelise asked, feeling betrayed already, but not yet sure by which of her associates.

"We were mostly interested in your forgeries. So we arrested Frank Morty. In exchange for information on only your work, we let him go."

Annelise growled under her breath in frustration. She was definitely going to thwack Frankie with his own stupid cane when she saw him next. Leave some crow-shaped bruises on *his* shins for a change. After all his talk of discretion being of highest priority, and promising retribution to anyone who might snitch on him, he gave her up in an afternoon!

Manny arrived with a glass of water for Annelise, snapping her out of her sour train of thought, and then left them to their business.

Once they were alone again, Annelise leaned into the Pendragons and dropped her voice. "Are we seriously going to finalize our plans to steal from government vaults here?"

Tristan glanced around the massive house. "Can you think of someplace safer?"

Annelise thought about it. "I guess not. And um... Mr. Manny was it?—" she started.

"Manny has been a part of this family longer than either Michael or I have. I trust him with my life."

"Yeah, but does he know what you're planning?"

"He knows our end goal and trusts us with the details. If we have a breach, I can promise you it won't be coming from him," Tristan said firmly, shutting down that line of discussion.

Annelise took a sip of water to cover her incredulous expression.

"So, how did you two come to suspect that the Dragon is being held in the Subraek?" she asked, changing the subject.

Tristan put the file of papers he held onto the table. "We've been looking into the cold case for years. Ever since we were hired as conciliar wardens, really. The loss of the Dragon was devastating for the Pendragon clan, and we want her back."

"It was devastating for all of the magical community," Annelise countered. Her mind flitted to the basin at the academy where the Dragon Blessed waters were ever dwindling.

Michael moved to stand on the other side of the table. "It wasn't until recently that we started making headway, and suspecting that someone in the government might have used their access to lock her away in the Subraek."

Annelise cocked her head. "What made you suspect that?"

Tristan pulled an old newspaper article out of the folder on the table and slid it over to Annelise. The paper was faded and yellowed, and the print had bled into the paper, causing the edges of each letter to blur slightly. "Michael found an account from the time the Dragon disappeared. It claimed that there had been strange lights out over Crater Lake, in Oregon. I doubt the previous investigators thought to look into sourceless newspapers."

Annelise nodded. "That makes sense. The Dragon disappeared before the Integration. Not many mages interacted with the sourceless at the time."

Michael leaned in over the table, picking up the narrative. "Since the Dragon often made her summer nest among the Cascade Mountains, we thought there might be a connection. We went up to Crater Lake ourselves to see if we could find any further clues or evidence, and we found an undocumented portal into the Subraek on the island in the crater. It's just sitting there, unprotected! They even call the island Wizard Island! I think we might be the only ones who know about it."

"Well, us and whoever used it to imprison the Dragon," Tristan corrected.

"Assuming our theory is correct," Michael amended further.

"Wait, wait, wait." Annelise held up her hands. "There's a portal to the Subraek in the middle of Crater Lake, and you didn't report it?" She knew they were planning to enter the Subraek, but she was not oblivious to just how dangerous that place could be. If something got out somehow… It would be disastrous. The last time something got out it caused the Black Death. It had taken years of work and countless lives to get the entity that originated the disease back into the Subraek. Leaving this entrance unreported seemed reckless.

Michael nodded. "Well, since the whole Subraek realm is locked, the portal is useless without the key. But I get what you're saying. It's unsettling to consider that it's just out there, waiting to be messed with. However, its anonymity has proved a good defense so far: you can't exploit a weakness you don't know exists.

"And we did inquire about the island. But as soon as we dropped the Subraek as a potential place where the Dragon might be kept, we were shut down: ordered to cease and desist, told to find a new cold case."

Tristan jumped in. "But then our uncle approached us. He works for the Government—"

"Who is your uncle?" Annelise interrupted.

"Fitzwilliam Cawthorne."

Annelise stared at him. "You mean Councilman Cawthorne?" She tried not to purse her lips. Councilman Cawthorne had singlehandedly villainized the use of blood magic and passed a swathe of laws restricting its use.

"Technically he's our great uncle."

Annelise snorted. "Your uncle doesn't work for the government, your uncle *is* the government." Councilman Cawthorne easily held the most sway in the council. He was a talented debater, and skilled politician. Annelise didn't like him, but she recognized that he wielded a lot of power.

Tristan chuckled. "Don't let him hear you say that."

"No, I like it. He really carved out a spot for himself in government. It's good to see someone other than a Pendragon at the top. I don't agree with all his policies, but I can admire his tenacity," Annelise said, careful to keep her tone light and breezy.

Tristan nodded. "I agree. And the Integration wouldn't have gone half as smoothly without him. Anyway, Uncle Fitz told us that our request had been locked down by the Subraek committee. It seems they were uncomfortable about the line of questioning we were following."

"And... Does your uncle know what you are planning?"

"No." Michael said. "As far as we are aware, he still thinks we plan to pursue this through official legal channels."

"Remind me why you aren't going through legal channels?"

"Because we believe that someone in the government is responsible for her disappearance. If we try to go through legal channels, they will catch wind of our plans and have plenty of time to move her... or worse."

Annelise paused. "How... How do we know that worse hasn't... you know..."

Tristan stared down at the table. "Until I find a body, I have to believe that she's alive." He looked up. "We can't give up if there still could be a chance, no matter how small."

Annelise considered his words. "What makes you so sure that it's someone in the government who caused her disappearance?"

Tristan opened the file on the table and pulled out a stack of papers with various lines on each page redacted. "Uncle Fitz managed to get us access to some of the Executive Session Council Meeting Minutes from just before her disappearance.

They spent a long time planning for the integration, but the matter of the Dragon was one that came up repeatedly. Some had concerns about how the sourceless community would react to the revelation that a dragon was living in their backyard."

He flipped to a page partway through the packet. "Here's some compelling evidence. Councilman Jackson—he was a junior councilman at the time—suggested hiding her in the Subraek for a while until the shock of the integration passed.

"Naturally, the mere suggestion sparked a massive argument and no official decision was made. However, only months later..."

"She disappeared," Annelise finished. Annelise tried to process all the information Tristan had just presented her with. She looked at the Pendragons.

"So you think that Councilman Jackson kidnapped the Dragon, and put her into the Subraek."

Michael and Tristan nodded.

"Your evidence seems very circumstantial."

"True. But no-one but a council member could have had access to the Subraek key. So it stands to reason that someone in the government was complicit in her disappearance."

"Councilman Jackson is still a Council Member."

"More than that, he's on the Subraek Committee," Michael added.

"So if he was responsible, he has both the resources and motive to shut down your investigation."

"He does indeed." Michael nodded. "One of Uncle Fitz's aides told us that shortly after we started making inquiries into the possibility of the Dragon being in the Subraek, he overheard a massive argument happening in Councilman Jackson's office rooms. All the council members' rooms have wards to prevent eavesdropping so he couldn't make out what they were saying, but it sounded heated."

"Clearly our theory and investigation is causing a stir. We think it's because we're on the right track—or at least in the right ballpark. Someone doesn't want us looking into this. Which is exactly why we can't back down."

Annelise took a moment to process the information coming at her. "So you think that Councilman Jackson kidnapped the Dragon, hid her in the Subraek, and is using his seat in the government to keep it under wraps?"

"Yeah. That's our working theory," Tristan said, collecting their evidence into a neat pile. "But we're holding culpability loosely at the moment. Our evidence is pretty circumstantial. But we are confident that the Dragon is in the Subraek. The government has looked everywhere else, so she must be where they haven't looked.

"Okay," Annelise nodded her head and stepped back from the table. "I see your reasoning. I think you have a fair chance of being right about the Dragon being in the Subraek. But why not have your uncle order a search of the Subraek for the Dragon? I'm sure he could make it happen if he asked."

Tristan chuckled. "Contrary to very popular opinion, Uncle Fitz is not the government. The committee which oversees the Subraek makes all decisions regarding opening its doors."

"A committee which Councilman Jackson sits on," Michael added.

"And they haven't deemed it necessary to open those doors in a very long time." Tristan continued. "They are absolutely convinced there was no way to get the Dragon into the Subraek without them knowing about it, and so she couldn't possibly be down there, and so there is simply no reason to open those doors and risk unleashing any of the creatures that were rightfully trapped there."

"So there's nothing your uncle can do?" Annelise asked.

"I'm afraid not. Also, Councilman Jackson and Uncle Fitz often bump heads, so he's not very likely to want to do Uncle Fitz any favors."

Annelise cocked her head. "Okay, then. How are we going to sneak into the vault? I imagine that security will be more robust than the Louvre; we can't just walk up with a ladder and construction vests."

Tristan chuckled as he pulled the last pieces of paper from the folder. The papers were long, but unwrinkled. "These are work orders for Michael and I to upgrade the security wards surrounding the Subraek key."

Annelise frowned. "I thought you needed my help to make the work orders?"

Tristan nodded. "We do. There's one final touch that will make these completely official."

"We need the High Council's official seal," Michael jumped in. "For sensitive work such as this, someone from the Subraek committee has to sign off by using the High Council's seal to certify the work order."

"So you need me to forge the seal," Annelise said.

"No. The seal has a unique magical signature that must be verified by the vaults. You can't forge it."

Annelise was stumped. "So... what then?"

"We need to use the actual seal to certify these work orders, and we need your help to do it."

Annelise frowned. "What are you saying?"

"There's a fundraising gala at the Government Building today. We got you a ticket. You and Michael will slip out of the grand hall, and find the High Council Chamber, and get the orders sealed."

Annelise stepped back, shaking her head. "No, no, no. I told you guys already, I don't do infiltration. It's way too risky. Why can't Michael do it by himself?"

"Because you will be much better able to hide these in the deep pockets of your dress."

"What dress?"

"We bought some dresses for you to pick from. All have pockets big enough to accommodate these," Tristan motioned to the work orders, ignoring her question.

"That's nice. Why don't you wear it?" Annelise snapped.

Michael snickered. Annelise shot him a sour look.

"I'm not a cat burglar," she continued. "The only reason I'm doing the vaults is because you're blackmailing me. This was not part of the deal. No way."

Tristan remained unphased by her refusal. He crossed his arms. "As a matter of fact, it was part of the deal. We said we needed help with the work orders. This is the help we need. Now, you can help us, or we can lock you up here while we get the key the hard way. Then, when the Dragon is free and we return, we will launch a full investigation into every forged and fabricated artifact you've ever sold."

Annelise paled. Her eyes darted to the door leading out of the dining hall.

Michael spoke, "Look Miss Windstarter... Annelise."

Annelise turned her eyes to Michael.

"We will be doing this together. We can do this. You can do this. Just stay close, follow my lead, and it will all be okay."

He looked like he believed it. Annelise glanced back at Tristan.

He uncrossed his arms and gripped the back of the chair in front of him. "Look, it's for the Dragon. None of this is easy. And we all have to take risks."

Annelise clenched her jaw. "And where will you be, while Michael and I are off taking risks?"

"I will be in front of the crowds at the Gala, giving a speech, keeping the people's attention focused on me, and away from the two of you as you slip out of the room."

Annelise ran a trembling hand through her hair. "Fine," she whispered. "I'll do it."

Michael grinned. Tristan's grip on the chair relaxed. "Thank you," Tristan said. "It's our best chance of getting the key and making a clean getaway. Now, once we have the work orders we will head straight for the vaults."

"So soon?" Annelise asked. She rubbed a hand over her face, stifling a groan.

Michael shrugged. "Why wait?"

Annelise downed her water, wishing for something stronger. She took a deep breath. The only way forward was through, it seemed. "Okay," she forced some pep into her voice. "How are we going to break into the government vaults then?"

Tristan grabbed a bag from one of the chairs, and pulled several rolls of paper out. He spread them on the table revealing a set of blueprints for the government vaults. It was a large warehouse.

"This is where the government keeps items deemed too valuable, powerful, or otherwise dangerous for the general population to have access to."

Annelise leaned in, peering at the blueprints. She couldn't help but feel a thrill of excitement at the thought of all the artifacts hidden away in the vaults. "So this is where all the fun magic has been sequestered to." She looked up at the Pendragons. "Do you know what's in there?"

Tristan and Michael exchanged a look. "That's going to remain classified," Tristan said.

Annelise smirked at them. "What? Don't you trust me?" she asked in a teasing tone, leaning her chin on her fist and batting her eyelashes at them.

Tristan hesitated.

Annelise felt an unexpected sting at his hesitation. "That's okay," she said, standing straight and forcing a carefree smile as she dragged her fingertips across the edge of the blueprints. She could not meet either of the Pendragon's gaze. "I don't trust you either." She glanced in their direction to see how the jab had landed.

Both Pendragons stilled.

Michael leaned in across the table, meeting her gaze. "Annelise,regardless of any hesitation we have about divulging government secrets to you, we are trusting you. We are putting our security into your hands for this. We all have to trust each other if we want to have a hope of freeing the dragon."

Annelise blinked, and nodded. "Okay." She believed him. They were relying on her. It both bewildered and terrified her. But Annelise was determined not to let herself end up in a position where she had to rely on them. She would take care of herself. "I won't let you down."

Michael returned her nod. "I believe you."

Tristan leaned in. "Look, "If everything goes right, they won't even know we were there."

"You know, everyone who has ever gotten caught has said those exact words," Annelise observed.

Tristan smirked. "Probably, but I bet some of the ones who haven't gotten caught have said them too. We just don't know who they were."

"Right." Annelise remained unconvinced. "So what's the plan?"

Michael pointed to a room near the center of the compound, "The key is in a vault here. Tristan and I can smuggle you into the grounds in the trunk of the car, while our work orders will give us access through the gate.

"After we have gotten past the outer gate, you will enter the building here." He pointed to an air vent that opened up to the grounds surrounding the compound. "You will have to crawl through the vents until you get to this junction box... here." He pointed to another spot on the map. "There, I want you to tap into the digital feed of the security cameras and keep us apprised of the movements of the guards. I'll also show you how to loop the feed so that the guards and security cameras don't register the switch."

Annelise chewed on her lip, thinking. "On a building like this, there are bound to be top-level security wards protecting it. As soon as I trigger those spells, we're going to have a massive warden response on our hands."

Michael chuckled, a quirk of overconfidence tugging at his mouth. "Tristan and I both specialized in security ward establishment at the academy and have spent many years inventing and perfecting the skill of interrupting wards without destroying or triggering them."

"What Michael means is that he invented and perfected it," Tristan said. "I am but his humble student in this matter."

Annelise was impressed.

Michael continued his explanation, ignoring the compliment. "The interrupted ward won't register as triggered or dismantled. It will still think it's running like normal, allowing us to slip past, undetected. We can get you past the wards before we head in through the front door."

Annelise was stunned. The possibilities of such a technique were endless. "And you've tested this?"

Michael couldn't seem to keep the proud smile off his face. "Works every time! It takes a minute to pull it off, but it works."

Annelise looked back at the plans. If they were as good as they said they were, this could work. A memory clicked into place, and her eyes snapped up to Michael's. She pointed a finger at him. "That's why my perimeter wards didn't go off at Mr. Aisel's Penthouse! You interrupted my wards."

Michael smirked. "Sorry."

"No, you're not."

He laughed, his eyes twinkling. "No, I'm not."

Tristan directed their attention back to the blueprint. "Michael and I will enter through the front doors." He pointed to the main entrance of the facility. "From there, we will make our way to the central vault. As we pretend to work on the security wards, Michael will interrupt the wards, and I will make the switch and drop the forgery in its place. Once we have the key, the wards will be reinstated like we were never there. We will all make our way out of the facility the same way we came in, and we head straight for Crater Lake."

Annelise gazed at the blueprints. If what they were saying was true... It seemed like a good plan. If nothing went wrong, it just might work.

***

They spent the next few hours poring over the blueprints, memorizing the layout of the building. Annelise drilled into her mind a map of the ventilation shafts until she could recite the path to the junction box, the front door, the secure warden transportation platform, and back out the way she came. Tristan wanted her to know every possible route, "Just in case." They drilled the placement of stationary guards, and learned the ins and outs of every security feature they had access to. Again, "just in case." They brainstormed backup plans, should their primary exits be unavailable and discussed every contingency they could think of.

Tristan showed her how to work all of the technology she would be using to cut into the security feed, and then made her practice it, over and over again.

Annelise's eyes started burning, and her mind buzzed. She didn't think she could fit another fact into her brain. "Guys, I need a break."

Drawing a hand over his eyes, Tristan nodded. "You're right. We could all use a break. Let's clean this up for now. We will do one last review right before we head to the Gala."

Annelise set about putting her equipment away, while Michael and Tristan rolled up the blueprints.

"Michael, Tristan," a voice came from the doorway. Annelise's head jerked up, and she did her best to not look guilty. An older middle-aged man of about one hundred and thirty, wearing fine clothes and a beautiful ruby that glinted in the warm lights of the house stood in the doorway, handing his jacket and staff to Manny, who whisked the items away. Annelise tried not to let her jaw drop as she recognized the man. From his impeccable posture to his lined face, shock of white hair, and cool grey eyes, it was unmistakably Councilman Cawthorne.

"Who is your friend?" Councilman Cawthorne asked, peering at Annelise.

"Uncle Fitz!" Tristan exclaimed, smiling as he continued to roll up the blueprints as though they weren't classified schematics to a heavily guarded facility—though Annelise thought his smile was more measured than she had ever seen him give.

"This is Annelise Windstarter. She's a painter. We are commissioning her for some new artwork."

"Oh yes, I remember you mentioning something about bringing in new art. How nice." The councilman turned to her. "Windstarter, was it? I've never heard your name attached to any of the national galleries."

Annelise had to work hard not to react to the snobbery in his voice. He always seemed much more likable on TV.

"Annelise is a local artist," Michael cut in. "We thought it would be nice to support a local craftsman — sorry, craftswoman." He gave her a gallant bow. "We looked into her work and thought it would make a nice addition to our collection."

Councilman Cawthorne smiled thinly. "Very well. Tristan, I hope you haven't forgotten to write your speech for the fundraising Gala tonight. I'd like you to actually practice your speech this year."

"Yes, uncle."

Councilman Cawthorne turned to Michael. "And I will need you to reach out to some key guests who haven't committed to a donation yet. Let's put that silver tongue of yours to good use."

"Of course, Uncle."

Tristan's nose flared as Councilman Cawthorne turned and swept out of the room. Michael had a vacant smile plastered on his face that fell away as soon as Councilman Cawthorne was out of view.

He shared a look with Tristan, and for a minute, they were having another one of their wordless conversations. Annelise wasn't sure exactly what was being said, but it was made up entirely of eye-widening, eyebrow-raising, and much rolling of the eyes.

"Wait, whose house is this exactly?" Annelise asked, her stomach clenching at the notion that she had just invaded the Councilman's home without his knowledge.

"It's mine." There was an annoyed edge to Tristan's voice as he closed the blueprint casing with an aggressive snap. "I inherited it after my parents died. Uncle Fitz likes the library and comes here most evenings to unwind."

"Or to wind him up," Michael murmured under his breath.

When everything was cleared away, Tristan went to occupy Councilman Cawthorne, while Annelise followed Michael out the front doors and onto the property grounds. There was a large gravel lane of chalky gray rocks surrounding the house. Beyond the lane, a rolling lawn with arrangements of vibrant flowers adorned the landscape. Framing the garden was a wall of tall birch trees with white trunks and bright green leaves. She loved birch trees. She breathed in the warm summer evening air, trying to calm her mind. The breeze rustled through the branches. She would have loved to sit out here and paint.

"So, tell me about your art," Michael said, strolling along beside her. The wind tousled his dark curls across his forehead.

Annelise frowned. "What about it?"

"What made you start painting?"

Annelise stared at him. "How is this going to help us achieve our mission?"

Michael shot her a look, his eyebrows slightly raised. "It's a way to unwind. Talking about something light. It refreshes the mind."

Annelise hesitated. "Tell me about yours first."

"Sorry?"

"You draw."

"I do." Michael didn't seem inclined to explain.

"Did you ever think of doing something with that?" she pressed.

Michael sighed. "To be honest? As a child, I was determined to be an artist. I wanted to be number one in the world."

Annelise waited for him to continue. He didn't. "So what happened?"

Michael's eyes fell to the ground as he scuffed the dirt beneath his shoe. "I discovered I only had craft, but no artistry."

Annelise cocked her head, waiting for him to explain.

Michael looked up at her and shrugged. "I attended a prestigious and competitive art academy as a child, and I flunked out. I thought I was making good work, but somehow my work never landed right."

He pinched his fingers together and adopted an exaggerated Italian accent. "Michael, where's the heart? I want to see the heart." He let his hands fall to his side. "Eventually, I gave up. I came to terms with my limitations."

Annelise's brow furrowed. "So what did you do?"

Michael looked off toward the horizon where the sun was disappearing behind the Sierra Nevada Mountains. "I had to find a new dream."

"Being a Conciliar Warden."

Michael nodded slowly. "It's what I do for now." He turned to look at her. "I'm more interested in finding the Dragon. I figured if I was incapable of making my mark on the world with my art, maybe I could change the world by making a mark on its history."

"Why do you have to change the world at all? Why not just live your life?"

"I guess I want to be able to look back on my life and feel like it mattered. Like, there was a point to all of it."

Annelise wasn't sure how to respond to that. "Well, to me it sounds like you have all the skills necessary to be an excellent forger." She gave him a light smile.

Michael chuckled. "Thanks. But it wouldn't be the same."

"Hmm. You're right. Recreation feels different from creation." She shot him a sympathetic look. "For what it's worth, I'm sorry about your art." She paused. "I can't imagine…" she trailed off, lost for words. She couldn't imagine ever having to leave it all behind. She definitely couldn't imagine trying to find a new refuge.

Michael sighed. "Come on. Let's go around the back to the kitchen. I want to keep you away from Uncle Fitz's scrutiny for now, and I want something to eat."

Annelise followed Michael through a small garden that led to a north facing entrance to the house. As they wandered through the grand hallways, her eye was caught by one of the paintings. It was a striking portrait of a young woman with bright golden eyes and curling black hair. She was dressed in a lacy white 1870s tea gown edged with bright red ribbons. Annelise searched for the signature. There in the corner, she saw the name painted in fine brushstrokes. She couldn't make it all out, but she could see that the last part of the first name was -Dee, and the last name was Finchley.

"Ahh, I see you've met Grandma Dee," Michael walked up behind her.

"Your grandmother painted this?" Annelise asked in surprise.

"Well, she's my great-grandmother, but yes."

"Any relation to Professor Finchley?" Annelise asked, turning to Michael.

Michael shook his head. "Grandma Dee was an only child."

Annelise turned back to the painting. "She was quite the painter."

"She is indeed."

Annelise looked at him, eyebrows raised. "She's still alive?"

"Yup. She's almost two hundred years old now."

Annelise inspected the painting again, looking for any family resemblance. "You have her hair." She decided.

Michael chuckled. "I suppose I do."

Annelise stepped back to admire the rest of the paintings hanging on the wall. "Do you have a favorite?" she asked.

Michael grinned as he led her down the hall to a large painting of a mage with bright golden eyes brimming with excitement that seemed to stare right at her. He stood, arms flung wide, with his heels dangling off the edge of a cliff. Wispy clouds stretched out behind him.

"This is Ambrose Pendragon." His face was drawn into an echo of the grin in the painting. "He is my great-great-great-great grandfather, and the last Pendragon blessed with the ability to take on dragon form."

"Neat."

Michael glanced at her. "You're not gonna push back? Some people prefer to believe that it never happened. That the tales of taking dragon form were all exaggerations and propaganda to consolidate power for the Pendragon clan."

Annelise shrugged. "We are mages. I think almost anything is possible. And there are many things that used to be possible when dragons roamed widely that are no longer within reach. Just because things are a certain way now, doesn't mean it's the way they always were."

They moved on and Michael led her into the kitchen. The kitchen was spacious with an island, and room overhead for hanging pots, pans, and spatulas for easy access. The walls were bright cream colors, giving the room a lively, but clean feel.

Manny was there, putting some dishes away. He greeted them with a friendly smile as they entered the kitchen. "Hello, there, Michael, Miss Windstarter. Is there anything I can get you? Coffee, or tea perhaps?"

"No, thank you, Manny. I've got it," Michael moved around the kitchen with ease. "I'm going to make some coffee, would you like some, Annelise? Manny, do you want your usual?"

Manny smiled fondly at Michael. "Yes, please." He went to the cupboard and pulled some cookies out, arranging them on a plate.

He offered the plate to Annelise. "You should try one, Miss Windstarter. Tristan makes excellent cookies."

Annelise tentatively took a cookie off the plate. "Tristan bakes?"

"Just chocolate chip cookies," Michael said. "But he's gotten very good at them. Coffee?" He waved an empty mug at her.

"Um, sure, if you're making it anyway. Thanks." She took a bite of the cookie. It was indeed the perfect texture and filled with chocolate chips that melted on her tongue.

Within a few minutes, the kitchen was filled with the rich scent of brewed coffee. Michael poured some cream into a cup, added a cube of sugar, and handed it to Manny. Manny nodded his thanks and snagged a couple cookies off the plate.

A bell above them chimed. "It seems that the Councilman has left, so I think I will retire for the evening unless there is anything else I can do for you?"

Michael smiled. "No, thank you, Manny. Just let Tristan know where we are when you see him?"

Manny nodded, bade them both goodnight, and swept out of the kitchen, sipping his coffee as he went.

"Goodnight, Manny," Annelise called after him. She turned to Michael. "How does he do that?"

"Do what?"

"Drink coffee while walking, and not spill anything?" She chuckled.

Michael laughed. "Well, I suppose it comes from years of practice. That man loves his coffee, and he refuses to make messes."

"He seems nice."

"He's the best."

"Who's the best?" Tristan asked, stalking into the room. His body language radiated with agitation.

"Manny," Michael replied simply.

Some of the tension seemed to drain out of Tristan. He tilted his head in agreement. "Too true. For one, I'm sure I would have ruined my relationship with Uncle Fitz by now if not for him. He really…" Tristan snorted in frustration in lieu of words.

"Uncle Fitz having a day?" Michael asked.

Tristan started pacing the kitchen. "I don't need that on top of everything else going on." He paused, sniffing the air. "Do I smell coffee?"

Michael slid a cup full to the brim in his direction. "You sure do."

They sipped their coffee in silence for a while.

Annelise's mind started flitting back over everything she had learned. She contemplated the evidence they had that pointed to a conspiracy within the government to imprison the Dragon. She ran over each piece of evidence again, analyzing it in her mind, trying to find holes in their logic or possible errors in their methodology.

She ran over the plan again and again, fretting over every possible thing that could go wrong. Her mind rehashed each step of the plan, each angle, rotating each part in her mind. They had covered every possible feasible contingency plan. Still, Annelise couldn't shake the nervous fear in the pit of her stomach. If something did go wrong, it was going to go very wrong.

"Do you really think this will work?"

Tristan looked at her, his face set with determination. "I think it's our best chance, and that we have an obligation to try, regardless of whether we succeed or fail."

Annelise nodded in agreement. He was probably right, but she didn't like being obliged to do anything. She much preferred her freedom.

When they finished their coffee, Tristan pulled the blueprints out again and laid them on the island counter.

"Let's go over this one more time." They reviewed the details of the plan, then double and triple-checked that they had all the necessary equipment properly stored.

"Have you picked a dress yet?" Tristan asked Annelise.

"Oh. No, I haven't."

Tristan looked at his watch, and said, "Well, we have about 30 minutes before we should be heading out to the Gala. Michael, can you show her where we put the dresses? We will meet in the entrance hall. And then..."

And then it would be time to commit the biggest crime of her life.

Chapter 4: The Gala

The woman in front of Annelise looked like she had stepped straight out of a Sargent painting. Her dark hair was swept into a french twist, while the fabric of her dress glimmered in the evening light. The line to the front doors of the Government building inched forward. People dressed resplendently packed the line, while other couples milled, arm in arm, around the plaza.

Annelise had thought her dress was over the top when she first put it on: The shimmering golden gossamer fabric was draped across her figure and fell in graceful folds down to just above her ankles. A scroll containing their forged work orders sat in each pocket. Now, as she looked at the finery around her, she felt underdressed.

The line moved forward once again. She was just shy of the security station. She fidgeted with the invitation that the Pendragons had procured for her. A scrawling line of golden ink on thick cream colored paper announced her invitation into the Gala. The Pendragon cousins were already inside helping their uncle with any last minute organizational details for the event. They had gotten in without the need to go wait in line. Annelise was not so lucky. A wave of nerves rolled over her, and she took a steadying breath. She just had to focus on getting through the front door. The rest would come later.

The line moved again, and Annelise stepped up to one of the four security guards checking people's tickets, and admitting people into the building. She handed him her invitation.

"Please place your staff in the circle." The guard did not look up from her invitation.

With a flick of her wrist, her staff was in her hand. She placed the butt of her staff in the center of a small circle of runes that glowed electric blue when her staff made contact.

"Please state your name," the guard said with an emotionless tone that could only be earned after saying the same set of words for hundreds of times.

"Annelise Windstarter."

A pillar of blue light burst upward from the circle, encompassing her staff and her hand. When the light faded, a delicate tendril of blue magic remained encircling her wrist.

"Your staff will become available to you when you leave the Gala."

Annelise nodded mutely. With a flick of her wrist, her staff retracted and her hand was free. The fine chain of magic remained around her wrist, joining the anti-tracing charm she had bought from Waylyn. She had given Tristan and Michael each one as well.

The guard saw the charm and gave her a questioning glance.

"Oh," Annelise said, acknowledging the bracelet. She gave the guard an embarrassed smile. " Bad breakup," she explained. "He got kind of controlling, and I didn't want him stalking me, so—"

"Enjoy the party," the guard waved her inside before she could explain any more.

Annelise walked up to the front doors that towered over her. She flicked her wrist, testing the magic that bound her staff. Her staff did not appear. Her hand felt empty without it. She tapped the earbud nestled in her ear that was supposed to connect her to her Pendragon associates.

"I just made it past security." She received no response. She flicked her hand again, wishing for her staff, but it did not appear. Frustration bubbled just below her ribcage. Forcing the feeling down, Annelise made her way through the gilded doors of the Government building.

Golden light filled the room. Columns of marble lined the walls. On each column, The impurities that flowed through the milky stone seemed to form the image of a water dragon. The room was already filled with dignitaries and guests in their glittering gowns and robes. They milled around the room, admiring the art and architecture. Here and there, a waiter in a smart white coat darted through the crowds with trays of drinks and appetizers made of ingredients so unpalatable only the very rich or very cultured would dare attempt them. Music wafted through the air from the string quartet playing on the small stage at the front of the room.

She took a few steps into the hall, her eyes darting from face to face. Her hopes of easily finding the Pendragons fizzled, and there was still no response through her communication device. A gentleman with angular features and ice blue eyes brushed past her. She plunged her hand into the deep pockets of her dress to double check that the documents were still there. The corner of the orders brushed against her fingertips, and she pulled her hand out of her pocket.

She caught a glimpse of Councilman Cawthorne being approached by a couple in absolutely dazzling regalia. The crowd shifted again, and the sight was swallowed up by jeweled fabrics. Annelise let the crowd pull her in its tide until she came near to one of the great marble columns that supported the gilded ceiling high above her head. Maneuvering out of the flow of the crowd, she tucked herself into the shadow of the column and tried again to find the face of anyone she knew. She struggled to see above the sea of people.

She raised herself onto her tiptoes, only gaining an extra inch beyond the heels she was wearing. A face appeared, but it was not the one she had expected.

"Professor Finchley," she exclaimed, relief flooding through her.

He was making his way toward her, a smile on his face. He wore emerald robes lined with bold golden stitching. More golden threadwork peeked out from behind his white beard. A panel of green and gold brocade fabric hung from each shoulder and almost reached the floor, giving him a courtly appearance.

"Fancy seeing you here, my dear," he said. "I didn't know that you cared for these kinds of events."

"I don't." A scowl pulled at the corners of her mouth. "But I was invited, and it would have been bad for business had I declined the invitation. So, here I am."

"Oh?" Professor Finchley asked. Annelise didn't particularly want to get into details, but he looked at her so expectantly she felt she could not avoid giving some sort of explanation.

"I sold a painting to one of the organizers, and he declared that I simply had to be here to connect with more art enthusiasts." Annelise said. "Now, I'm all for connecting with more potential clients, but I prefer more intimate settings. Still, I hope to do business with him again in the future, and so... at this party I must be. I was actually looking for one of them. The organizers, that is."

"Well, who are you looking for? Perhaps I will have a better chance of seeing them over the top of all this crowd."

"Do you happen to know either Tristan or Michael Pendragon?"

"I do indeed. And where you find one, you will soon find the other, in my experience." Professor Finchley pulled himself to his full height and scanned the room. "Ah, yes. Just there." He offered his arm to Annelise, and she accepted it, allowing him to lead her across the room.

"So why are you here, Professor?"

"Oh, I like to stay in the loop. I've been doing a bit of advising on a security matter and, much like you, making an appearance at an event like this is good for business."

"Professor, lawyer, security consultant. You're absolutely everywhere. How on earth do you manage to have your fingers in so many pots?"

"My dear, when you are as old as I am, you learn that true power is in who you know. I've just spent a very long time getting to know a great many people. Now I'm at a place where I can make my voice heard, and encourage practices that will benefit everyone."

"Hmm. Sounds exhausting." Annelise said. "All I want in the world is to be left alone with my work."

Professor Finchley chuckled. "An understandable position, but it may change over time. Ah!" They broke through a particularly dense cluster of people and found Michael, dressed in a crisp white suit, giving instructions to some of the waiters. He glanced at Annelise as she approached and flashed her a smile. He gave a few final words to the three waiters he had assembled, and they dispersed to carry out whatever instructions he had given them.

"Professor Finchley, it is good to see you," Michael offered his hand for a handshake.

"It is good to be seen," Professor Finchley replied with a polite smile, either ignoring or not seeing the handshake. Michael let his hand drop.

Professor Finchley turned to Annelise, and patted her hand. "I will leave you here. There are some people that I, too, am looking for."

Annelise thanked him and he turned and disappeared into the crowd.

Michael watched him disappear, gave a minute shake of his head and turned back to Annelise.

"How are things going?" Annelise asked.

"I think everything is ready. How is that dress treating you?"

Annelise gave a slow nod, her hand drifting to the folds of her dress where the documents were tucked away. "It's doing the job."

"It is indeed." His mouth quirked with a small smile as he offered her his arm.

Annelise rolled her eyes but took his offered arm. Another wave of nerves assaulted her, and she tried to dispel them with a slow, controlled breath.

Michael squeezed her arm. "It's going to be okay, this is the easy part."

Annelise tried to believe him. But all she could see was that there were far too many potential witnesses for this to go off without a hitch.

Tristan appeared through the crowd, concern lining his face. He glanced around the room, and then leaned in close. "Uncle Fitz was just complaining that some of the other council members want to pull him away for some business."

Annelise looked up in alarm. "You mean business, like, they'll be working where we are snooping?"

Tristan nodded, his mouth set in a grim line. "Look. This doesn't have to change anything. I will do what I can to keep the council members engaged as long as possible. The two of you need to get in, seal the orders, and get out."

Annelise's palms were sweating. She glanced at Michael who was running a hand through his black curls. She saw the first signs of strain flash across his face, but he smoothed them away and flashed her a smile.

"We will be quick. If something comes up, you'll hear from me."

"They locked my staff," Annelise commented. "Any chance you can unlock it for me?"

"I'm afraid not. It's standard procedure for events like these. Ours are locked too. It will automatically unlock when you leave the building."

Annelise shifted her weight in frustration. "So we have no magic, and no time."

"No, just… less magic, and less time," Michael said.

Annelise huffed. "Whatever. The sooner we get this over with, and I get my staff back, the better."

Tristan nodded. "Let's do this."

Michael made to guide Annelise away, but Tristan stopped him with a hand on his shoulder. "For the Dragon."

Michael covered the hand on his shoulder with one of his own. "For the Dragon," he echoed.

Tristan gave Annelise a curt nod, and then disappeared into the crowd. Michael stood there a moment, his eyes not leaving the spot where Tristan had just been standing.

"You ready to get this over with?" Annelise asked, her nerves already starting to ramp up again.

He looked down at her, and gave her an almost-perfect smile. It did not quite reach his eyes, and there was too much tightness around his mouth. "Yes. We should go." He offered her his arm, and whisked her across the room. Along the way he snagged a glass of champagne off the tray of a passing waiter.

"Some courage for the road?" He offered her the glass.

Annelise's stomach turned at the sight of it. "No." She didn't want to give up her control to any amount to alcohol.

Michael downed the glass in one go, grimacing as he did. It only lasted for a moment, before he had arranged his face back into a smile.

"Try not to look so scared," he said as he led Annelise to a door on the far side of the room. "It's gonna be okay."

"I'm not sure I believe that," she murmured back.

A guard stood between their door and the next one to ensure that nobody did exactly what Annelise and Michael intended to do: venture into the secure parts of the government building.

Annelise's mouth was suddenly dry. She swallowed.

Michael paused, leaning against the recess in which the door was set. He rested a hand on the small of her back and looked down at her. His smile had softened, but it seemed more real now. "Smile up at me, like I've just said something you find absolutely delightful."

Annelise was sure her smile looked more like a grimace, but it was the best she could manage. She reached a trembling arm up, and hooked it around his shoulder for support.

Michael's smile grew. "We'll work on it," he chuckled.

Annelise glanced out across the sea of people.

Tristan was making his way to the small stage that stood at the front of the hall. His bright teal suit contrasted against the cream colored marble behind him.

A hush fell over the crowd as Tristan welcomed the guests to the event. He began his speech, thanking various guests and donors for their contributions. As he launched into the account of everything the charitable event had accomplished in the last year, he made to lean casually against the podium. The podium tipped, and there was a moment where the podium, Tristan and the audience were suspended in time, before gravity reasserted itself. The podium crashed to the marble floor. Every eye in the room snapped toward the stage. Tristan disappeared beneath the surface of the crowd as he toppled off the platform. The audience gasped. Annelise glanced at the guard to ensure that he too was focused on the commotion taking place on stage.

"Let's go," Michael said.

Annelise darted through the door behind him into the dimly lit corridor. It was quiet. The muted sounds of Tristan's profuse apologies butted up against the door, but only a small amount of the sound managed to force its way past. Annelise felt some of the tension drain out of her. Michael grabbed her hand.

"In case someone comes along," he explained. "We can pretend like we were looking for a moment alone."

Annelise shot him an incredulous look. "I don't know, Michael. I think you just want to hold my hand," she teased.

Michael said nothing but blushed deeply, which then caused Annelise to blush. Now she wanted to pull her hand away. But Michael was right. It was better to pose as a lovestruck couple looking for a quiet moment away, should they be caught. They would be considered foolish, but not criminal.

A few hallways down, the lights were dimmed. Annelise's shoes echoed loudly against the stone flooring, so she stopped to pull them off. She breathed a sigh of relief as the coolness of the stone floors seeped into her bare feet. Much better.

They scurried through the halls. Annelise's ears strained down every hallway for the sound of footsteps, but her heart was pounding so loudly in her ears that it sounded constantly like someone was running in their direction.

Finally they came to the Council Chamber. The room where every law pertaining to magic and the magical community for all of North America was deliberated and acted upon.

Annelise had only ever seen the room on television. Never in person.

The room was large. A raised platform stretched along three of the four walls of the room, and on the raised platform stood a large ebony table that formed a half-circle arch.

Along the fourth wall of the room was the Dragon's seat. It was massive—made of a wide stone platform, the edge of which was decorated with golden dragon figurines. In days long gone, dragons held respected positions on the High Council. And now, long after dragons stopped bothering to involve themselves in the political affairs of the magical community, they still kept a ceremonial seat here in the heart of government.

Decorative marble vaulted arches lined the walls, with small alcoves recessed into each arch. Each alcove was adorned with some attraction from art to floral arrangements, to a bookshelf. A rich pale golden carpet covered the floor while the ceiling reached high above them into a dome decorated with some mosaic which was currently too dark to make out. A crystal window set in the center of this dome would let light pour into the chamber during the day. Now it was just a dark shadow reaching above them.

Annelise ran a hand over a small dragon figurine. Perhaps, they would see a dragon in the Dragon's Seat once again.

Michael sprang forward, and started pulling drawers open, looking for the seal. He started near the seat at the center of the table. Annelise followed his lead. She pulled open a drawer, finding papers, and writing supplies. She rifled through it before carefully shutting the drawer again, and moving to the next one. This one contained only files. The next drawer contained only an ornate box. Annelise gasped with excitement. She opened the box. It was empty. She snapped the drawer shut in frustration, and looked around the room.

Her eyes fell on the alcoves. Perhaps they were looking in the wrong place? She made her way towards one of the alcoves with a large painting held in a gilded frame. She reached out with her magic, trying to see if she could sense any wards or spells near it. Nothing. She moved to the next alcove and then the next. When she reached the bookshelf, she stilled.

There, humming beneath her fingertips was the telltale thrum of magic.

"Michael," she whispered. He looked up from a file he was flipping through. Annelise frowned. Now was not the time to get distracted. "Here."

Michael put the file away, and hurried to her side. Annelise could feel where the magic was centered, but it was behind several of the books. She reached up to move them, but Michael stayed her hand.

"Wait." Reaching out, he found the trail of magic, and with a twitch of his fingers, suddenly the tendrils of white magic were visible running through the bookshelf, and along the books. They all seemed to cut through one particularly large tome. Michael pulled the book back, and a section of the shelf swung out.

Annelies ducked as the heavy wooden shelf swung at her face, while Michael sprang away. The removed section revealed a door to a safe. The door was small, no more than a foot tall and wide. Reaching out once again, Michael flared the wards to life. These ones burned a violet blue.

Annelise stepped aside, and watched as Michael used the technique he had invented to interrupt the wards without breaking them or triggering them. As she watched, she tried to discern how his technique worked.

"Go keep watch," Michael's eyes did not leave the tendrils of light he was attempting to manipulate.

Annelise peeled herself away from the fascinating display of novel magic. She darted around the great table to the door. She cracked it open and peered down the hall.

Every so often she glanced back at Michael to see his progress. Several of the blue threads of light seemed to be separated, but still active. Annelise was amazed. If she could learn this skill, the possibilities would be endless.

She stilled. The sound of footsteps echoed down the hall. They were getting closer.

"Michael," she whispered. "Someone's coming."

"Just a moment more." He was working on the last two strands.

Two figures appeared from around the corner of the hall, walking straight towards the Council Chamber.

She pulled back from the door, and ran towards Michael.

"No. Now."

Michael looked at her, his jaw clenched with frustration. But the voices of the council members were quickly approaching the door. He released his hold on the tendrils of magic and they snapped back to their original course. Together they swung the shelf back into place.

They ducked down behind the table just as the doors to the council chamber opened. Annelise's heart pounded in her chest.

"Well that's something I won't soon forget," one of the voices said.

The other voice chuckled. "Me neither. The most interesting speech I've had the displeasure of sitting through in a long time. I swear these speeches get longer every year."

The other voice snorted. "It's because they have so many more donors to thank."

Annelise looked around. They were hidden for the moment but if the council members came to this side of the room, they would be found. She glanced at a nearby alcove. It was decorated with a well crafted painting that was not at all to her taste. But, if they stayed low, they were less likely to be found tucked away in the alcove behind the great table. Glancing back at Michael she gestured to the hiding spot. He nodded at her.

They crept along the carpeted floor. Annelise's foot got caught in the long skirt of her dress and she nearly fell on her face. She stilled, held her breath, and then continued on again. Michael was already tucking himself into the alcove, and she slid in beside him. It was cramped. Annelies's knees pressed against Michael's and the gilded frame of the painting dug into her shoulder.

"Will Cawthorne be joining us?" The first voice asked, as he tossed an orb of light into the air. Light filled the room. Annelise tried to melt into the floor and wall as much as possible. She barely dared to breathe.

She craned her neck to see who it was who was talking, but she couldn't see past the desk. This was good. If she couldn't see them, they probably couldn't see her either.

"As soon as his nephew finishes his speech. After that start, I don't blame him. The young man will need all the moral support he can get." The other voice replied.

The door to the council chamber opened again. Annelise craned her neck. Between the edge of the alcove and corner of the great table, there was a thin sliver where she could see the activity at the door. A petite, brown-haired woman entered the room, followed by Councilman Cawthorne and the new Councilman Verdre. All she caught was a glimpse of each person before they disappeared behind the table.

"Ah, good. We're all here. Jackson, Trewson, this is Detective Poe," Councilman Cawthorne said. She heard the sound of the bookshelf being swung open, and the safe behind it opening too.

The voice of Junior Councilman Verdre spoke. "There have been some concerns raised of late by certain members of the council about the security surrounding the key to the Subraek."

Annelise stifled a gasp. Michael tapped his earbud to activate it. Annelise could now hear the conversation coming through her earpiece as well with a slight delay. Somewhere in the building, Tristan would be hearing this too.

Verdre continued, "Although the security surrounding the key is top notch, there have been attempts to get access to it in the past. And as much as I have faith in the competence of our security systems and personnel, we cannot ignore the possibility that one day someone is going to make it all the way through. Therefore, on advice from consultation, we have decided that the best option would be to protect the key with a rolling transfer from secure location to secure location every few years."

"I would like to state for the record that I do not think this is the best plan of action." Councilman Jackson said. "I think keeping the key where it is and increasing the security around it is our best plan of action. Moving the key introduces too many variables—"

"Thank you Jackson," Councilman Cawthorne's voice rang out, laced with weariness. "Your concern has been noted. Please continue Verdre."

Verdre obliged. "We are entrusting this task to you, detective. You may assemble a small team, but they must be people that you absolutely trust beyond a shadow of a doubt. I will also advise you that Mr. Robin Finchley has offered his insight and expertise should you choose to make use of it. But ultimately, how you secure the key is up to you. It must be moved in absolute secret and to a location that none but you, your team, and this committee know. Once it's moved, you will inform the committee.

"In the meantime," Councilman Cawthorne's voice cut in, "we are giving you the High Council seal."

Annelise closed her eyes in frustration. They had been so close!

Cawthorne continued, "You have latitude to take whatever reasonable action and use whatever reasonable resources you deem necessary in order to assemble your team, and secure the key."

There was a moment where no one spoke. Then, "Understood," the detective said. She sounded slightly dazed. If Annelise wasn't choking on her own frustration, she would have sympathized.

"One more thing," Councilman Cawthorne said. "Certain rumors have been brought to our attention, unsubstantiated and lacking much-needed relevant detail, about a plan to steal the key within the next month or so. The sooner you can get the key moved the better. Secrecy of location will be its best defense."

Annelise looked at Michael, her eyes wide. His hands were clenched and his knuckles stood pale against his skin. How could anyone even remotely know of their plan?

"If it is as you say," the detective replied, "then I will have the key moved by the end of the week. I would move it right now, but it will take some time to make suitable security arrangements."

"We appreciate your service in this matter," Councilman Verdre said.

"Please excuse me. It would seem I have work to do," the detective said.

"Yes, of course. We should get back to the party." Councilman Cawthorne's voice was laced with eagerness.

Annelise watched several of the councilmen disappear through the door. As the delicate looking detective approached the door, she stopped, then turned around. She looked straight at Annelise. Annelise didn't dare breathe, trying her best to look like an inanimate object.

The detective frowned, started, and then extracted her staff. Annelise's stomach dropped. They had been found. She flicked her wrist. Still no staff.

"Who's there?" the detective demanded in a loud voice. She held her staff in a combative stance.

There was a beat, where nobody moved. Then, "Conciliar Warden Michael Pendragon, ma'am." Michael jumped to his feet at attention.

The council members erupted in commotion.

Annelise gaped at him. The room seemed to shrink. The muscles around her ribcage seemed to constrict, making breathing difficult.

He glanced at Annelise and gave a miniscule jerk of his chin. Annelise shook her head. He repeated the gesture. Annelise rose to her feet, remaining half tucked behind the wall of the alcove. Her eyes darted to the door. It was blocked by council members who now crowded the exit.

"This is Annelise Windstarter," Michael continued. He nodded in her direction, raising his voice above the clamor of the council members.

"Michael, what is this about?" Councilman Cawthorne called out in astonishment.

"What are you doing there?" the detective demanded.

"We're on assignment Ma'am," Michael replied.

"Assignment."

"Yes ma'am."

"What kind of assignment gives you the right to go skulking around the government building after hours, and eavesdropping on highly classified meetings?" Councilman Verdre scoffed.

"The classified kind," Michael replied. "Windstarter, give her the orders."

Annelise did not move.

Michael turned to look at her. "Now please."

Annelise could hear the stress in his voice. She clenched her hands into fists to keep them from shaking. Every instinct in her body screamed at her to not hand over very incriminating evidence to the detective with the staff pointed at her.

Michael grabbed her arm, and plunged a hand into one of her pockets. Annelise tried to twist out of his grasp, but he was stronger than her.

"I promise I have a plan," he whispered so quietly, she almost didn't hear him.

Annelise wanted to believe him. But she didn't.

He managed to pull one of the orders out of her pocket. Annelise gave him a shove to force him back so that he couldn't reach her other pocket.

A spell struck the concrete just above their heads. They both froze.

Detective Poe looked positively livid. "If one of you doesn't bring me those orders in the next five seconds, I'm going to arrest you both for political espionage."

Annelise believed her. She looked at Michael. He held out the scroll that he had taken from her. She looked back at the detective.

Not seeing a better option at the moment, she took the scroll from Michael with trembling hands, and pulled the other one out of her pocket. Her legs shook as she walked them over to Detective Poe. Michael followed close behind her.

Her mind went numb as she handed over definitive proof that she was involved in a plot to go after the key to the Subraek.

Detective Poe turned the orders over in her hand and Annelise's stomach dropped.

"Detective," Michael said before she could open the orders. "You don't have clearance to open those. We are on a highly sensitive special assignment from Director Desmedt. You need to be read in first."

Detective Poe's eyes snapped to Michael's face, irritated. "Then read me in."

"I'm afraid only the Director can do that."

"You really expect me to trust you after that little show just now?"

"I apologize for my associate. She is passionate about the security of this mission."

Councilman Cawthorne scowled then pointed at Annelise. "I thought you said she was a local artist."

"She is. She's an informant. Tristan and I needed her skills, and she agreed to help." He turned to the detective. "Tristan Pendragon is my partner on the warden service. We are working this case together."

Detective Poe eyed Annelise. "And you, Windstarter, was it? Have you been read in on this?"

Annelise considered her words. "I know enough to do what I need to."

The detective threw her hands in the air. "Fine. Councilman Trewson, please send for Director Desmedt. If he's the only one who can tell me why the two of you are eavesdropping on classified—," she emphasized the word glaring at Michael, "—committee meetings, then he had better get here fast. You two," she pointed to Michael and Annelise. "Sit." She pointed to the base of the raised platform.

Annelise's feet moved of their own accord. Her eyes darted around the room, and her mind raced, looking for any way out of the situation. Maybe if they ran? If only the detective hadn't looked back when she had...

"To be fair, detective, we had no intention of eavesdropping on your meeting." Michael said as they made their way to the platform step. "We just happened to be in the room working our assignment when the honorable Councilmen entered, and we didn't reveal ourselves because our assignment is—"

"If you say classified one more time," The detective warned.

Michael fell silent and took his place on the step beside Annelise. The detective checked them for weapons. Since their staves were locked away, she was satisfied. She pulled out a pair of cuffs, and cuffed Michael's wrists behind his back.

"Detective, is this really necessary?" Councilman Cawthorne gestured to the handcuffs.

"Yes," the detective shot back. She pulled out a zip tie, and bound Annelise's hands behind her back as well.

The remaining Councilmen filed into the room and took seats behind the table. The shape of the table meant that all of them were facing Michael and herself. Was this what her trial would look like? Annelise had the foreboding feeling that she was going to find out sooner rather than later. Maybe she could get Professor Finchley as her defense attorney? Because if she didn't figure something out soon, she was definitely going to jail.

Annelise's mind raced. Michael had stalled for time, but as soon as this Director Desmedt arrived, the gig would be up. What was worse, they had just handed over *very* incriminating evidence. One look at their fake orders would make it clear that they were going after the key to the Subraek. Her diaphragm spasmed, and her stomach flip flopped as she felt a panic attack coming on. She stared at the ground and tried to focus on her breathing.

"What can you tell me about your case?" the detective asked once their hands were bound.

"I can tell you it's important. And that if you knew what we were working on, you would let us go." Michael's voice sounded earnest, and Annelise supposed that if their assignment was legitimate it would be true.

The minutes passed by, and Annelise dreaded the moment when the doors would open, the Director would enter, and their freedom would be forever a thing of the past.

The detective started pacing the floor. Finally, she turned to the council members. "Can one of you see what is taking them so long?" she demanded.

As she spoke, the door to the Council Chamber burst open. Annelise's stomach dropped. Detective Poe whirled to face the door.

But it was Tristan who all but tumbled through the door, out of breath. Annelise felt a flicker of hope kindle within her.

"Who are you?" The detective demanded, pointing her staff at Tristan.

Tristan fished a badge out of his coat pocket. "Conciliar Warden Tristan Pendragon," he said. "Why are you holding my partner?"

"He and your informant were found spying on a highly classified meeting. He's not going anywhere until I have some answers." She waved the still sealed orders in front of his face. "I've been told that only Director Desmedt can read me in on your assignment."

"This is true. He needs to be the one to read you in. But I need these two to come with me now." Tristan said. "There's been a development, and a very time sensitive situation is in play. If we don't act now we will miss our window of opportunity."

"I can't let these two go until I know at least something about what is going on here," Detective Poe insisted.

Tristan seemed to consider her words. "Look, I can't reveal all the details, but—"

"Tristan, no. If this information reaches the wrong people," Michael interrupted.

The detective whirled to face Michael. "Do you want me to book you for espionage?" she demanded.

"No ma'am." Michael replied. "Only… we don't know who to trust." His eyes locked with Tristan's and flicked over to Councilman Jackson. "There's a reason this mission is classified."

"If this goes right," Tristan continued deliberately, addressing the detective, "we just might get the Dragon back."

A hush fell over the room. Annelise flicked her eyes over to Councilman Jackson to see his reaction to this information. She could see astonishment in his face, but little else. Nothing that would unmask him as the traitor who locked the Dragon up.

"Look, keep the orders, and if Desmedt wants to read you in, then fine. But we have to go or our opportunity will be lost. We might never get this chance to get her back again."

There was a beat. A pause. Annelise turned her eyes back to the detective and held her breath.

Finally, the detective waved them away. "Go. If what you're saying is true, I can't hold you back. But so help me, there had better be a really good explanation for all of this." She waved the work order scrolls in her hand.

Tristan hurried to release Michael's cuffs, and cut the zip tie that bound Annelise's hands together. Annelise rubbed her wrists.

Michael stood up and turned to the detective, "Thank you, Detective. You won't regret this."

"I'd better not. Or I promise you I will hunt you down to the ends of the earth."

Annelise nodded to the detective, not trusting herself to say anything, and then scampered after Tristan and Michael.

No one said a word as they ran through the dark halls. The light of the main hall assaulted her senses as they waded through the unrelenting cacophony of the gala. When they finally burst out of the front doors of the government building, leaving the sounds, sights and smells of the party behind them, Annelise stumbled to her knees and retched. Nothing came out. Her vision greyed, then faded back into focus. She flicked her wrist, and extracted her staff. The familiar cool wood of her staff materialized beneath her fingertips. Her vision started to clear.

A steadying hand fell on her back.

Annelise wiped her mouth and looked up at Michael's concerned face. "I'll be okay. Let's get out of here." She leaned on her staff as she clambered back to her feet.

They piled into Tristan's car. Annelise nearly dove into the back seat. She was still pulling her door shut when Tristan started driving.

"That... sucked," Annelise gasped.

"Yeah. It did," Michael agreed.

"How did they know about your plan?" Annelise asked, her mind flitting back to the information revealed in the council chamber. She slid to lie down across the back bench of the car, clutching her staff to her chest.

"I don't know, and honestly, we really don't have the time to figure it out," Tristan replied, turning the car so sharply that the tires squealed across the pavement.

"What? Why?"

"If we're going to get the key, we have to do it now."

Annelise sat up and stared at him. "You *are* joking. There's no way we can keep going. As soon as they open those orders, they'll be on to us. We need to run."

"Look. We either run with the key, and have a chance of freeing the Dragon and maybe clearing our names, or we run without the key and we get hunted as terrorists for the rest of our lives, and never free the Dragon and never clear our names." Michael said.

Annelise rubbed her hand across her face. "You're on board with this?"

"We always planned on going for the key whether or not we managed to get the seal. We just have to move to plan B. That's all."

Annelise crossed her arms. "What is plan B?"

"Plan B is that we enter the building through the ventilation shaft along with you," Tristan explained. "We will drop down near the vault with the key. Your job is pretty much the same, only you'll use your access to the security feed to help us avoid any guards on patrol. We get into the vault, get the key, and we all leave via the secure warden transportation platform. If we can make it before the alarms go off, we can make it to the Medford precinct with the key, shaving hours off our time in the open."

"Your escape plan from pulling a heist on the most high security facility is to walk through a law enforcement office?" Annelise asked, panic creeping into her voice.

"We are wardens. We have every reason to be there."

"We'll never make it in time."

"I bought us some extra time," Tristan said, as he made some dubious lane changes at breakneck speed. "When I heard that they were calling for Director Desmedt, I pulled the crystal from the transportation pad in the Government building. It will be out of commission until they find it and re-install it. He's going to have to get to the government building the long way. Also, we sealed the scrolls with some binding wards. It will take them another 15 minutes or so to actually get them open and find out what we are up to."

"So what does that add up to? An hour? Tops?" Annelise asked.

"Something like that," Michael agreed.

"And you expect us to get to the vaults, break in, and get out in under that time?"

"We're going to try."

"And what if I refuse? What if I would rather run?"

Michael glanced over his shoulder at Annelise. "Then I can warn you that you'll have the best and the brightest of the Conciliar Wardens after you."

"They'll be after me either way."

"Only the difference will be that you'll be on your own," Michael replied. "And when they inevitably capture you, it will be for nothing. Or you can stick with us, and have a chance of making a real difference in the world."

Annelise groaned. She was pretty sure she hated these two Pendragons. But she also thought they might be right. And the ever fading but not yet faded hope of one day freedom beckoned to her like a siren, leading her into ever deeper trouble.

If only she had taken the five years at the start of it all. Then again, if they somehow did manage to find the Dragon… they would right a great injustice. And maybe the waters of the fountain at the academy would fill the basin once again.

She wanted to scream. Instead, she retracted her staff and sat up. "Fine. I'll do it." She felt like she was going to be sick, and it wasn't just from Tristan's driving.

Michael grinned at her. "I knew we could count on you."

Annelise gripped her seat.

"The good news is that we have all of our equipment with us." Tristan said, as he finally slowed the car to a stop.

"And the bad news?"

Annelise received no reply as he and Michael both stepped out of the car.

Tristan knocked on her window. "We have to get into the trunk."

Annelise looked at him unimpressed, but got out of the car.

Tristan opened the trunk. There was a duffle bag of equipment for Annelise, and another with the uniforms that they had planned to change into for the heist. Annelise chucked her heels into the trunk, grabbed a pair of pants and pulled them on under her dress.

"We don't have time to change."

"We have enough time for shoes." Annelise insisted. "Or we don't have enough time at all." She yanked on a pair of boots, and then turned to the trunk. Why did it look more like a coffin than anything else to her at the moment?

"Well," Tristan's golden eyes glinted in the dark. "Good luck to us all."

He slipped into the trunk, graceful as a cat, scooting as far back against the equipment as he could.

"You've got to be kidding me," Annelise said as she observed the small space she was supposed to fit into. But she climbed into the trunk after him, curling into a tight ball beside him, stuffing as much of the skirt from her dress into her pants as she could. She didn't want it getting in the way. The sooner they got this job started, the sooner they could be done, and the sooner she could hopefully move on with her life.

Her eyes met Michael's steady gaze as he closed the trunk over their heads. His eyes lacked the playful mischief she usually saw, but instead were alert, tense, and serious.

Then the trunk closed, and everything was dark.

Chapter 5: The Job

$\mathbf{T}$**he gravel crunched** beneath the sleek car as it rolled to a stop. There was a pause, and then Annelise heard muffled voices. She could not make out what they were saying. The voice that did not belong to Michael laughed suddenly. It seemed Michael was putting his "silver tongue" to use.

Annelise squirmed a bit where she lay, stuffed into the trunk. A buckle was digging into her back, and it was driving her crazy.

The voices outside went silent. Annelise was sure that Tristan could hear her heart pounding as they waited for Michael to get clearance to pass through the gate. Finally, they rolled forward once more, bouncing over the uneven road. Annelise grimaced. After a few more minutes of driving, the car stopped, and the trunk opened.

Annelise was greeted with Michael's face, lit only by a sliver of moonlight. His previously playful eyes now scanned their surroundings, on alert for any threats.

She hopped onto the pavement of the parking lot. After a moment's hesitation, Michael chucked his formal jacket in the trunk and grabbed the two warden uniform jackets. Annelise grabbed the bag of equipment she would need and closed the trunk.

They scampered to the long building. Tristan and Michael pulled on their warden jackets as they ran. They were much more subtle than the brightly colored dinner jackets they had previously worn.

Outside of the warehouse, there was not much visible security — just the gate and the guard. The building itself was a nondescript dark gray block, designed to be unassuming. The outer wall stretched out of sight, disappearing into the night. How many magical artifacts was the government hiding away from the public?

Michael had parked as far from the front door as possible. Annelise followed Michael as he led them around the side of the building to the vent they would enter through. The parking lot lamps faded behind them as they ran to a less inviting part of the property. They stopped. The vent was about ten feet off the ground, so Tristan and Michael boosted her up so she could remove the vent cover. Annelise plunged her hand into the duffel on her shoulder and pulled out the small electric screwdriver. It whined loudly in Annelise's ears as she removed screw after screw. Why did there have to be so many screws? She felt one of the Pendragons adjust their grip on her leg. Finally, the last screw spun its way out of place, and Annelise grabbed the grate, letting Tristan and Michael lower both her and the grate down to the ground.

Michael was the next person to get boosted up to their makeshift entrance. Annelise grunted as the weight of his right foot settled in her hands. Michael was tall and, while not bulky, definitely muscular. Half of all his weight now rested in her hands. She maneuvered her fingers to lace underneath his foot to let friction help keep her grasp.

"You doing okay there, Annelise?" Tristan whispered, seeing her squirm.

Annelise nodded. There was no other option. She had to be okay. This had to work, and fast. Or they were all going to jail. How much time had passed since they had left the Government building? Twenty minutes, maybe? That left them with forty if they were lucky. Annelise wished that Michael would hurry up.

Above their heads, Michael worked soundlessly as he used his invented technique to interrupt the wards and alarms guarding the vent. By the time he was done, Annelise's forearms were on fire.

"Okay," Michael whispered, grabbing the edge of the vent.

Carefully, Annelise and Tristan let go of Michael, leaving him hanging from the edge of the vent while his magic actively held the dancing lights of the wards back. They looked like small threads of light pulled apart like a curtain... or like bent prison bars.

Tristan boosted Annelise up through the vent.

She clambered around Michael, trying not to kick him as she pulled herself into the vent. Once she was in, she reached her arm down for Tristan to grab. Using her hand to pull himself up to the point where he was able to grab the edge of the vent himself, Tristan let go of her hand and climbed around Michael as well, sliding into the vent without a sound.

Once the other two were safely in the vent, Michael pulled himself through, letting the wards snap back into place behind him. The dazzling lights from the wards faded as they resumed their usual path, leaving them in the dark.

The vents were pitch dark, but they had memorized their path forward. First straight, then a left. Now, the occasional grate looked down into the vault hallways, and some light filtered through into the vent. When they reached the next junction, it was time to split up. Annelise went left, and the Pendragons turned right. They would wait above their drop spot until Annelise was in place and set up.

She pulled herself forward on her belly once more. The ventilation shafts were dusty, narrow, and slippery. The smooth metal gave little opportunity to grip onto it to pull oneself forward, and the small layer of dust on top of that made it even harder. In addition to of all of that, a section of her dress had come free of the waistband of her pants and kept getting caught under her knee.

Footsteps drifted up to her from the hall beneath her. Two security guards were doing their sweep. Their clipped footsteps sounded like the tick tick tick of a clock.

Annelise stopped moving and waited for them to pass. Her heart pounded in her chest, and she barely allowed herself to breathe.

The dust was irritating the back of her throat. She felt a cough scratching its way into existence. She swallowed and held her breath. She covered her mouth. Her diaphragm spasmed.

The sound of the guards' boots below her seemed to slow down. Still, the guards' boots ticked below her. Her eyes watered. The footsteps below her faded, and Annelise inched her way forward once again. Her eyes were watering, and now her nose was dripping too.

Finally, she reached the junction and climbed out of the ventilation shaft into a maintenance room. Grabbing a tissue, she blew her nose and released the cough she had been choking back.

With a flick of her wrist, her staff extracted and appeared in her hand. With a whispered word, draconic runes flickered to life along her staff, glowing a pale blue. They illuminated the room in a gentle glow. The room was barely more than a closet and was not tall enough for her to stand without stooping. A ceiling beam jutted up from the floor through the center of the space, and the far wall was a mass of intersecting wires. She stepped over the beam and took a deep breath, letting it out slowly as she looked at the maze of wires in front of her. They had gone over this. She could find the ones she needed.

She set her backpack down and started analyzing the wiring. Working methodically, she found the appropriate feeds, hooked her devices up to them, and took control of the cameras. The black and white images flickered to life on her small screen. So far, so good. She sat down on the beam to continue working. She could see their target: a larger rusted copper key seated on a pedestal in the middle of a dark room. She could also see armed security patrolling down the long corridors, their staves always out and ready for action.

She cycled through some of the other cameras to get a sense for the layout of the cameras and where all the guards were. As she did she snuck a peek at some of the other "classified" items that were being stored in the vaults. She saw several blades, gems, and various other items that she could not quite make out on her tiny screen. One of the rooms held nothing but a large, smooth stone, which intrigued Annelise greatly, but she pushed her curiosity aside. There was no time to indulge it. Their time was ever dwindling. She estimated they only had twenty-five minutes before this place was swarming with wardens.

She tapped her earbud. "I'm in position," She would need to loop the feed of the hallways as Tristan and Michael entered them, and then unloop the hallways once they had passed through, to stay undetected.

"Okay." Tristan's voice came clearly through the device. "We're on the move."

She watched on her tiny screen as the two Pendragons dropped down from their ventilation shaft and into the hallway. They extracted their staves, brandishing them at the ready as they moved forward.

"You're clear on the next hallway, but you'll have to wait before you turn. Some guards are doing a walkthrough of the next corridor you need to enter."

The Pendragons dutifully waited until she gave the all-clear before continuing. Annelise glanced at the time. They needed to speed things up. "If you want to make it past the next intersection before the guards come and make you wait again, I advise that you run," she said. The Pendragons broke into a run and cleared the intersection just before the guards turned the corner at the other end of the hall. They did not seem to notice any disturbance as they wandered along their route.

"Good work," Annelise told them. She guided down two more corridors until they had reached the central vault. She looped the feed for the central vault so that the Pendragons' presence would be invisible to the security guards' cameras.

She glanced at the feed again. There was a patrol coming.

"I need you guys to backtrack one hallway and hide. A patrol is about to swing past the central vault," she instructed them.

Tristan and Michael scampered back the way they had come and waited. The security guards walked with a pace more suited to a garden party. Annelise tapped her finger against the side of the small screen. She glanced at the clock. Only twenty minutes left before their presumed hour was up. What if the Director had managed to get to the Government building faster than expected? What if the Pendragons' locks on the scrolls failed too soon? A swarm of wardens and one Detective Poe could be on their way here right now. Finally, the guards disappeared around some distant corner. They had a while before the guard's patrol took them that way again.

"You're good to go," Annelise whispered into her com. The Pendragons crept down the hall to the vault door.

Annelise watched on the tiny monitor as Michael grabbed hold of his staff and placed his palm against the doorframe. She could see faint tendrils of light pulsing beneath his hand as his magic made contact with the various wards and alarms surrounding the room. Far too slowly, the lights were pushed away until the area surrounding the door was dark. Annelise leaned forward, peering at the screen, watching him work. The lights pulsed at the edge of the doorway as though eager to rush back into their previous channels, but Michael continued to hold them back. Annelise couldn't help but be impressed by his ingenuity in inventing the skill.

Tristan pushed open the door and slipped through the gap in the wards into the central vault. She watched as he, too, held his staff and placed his hand against the base of the pedestal holding the key. One by one, he pushed back the alarms connected to the key.

Suddenly, something on one of her monitors caught her eye. Her eyes went wide, and her heart pounded.

"Guys," she said. "Those guards from before, they're coming back early." She tried to keep the panic out of her voice, but she wasn't sure she managed. On her little monitor, she could see Tristan look at Michael in alarm. Michael was standing in the open door to the vault, holding back the threads of the wards, and Tristan was halfway through the wards around the key. She suspected that if they dropped their magic holding the wards back recklessly, they risked setting them off. Tristan was speaking to Michael, gesturing with his head, but his comms unit wasn't activated, so Annelise didn't know what he was saying. She saw some faint movement in the corner of the vault camera, and glancing over to the hallway camera, she saw Michael slipping through the door, still holding the tendrils of magic apart, and the door appeared to close.

The guards stalked through the hall, approaching the vault holding the key and the Pendragons. Annelise's heart pounded, and she had to force away the beginnings of grey spots at the edge of her vision. She shook her head. She could not succumb to panic now.

The guards marched right past the vault and continued on their way. Annelise's deathgrip on the small screen lessened.

"They're gone."

In the vault, Tristan had not stopped working on the wards. The last ward separated, and Tristan used one hand to hold all of the wards in place. With the other hand, he reached out to take the key from the pedestal. Annelise held her breath. He picked up the key. No claxons sounded, and no lights flashed. It was a good start.

Tristan placed the key between his teeth and reached his hand into a pocket to bring out the fake key. He placed it on the pedestal. Then, one by one, he allowed the magic of the wards to resume their original paths.

Annelise bit her lip as she watched the little blue lights resume their place dancing over the key. If anything was going to go wrong with her decoy, it was now. After a few moments, she breathed a sigh of relief. The alarm was back in place. If they moved fast, they might make it out of the vaults, and no one would be the wiser that they were ever there. Tristan and Michael slipped out of the room, and Michael released the magic interrupting the wards to the vault. She watched as the blue lights rushed into their usual channels across the door. Silence. Annelise smiled. She would have cheered if it were possible.

"We're out. Annelise, what's our situation?" Tristan whispered over the coms.

Annelise scrambled to see where the guards had gone. She had been so wrapped up in the action taking place in the vault that she had lost track of the guards.

"You're good for the next two hallways." As quickly as she could, she guided them out of the main vault area and to the corridor that led to the secure warden transportation pad.

Since there were no artifacts stored in that section of the building, and since it connected straight with law enforcement, no guards were patrolling that part of the building. No one expected any potential thieves to consider it as an escape route. Annelise had to admit, it had the potential to be an ingenious plan.

The Pendragons made it safely to the transport corridor and waited there in the shadows. Annelise left her equipment where it lay and scrambled through the ventilation shaft to the Pendragons' position. They were so close, but their time was running out. She dropped down from the ventilation shaft into the hallway. Tristan and Michael were grinning. Annelise would grin when they got out of here.

They hurried down the last corridor to the room that held the transport platform.

An alarm pierced the compound, echoing off the wall. Annelise clutched at her ears as red alarm lights flashed across the walls around her. Their time had run out.

She extracted her staff with a snap of her wrist. Beside her, Tristan and Michael held their staves at the ready.

"Keep going!" Tristan yelled over the blaring alarms. They raced down the hall toward the transportation platform room, hoping to make it before the wardens arrived. The door ahead of them burst open, and half a dozen wardens poured into the hall, brandishing their staves. Annelise skidded to a stop.

"Halt," Detective Poe stepped forward, brandishing her staff in both hands, ready for anything. "I told you I would hunt you down, Pendragons."

"Second exit! Go!" Tristan shouted, urging them back down the hallway they had just come down, covering their retreat. They dashed around the corner as a barrage of spells impacted on the walls around them. No one fought with the Conciliar Wardens. Usually, only the foolish bothered to flee, but today was a special case.

Her heart pounded as she sent a couple of knockback spells down the hallway before ducking around the corner and following Michael, who was at the front. He tore down one hallway towards their secondary exit plan—the front doors. More security personnel appeared, blocking their path and forcing them down a different hallway, the additional security advancing on them from behind.

Halfway down the hallway, a pair of double doors blocked their progress. Michael pulled on the doors. They were locked. He grabbed his toolkit to pick the lock. There wasn't enough time. The troupe of wardens and vault guards burst around the corner. They were trapped.

Annelise fired off a few stunning spells. The pulse of magic ripped through the air but glanced harmlessly off the wardens' hastily erected shield spells. Tristan was next to her a moment later, adding his attacks to hers. The wardens didn't stop. They continued to advance, firing off an overwhelming barrage of magical attacks that ricocheted all around them. One cracked into the cement wall near Annelise's head, sending sparks flying like shrapnel. She flinched. This wasn't going to work. She needed a new strategy.

She aimed her staff at the feet of the cops and chanted in ragged breaths. Water blasted from the end of her staff. A couple of the wardens lost their footing, but most were unfazed. With another breathed word and a hastily drawn rune, the temperature in the room plummeted, and the water froze. Two of the cops who had been standing in the water ended up with their feet frozen to the ground. The spells of others flew wide as they lost their footing.

Annelise and Tristan doubled down on their advantage, shooting off knockback spells, stunners, and anything they could think of to drive the wardens back.

Detective Poe was unfazed by their tactics and continued to advance. She bit out a word in the draconic language, drawing a rune with the now crackling end of her staff. A pulse of energy seared through the room, and the ice evaporated. She nailed Tristan with a knockback spell. The pulse of magic sent him sprawling to the floor.

Annelise was now the only defense between Michael and the advancing wardens.

Leaping forward, she planted her staff into the ground and chanted the words to the strongest shield spell she knew. A pale yellow light leapt up between her and the wardens, stretching out to reach from wall to wall. She could feel the magic moving through her, almost alive as it leapt around her. The warden's violet columns of magic seared through the air and slammed into the shield, sending shockwaves through Annelise's staff. Her glimmering shield was not going to last.

Behind her, Tristan had clambered back to his feet, and just in time, as Annelise had to let the shield spell shrink or risk losing it entirely. He took cover behind her and her shield, sending electric blue bolts over the top.

"Hurry up, Michael!" Trisan shouted, dodging a spell that whizzed by his head, ruffling his golden hair.

"That's not helping!" Michael shouted back.

Annelise glanced back and saw that he was now dealing not only with the physical lock but with several locking spells he had to unravel as well.

More bolts of magic burst against her shield, and she could feel the magic of her shield spell shuddering beneath her hands.

She poured more strength into the shield spell, the staff beneath her hands going frosty at the amount of power pouring through it.

Through the pale light of the shield and the continuing onslaught of the wardens' spells, she saw Detective Poe step forward among the wardens. "You're trapped with nowhere to go," she called out. "If you lay down your staves and surrender peaceably, nobody has to get hurt." Her voice rang out over the din of spellfire and cracking concrete.

The only response Tristan gave was to fire more spells in their direction. A ball of crackling golden light whizzed so close to Detective Poe's head that it ruffled her brown curls. Detective Poe was forced to dive behind the warden shield wall. Tristan's expression was grim. If they gave up now, it would all have been for nothing. Annelise glanced over her shoulder to where Michael was. It looked like he was making progress. They just had to hold out a little bit longer.

In one swift movement, the brown-haired detective dropped into an offensive stance and thrust her staff toward Annelise's shield, sending a white lance of light catapulting toward her.

The air around it rippled with heat as it burned across the room.

The spell crashed against her shield in a wave of light but did not dissipate. It continued to burn against her shield, a high-pitched whine emanating from it as the two magics collided. Annelise's staff burned with ice beneath her hands as she poured more magic through the conduit, trying to sustain the shield. But the magic of her shield shook beneath her hands, buckled, and then crumbled just as the detective's burning spell exploded, blowing her back toward Michael. She watched, stunned, as her staff turned to ash in her hands, crumbling beneath her fingers.

Annelise stared at her empty hands in horror and disbelief. Her staff was gone.

"Let's go," Tristan cried, as he grabbed her arm and pulled her through the doorway. Michael had gotten it open. They fled down the halls, and Tristan fell to the rear to shoot bolts of light at their pursuers while Michael led the way. Annelise no longer knew where he was leading them. All the hiccups they had anticipated and all of their backup plans seemed useless at the moment. They reached a hall that had doors on only one side of the hall.

"Here!" Michael shouted, stopping at an unassuming part of the wall.

"What's here?" Annelise cried over the din of wardens shouting and spells flying. Tristan grabbed her and pulled her low as Michael provided cover for them.

"On the other side of this wall is the river. Make us a doorway! We will hold off the guards," Tristan shouted.

"I don't have my staff!" Her panicked voice rang through the din. "And even if I did, it would take forever against this stone!"

Tristan grabbed her hand and pressed something into it. It was a pin from his uniform jacket. "You can perform blood magic, right?"

Annelise gaped at him. Nobody knew that. How did he know that?

"There's no time!" she cried.

"We will buy you time," he shouted back.

Annelise hesitated. She would be useless if she cast a spell this big with blood magic. She would probably pass out. She would be defenseless and utterly dependent. She wanted to scream. She felt like the world was closing in around her, and she forced herself to breathe.

"Annelise, I promise, if you make this door, I won't leave you behind," Tristan shouted, as though he had read her thoughts.

Michael made a strangled sound of pain, and Annelise's head snapped to where he stood. His shoulder had an awkward extra lump that should not have been there. Probably dislocated. His shield was flickering as he tried to hold the shield spells despite his injury.

Tristan flinched as more spells impacted near them. "Just make a doorway!" he shouted, pointing at the wall. He then stood up and joined Michael in sending spells back at the wardens and guards, keeping them at bay.

Annelise turned to the smooth wall of gray concrete. It seemed impenetrable. She fought the desperation that welled inside her. She wanted out, to run away. A stray spell whizzed through her hair, jolting her into action. This *was* the way out. A plan started to form in her mind.

Annelise barely winced as she dug the tip of the pin into her palm. There was so much adrenaline in her system that she hardly felt the pain. She dug deep in desperation. She didn't have the luxury of time or a shallow cut. The blood welled up freely from her palm. She dipped her finger into it and started drawing runes on the wall in the shape of a door. She then added the runes she would need to burst through the concrete.

She wasn't just going to make a hole. She was going to blow the wall to bits. With any luck, the wardens would be stunned long enough by the percussive force of her spell to give Annelise a chance of making it out of the building and into freedom. It was dangerous, but it was better than going to prison.

The runes glowed red as she started chanting.

Her head spun as the magic moved through her, taking hold of her. Soon, it was no longer clear who was wielding whom. She couldn't stop the spell even if she wanted to. And if someone somehow forced her to stop—like getting hit by a stray spell—the consequences could be dire for both her and anyone near her.

Her whole body shook with magic passing through her. It seemed to fill her and drain her at the same time. She was only vaguely aware of the fight still raging around her. Time seemed to slow down and then raced to catch up as spells passed by her slowly enough that she could watch each individual spark shatter into nothingness and then disappear abruptly into the distance.

The whole corridor seemed to ripple around her as the smooth concrete wall shuddered. The ruins burst in an explosion that threw Annelise back and tore a gaping hole in the wall. Concrete dust floated through the air everywhere, some of it pouring out of the hole and into the black night beyond.

There was silence. She wasn't sure if it was because the fighting had stopped or because her ears were ringing too badly. Her head spun as though she were still in the throes of spellcasting.

She had to get through the gap. She braced a bloody hand against the wall and tried to get to her feet. The ground beneath her tipped, and she tumbled back to the ground. She landed on a stray piece of concrete wall that dug into her ribs. Her breath came in short, panicked gasps. She had to make it through the hole in the wall.

The cloud of concrete dust shifted. Tristan appeared in front of her, grabbed her arm, and pulled her forward. She stumbled behind him, darkness dancing at the edge of her vision. She could barely walk, but Tristan supported most of her weight as they moved towards their makeshift exit. He dragged her through the hole in the wall towards the precipice that overlooked the river. The black edges of her vision closed in on her, and then, she was falling. She wasn't sure if it was because they had leapt off the precipice into the raging water below or because of the darkness enveloping her. She knew no more.

Chapter 6: The Escape

Tristan's heart pounded as he sent volley after volley of spells toward the wardens. Stunner pulses, knockback hexes, balls of burning magic, concussive blasts of electric blue... the list went on. He cast shield after shield to block incoming spells. He had done plenty of sparring in training before. This felt... different. He could feel through his shields that the wardens were no longer pulling their punches. Each spell that burst against his shield reverberated more. Soon, he was holding his staff in both hands, trying to block spells he normally would have dodged from reaching Annelise. If not for his own training with the wardens, he would have succumbed to the onslaught by now. His arms shook beneath the impact, and sweat poured down his back. He wished Annelise would hurry up already and blow a hole in the wall, if only for the sweet relief of the icy water that awaited them down below.

Behind him, he sensed a slight slowdown in Michael's spellwork. Michael had stretched his magic to the limit today, taking on the bulk of the magical wards and locks, and Tristan worried it was starting to take its toll. He wasn't sure how much longer Michael could hold out.

The delicate-looking Detective was sending off an impressive array of spells. She swung her staff in crisp strokes, sending volley after volley their way. She spun her staff over her head and sent another spell barreling towards Michael. Tristan stepped between them, throwing up the strongest shield he could manage. The warden's spell impacted against his shield and cut through it like butter. His staff took the impact with a crack and snapped lengthwise clean in the middle.

Tristan gaped at the broken halves of his staff. A leaden weight settled in his stomach. His staff was gone. It had been his constant companion, the tool of his craft, his art, and his play for years. How could it be gone? He pressed the smoldering halves that used to fit together, willing them to rejoin once again.

A stunner flew so close to his head that it singed his ear, forcing him out of his stupor. He ducked out of the way and dropped the useless pieces of his staff. It was now up to an exhausted Michael to hold off the guards and the wardens until Annelise finished her spell. Not a moment too soon, he saw the runes flare to life, glowing bright red.

The magic in the hallway shifted like the tide pulling out before a tsunami. Tristan hit the deck, covering his head. A shockwave of magic bowled him over as the wall erupted in an avalanche of concrete and rubble. Concrete dust filled the air, causing him to cough and sputter. The din of battle from a few moments ago was silenced. The wardens had been pushed back and thrown down by the shockwave. They were sprawled through the hallway, sometimes piled on top of each other, stunned, and covered in a thin blanket of concrete dust. Down the hall, someone coughed.

A few feet away, Michael picked himself up off the floor. He had known the impact was coming and was able to prepare himself, but even he looked rattled by the blast. He was covered from head to toe in pale concrete dust. Tristan motioned him towards the new hole in the wall. Michael nodded, stumbling in that direction. Annelise had been thrown against the wall opposite her spell and seemed disoriented. She looked pale, but he wasn't sure if it was because of the impressive spellwork she had just done, or if it was because of the fine layer of pale dust on her skin and hair.

He grabbed her arm and pulled her through the gaping hole in the wall. She moved much more slowly than he would have liked.

Tristan grabbed hold of Annelise's waist as she swooned. He dragged her to the precipice and leapt without a second thought. The black water rushed up to meet them. When the cold water met his chest, it nearly took his breath away. He fought to hold his breath against the cold. He scrabbled against the water and finally managed to drag both himself and Annelise to the surface. She was still out cold. From the little he knew about blood magic, it tended to take a large toll on the caster. What she had done was no small feat. He gasped for air as he broke the surface of the water. He could hear someone else in the water, but in the dark, he couldn't see anything.

"Michael!" He called, hoping that he had made it into the river safely despite his exhausted state.

"I'm here," came the breathless response. Tristan would have breathed a sigh of relief if a surge of water hadn't caught him in the mouth at just that moment. He spat the water out and kicked with the current, careful to keep Annelise's head above water.

He felt more than saw Michael come up beside him and take hold of Annelise from the other side. Together, it was much easier to support her dead weight as they struggled to navigate the currents in the dark. The compound was on the outskirts of the city, and the river was flushing them rapidly away from civilization. They would need to get out soon, however. As fast as the river was moving, he was sure that the wardens could move faster, and it wouldn't be long before they were found. He was relieved that none of the wardens had followed them into the river. At last, it seemed they had a bit of luck.

With much struggling and spluttering, they managed to drag Annelise to a shoreline. They hauled her out of the water. Tristan stood and looked around them for any options or threats, while Michael sat panting in the gravel and the mud, gripping his shoulder.

"How's your shoulder?"

"Not great, but not dislocated anymore." Michael looked up at Tristan. "How about you. You good?"

"My staff is gone," Tristan felt as numb from the shock of losing his staff as he did from the icy bite of the water.

Michael swore. "Okay, first things first. We need to get out of here."

Tristan nodded, locking the crushing disappointment about his staff away for a later time. He needed to work the problem at hand. "You need to make a portal."

Michael clambered to his feet, leaning heavily on his staff. "I don't think that's a good idea."

Tristan knew he was exhausted. "We need to get off the riverbank. The wardens will be here any minute. The farther we get away now, the better chance we have of actually escaping," Tristan argued.

"Portals can be traced, and I won't be in any shape to move when we get where we're going. You can't lug two unconscious people around behind you!"

"But it will buy us time, during which I'll think of something! Just make me a portal!" He knew Michael was right. He couldn't lug two unconscious people around with him, but he could only handle one problem at a time.

Michael's nostrils flared. "Fine," he bit out. "Where would you like to go? Oh, wise and mighty one?" His tone was clipped, and he gave a slight mocking bow. His eyes were hard. Tristan knew that he was angry. He would deal with that later.

"Any parking lot north of here," A plan started to form in his mind. They had committed high treason this evening; why not add a bit of grand theft auto?

Michael nodded curtly, catching on to his plan. He drew a large circle around them in the dirt and added a rune to tie the circle off. Placing his staff on the thin line of the circle, he started chanting. Sweat dripped from his brow, and his body shook as he seemed to grab onto his staff for dear life. After a moment, the blue light flared, momentarily blinding Tristan. When his vision cleared, they were in a parking lot. There was a soft thump as Michael fell to the ground beside Annelise. Michael had been right. They were now both out cold from magical overuse.

Plucking Michael's staff out of his hands, he walked over to an old-looking car and used the staff to break through the back passenger side window. He reached through and unlocked the car. One by one, he managed to drag Annelise and Michael into the back seat of the car. With a little bit of rest and some food, they would both be okay again soon.

He placed Michael's staff next to him. He wished he could use it, but it was useless to Tristan except as a blunt instrument. Each staff was uniquely attuned to its wielder's magic during the year-long process each sorcerer went through to grow and craft their staff. In Michael's hands, his staff was a conduit through which he could wield his magic. In Tristan's hands, Michael's staff was nothing but a beautifully carved short staff made of hard white oak.

He slid into the driver's seat of the car and pulled apart the wires under the steering wheel. The wires clicked with zaps of electricity as he tapped the wires together, and on the fourth try, the engine rumbled to life.

He drove them out of the city, eager to put distance between themselves and the portal they had created. Michael was right. Portals could be traced, and once the wardens found out where the portal had come out, that area would be swarming with wardens.

He pulled out his cell phone as he drove. It was only fair to try to warn Manny of the storm about to arrive on his doorstep. His phone was dead. Drenched from port to lens, it was completely unresponsive. Tristan groaned and chucked his phone out the window as he drove. It was probably for the best. This way, they couldn't be traced.

They left the city and headed North. The city gave way to suburbs, which gave way to the occasional small town dotted through the countryside. Every once in a while, Tristan would grab at the large key in his satchel. It was hard to believe that they really had it. After all these years, the last dragon was finally going to be free. She would finally have justice. The Pendragon clan would have their emblem back. She was more than just a mascot. She was like a patron sister to the Pendragons — an unofficial royal — and she was finally coming home.

Several hours later, Tristan finally pulled into a small public parking lot in a town just over an hour north of Sacramento. The first hints of dawn were stretching across the horizon, and Tristan was crashing after the adrenaline of the fight, the cold of the river, and the long drive. He glanced into the back seat where Annelise and Michael were still out cold, but safe. Then he slid down in his seat, closed his eyes, and fell asleep.

***

Annelise groaned as she came to. Her head was pounding, and her neck was incredibly stiff and sore. She was also freezing, and there was a cold draft blowing on her face. She pried her eyes open. She was seated in the back seat of a shabby car. Her window was shattered, allowing the cold morning air in.

She twitched a muscle in her hand and immediately felt discomfort. She felt a weight pressing down on her left shoulder. She managed to turn her head to look at what it was. It was Michael's head. With a little shove, she pushed him off of her. He grunted at the movement and started to come to as well.

He blinked and pressed a hand to his forehead, groaning. Annelise looked around and found that they were in a car. Tristan was slouched down in the driver's seat, his chest softly rising and falling as he slept. Outside the window, she saw nothing recognizable. She wasn't sure how she had gotten into a car, or how they had gotten here.

She reached for her staff only to remember with a sickening feeling that it was gone. She stared at her empty hands.

"Tristan," She whispered, wincing as even the whisper lanced through her head like a hot iron. He started awake, sitting upright in his seat, alert and looking for danger. When he saw that there was none, he sighed and slouched again, looking for the source of what had woken him.

"What happened?" Annelise asked. "And where are we?"

"What happened is everything went to crap," Michael snapped, still pressing a hand against his forehead. "We ran out of time, and they wiped the floor with us." He leaned forward, groaning as he pressed a second hand to his head.

Annelise looked at her empty hands again. "Unbelievable," she spat. "I thought you two had thought this plan through. Instead, we go and hand incriminating evidence right over to the detective whose job it is to hunt us down and throw us in prison," she scoffed. "Great plan."

"Yeah, well, maybe if you hadn't acted like such an idiot in the Council Chamber, they wouldn't have been so suspicious, and we would have had more time," Michael shot back.

Heat bloomed on Annelise's cheeks. "How did they know about your plan, anyway?" she snapped. "Somehow the highest levels of government knew a startling amount of information about your *highly classified mission,"* she made air quotes as she spoke, "and that was *before* you had me hand over the blueprints to our plan."

"I don't know how they found out. It's not like I wanted this to happen."

"Kind of surprising considering how—"

Tristan cut her off. "Look. We took a hard hit, getting the key."

Annelise was about to complain about losing her staff, but Tristan cut her off again.

"I know you lost your staff. I lost mine too."

Annelise stilled. Two staves in one battle? They would not last a third.

Tristan continued. "But the good news is that we got the key. We still have a hope of freeing the Dragon, and maybe even clearing our names."

"Assuming Annelise's key holds up to scrutiny," Michael grouched. He had gone back to pressing his hands against his head. "How do we know your *fake key* didn't trip some alarm, bringing the wardens to us even faster?"

Annelise's eyes snapped to his, blazing. Her heart pounded, and she pursed her lips to restrain herself from saying something foolish.

"Michael—" Tristan started to say.

But Annelise cut him off. "Give me the key," she ordered, holding her hand out to Tristan. Tristan hesitated before reaching into the satchel and handing it over. She spun it in her trembling hands, critically analyzing every aspect.

"My work was flawless," she fumed and shoved the key into Michael's hands, knocking him back against the car seat. "Check it yourself. Unless there was some magical component of the key being sensed by the wards, there is no way the replica was detected. Short of making an actual key to the Subraek, which is impossible," she emphasized the word, "the replica is perfect. The wards didn't go off as soon as my key was in place, so we can conclude that there was nothing wrong with my key. The problem was with your plan: Trying to go after the key when they had all the information to tell them exactly where we would be and what we were after. I'm not the weak link, here, so who?"

"We don't know," Tristan said.

"Well, who did you tell?" She pressed. "Did you consult with anyone about your theories? About your plan?"

"About our theories, maybe. But the plan was kept strictly between the two of us," Michael said.

"Maybe you let something slip to the wrong person. What about your butler?"

"You leave Manny out of it!" Tristan pointed his finger at Annelise. "I trust him a lot more than I trust you right now. How do I know it wasn't you who spilled our secrets to your criminal friends?"

"Excuse you?" Annelise gaped at him. Her hands were shaking with anger and frustration. "It is not my fault that we are in this mess. In fact, I got us out of that death trap of a situation. I can't believe I lost my staff for this stupid job. I never wanted to be there in the first place!" She took a breath as she struggled to regain some semblance of calm. "I'm done. Consider my part in this plan finished and my commitment fulfilled. I'm leaving." She grabbed the latch to open the door. "You owe me my money," she spat over her shoulder.

Michael reached around her and grabbed the door handle, holding the door shut. "If you leave, you'll be caught. And if you're caught, our mission goes up in smoke. What we're doing matters."

"My freedom matters!" she shot back.

"I won't let you ruin this for us. It won't be long before they know who we are, and our faces are plastered across every newspaper and TV station. You can't leave."

"Unlike you, I know how not to get caught." She jammed her shoulder into his chest, trying to force him to let go of the door so she could get out of this circus of a disaster. Michael didn't budge.

"If you leave now, I'll tell the wardens you used your blood magic to enslave us to your will," Michael threatened.

Annelise stilled.

He continued, "Everyone knows that blood magic is corrupt and those who wield it are not to be trusted!"

Annelise lunged at Michael, ready to smash his pretty face through one of the windows that wasn't yet broken. He scrambled back to the opposite side of the car, snatching up his staff and pointing it at her, keeping her at a distance.

"That's enough!" Tristan yelled, halfway climbing into the back seat to get between them. He grabbed Annelise's shoulder, keeping her from grabbing Michael's head. "Pointing fingers is not helping. Yes, the vaults were a disaster. No, we don't know how our plan was found out, but there is still a chance we can accomplish what we set out to do. But only if we stick together. Look," he addressed Annelise. "I'm sorry I accused you of indiscretion. I don't actually think that you let anything slip." He looked pointedly at Michael.

Michael folded his arms and looked out the window. "I'm sorry about what I said about blood magic. I wouldn't actually claim you used it to enslave us." He sounded more like a petulant child forced to apologize than an adult who was feeling contrite.

Annelise huffed. "Whatever." She flung the car door open. "I need a minute."

She stepped out of the car and paced in the pale light of the cloudy morning. The cool air blew into her face. Her breath came in heated puffs. She wanted to scream, to run, to do anything other than get back into the car. She was seriously considering walking away when she heard another car door open and shut behind her. It was Michael. He came and stood beside her.

"I *am* sorry about what I said." This time, he sounded sincere. "It was childish."

Annelise snorted.

He pressed something cool into her hands. It was the key. "We still have this. We can still do what we set out to do." He turned to face her. "If you need to leave, I understand. But I'm asking you to please come with us. We could really use your help. And the Dragon, she deserves our best efforts to set her free."

Annelise shook her head. "I can't afford to lose any more just because Michael Pendragon wants to leave his mark on the world."

Michael ran a hand through his hair. "It's not about me. It's about her. She doesn't deserve to be imprisoned any longer. I can't promise you that we won't have more setbacks. But I promise you we will look out for you as you have looked out for us. We're a team."

"Some team."

Michael nodded. "Every team has its moments. But if you stick with us, we won't let anything happen to you. We all have a better chance of coming through this without spending the rest of our lives in prison if we stick together."

Annelise smiled ruefully up at him. "I'm no good at teamwork."

He nudged her with his shoulder, a playful twinkle in his eye. "Well, then you'll just have to practice."

Annelise huffed and swatted him on the shoulder. He hissed in pain at the impact. It was the shoulder he had dislocated the night before.

"Sorry." Annelise hadn't meant to hurt him this time. She returned to the car, shutting the door behind her with a sharp click.

Michael slid into the front passenger seat.

Annelise bit the inside of her cheek. "I'm sorry. I shouldn't have said that about Manny. It was unfounded."

Tristan nodded in response.

Annelise looked down at her empty hands. She kept wanting to reach for her staff, but kept finding that there was no staff to reach for. "I'm not going to be much use to you with my staff gone."

Tristan twisted in his seat to face her. "I think your actions in the vaults proved that to be untrue." His mouth pressed into a hard line. Annelise remembered that his staff was gone too.

"We cannot change what happened," Tristan said. "All we can do is focus on the task at hand."

Annelise drew in a breath. They would not survive getting caught off guard again. "We can't go on like this."

"We don't really have a choice," Michael said. "We are well past the point of no return."

"Things could get worse. We could disappear now and cut our losses." She was thinking about the new identity that still sat inside her kitchen sink.

"It wouldn't buy us much time. And if we give up now, we might as well give this back," Tristan waved the key around, "and we will have lost our staves for nothing. Our best chance is to push through. And if we can make it to the Subraek, we will have the wardens off our backs for a little while. Nobody can get into the Subraek without this," he waved the key at her.

"Right. All we will have to worry about then are the untold horrors and monsters that defy description."

"Which we will face, together. Are you with us?"

Annelise wasn't sure she wanted to be. Surely she had given up enough already? But when she analyzed the situation, she realized that the Pendragon cousins were probably right. If they stuck together, they had a higher chance of evading capture. That was if nobody bailed and sold the rest out to save his own skin. She regarded the cousins. They were loyal enough to each other. She didn't think either of them would bail. In all honesty, she saw herself as the weakest link. She slumped in her seat.

"Yeah, I'm with you." She could see no better option at the moment. Perhaps if they actually found this dragon, the goodwill that would produce would wipe out the crimes they had committed to set her free.

"Good," Tristan said. "Here," he handed Annelise some cash. "I found it in the car. We all need some food. Since you're the least likely person to draw attention, you'll take point."

Annelise took the money he offered and shoved it into a pocket. The three of them stepped out of the car. They were in a small town. A quaint metal arch spanned the width of the main road, and a few shops ran along its length. None were open. It was still early. Tristan made his way across the road towards a small diner that looked like the only shop awake yet.

She glanced at her outfit, and then at the Pendragons. They made quite the collection.

Annelise wore her gown over her pants, but it was now river-stained. Luckily, her clothes had dried, but they still felt uncomfortably stiff from the river water. Michael and Tristan also wore an unusual combination of wrinkled gala attire and warden's uniform. Michael's curls were frizzing from the river water. Tristan's face sported a small cut, and the hair near his left ear was singed. They were a painfully conspicuous bedraggled trio.

"Do either of you have your phones on you?" Tristan asked as they approached the diner.

Annelise pulled her phone out, pleasantly surprised to find it where she had left it in the deep pockets of her dress. She was less pleasantly surprised to find that it was dead. The screen was cracked, and she could hear the faint sounds of water sloshing around inside the small device.

"My phone is cooked," Annelise held up the ruined device.

"Mine too," Michael said.

"Okay. We may have to find one along the way. But for now, it's probably best that we be as untraceable as possible." Tristan said. Annelise touched a hand to the traceless charm on her wrist.

The bell in the diner door jangled as they pushed it open, then again when it swung closed.

"Table for three, please," Annelise told the waitress as she looked around the diner. The floor and the furniture were worn but clean. The once bright red seats were faded where years of sunlight had bleached the colors. There was a small TV playing above the counter, which was currently lined with clean coffee cups that would be used as the morning rush started. They seemed to be among the first patrons of the morning. Only two others sat around the diner, one staring blankly into his coffee cup, and the other wolfing down his meal.

The waitress pointed them to an open booth. Tristan and Michael slid into one side, while Annelise took the spot opposite them.

"Where are we?" Michael asked Tristan as they settled into their booth.

"About an hour north of Sacramento," Tristan replied.

A waitress approached with a pot filled with coffee and a big smile. "Good morning, what can I get started for you?" Her voice was cheerful as her dark ponytail swished behind her with entirely too much pep for this time of the morning. "Aren't you all dressed to the nines?" she asked.

Annelise gave a forced laugh. "Yeah. We partied a bit too hard last night. Now we have a long road ahead. We'll take some coffee for the three of us," Annelise put on her best smile as she made eye contact with the waitress, "and a plate of pancakes, sausages, and eggs for each of us."

The Pendragons subtly obscured their features with their menus while she ordered.

"All right, that will be right out for you."

Annelise handed the waitress their menus as the Pendragons murmured their thanks, and the waitress whisked off to put their orders in. Annelise's smile dropped.

During the short wait for their food, their eyes were drawn to the television broadcasting over the counter.

Annelise paled when she saw what was being broadcast. A news anchor stood in front of the compound, a breaking news title bar flashing across the bottom of the screen. She caught Michael's eye and nodded towards the screen.

He looked nervous as he watched the small TV. "They haven't shown our faces yet." The relief was evident in his voice.

"Yet," Tristan mumbled. "We shouldn't stay long," The scene flashed to the parking lot where he had stolen the car. Annelise stared at the screen, dreading when a picture of her face would flash across it.

The scene changed, and Annelise saw Detective Poe. The same woman who had destroyed her staff in one fell swoop. She was presiding over some sort of press conference. The detective's name flashed across the bottom of the screen. She was heading up the investigation.

"What do you guys know about her?" Annelise asked the Pendragons. Tristan glanced up at the screen again.

"I've never met her before the gala, but I know her work. She's a good detective. Fair."

"Great," Annelise grumped, her voice barely more than a whisper. "Of course she is. Why couldn't it have been the detective renowned for her laziness who was after us?"

"Well, I'd rather have an honest detective on our case than a lazy one," Tristan whispered back. "A lazy detective will bend the truth to line his resume. An honest one will want to find the truth. So really, we all want the same thing."

"I'm pretty sure we want to stay out of prison, and she wants to put us into prison. That's not the same thing." Annelise shot back.

The waitress came back out with their food, and the three of them wolfed down their meals, too focused on eating to say anything. The last day had been strenuous for them all, and even though the food started to taste like ash in her mouth, Annelise knew that there was no guarantee when they would be able to have their next meal, so she forced herself to eat.

She stole glances at the screen as they ate, trying not to draw attention to the news broadcast. Annelise was befuddled as to why their faces weren't all over the broadcast already. The wardens knew who they were.

Instead, they showed the law enforcement forces amassing at every known entrance to the Subraek, ready to catch them when they arrived. The Crater Lake entrance was not shown. If it really was an entrance, they did not know about it. It was the first piece of luck they had had since this whole thing started.

Tristan downed his coffee in one go. As he did, the owner of the establishment approached with a pot of coffee in his hand. At least, Annelise assumed it was the owner, because the diner was called Marvin's Place, and the man's nametag read "Marvin".

"Anything else to drink?" Marvin asked, swirling the coffee pot in their faces. Both Tristan and Michael lowered their golden eyes, no longer having menus to hide behind.

Annelise looked up and smiled sweetly. "No, thank you. We're just about finished here."

"All right, then, have a good day." The owner said in a sing-songy voice and moved off to other customers.

They hurried through their meal, casting nervous glances at the TV screen throughout. Michael jumped when his face finally flashed across the screen. Luckily, no one else was paying very much attention to it at the moment.

Tristan noticed the update as well. "Come on, let's go." He looked a bit pale. Then again, Annelise felt a bit pale.

"I'll drive," Tristan said. The two Pendragons slipped out of the booth while Annelise paid for their meals.

Chapter 7: The Journey

They drove north, making their way toward Crater Lake.

Annelise had found a stray sweater in the trunk and pulled it over her head. There was also a half-filled notebook kicking around in the trunk. The first half of it was filled with math homework. Annelise felt a brief pang of guilt knowing how much this car might mean to a student, but she pushed it away. What was done was done. They could only move forward.

"So," Michael turned to where Annelise sat in the back seat. "About that fake ID."

Annelise leveled her gaze at him.

"What made you want to run?"

"You mean other than the fact that I was blackmailed into this job, and that I had no reason to trust you, and that this job most likely meant spending the rest of my life in prison? —which, I might add, is absolutely in the process of coming true."

Michael chuckled. "Yeah, other than all of that."

"Isn't that enough?"

He thought for a moment. "So what made you stay?"

"Momentary insanity," Annelise shot at him, a rueful smile tugging at her mouth. Her gaze fell to her lap. "I don't know. I felt guilty, I guess. Guilty for abandoning the Dragon. Guilty for going back on my word, no matter how coerced it had been given."

"So the thief has some honor after all."

Annelise's eyes snapped to Michael as she glared at him. His eyes were twinkling with mirth, but he had hit too close to home for her to join in his amusement.

"What were you expecting? Someone only out for the money, looking for every opportunity to swindle you, and dying to stab a couple of wardens in the back, the moment the opportunity arose?"

"Kind of."

Tristan swatted him on the back of the head. "We had considered the possibility."

"Let me say, so far, we've been pleasantly surprised." Michael rubbed the back of his head.

Annelise turned to look out the window, where the trees were flitting by. "Well, so far, I'm only regretting my decision."

Michael fell silent. "For what it's worth," he said at last, "I'm grateful you stuck with it. It's been a mess, but we would have been captured with no hope of success without what you did back at the vaults. This mission…it means a lot to Tristan and me." He looked as though he was going to say more, but he fell silent instead.

"Yeah, well, the sooner we can get this done, the sooner I can get on with my life. That is, if I don't end up in jail with three life sentences."

Michael grinned. "What do you plan to do when this is over?"

"I hope to disappear. Go somewhere where I'll be left alone, and—" She broke off, her ears picking up the faint sound of sirens in the distance. The distinct siren marked it as a sourceless police car. The faint whine grew louder as it grew closer. Michael glanced at Tristan, his posture tense.

"They might not be for us?" Michael asked, hopefully.

Tristan shot him a look. "Hope for the best, prepare for the worst. Michael, give Annelise the key. Annelise, if I say run, you run. You disappear as well as you can and make your way to Crater Lake.

"What, you want me to go to Crater Lake without you?" Annelise asked as Michael handed her the Subraek key, her voice rising with panic.

"Only as a last resort. We will meet you there." Tristan's voice was frustratingly calm.

"And if you don't?"

"You're just going to have to trust us."

Annelise jutted her chin up. "Why?"

"Because you have no other choice."

Annelise fumed. He was right. She didn't see any better option. She hated that he was right. She hated that she was on the run. She hated everything about this situation.

"You still have that pin?"

Annelise nodded. "Yeah."

"Good. Michael, if it comes to it, I will hold them off. I want you to be the decoy. You keep them away from Annelise and the key."

The sirens were growing louder.

Annelise's mind was whirling. Now that it came to it, she didn't want to be on the run by herself. It was bad enough with the Pendragons, but she had to admit: it was nice to know they were looking out for each other. The thought of having to run alone suddenly made her feel vulnerable and exposed. There would be no protection from the warden forces after her.

She turned to Michael." Do you think you can manage a perception ward?"

His eyes locked on her, and the glimmer of hope she offered. "I've never cast one before, but I'm willing to try."

Annelise wasn't surprised. She hadn't learned it at the academy, and what she had learned she had modified to give it her own unique twist. "I can help you, but you'll have to come back here," she said, scooting to make room for him in the back.

With surprising agility, Michael climbed into the back seat and extracted his staff with a flick of his wrist.

"Face that way." She pointed to the side of the car where the sirens were becoming louder and louder. He swung his feet up on the seat, and Annelise crouched next to him, guiding his staff as he drew the necessary combination of runes on the window. It was a similar spell to what she had cast on the fake key, but did not require blood as a conduit. With any luck, when the spell was cast, anyone who saw their car would want to ignore them.

"Good. Now repeat after me." She spoke the spell, and he repeated her word for word, his voice mingling with hers as their words and phrases in the old draconic language overlapped. It was strange, going through all the motions of casting a spell, but feeling none of the magic move through her. The runes flared bright blue before fading. It had worked. It helped that Michael had such a strong understanding of wards for him to manage this spell on his first try.

The sirens were almost upon them, the pitch of the whine rising in agitation. The cars directly behind them pulled over, and Tristan followed suit. They all lowered their heads to hide their faces.

Annelise peered out the window of their car, looking for possible avenues of escape. Flat green fields stretched out on either side of the car. In the distance, electric wires stretched up like spines across the flat ground. There would not be much cover if she had to run. She looked around. Just down the road was a large field with some species of tree growing in precisely calculated rows. If she could make it there, she could potentially disappear among the branches.

She slung the satchel over her shoulder and palmed the pin, hoping she wouldn't have to use it.

The sirens rose to a fever pitch, and the tension in the car was taut as a bowstring. The lights pulsed behind them... and then sped past them. All three mages sagged into their seats. Either they hadn't been aware of them in the first place, or the perception spell was working its magic. Michael let out a bark of relieved laughter, and Annelise drew a shaky breath. Traffic crawled back onto the road, and Tristan followed suit. They had gotten lucky...this time.

"You'll want to dismantle that ward now," Annelise said. "We don't want the rest of the traffic to forget that we are here. It's a sure way to end up in a wreck."

"Right." With a word, Michael dispelled the perception ward that he had cast.

They settled into silence after that.

Michael asked Annelise for the key and spent his time reading and analyzing the runes. After a while, she started reading over his shoulder.

Most of the runes were predictable. Runes of binding, locking, sealing, protecting... Some of the runes were unfamiliar.

"Can I try something?" Annelise asked.

Michael held the key out to her. Reaching out to the key as she would with her staff, she sent a pulse of magic through it.

More runes, previously unseen, glowed along the key in a cold white.

"Whoah." Michael peered at the new runes with interest. "Do me a favor, Windstarter." He did not take his eyes off the key. "Don't do that again."

"Why?"

"I don't want to mess too much with this thing. I'd hate to open something we shouldn't."

Annelise scoffed. "You mean like opening the portal to the most dreaded subrealm known to man?"

Michael did not respond to her comment. Instead, he leaned over and pointed to a combination of draconic runes. "What do you make of these?"

Annelise peered at the faint lines in the glowing metal. There was a rune related to the growing of roots, one that spoke of sunlight, and the last was some sort of blade. "Huh." It didn't make any sense.

"I agree. I'm stumped."

"It would help if we had a dragon, I suppose."

"Maybe I'll ask her when we find her." He was now holding the key close to his face, trying to unravel the secrets of the runes. "You know, it was Pendragons who created this key."

"Yup. And it was also Pendragons who ripped a hole through the seven subrealms, almost destroying the world, and necessitating the creation of the key."

He finally looked up from the key, a frown on his face. "What, are you some anti-dragon mage?"

"No! I want the Dragon to return. I just think that magic needs to be used responsibly."

He gave her an incredulous look. "Responsibly? Like using it to cheat and swindle people who are defenseless against it?"

"I don't take anything. They give it to me and are always pleased to do so. This, on the other hand," she gestured to the key, "launched the civil war that decimated the dragon population. If the Pendragons had only been a bit more responsible, we would have more dragons around, and magic itself would not be on the verge of collapse."

"It's not our fault that the dragons died!" Michael retorted. "It was clanless mages who sided with the sourceless to slay dragons."

Annelise could hear the accusation in his voice directed at her, just because she was clanless. She pointed a finger at Michael. "Because you were so reckless with your curiosity that you almost destroyed the entire world!"

"Guys," Tristan interjected from the front seat. "Keep it civil. None of us were directly involved, so let's not accuse each other of the crimes of our ancestors."

He was right. Annelise settled into her seat.

"Yes, Mom." Michael slumped in his seat, crossing his arms.

"Don't make me turn this car around," Tristan retorted.

Annelise thought she heard a tinge of humor in his voice. "If only you could. How about we just boot Michael out of the car instead?"

"Hey!" He sounded indignant, but he was chuckling too. "How about a truce?" He held out his hand.

"Hmm. For now, I suppose." Annelise shook his hand. They rode in silence for a while. Michael continued to inspect the key. Occasionally, he consulted Annelise for a second opinion, but she now left most of the reading to him.

Instead, she gazed out the window as field after field flitted by. The landscape occasionally gave way to sparse natural vegetation before being caught up in the endless parade of fields once again. They spent the last of their money on gas, hoping to get as close to Crater Lake as possible.

Not ten minutes after they had bought gas, the front of the car started to smoke.

Tristan swore and pulled over to the side. Michael hopped out of the car before it rolled to a full stop and ran to the front of the car.

"Pop the hood." He tapped on the hood once the car had reached a standstill.

Tristan popped the hood, and the view out the front windshield was obscured by the dusty engine cover. Annelise and Tristan both slid out of the car.

"Can you tell what's wrong?" Annelise asked as she came around to the front.

"Something is causing the engine to smoke." He held his hand a few inches above the engine. "It's way overheated."

Tristan reached into a small compartment near the back of the engine and popped it open. He pulled out a small crystal, which was also blackened and charred.

Michael swore.

It was the absorption crystal. Every car that frequented a magical settlement needed one to prevent the ambient magic from overloading the car and setting the engine on fire. In fact, any form of technology with electrical components required a crystal if being used in high magic areas. It was one of the wonders developed during the integration, but it required regular replacement. It was like a sponge, and when the sponge was full, it could no longer protect the car. Regulations required them to be assessed and replaced every year. Apparently, the college student who had owned the car had neglected to look after it.

Michael snapped the hood shut with unnecessary force. He turned on Tristan. "You didn't check the car before you stole it?"

"How was I supposed to know the owner wouldn't be up to date on his maintenance. I picked a low-profile car that I could hotwire."

"Guys, it's probably the key. It's so potent that it burned through the rest of the crystal." Annelise said.

Michael shot her a look. "I doubt it," he grumbled. But he did not pursue his argument with Tristan.

"You're right." Tristan looked at Michael. "I should have checked. It was my responsibility. I failed." He ducked his head. "I'm sorry."

Michael gave him a nod.

The two Pendragons then turned and started walking down the road. Annelise scampered to catch up. "Any ideas?"

"I was actually hoping you could help us with that," Tristan said as he ambled along the side of the highway.

"I don't know how to empty an absorption crystal," she said as she came alongside him. "Even if I did, Michael has a staff. He would be better off doing it."

"I wasn't thinking that. I was thinking that if you were the one asking, we're more likely to hitch a ride."

"Oh." Annelise was not sure of this plan of action. "Won't we get caught?"

"I mean, it's possible, but we've been on the road for several hours, and they have no idea where we are heading. Nobody knows that Crater Lake holds a portal to the Subraek. Also, it's unlikely that their search perimeter has managed to keep up with our travel so far. And most of the people out here are sourceless. They are less likely to care about a break-in of the vault of magical artifacts beyond mild curiosity. Either way, it's our only option."

"Okay, but I don't think hitchhiking is a thing that happens anymore. Nobody's going to stop."

"I'd stop for you," Michael chimed in.

"Michael, you'd stop for any face you thought was pretty," Tristan said.

Annelise blushed.

There were no cars in sight at the moment, so they started walking. Michael extracted his staff and used it as a walking stick, swinging it like a gentleman's cane.

"Annelise, I'm curious. How did you get into all of this?" Michael turned his head to her.

"You invited me," she deadpanned.

Michael threw back his head and laughed.

Annelise couldn't help but join in and chuckle. "You mean the forgery and grifting?" She thought for a moment.

"Do you want the short story or the long one?"

"Definitely the long one."

Annelise plucked at the skirt of her dress. "I grew up loving art. Even as a kid, I was always drawing, painting, whatever. I always knew it was what I wanted to do with my life.

"When I was about ten, my mom got injured, and then she got sick. Very sick. My dad couldn't take it, and he split, so things got tight." Annelise kicked at a pebble, sending it clattering ahead of her as she tried to force down the bitter taste of betrayal.

"But my mom, she um… she did her best, you know?" Annelise bit the inside of her cheek hard to force the sudden torrent of emotions back down and out of reach. She took a steadying breath, hoping to cool her burning cheeks.

"Anyway, a few years later, Jimmy reached out to me. I don't know how he had gotten wind of my artwork, but he offered me money in exchange for a forgery. I was pretty desperate at the time, and it was a much-needed lifeline. I took it. When he saw that my work sold well, he recruited me more and more.

"Soon enough, I branched out. Started making up stories about artworks that never existed and selling them to people who didn't know any better." Annelise shrugged. "That's pretty much it, really."

"Did it ever bother you that you were cheating people?" Michael asked.

Annelise glanced at him, ready to be defensive, but this time his expression was carefully neutral, and his tone betrayed no judgment, only curiosity.

She lowered her eyes. "Not really. I was so desperate at first, I couldn't think about it. Once I gained some stability, I was past thinking about it. But I do have some ethics. I never take money from anyone who can't afford to lose it. Most of the time, it's sourceless tycoons who have more money than they know what to do with and can't be bothered to learn a bit of history or theory. At some point, I think they deserve to be swindled. Goodness knows people rarely get that rich without doing some swindling themselves. And from another point of view, I've never cheated anyone in my life."

Michael glanced at her. "How do you figure that?"

"Because ultimately what I sell is stories, and all stories are fabricated or curated to some extent. So the buyer is getting exactly what he paid for. A great story. I don't think it matters all that much if it's true or not."

"Would you ever walk away from it all?"

Annelise stopped in her tracks. "The art?" She would have thought he already knew that answer.

Michael chuckled. "The swindling."

Annelise continued walking. "I'm not sure what else I would do."

"You could sell your art. Your original art. It's really good. It's moving, you know." His eyes dropped to the ground. "I think there would be a market for it." He looked up at Annelise, his eyes earnest. "It's full of heart."

"Hmm. Maybe. I never imagined there would be any market for it." She nudged him with her shoulder. "Perhaps if we manage not to go to prison for the rest of our lives, it could be interesting to give it a shot. But, you know, old habits and all that. I make no promises." She shot him a smile.

"Well, then I'll just have to arrest you for it," Michael said, a playful lilt to his voice. "Old habits and all."

Annelise narrowed her eyes at him. She did not intend to let herself get caught ever again.

"How do you decide what to paint?" Michael asked.

Annelise released a long breath of air through puffed cheeks as she thought. She glanced at Michael. "I don't know. I guess I paint what I want to see. And what I want to see is probably determined by whatever is on my mind and how I'm feeling. I don't know. It just... comes to me, and I paint it."

"Huh. Do you ever have a way you are trying to make your audience feel?"

"With my own art? Not really. I just wanted to expel whatever emotion or problem I'm wrestling with onto the canvas. I never really meant for anyone to see them but me."

"Hmm."

She glanced at him. "You thinking about your own art?"

"I suppose. It's so different from how I approached my art. I was always trying to make the audience feel something. You manage to do so without even trying."

"Well, maybe that's why."

He cocked his head. "How so?"

"Maybe you were focused too much on what you thought the audience wanted, instead of imprinting your heart onto the canvas."

"Hmm. Sounds painful."

She smiled. "It can be, at times, but it's often cathartic."

"So, how do you know when you're doing it right?" There was frustration in his voice.

She thought about it for a moment. "The same way you know when you're being honest. And not every piece will resonate with every person. But that's okay. As long as you are honest with the painting, I think someone will recognize themselves in it."

They fell into silence after that, holding out their thumbs in classic hitchhiking technique at the cars that whizzed by. The sun started to beat down on them as the last of the puffy clouds melted under its heat. Finally, a brightly colored van pulled over, kicking up dust as it pulled to a stop.

"You have got to be kidding me," Annelise said, staring at the offending vehicle.

Chapter 8: The Assist

It was a classic hippie van with aggressively bright paintings of sunshine and beach scenes, awkwardly mixed with Hindu art motifs and styles. Annelise felt sure that the occupants were ecstatic to be performing the classic hippie maneuver of picking up hitchhikers as a validation of their super authentic hippie-ness.

The passenger side window rolled down. Inside, a young man and woman, both sporting long dreadlocked hair, peeked out.

"Dudes, I like the fits!" The guy in the driver's seat grinned at them through his rose colored sunglasses, dreadlocks swinging over the steering wheel.

Annelise was sharply aware of their unusual attire, her mind scrambling for a suitable explanation. "Thanks!" was all she managed.

"Where are you headed?"

"We're headed North. Trying to get to Crater Lake." Michael flashed them a charming smile.

"You guys hikers or something?"

Michael didn't hesitate. "Yup! We're avid backpackers. We're going there for a...photoshoot." He tugged at the sleeve of his wrinkled and ruined shirt.

"Excellent vibes! And we love hiking!" He waved his hand in invitation. "We're heading north as well. Hop on in. We can totally drop you guys off."

The three clambered into the back of the van. Two long, cushioned benches faced each other lengthwise down the van. The van smelled of incense, and several dream catchers hung from the ceiling, swaying as the van pulled back onto the road.

The woman craned her neck around to see her guests. "I'm Clara, and this is Dylan." Her voice was mild and gentle.

The trio introduced themselves and learned that Clara and Dylan were traveling north from Sacramento to visit family.

"So you two are married?" Tristan asked.

"Nah. But we are in love." Clara gazed adoringly at Dylan. "It's his family we're seeing. They live in Idaho."

"That's quite the drive. Why not use the transporter pad facility?" Annelise asked.

"Instantaneous travel is amazing, but it takes the journeying out of the journey." Dylan gestured to the road ahead of them. "We wanted to take the scenic route."

"I agree." Michael leaned forward. "There's nothing quite like being on the open road, and seeing the world pass you by to remind you that you are only a small part of it."

"Exactly, man!" Dylan's head bobbed up and down. He made eye contact through the rearview mirror. "Hey, so what's with your eyes?"

Michael and Tristan shared a look, trying to decide on a story. Annelise rolled her eyes. "They're Pendragons."

The two Pendragons turned to Annelise with nearly identical disapproving stares.

"What? You weren't going to come up with a convincing story, and I'm sure that these lovely folks won't care. Do you?" she asked hopefully.

"Nah, man. It's cool. People are people, you know." Dylan nodded, his head bouncing to some unheard island rhythm. "So what's a Pendragon?"

Annelise had to stifle a smile as Michael's eyebrows shot up and Tristan shifted in his seat.

"It's a clan of mages," Tristan finally said.

"Wow, you're mages? Like, all of you?" Clara asked, her eyes sparkling with excitement.

Annelise nodded.

"A clan. That's cool. Do you guys wear kilts or something?" Dylan asked.

If Michael's eyebrows went any higher, they were going to disappear entirely beneath his dark brown curls.

"So what do you guys do in Sacramento?" Annelise jumped in, trying to redirect the conversation without laughing. The Pendragons clearly weren't comfortable with this line of conversation, and, as much as she enjoyed watching them squirm, it was probably safer to steer clear of any questions about their background while they were on the run.

"Oh, we were just visiting my parents for my mom's birthday. We live up in Ashland." Clara gestured northward. "We're going to school there, at the University."

Annelise nodded. "Cool. What do you study?"

Clara cocked her head. "Oh, you know, a little bit of this, a little bit of that. We're not really declared yet. Haven't figured out what we want to do with our lives."

"How about you guys, do you all have to study to do magic?" Dylan asked.

Annelise nodded. "All magic users study at the academy to learn how to properly and safely wield magic."

"Unless they are homeschooled," Michael amended.

"So magicians go to school, too. See, I told you," Clara said, turning to Dylan, and poking him in the shoulder.

Annelise bit her tongue at the comment and had to stomp on Michael's foot to make sure he did too. Mages disliked the term magicians. Magicians did card tricks on the sidewalk. The three mages in the back seat were most definitely not Magicians.

"You were homeschooled?" Annelise asked Michael, trying to move past the "magicians" statement.

Michael allowed her to redirect the conversation. "Yup! Tristan and I both were. My parents hired private tutors to guide us through our spellwork. They wanted us to have more freedom to pursue study in any area of magic we were interested in, and to work at our own pace."

Annelise whistled. "Wow. And here I thought everybody on the West Coast learned their first spells from Professor Finchley."

Tristan laughed. "We *did* learn our first spells from Professor Finchley. He is the best there is, and my Aunt and Uncle only hired the best. Besides, I think they had fond memories of their classes with him. Heck, even our grandparents and Uncle Fitz had Finchley as a teacher. He's a legend."

Michael grinned. "He just says that because he was Finchley's favorite."

"And here I thought I was his favorite," Annelise crossed her arms, pretending to be offended. "His class was the best. What an introduction to spellwork, huh?"

Michael jumped in, his eyes sparkling. "Did he do that thing with you all where if you answered a question right, he'd bop you over the head with his staff and shout— "

"Huzzah!" Annelise finished. "Yes! He absolutely did that! Come to think of it, I'm surprised he gets away with it in this day and age."

"It's because he's so old," Tristan chuckled. "And he's earned the trust and respect to be as quirky as he likes."

Annelise leaned in, her eyes sparkling. "Did you know he's actually starting a second career?"

"No!" Michael gasped. "He can't stop teaching! He would deprive future years of students of the iconic experience of learning from Finchley."

Annelise chuckled. "I think he's doing both at the moment."

"That sounds about right for him." Tristan nodded. "It feels like he's always had his hands in a million pots. I don't know when he sleeps."

"So what do you all do for work?" Dylan asked, jumping into the conversation.

Tristan and Michael exchanged a glance, deciding who would do the talking. Tristan won. "Michael and I are wardens."

Dylan nodded. "Oh yeah. That's like a magic cop, right?"

"More or less."

"That's pretty cool. How about you, Annelise?"

She flashed a bright smile. "I'm an artist."

He grinned at her. "Neat! I like doing art myself. I painted the van."

"Wow. I noticed it's very... colorful." Annelise scrambled to find any moderately truthful and complimentary adjective.

Dylan frowned. "It didn't turn out the way I wanted. I feel that something just clashes, you know?"

"Hmm," Annelise considered what she had seen of the paintings on the van. "If you like, and if you have some paper I could borrow, I could brainstorm some ideas on how to tie it together better."

He glanced at her, a hopeful look on his face. "You would do that?"

"I'd be happy to! And it's the least I can do for you after all the help you're giving us. Plus, I enjoy every chance to be creative."

Clara guided Annelise to where she could find paper, pencils, and some colored pencils. Annelise sketched as they talked.

"So what's up in Crater Lake for you guys? You mentioned you have a photoshoot?" Dylan asked.

"Yeah, it's… um. For a brand. Doing a buddy a favor. We can't really talk about it yet." Tristan shifted in his seat.

"Okay, that's cool. Everybody's got to have their secrets. Like the government." Dylan adjusted his rose colored glasses on the bridge of his nose. "Not to sound all conspiratorial and stuff, but man, have they got some whacky stuff going on."

Annelise widened her eyes at her artwork but said nothing. Hopefully, if she didn't prompt him, he would change the subject. She wasn't in the mood to listen to a rant on conspiracy theories. She was living a conspiracy theory.

"What sort of stuff?" Michael asked, his eyes dancing between mirth and curiosity.

Annelise rolled her eyes. *Here we go.*

Dylan looked at him, eyes wide, and his gaze fervent. "I don't know the details, but let me tell you. When our governments merged in the early 1900s, and everything was supposed to be super transparent and open all of a sudden, they hid a lot more secrets than they revealed."

Annelise looked up from her drawing. Perhaps he was actually onto something.

"I mean, do we even know what our government is doing anymore? It's like they dazzled us with magic and technology, but behind the scenes, there's no oversight to what they're doing. I think that they're combining magic and technology to build a super-weapon that will destroy the whole world!"

Annelise sat back in the seat. Just like that, her interest was lost. He was clearly off his rocker. Anyone who studied magic knew that magic and technology were like oil and water. Any new integration between the two happened in small increments and was very time-consuming and delicate to accomplish. And besides, what could they *possibly* gain by destroying the world?

Michael continued entertaining Dylan's conspiracy theory while asking pointed questions that poked holes in many of the theories. He had a way of inflecting his voice when asking questions that diffused defensiveness and allowed one to take the question at face value. Clara swapped places with him after a while to let them interact more easily. Michael moved to the passenger seat, while Clara came and sat next to Annelise, looking over her shoulder and giving clarifying details about what they might want on their van.

Annelise looked up at Clara. "Thank you, again, for helping us out."

Clara gave her a warm smile. "Of course, it's our pleasure."

"Do you stop for hitchhikers often?"

Clara grinned. "We don't see a lot of them, but we've stopped a couple of times."

"Do you ever worry about the people that you pick up?"

"What do you mean?"

"I mean, do you ever worry about your safety? You could be picking up anybody. You could be picking up fugitives."

Tristan shot her a sharp look, but Annelise pretended not to notice.

Clara shrugged. "It's true... we could run into some rough folks doing this, but so far, we've been lucky."

"Why do you do it then?"

Clara gave a small smile. "Because anyone out in the middle of nowhere, holding out their thumb, needs help. The world would be a little kinder if everyone would help, but until then, we just want to do our part. Share some kindness. And I think if you treat people like they are worthy of trust, most of the time, they will rise to the occasion."

Annelise fell into a contemplative silence, chewing on her words. She had not had the pleasure of meeting people so openhearted beyond Professor Hale. She hadn't thought there were more people like that out there in the world.

The flat Californian fields gave way to mountains, and then to the steep forests of Oregon. Eventually, Clara took over driving, Dylan moved to the passenger seat, and Michael moved once again to the back.

"Mind if I put on some music?" Clara asked, craning her neck to look at them from the front seat.

"Not at all," Tristan said.

Obnoxious, cheerful music bopped through the van as it bounced along the road north.

The three mages tensed when the DJ came on the air, talking to the co-host about the break-in at the vaults. They exchanged a look.

"...can you believe that three people broke into the Magical Government's Vaults, stole something, and got AWAY with it? The wizarding council is being all hush-hush about what was stolen, but one source from the Wardens says this is the biggest manhunt they have had in over one hundred years. Apparently, the last time this many people were mobilized, they had lost a dragon. A dragon! Can you believe that? How do you lose a dragon? It's a shame, too. I'd love to see a dragon.

"As usual, we want to hear from you, and it looks like we have our first couple of callers on the line. We have Toby from Grants Pass, Oregon, and Carl from Grangeville, Idaho. Welcome, Toby and Carl. Tell us, what do you think about this latest news? Toby, we'll start with you."

"You know, I think that these sorcerers are just too dangerous to be walking around." Toby had a nasally voice. *"We never think about it because the magical community seems to crack down hard on anyone breaking the law, but then you see something like this*

happen, and what good were the wardens? Every one of these mages is walking around carrying a lethal weapon with them. I think they should crack down on people like this and take away their staves."

"And Carl, what's your response to all of this?" the DJ prompted.

"Well, if I may respond to some of what Toby said." Carl sounded like an older man. *"I don't know that taking away the staves of these sorcerers would do any good. I heard that one of the fugitives blew up a whole building with his bare hands."*

Annelise clenched her hands in her lap so tightly her knuckles turned white.

Carl continued, *"Magic exists, and it's out there. I think we need to come to terms with this reality, no matter how uncomfortable it is."*

"An interesting take. Toby, any response?"

"Yeah. Look, I see what you're saying, Carl. But I still think that they need to crack down on people like this. Some people want to see more magic in their lives, but I want to see less. Unlike the majority of the people out there, I have a brain, and I've actually used it to realize the absolute devastation these people could rain down on us if they wanted. These people are dangerous, and I don't want them in my back yard.

"I also want to know what it is these fugitives stole, and what else the magical community is hiding. Let me tell you, there's a lot less transparency from the magical government than I would like. And you have to wonder, how did they get away with it? Could it have been an inside job? Someone working with the wardens who facilitated this break-in? I'm telling you, these magic folk are not to be trusted. It's just not natural."

"I see where Dylan gets his conspiracies," Michael murmured, his tone light, but his eyes held concern.

"Yeah, but this time, they're actually right," Annelise murmured back. She was concerned with how their actions might damage relations between the magical community and the sourceless one.

She knew that the Magical government worked very hard to ease concerns with the sourceless about these sorts of things.

She hated to think that what she had done would cause any among the sourceless to overlook all the benefits of the integration and become hostile towards the magical community — and heaven forbid the government followed suit. The magical community was too small to withstand all-out war, even with magic at their disposal. They *needed* to remain on good terms with the sourceless governments.

"I'm amazed at the lack of communication between our government and the sourceless one," Tristan added in a voice barely breaking a whisper.

Annelise looked at him quizzically.

"They know all of our involvement, and they know that Michael and I are wardens. But none of the sourceless news broadcasts are advertising that we are wardens. I don't think our government has shared this information."

"Maybe they're trying to save face?" Annelise suggested.

"We should be grateful; this can only work in our favor," Michael murmured.

Tristan looked thoughtful. "For now."

"I know it's kind of late in the game to be asking this, but do we know that there won't be wardens at Crater Lake?" Annelise murmured, the unsettling thought forming in her mind.

Tristan glanced up to the front of the van. "I doubt it. We played our theory about Crater Lake pretty close to the chest. They have no reason to suspect this is where we are going. They will be rushing to defend all known entrances to the Subraek. With any luck, this will divert manpower from the investigation and give us room to move where we need to."

"So what do you all think about this break-in?" Dylan interjected from the front seat. The three mages jumped. They had varying levels of success at schooling their features into something resembling not guilty.

Annelise recovered first. "I don't know much about what's being said about it. All I saw on the news was that there was a break-in and that it was being investigated. I think they've managed to ID one of the folks, but I don't know much more about the case than that."

"What do you think they stole?"

Annelise stared at her drawings. "I don't know much about what's kept there myself. Generally, items that the government deems unsafe to be in the public's hands." She turned to look out the window. "Whoever broke in, I hope they know what they're doing."

"Well, it's a good thing I've got two magic cops in my van. If those people show up, they won't dare try anything with you around."

Annelise had to bite the inside of her cheek to keep from reacting.

"Don't worry," Tristan said seriously. "Nobody will be trying anything. I can promise you that."

Dylan and Clara switched who drove again, and Tristan offered to drive for a while as well, so the two of them could get some rest. The sun was only just changing its angle in the sky when Annelise spotted the Cascade Mountains in the distance. Their peaks were adorned with snow even during the heat of August.

They pulled over at a rest stop to stretch their legs and use the restroom. Tristan decided to go for a short walk after all that time sitting in the van.

Annelise used the extra time to enjoy the scent of the warm summer air. It always smelled like promises and happiness to her. She felt someone come up behind her. It was Clara. Dylan followed her, not far behind.

"So, we were wondering... Can you show us some magic?" Clara asked.

Annelise frowned, confused. "You want to see magic?" Performing magic in the presence of the sourceless was generally discouraged because it was thought they would find it unsettling or unnatural.

"Of course! It's got to be the coolest thing, and other than transporter pads and the time when the mage doctors saved my grandpa's life from a heart attack, I've never seen any. It seems like nobody ever wants to show any real magic," Dylan said.

"Oh, um, I'm sure we could show you something." Annelise looked over to Michael. "Would you do the honors?"

"...Sure." Michael put his hands on his hips. "Just give me a minute to think of something that would be cool."

"Can you turn into a dragon?" Dylan was looking at Michael with barely restrained hope and anticipation.

Michael gaped at him, his brow furrowed in confusion. "You want me to turn into a dragon?"

"Yeah. My buddy at school is taking a magical history elective, and said that some mages can turn into dragons. That would be the coolest thing to see."

Michael nodded. "It would be very cool, but unfortunately, I don't have the ability to turn into one."

"Are dragons actually real?" Clara asked.

Annelise nodded. "Yes. They are real. There aren't many of them left. Actually, practically, there's only one left, and she went missing a century ago. But there used to be a lot more."

"What happened to them?"

Annelise hesitated. "The Dragon Wars."

Dylan looked at her with wide eyes. "You guys fought dragons?"

"Actually, *you* guys fought dragons." Annelise nodded at Clara and Dylan's incredulous expressions. "The sourceless waged war against the dragons for a hundred years between the 3rd and 4th centuries. You can still see echoes of this war in stories such as St. George and the Dragon, Sigurd and Fafnir," she ticked the stories off her fingers as she listed them, "St. Theodore and the Dragon, St. Donatus and the Dragon, Beowulf Killing the Dragon, and St. Sylvester and the Dragon. And these are just the stories that survived to the modern day in the sourceless world."

"Why? Did dragons eat people or something?"

Annelise chuckled. "No. Not normally. People are far too crunchy. Too many bones, not enough meat."

Michael snorted.

Annelise ignored him. "The conflict was about their magic. Dragons are powerful sources of magic. Basically, they give magic its…magicalness. Some overly curious sorcerers and dragons started experimenting with very dangerous magics. Like, get it wrong, and you destroy the world kind of stuff. It was reckless." She glanced at Michael, then turned her eyes back to Dylan.

"It caused a great divide in the magical community. The sourceless decided to wage war on the dragons. Less dragons meant less magic, and less magic meant that the reckless actions of a few would no longer be able to endanger the world.

"Even some mages joined the sourceless against the dragons. It was a terrible decision to have to make. But, for the preservation of the world, they felt it was necessary. By destroying many of the dragons, a large amount of magic was drained out of the world, too. And the power to perform the kind of magic that almost tore apart the world was lost."

"So St. George really killed a dragon?" Clara's eyes were wide.

Michael hesitated. "Well… St. George led the army that killed a dragon, yes."

Annelise continued, "After the wars, the sorcerers went into hiding along with the last few dragons, and took their magic with them. The dragon population never recovered, but dwindled over the centuries. The missing Dragon was the last of the great dragons."

Michael cocked his head at her. "Unless you count the Obsidian King."

"Who was the Obsidian King?" Dylan asked.

"He was an ancient and powerful dragon," Michael explained. "He waged war on humanity. He could devastate entire regions in a single day. It took a coordinated effort by the strongest mages of all the clans of the day to take him down. No matter what they tried, he would not die. But they managed to imprison him in stone, deep in a mountain."

"Luckily," Annelise cut in, "He doesn't count."

"Still." Dylan stuffed his hands in his pockets. "I'd love to see a dragon."

"Not that kind of Dragon," Annelise countered.

"A good dragon," Dylan clarified.

"What happened to the sorcerers who joined us normal people against the dragons?" Clara asked.

Michael glanced at Annelise. "Things were tense for a long time, but eventually we found a way to get along again."

"Well..." Annelise teased. "I don't know. Some of you Pendragons are pretty hard to get along with."

"Anyway..." Michael clapped his hands together. "You wanted a display of magic, not," he gave Annelise a pointed look, "a history lesson."

"What? I appreciate people who are willing to learn about our history!"

Dylan bobbed his head. "Yeah, no worries! It's super interesting." He turned to Michael. "Actually, I was thinking, could you do something so that the birds stop dumping on the van?" He gestured to the vehicle. "I swear they use it for target practice."

Annelise turned to look at the van and, sure enough, there were a substantial number of bird droppings plastered across the van.

She had initially thought they were part of the artwork. Apparently, she was wrong.

"I washed it just last week," Dylan complained.

Michael chuckled. "Let me think about what would work, but I'm sure we can come up with something to help. You have an absorption crystal in your van?"

"Yeah. We got one on the off chance that we might visit Canol Dinas. I mean, they give them out for free, so why not?"

Michael considered the van. "I have an idea." He extracted his staff with a flick of his wrist. Dylan and Clara oohed and aahed as the staff seemed to appear in his hand out of thin air.

Michael chuckled. "Just wait. I'm only getting started." He approached the van and snagged a bit of chalk that the hippie couple had kicking around in the van. Then he drew some runes on the outside of the van that made up a shield spell. He held his hand over the runes and chanted in the draconic language. The chalk runes and the grain along his staff glowed bright blue before fading.

"That should help. It will only last you up to a couple of weeks, depending on how many birds take a shot at you, but it will help, for now."

"Cool! What did you do?"

"I cast a shield spell. If your car is under attack from birds, I figured that a shield would be the best way to protect it."

"What about if it rains?" Clara asked, observing the chalk.

"The magic will hang around even if the chalk washes off. But, like I said, it won't last more than a couple of weeks. And you'll want to check on your absorption crystal every week or so, just to make sure it's still in good condition."

"That totally rocks, dude!" Dylan clapped Michael on the back.

Just then, Tristan returned from his walk, wearing a new pair of sunglasses. "I found a shop," he explained, as he passed a pair to Michael and Annelise as well. Annelise nodded. It would be good to hide Tristan and Michael's unusual eyes. The group piled back into the car.

They followed the winding road that led them up the mountain. Once it reached the rim, the road followed the mountain, often dipping below the edge, but once in a while coming up just enough that they could all gaze out over the beauty that was Crater Lake. Vivid blue water sparkled in the caldera, lined with sunburnt grass, and dotted here and there with trees so dark green they looked black. Annelise would have enjoyed stopping to paint the scene if they had been there on vacation like everyone else.

Eventually, they reached the crossroads where they would part ways. Dylan and Clara would continue North, while Annelise, Michael, and Tristan would take the road east to the trailhead that led to the boat dock. A gravel parking lot crunched under the wheels as they pulled off the road.

Annelise climbed out of the van and turned to their hosts. "Thank you so much for all your help."

"And for the engaging conversation," Michael added, his eyes sparkling.

Tristan shook hands with Dylan. "We appreciate you going so far out of your way to help us."

"Hey, no problem, man. It was our pleasure. If you're ever in Coeur d'Alene, look us up!" Dylan replied.

"Here," Annelise handed Dylan the various concepts she had come up with for the van. "Some ideas to get you started."

"These are amazing! Thank you!"

Clara peered over his shoulder. "Wow. Babe, this would look so cool! And they don't even look complicated." She turned to Annelise. "Thanks!"

"It was my pleasure."

Clara and Dylan waved their goodbyes, and the van pulled out of the parking lot. The three mages watched the smiling and waving folks in the happy hippy van shrink along the winding road.

***

Their walk along the rim of the volcano took about an hour and a half. Luckily, after the first half mile uphill, the road became a downhill slope, and they made good time. The occasional pack of cyclists whizzed by them along the winding road. The trail itself was another matter. The steep gravel path switched back a few times, and occasionally their feet would slip along the path, kicking up dust and sending a small avalanche of pebbles down the slope. Further down, they could see more people picking their way down the trail.

When they reached the shore of the lake, Annelise couldn't help but stop to appreciate the view. The bright early evening sun glittered across the water and reflected the mountain and the trees surrounding them. Vibrant blues, golds, and whites played across the sky, causing the world to gleam.

A crowd of people was gathering around the ramp that led onto the docked boat, but they had a while to wait before they could board the last tour of the day.

Annelise lifted a tour ticket off a guy who was too busy staring at the world through his camera to notice what was going on around him. She handed it to Michael, who grabbed a few napkins he had requested from a picnicking family. One reflection spell later, the napkins looked identical to the tickets. Tristan generously returned the ticket to the man, who thanked him profusely for rescuing his dropped ticket.

The boat shuttle took them directly to the island. The icy meltwater sprayed over the bow of the boat as they raced through the windswept waves. When the boat was secured to the dock on

Wizard Island, the three mages meandered onto the island with the rest of the group.

Annelise did not want to meander. She wanted to run off the boat and get this over with. Everything had moved so fast. It was hard to believe that this time yesterday, they were poring over blueprints, preparing for their doomed break-in.

Everything from getting blackmailed into this job to arriving on the island seemed like a blur, and she hadn't had much time to process the fact that they were actually going to enter the Subraek. She had no idea what they would find there, but seeing as ancient wizards had used the underrealm to banish all manner of foul and dangerous spirits and creatures, she didn't imagine it to be a pleasant place. Her heart was pounding, and her mouth dried out as the reality of what they were about to do set in.

Tristan waved them off the beaten path, and they followed him through the underbrush to where the entrance lay. A large outcropping of rock jutted out from the dirt, trees, and underbrush.

There, etched in the stone, was the rune for a locked door. It was faded and old, with lichen and moss creeping across the rock, but it was still readable.

"Hey, that's cool! A wizard's rune!" Three sets of eyes snapped toward the sound of the voice. It was the guy with the phone camera. "Oh, hey!" He recognized Tristan as the one who had found his *'dropped ticket'*. "Hey, did you know that Wizard's Island is actually the entrance to a super-secret magical dimension?"

"Is it really?" Michael responded with polite disinterest, only the faintest amount of strain leaking into his voice.

"Yeah, people disappear here all the time and are never heard from again. Here, move to your right a bit. I want to get a close-up of this rune."

Annelise obligingly stepped out of the way so the man could get right up close with his camera.

"This is gonna be great, my followers are gonna love this!" He snapped a few pictures with his phone. "Have either of you guys ever actually seen a wizard perform a spell?"

Annelise smirked. "Once or twice."

His expression filled with awe. "Awesome. It's a bummer that the wizards don't come out much. I kind of wish that magic was a bigger part of everyday life. I don't see why it's not, what with us being Integrated, and everything."

Annelise was starting to wonder if the policy of keeping magic out of sight of the sourceless was achieving its goal. The government discouraged displays of magic around the sourceless. There were concerns that if the sourceless got spooked by magic, they might turn on the magical community. So, to give the sourceless a sense of security, any magical infractions, particularly against the sourceless, were heavily punished. Magical displays were discouraged.

"I think maybe they are just trying to be respectful." Annelise kept her tone diplomatic.

The man nodded. "Yeah. I guess. I wouldn't mind seeing some magic, though. Did you see on the news? One of those mages that broke into the compound blew up a wall with nothing but her bare hands!" He had a gleeful smile plastered across his face. "Wicked."

Annelise's eyes were wide as saucers at this point. "Did they say who was behind that?" She was using all her willpower to keep her panic from her voice. How much did this guy know? What if he turned them in?

"I don't know." He fiddled with a setting on his camera. "Something called Pendragons, and some chick. Hey, I'll catch you around. I want to get a panoramic shot from the peak of the island."

Tristan nodded at the man as he bounded away, disappearing around the corner of the path. He then turned back to Annelise and Michael, his face pale but resolute. "We should wait until sunset. The last shuttle off the island is in about an hour. We can use the light of sunset to disguise the magic, and... we don't want to be interrupted." He nodded in the direction of the cameraman.

"Do you think we should snag a camera from someone?" Annelise asked. "We might need proof of what we find."

"We will have proof enough when the Dragon walks out of the Subraek," Tristan countered.

"What was it you said earlier? Hope for the best, plan for the worst?"

"I don't like stealing from people."

"You've already stolen a car."

"And I didn't like it."

Annelise looked at Michael.

Michael turned to Tristan. "I think she's right. It's better to have it and not need it than to need it and not have it."

"With any luck, we can give it back when we're done." Although Annelise doubted it would be possible.

Tristan looked out across the water of Crater Lake, his posture rigid. "Fine," he said. "Let's do it."

They set out to find a suitable device.

Their first pick was a point-and-shoot camera. Michael held the owner's attention while Annelise made the lift. She ducked behind a tree and pried open the casing of the camera, looking for an absorption crystal. They would not make the same mistake twice.

The camera did not have one, so Annelise slipped the camera back into the woman's backpack without her noticing.

The second time, they had more luck. This time, Annelise flirted aggressively with a man while Tristan lifted his phone. Not long after, she saw a thumbs-up. She extracted herself from the conversation and slipped back to their spot by the portal.

"Perhaps you should create another perception ward," Annelise told Michael. "So nobody finds our hiding spot."

"On it." He drew the necessary lines and runes in the ground around the portal, and Annelise guided him through the chant again. The faint blue light of the perception ward shimmered in the air around them before fading.

They hid on the island until the sun sank low on the horizon, casting a striking golden haze over everything in sight. The boat tour left, leaving them alone on the island.

Annelise's heart pounded.

Michael stood up and collected the key from Tristan.

"So... Do you know how to use the key?" she asked. "I don't see a keyhole."

"I think the key will do that part for us." Michael placed one palm on the rune. The stone beneath the rune seemed to melt away to reveal a large, ornate copper keyhole. "Grab on to me."

Tristan and Annelise each grasped one of Michael's shoulders as he slid the key into the keyhole. The rune in the rock glowed white before engulfing all of them in a bright white light. The light faded, and they were left standing exactly where they were before.

And yet, it wasn't the same. The shadows seemed deeper, and the sunset a little richer. A nearby tree held deep gouge marks, though what creature had caused such destruction, Annelise didn't know. Michael released the rune and let his breath out slowly, regaining control of his magic.

Annelise gestured to the slashed tree. "We're going to have to keep a very low profile while we're here."

The three shared a look of concern. They were in the Subraek now. The place where dark creatures roamed freely.

Chapter 9: The Monster

They hiked in total silence to the very top of the island in the fading light, wary of any creatures that might come upon them. The pale evening sky glowed above the darkening waters of the Subraek's version of Crater Lake. The Subraek was, in most aspects, a reflection of the world above. The normal world. Their world. And yet, it was different. There was no birdsong here, and everywhere they looked, they could see evidence of creatures whose names and aspects were long forgotten to history.

They found a patch of dirt clear enough of trees and bushes to perform a finding spell. Michael drew the runes for the Dragon's name into the dirt with the butt of his staff.

Annelise bit her lip as worry, anticipation, and excitement battled within her. If the finding spell failed, they would be back to square one. Worse than square one, because they were down two staves, and the entire warden service was after them. But if they were right...

They set to work drawing the runes for the finding spell. It required several runes to be etched into the landscape in a circular pattern. Tristan carved one into the dirt, Annelise picked up a pebble and scratched one on a boulder that jutted out from the ground, while Michael drew one at the base of a shrub with his staff. Luckily, for this spell, they only needed one working staff for all of them to participate. Michael gripped his staff in his right hand, while Tristan grasped his wrist with his left. Annelise grasped both the Pendragons' open hands. The chant for this spell was long and languid, rolling over her tongue in a hypnotic rhythm. They chanted the words in little more than a whisper. Annelise's quiet voice mingled with the deep voices of Tristan and Michael, as images flashed through their minds.

The gouged tree they had seen by the door.

A great stone covered in bright green moss.

The deep blue waters of Crater Lake.

The rim of the caldera, with snow-capped mountains glinting in the distance.

A barren flat of reddish-brown earth.

Sunlight pouring in dappled splotches through the trees.

A glittering lake lapping at the sandy shore, framed on two sides by mountains.

And a great cave, with…a dragon. She was curled up in the entrance, her green scales glinting in the evening light.

Annelise blinked and opened her eyes as the vision of the markers to their objective faded. She was breathless from the sight. The Pendragons had been right! The Dragon was trapped here. It was a small glimmer of hope that they had not thrown away their futures for nothing. Relief and excitement shone on the faces of the two Pendragons.

"We found her," Tristan breathed. He and Michael shared a look, grabbing each other's shoulders in congratulations.

Following the first clue in their visions, they made their way back down the hill towards the gouged tree by the door, and continuing in as straight a line as possible, they worked their way down to the lake. When they had nearly reached the water, Annelise stopped dead in her tracks. There, to the right, several yards away, was a large rock covered in bright green moss.

"Psst," she whispered, getting the Pendragons' attention. Michael nodded when he saw the stone, and they made their way toward it. Letting the clue correct their course, they continued down the hill from there.

Soon they had reached the shore of the Lake. Tristan reached his hand into the water and shivered. It was frigid, and the waters were darkening under the fading light.

"I don't want to swim this water in the dark," he said. "Let's get some rest and continue first thing in the morning."

Annelise agreed. The light was now almost all gone, and she was no longer certain where the far side of the lake was. It would be foolish to try the crossing in the dark. Besides, they might miss their markers.

No one spoke as they settled down for the night. They were all too tired for conversation and too wary of what might be just beyond their sight to attract any attention to themselves. They lit no fires.

Annelise and Tristan both set about looking for something to serve as a makeshift staff. Not to perform magic with—that was impossible right now—but to use as a blunt weapon. It would be better than nothing, at least, and it was something they knew how to work with. All students at the Academy learned basic martial skills with the short staff since the discipline and precision of movement translated well to spellwork.

Perhaps one day she would be able to carve herself a new proper staff—to once again find a seed that resonated with her, to water it from the waters of the Dragon Blessed fountain, and then to carve it into its shape, but not today. The whole first year at the Academy was spent growing, shaping, and crafting the new mage's staves at the beginning of their magical training. They did not have that kind of time right now.

Annelise found a nice branch that fit into her hand, seemed sturdy, and was straight. Satisfied with her choice, Annelise used a sharp rock to try to smooth the sides down a bit more and peel the bark off her branch.

As the last light faded from the sky, Annelise picked the most comfortable patch of dirt she could to settle down on. Tristan, too, had stopped working on his staff, and he and Michael settled on the ground near her.

The stars glittered, more radiant than she knew was possible.

Then the night grew dark. Darker than they had ever experienced before. There was something off about this night.

Annelise's skin prickled like there was someone, or something, watching her. A heavy darkness pressed against her eyes and seemed to dim the light of the stars to barely a glimmer. Annelise's heart pounded. She scooted closer to Michael.

"Do you feel that?" She whispered as quietly as she could manage.

"Yeah." His voice sounded muffled.

"What do you think it is?"

"I don't-"

Just then, a piercing scream tore through the forest around them. Annelise clutched Michael's arm with one hand, grabbing her makeshift staff with her other. The stars went out completely. She could not make out where Tristan was.

"Tristan?" She called in a rough whisper. But he didn't reply.

Another scream rang through the forest. It sounded like a mountain lion, except that normal mountain lions didn't put out the light. Next to her, she heard Michael's illumination spell fail. They were swallowed in utter darkness.

"Don't let go of me," Michael said.

"Where's Tristan?"

"I don't know."

"We need to find him."

"I know. Come on. But don't let go of me."

Together they stood, clutching each other against the pressing darkness; another scream, closer this time. Annelise gripped her staff.

The hairs on the back of her neck stood up. In one fluid motion, she let go of Michael's arm and slid to the side, swinging her staff in a wide arc. It connected with something big; something big and furry; something big and furry with a scream that seemed to come right out of the very depths of Sheol. She heard the faint thud as her staff connected with the creature, but she could not see what damage, if any, it had taken.

She reached for where she thought that Michael ought to be, but he was no longer there.

"Michael?" she whispered. But there was no response. She refused to feel the pang of loss at his absence. She fought best alone, anyway. She repositioned herself at the ready.

Annelise could feel the creature prowling around her. She couldn't hear it, and she couldn't see it, but the darkness was so thick that she could almost feel the reverberations in the air around her as the creature moved through it. She knew where it was. Her heart pounded, and her mouth went dry. Every sense was on high alert. She tried to gauge when the creature would strike next as she rotated in a slow, tight circle to keep her stick between herself and the creature.

Annelies felt the creature lunge. She ducked low, jabbing upward with her staff. She felt it connect, her staff reverberating in her hands. It was a good hit.

The creature fell back, pacing just out of reach.

Where was Michael? She wondered desperately. He had been right next to her, and she would have thought he would have either found her again by now or she would have heard him moving around, but it was as though the darkness had swallowed him up.

She felt the creature creep in a large arc around her, trying to get behind her. She spun around, trying to cover her exposed back.

Her skin tingled as she felt the creature pacing ever closer, as if testing to see if she would notice its approach. Taking the offensive this time, she lunged forward, bringing her staff down in a decisive strike. It cracked against some part of the creature. Another horrible scream ripped through the air as it moved away. Then there was silence.

Annelise panted as she tried to slow her racing heart. It must have thought she was too challenging a meal. As the creature moved away, the thick darkness dispersed, and the light of the stars returned.

"Michael?" she whispered.

There was no response.

"Tristan?" she called again, as loudly as she dared. Nothing.

Moving cautiously by only the faint light of the occasional star that passed through the canopy, Annelise spent the next hour looking for Michael and Tristan. She strained her ears and tried to see through the dark forest, but they were nowhere to be found. She did not dare call out, for fear of the creature—or something worse— coming back again.

Dejected, she curled up next to a tree, finding comfort amongst its roots as she pressed her back against the trunk and clutched her staff. She didn't sleep for fear of the creature returning. Her mind replayed the night's events over and over, hoping for any clue to assure her that Tristan and Michael might be okay, but her memories gave her no further insight. She stayed on watch until the sun rose and dispersed all traces of the darkness.

When the sun did rise, Annelise resumed her search for her companions.

***

Two hours later, Annelise had to conclude that they were no longer on the island. A sick feeling settled in her stomach. What if they had left her behind? What if they had been eaten by some nameless creature?

Her mind swung wildly between the hope that they were merely waiting for her at the next clue marker and the despair that they had definitely left her behind due to either callousness or death.

When she remembered that she could not return home without the key, which was with Michael, Annelise thought she might be sick. She was going to be stuck here for whatever was left of her short, miserable life.

The more she searched, the more she was sure that they had abandoned her.

A small, persistent voice in her head kept countering her despair with the memory of Michael telling her that they would look out for each other. Annelise was torn between squashing the beautiful memory and holding on to the useless hope.

Of course, they were gone. It's what people did.

And yet, that voice persisted. She figured that she might as well go to the next marker and prove to that dogged voice that it was wrong.

Annelise wiped away tears with an impatient hand. She was more alone than she had ever been in her life, and, for the first time, she didn't want it. More tears sprang to her eyes. She groaned. She did not have time for this. Wiping her face with her arm, she cursed. She cursed her tears. She cursed the creature that had nearly killed her. And she cursed the Pendragons who had gotten her into this mess.

She felt a little better.

She picked her way through the trees to the shoreline. The next marker was on the rim of the volcano. She would need to cross the lake and hike up the inside of the caldera to get to it.

She crept to the water's edge and dipped her hand in the lake. It was frigid. But she looked to her left and saw that the distance between the island and the far shore was only a few hundred yards in that direction. If she had to swim, she preferred to minimize her time in the icy water as much as possible. A long flat section of the island reached for the edge of the lake. That would be her best bet.

She peered into the water for a while, praying she did not find some monstrous creature from the deeps. After last night, she was wary of every rustle of leaves and every lap of water on the island shore.

Eventually, there was nothing left to do but begin. She had seen nothing, and if there was something in the deep waters of the lake, she would find out soon enough. She tried not to dwell on the fatalistic thought that it wouldn't really make much of a difference—she was likely dead anyway. At least her route took her over a shallow shelf that stretched under the water about halfway to the rim of the lake. Her exposure to the unseen deeps of the lake would be minimal.

She tore a strip of fabric off the bottom of her dress and tied her makeshift staff to her back so as not to lose it. Her new, far inferior, non-magical staff was not retractable as her magical one had been. She then tore a large swathe of fabric off her skirt so that it fell above her knees. She did not need the extra fabric dragging her down.

She waded into the water, the frigid chill creeping up her legs. When the water hit her waist, her breath came in uncontrolled gasps until she managed to master it again. She scanned the water as she went, on alert for anything that might want to eat her.

Finally, she had no choice but to leave the safety of the rocky bottom and strike out across the lake. Her fingers were already numb, and she felt little through her skin, but she kicked hard and swam as fast as she could. She wanted both to limit her time in the water, as well as to work her body temperature up as much as possible.

Her heart pounded as she swam. It was a small mercy that the sweet water of the lake could quench her parched mouth. Every glint of light became a threat. Every rolling wave, moved along by the breeze, became the ripples of something moving towards her. Annelise pushed and pulled the water with all her might, desperate to get to the end of it.

The swim did not take long, but her muscles were slowing down by the time she reached the far shore. They no longer moved with precision, and Annelise was bone-chilled.

The slope on this side of the caldera was steep, and she had to grab at trees and brush to keep her balance as she pulled herself up and out of the water. Flopping on the high side of one tree, she shivered. Slowly, her heart rate returned to normal as she let the warm summer air bring life back into her frozen limbs.

After a few minutes, she decided that the better way to warm up would be to climb back out of the caldera. It would get her blood pumping, and she had to get there anyway. Her dripping clothes stuck unpleasantly to her skin as she scrambled through the underbrush up the steep climb to the rim.

The icy swim had diverted her attention for a while. Now, her gloomy thoughts returned. With every step towards her goal, Annelise was more sure that she would find it empty. She tried to focus on the ground in front of her. Who knew? Maybe she could find the Dragon on her own and at least have some company in this unforgiving place.

The hike to the rim took her well over an hour, as she had to stop frequently to rest or plan her next moves. There were no convenient hiking trails on this side of the Subraek door. When she finally reached the rim, she had worked the warmth back into her body, and she was thinking longingly of the icy waters below once again.

She headed north along the rim of the caldera. The first two landmarks of their vision had led in a northerly direction, and so the third landmark should be in that direction as well.

The closer she got, the more knotted her stomach became. Would they be there? Probably not. Would they be safe? Who knew. Would they have moved on without her? They had no reason to stay.

The idea of having been left behind in such a place filled her stomach with lead. She hurried forward, desperate for answers, and dreading what she would find.

By the time she approached the part of the caldera directly north of their starting point, Annelise was ready to be sick or start crying. There was no way they would have waited for her. They would have left her behind rather than have her slow them down. Her stomach cramped so hard she doubled over. On the second wave, she retched. There was nothing but bile.

She stood up and stumbled forward. She must be close to the next marker. She leaned against a great rock that towered several feet above her, blocking her way forward. Her hands were trembling. She wasn't sure she could bear to find the marker and not find the Pendragons.

She sank to the ground at the base of the rock, her breath coming in short gasps. She fixed her eyes on the ground and focused on taking slow, steady breaths. Finally, her panic subsided.

She knew she should continue forward, but she couldn't bring herself to get up. She sat there a while and watched the trees sway. The only sound she could hear was the wind through the branches. It was eerily quiet.

She got up. She could not linger forever in this in-between state—between hope and reality. She had better find the marker, come to grips with what was real, and move forward from there.

Her self-talk did not stop her legs from shaking as she picked her way around the rock. She glanced up from the uneven ground. Ahead of her was the sight she had seen in the vision of the finding spell: A clearing on the rim of the caldera, with snow-capped mountains glinting in the distance. The only difference was that there were two figures, sitting on the ground, gazing down the north slope of the volcano. A small fire crackled between them.

A sob escaped Annelise.

Both of the Pendragon's heads snapped towards the sound of her voice. In an instant, Michael was on his feet, running towards her. He wrapped her in a fierce hug, which she gingerly returned.

Her heart, which had been previously pounding with anxiety, finally slowed, and her legs shook as the tension left her. She blinked back tears.

Michael pulled back from the hug and held her at an arm's distance, checking her over. "Are you okay? I was so worried about you! What happened? Where did you go? When we couldn't find you, we feared the worst!"

Annelise wiped her eyes. "I was on the island. After I fought off... whatever that was, I waited for the sun to come back up, and then I looked for you," she hiccuped, "but couldn't find you anywhere. So I decided to make my way here. Where were you?"

"We were looking for you." Michael squeezed her shoulders before letting go.

"Michael found me not long after he lost you," Tristan said. "We searched for hours together to try to find you, but found no trace. We hoped you would find your way to us at the next clue marker. I'm glad you're okay."

"For a while, we feared..." Michael trailed off.

"You feared I had been eaten by some terrible monster of utter darkness? Yeah. For a while, I feared that would happen too. But luckily, I'm too much trouble for not enough food, and it left me alone." A hysterical giggle welled up inside her, while her eyes gathered with tears again.

"Speaking of food, have you eaten?" Tristan asked.

Annelise's giggling stopped abruptly. "No. Do you have food?" Now that her attention was brought to her stomach, she realized that she was famished.

Tristan produced some roasted fish that Annelise did not recognize on a long, semi-flat rock.

"How?" Annelise asked, popping a piece of the roasted fish into her mouth. In her ravenous state, it tasted exquisite. It melted on her tongue, filling her mouth with the rich flavor. It was some of the freshest fish she had ever enjoyed. She sat down to eat.

"There's a stream not far from here," Tristan said. "With a little patience—"

Michael scoffed, but Tristan ignored him.

"I managed to catch some. Michael roasted the fish, so if it's burned, you can blame him."

Annelise took another bite. "No, it's great." She paused. "So, how did you two get away?"

"I think it was most interested in you, actually." Michael sat down next to her. "When you let go of me, I tried to find you again, but instead I stumbled out of the oppressive darkness and into Tristan."

Tristan poked a stick at the small fire. "I was looking for the two of you and had wandered out of it as well."

"We could hear the sounds of your fight in the distance, but when we shouted, it was like the darkness swallowed up all the sound." Michael's eyes fell to the ground. "We went in together, and though we were holding onto each other and shouting, we could barely hear each other. Every few minutes, we found ourselves back on the border of the unnatural darkness."

"It was like it was spitting us out," Tristan added.

"Finally, the fight seemed to end for better or worse, but we still couldn't find you. We didn't want to shout in case we called that thing back. We waited until dawn, and gave the island one final look over before deciding to come to wait here in the hopes that you would make your way to us rather than us endlessly circling each other on that stupid island."

"I did the same thing. How long have you been waiting here?"

"A few hours."

"We must have just missed each other."

Annelise licked her fingers as she finished the last bits of fish. She felt much better now that she had eaten. Not great, but better.

"What would you have done if I hadn't found you?"

Tristan frowned. "We would have gone back to look for you. Until we knew there was no other explanation than you being eaten, we would have looked for you. You're a part of the team."

"But what about the mission? You need to free that Dragon."

"We are a team. We do this together," Michael said.

A deep-seated fear seemed to dislodge itself in her gut. Annelise suddenly felt like crying, but from something other than anxiety this time. She refused to let the tears fall.

"Well, just promise me one thing." She tossed a small stick into the fire. "If I *do* get eaten by some crazy monster, don't let that stop you from setting the Dragon free. She deserves to be free. Besides," she managed a smile, "You need to make your mark on the world. You should get that chance."

Michael smiled. "I'll promise you this: until you get eaten by some crazy monster, we will stick together, look after each other, *and* set the Dragon free."

Annelise liked the sound of that.

They set out again, towards the snow-capped mountains in the north. There were no paths, roads, or trails in the Subraek, so they had to pick their way down the slopes of Crater Lake through the underbrush. Tristan had snagged a topographic map from the visitor's kiosk near the boat docks, which helped them keep track of where they were. The terrain of the Subraek should, for the most part, reflect the terrain of their realm. They focused on maintaining a northerly route from their origin point, but it was slow going.

They were picking their way through a sparse juniper forest when Tristan plunged his hand into his pocket, pulling something smoking out. He flung it away from him with a curse, and the object burst into flames.

Michael stared at it dispassionately. "That sucks. I guess we're not getting any photos."

It was the phone they had lifted.

"I thought it had an absorption crystal?" Annelise asked.

Tristan nudged the now smoldering husk that was once a phone with his foot. "It did. But this place, it's soaked with magic. It must have overloaded."

Annelise had noticed that her magic seemed to be flowing better, but she hadn't made the connection. She was too tired to think critically about much of anything. It had been a long time since she had slept properly.

By the time the sun was starting to set, they found themselves on the edge of the plain of barren earth that they had seen in the finding spell. Annelise's steps were becoming more like a stumble than a steady forward march. Her feet and lower back ached, and her eyes burned. It was a pleasant distraction from the pounding headache that had developed in her temples.

"We need rest," Tristan said when Annelise tripped over yet another rock. She was spared tumbling to the ground by stumbling into Tristan. "We will camp here and continue on in the morning."

Annelise could have cried with relief. How long had it been since she slept? Not since she passed out from the blood magic, if you could count that as sleep. She wanted nothing more than to flop down on the ground and drift into sweet oblivion. If some monster decided she was a tasty snack, as long as it didn't wake her, it could have her. With no new food available to them, they drank some water and curled up on the ground near a juniper tree.

Tristan took the first watch, Michael would take the second, and Annelise would take the last. They pressed in close together. Nobody wanted to get separated if that thing attacked again. Annelise fell asleep as soon as her eyes closed.

She woke to Michael gently shaking her shoulder. His golden eyes glinted at her in the rapidly paling eastern sky.

"You let me sleep in?" she asked.

Michael smiled at her. "Tristan and I agreed that you could use a little extra rest since you had none the night before."

"Thank you." She sat up and stretched her stiff and sore muscles. Michael laid himself back on the ground with his back to Tristan and was soon sound asleep.

Annelise didn't have a drawing pad or pencil with her, or she might have drawn the scene. Something about seeing those two back to back, even in sleep, reminded her of her favorite painting. These two really embodied what she had imagined only existed in fairy tales when she had painted it. They trusted each other and relied on each other. And they were able to achieve more through it. She admired Michael's loyalty to Tristan and Tristan's confidence in Michael.

A pang of longing struck her: the desire to have such complete trust in someone else, and to be trusted in return. It was not something she had ever imagined wanting in the past. She had lived her whole life avoiding situations where she would be forced to depend on anyone other than herself, because she was afraid of being let down and left holding the bag.

A rustle through the trees behind her drew her attention. A horrific screech tore through the trees in the distance. She jumped, gripping her staff with white knuckles as she heard what sounded like some poor creature becoming another creature's early breakfast.

Her eyes scanned the trees, searching for the source of the noise, but whatever had made the sound was hidden amongst the trees.

The noises faded, and Annelise couldn't decide if that was better or worse. All she could do was hope the creature had eaten its fill and wasn't in the mood for human.

The first splendid rays of sunshine poured over the mountaintops to the east, bathing the world in golden light. When the sun had finished rising, she nudged Michael awake. As he stirred, Tristan woke too. In the morning light, Annelise spotted some blackberry brambles. The three sorcerers gorged themselves on the ripe black fruit. Now, energized and rested, they were ready to continue on.

The trees gave way to a barren plain, dotted sparsely with grasses, and containing an abundance of porous rock. The occasional intrepid bush was found, but most of the plain was just rock and sun-cracked earth.

"How did you know that I could perform blood magic?" She asked as they walked. It wasn't something she advertised, and the fact that they had found it out about her had been quietly bothering her since the vaults.

"When we saw the way that you blended magic into your forgeries with the VanTover, we took several of your artworks to a consultant. He discovered the blood magic element in a couple of your pieces," Tristan said.

"Who was the consultant?" Annelise asked, curious and a little indignant to know who had outed her.

Tristan exchanged a look with Michael. "Professor Finchley. He knows more about magic than anyone else I know. In addition to teaching, he occasionally consults with the wardens when they come across something new. And most importantly, he's someone I can trust."

"Huh. Did you tell him who had done the paintings?"

"No. We wanted to keep our future conspirator as anonymous as possible, so we only asked about the magic used. And Professor Finchley is a professional. He knows that we can't always tell him all the details, and he knows better than to ask."

Annelise breathed a sigh of relief. "I guess that makes me feel marginally better. I really try to keep that fact close to the chest."

"Don't worry. We won't advertise." A smile pulled at Tristan's lips.

"So, Tristan, what made you want to be a warden?" Annelise asked, changing the topic. There was a lot about these two she didn't know but they knew a lot about her. It was only fair to turn the tables on them.

She saw Michael shoot a concerned glance at Tristan.

"It was my parents," Tristan said. "They died when I was a boy."

Annelise wanted to reach out and place a hand on his shoulder, but she didn't. She just kept walking beside him. "You mentioned this, yes. You inherited the house. I'm so sorry. What happened to them?"

Tristan shrugged. "We don't know. It's a cold case that nobody has solved. They were just found dead in our home one day. Very little evidence beyond that." He paused. "It's a special kind of torture, not knowing what happened or why. Nobody should have to go through that. That's why I became a warden. I wanted to solve cold cases."

"Did they ever find your parents' killer?"

"No."

"And so instead you went looking for the dragon?"

Tristan gave his makeshift staff an aggressive swing as he walked. "I guess I figured if I couldn't solve my personal tragedy, perhaps I could solve a public one."

"How old were you when your parents passed?"

"Eleven."

Annelise felt a wave of empathy for him. "That's awful. I'm sorry."

"It was. But I was fortunate. My aunt and uncle, Michael's parents, took me in. They raised me like one of their own."

"One of their many own." Michael smirked.

"You have a lot of siblings?" Annelise asked.

"Four amazing sisters," Michael said. "And now, of course, this one." He jerked his thumb in Tristan's direction.

Tristan rolled his eyes, but there seemed to be a smile tugging at the corner of his mouth.

"So you grew up together and decided to go into business together."

They looked at each other and shrugged.

"What's that supposed to mean?" Annelise asked.

"It means that as much fun as it is having to put up with this one's bossiness all the time," Michael dodged a thwack from Tristan with a grin, "and the abuse, I don't know that I plan to continue being a warden forever."

Annelise chuckled. "Michael, I hate to break it to you, but I think that ship has sailed. Unless they allow people who commit treason to be wardens."

"They don't." Tristan pinched the bridge of his nose. "But that's a problem for another time."

"So what do you want to do?" Annelise asked. "Assuming all our dreams come true, and we find the dragon, and all our crimes are miraculously forgiven."

A smile tugged at the corners of his mouth. "Assuming all of that," he paused. "I don't know…I mostly followed Tristan into being a warden. After I flunked out of art school, I didn't know what I wanted to do with my life. Tristan was so sure, so I figured I'd help him out for a while. I'd like to help him solve his parents' case, you know?" He shrugged. "Beyond that, I'm not sure. I really liked the stuff we got to learn in our training to be wardens. The advanced spellwork involved with ward establishment particularly fascinated me. But honestly, developing the technique to interrupt wards was what made me feel alive. I might want to be a spell developer someday. I like how it combines creativity and magic to create something completely new."

His eyes lit up when he spoke about developing spells.

"That's beautiful," Annelise said. "And judging by what I've seen of your inventions already with the ward interruption, I think you'll be really good at it."

"How about you?" Tristan asked.

"What about me?"

"Do you have any siblings?"

"Nope. Only child." Annelise stared intently at the bare ground ahead of her as she walked.

"Huh," Tristan said. "And you live alone."

"I have since I was a teenager."

"And you have no friends," he continued.

Annelise's head snapped towards him. "What makes you say that?" Annelise wasn't sure if she should be offended or not.

"The furniture in your house. You obviously never have people over. So I was really surprised to see your painting of the two mages battling back to back in your living room."

"Where else would it be?" She kicked at a stone as she walked.

Tristan tilted his head. "Probably somewhere with more furniture."

Annelise was stumped. "I don't know what to tell you. I suppose I like painting fairy tales."

"Do you really think it's all fairy tales?" Michael cut in; his golden gaze seemed to pierce through her. He seemed almost hurt that she didn't believe in such things.

Annelise glanced from Michael over to Tristan, and then back to Michael. "Maybe not for some. I just don't know if it's possible for everyone."

Michael put a hand on her shoulder. "I hope that you discover that it's more prevalent than you think."

"I'm not sure I can afford the risk if I'm wrong," she replied.

"If you give—" Michael stopped.

A rumble under their feet sent small pumice stones rattling around on the plain. All three mages stilled, looking at each other in concern. Tristan and Michael immediately fell into formation, shoulder to shoulder. Another rumble rolled through the plain, and a sound like rock grinding against rock started emanating from the east.

Annelise whipped around to face the source of the sound, her makeshift staff in both hands.

A bulge had appeared beneath some of the rock that was growing by the second. The pumice was shifting and sliding around as it was pushed higher and higher, as though something beneath the surface was burrowing its way out of the ground.

"Run," Tristan said. He didn't raise his voice, but the note of fear rang through his tone.

Chapter 10: The Oath

Annelise broke into a sprint. Tristan and Michael matched her pace. All around them, more bulges were appearing in the rocky ground, grinding and rumbling as whatever was below worked its way to the surface.

"What is it?" Annelise screamed as she ran.

"Nothing good!" Tristan hollered back.

A plume of black gas burst from one of the bigger bulges. It looked like volcanic gas, but the gas seemed to coalesce into an inky droplet the size of a bowling ball and plummet back toward the ground. It pursued the mages, looking like a drop of mercury racing along the pumice stones.

All around them, inky black puffs burst from the ground. One by one, they coalesced and fell to the earth with an ominous crunch. They surged towards the sprinting mages. As their numbers grew, they merged into a thick black menacing ocean that seemed to rise and fall of its own accord, or to the rhythm of some unfelt wind. Always, the black substance pursued them.

Annelise's lungs burned. Her heart was in her throat, and it felt like it was about to burst. Too many ink monsters were coming from the ground now.

Tristan skidded to a halt, forcing Annelise and Michael to stop too. Their way forward was cut off. All the while, more and more droplets were joining their ranks, and the ocean of black ink grew. The trio circled up, facing out.

About half a mile away, they could see the edge of the plain, lined with trees. Beyond, a thickening forest grew. Whatever this stuff was, it didn't seem to want to pass the tree line. If they could just make it there...

"Whatever you do," Tristan's voice was urgent. "Stay together."

There was a moment of quiet as the roiling liquid frothed just out of reach. The mages stood, weapons ready.

The inky ocean was eerily quiet. There were no shrieks, no roars, no screams. There was only a low burbling sound against a high-pitched whine emitted by the mounds leaking a malodorous gas.

Annelise wondered if these things were even solid. If she hit one with her staff, would it connect to anything?

She stretched her staff out to touch the inky substance.

"I wouldn't..." Tristan warned.

As soon as her staff connected with the liquid, a black tendril of the stuff coiled around the end of her staff and pulled. Annelise gasped and would have tipped forward into the mass if Tristan hadn't grabbed her and held her steady. With a yank, she pulled her staff free of its grip.

A low, boiling sound emanated from the black waters all around them, building to a crescendo.

The oily ocean around them surged towards the three mages. Annelise swung her staff. It was like connecting with water. It resisted, then gave way. Some of the black stuff seemed to dissipate into the air. The viscous sea shrank back a bit where she had hit it and then surged forward once again.

Michael leveled a blasting spell at the amorphous entity, and a whole section recoiled, drawing back like the tide. Magic was much more effective than physical force.

"We could portal?" Annelise suggested.

"Easy for you to say," Michael retorted.

"I'd rather not have the only member of our team still wielding his staff out of commission while we're stuck in the Subraek," Tristan said. "We will save it as a very last resort." He assessed the situation, his face set with determination. "Okay. Michael, I need you at the front blasting a way through this stuff so we can move. Annelise and I will bring up the rear. We make for the tree line. And whatever happens, stay together."

Progress toward the tree line was slow and exhausting. The strange, semi-sentient substance did not seem to be sure what to make of them. But as the three mages moved across the plain, the burbling sound got louder. With each spell that Michael cast, it seemed to get more agitated. The inward rushing, like waves on the shore, was more aggressive.

Annelise swung her staff against the new wave, forcing it back, but this time, it seemed to grab hold of her staff and almost yanked it out of her fingers. Annelise was pulled forward, stumbling into the ink-monster with one foot. Inky blackness surrounded her leg, pulling at her. Digging her staff into the ground, she yanked it free and stumbled back.

Next to her, Tristan had just managed to wrestle his staff free from the strange mass and brought it with a crack against the ever-thickening liquid again. Ahead of them, Michael's spells seemed to be less effective. Something was changing.

Annelise looked around. They were going to be devoured by this ocean of oily mercury. Their progress forward had slowed to a crawl. At this pace, they would collapse from exhaustion before they reached the safety of the trees. Her breath came in ragged gasps, but she couldn't seem to get enough air. She did not want to die like this. Prison would be preferable to this. Her eyes darted around, looking for any hope of escape.

Then, as though by an answer to prayer, she saw a path open ahead of her. A section of plain that the black swirling sea did not seem to want to traverse. It led the few hundred yards to the line of trees and the end of the black sludge.

"I can see a path!" she cried. "We can get out of here!" Hope poured through her, and she darted onto the path. "This way, come on!"

"Annelise, no!" Tristan and Michael's voices mingled.

Annelise looked back in confusion and frustration. Tristan and Michael had not followed but were screaming her name, horror on their faces.

Then, the pumice under her feet slipped and slid, and more black ink poured out from the rock under her feet as though she were squelching her way through sponges filled with the stuff. It swirled over her feet. Annelise only managed a moment of sickening dread before a tentacle of swirling oily ink latched onto one of her legs and yanked.

Annelise screamed. Her stomach seemed to stay behind as her body was dragged beneath the surface of the inky blackness to her certain death. She couldn't breathe. She could barely move her staff, let alone swing it to any effect.

Some deep current dragged her across the rough pumice stones. They scraped against her back and tore at every bit of exposed skin. She barely noticed the burning pain it caused. Her lungs burned, and her diaphragm spasmed as it demanded air. She struggled, trying to flail her arms, legs, and her staff to no effect. She could hardly move.

Using all her strength, she pressed her staff up towards the surface, breaking into the air with a burble. By some miracle, she also managed to lodge the other end into the ground and pull her face out of the river of liquid obsidian just enough to take a gasp of air before she was pulled under again. She hadn't even had time to scream. But the top of her staff still rose above the surface. Her only hope was that Tristan and Michael might manage to save her. She prayed desperately that they would succeed soon.

The torrent of black liquid pulled at every part of her, threatening to rip her away from her staff, but she clung to it all the tighter. Her breath burned in her lungs, and her arms screamed with the effort of holding onto the staff. She couldn't hold on much longer. Two fingers on her left hand slipped off the staff. Annelise screamed, wasting her precious air, but unable to contain the horror, fear, and rage of such an end.

There was a blast of blue light all around her. Annelise fell to the ground, no longer drowning in the black, mercurial liquid. Tristan was next to her, striking at the roiling ocean with his staff, pushing back the sludge. He pulled Annelise up from the ground, his mouth set in a grim line. His golden eyes flashed with ire as he beat back the waves of ink. Michael was right behind her, protecting their backs. Annelise staggered back from the edge, dazed, and looked around.

They were farther from the treeline. Much farther.

"Now!" Tristan shouted.

In one smooth movement, Michael drew a portal circle around them and started chanting. The black sea surged again, with more ferocity than ever, but Tristan had grabbed hold of Michael to keep him steady with one hand and was beating the waves back with the other hand. Annelise followed suit. They did not need to go far, just past the treeline. She swung wildly. Every form that had been trained into her at the academy was gone.

The portal flashed blue, and the three tumbled to the ground, surrounded by trees. The few tendrils and drops of black ink that had been caught in their portal evaporated into nothing. Every muscle burned and shook as Annelise clambered back to her feet. She was scraped up and bleeding in a few places, but she was alive.

Tristan stumbled over to a nearby log and sank onto it.

Next to her, Michael was leaning heavily on his staff, his face white as a sheet. "You said you didn't think you could afford to risk trusting someone and being wrong," he panted, "I don't think you can afford not to risk it anymore." He stumbled to a nearby bush and vomited.

Annelise stared after him. She would certainly be dead if not for Michael and Tristan coming to her rescue. She glanced at where Tristan was still sitting with his head in his hands.

"Tristan?" She approached him tentatively, not sure how he would react.

He flung up a hand. Annelise's words died on her lips.

"I am trying to keep us all safe." His voice trembled with anger. "Your life, Michael's life…if something happens to you, I am responsible." He looked up at her, his gaze burning into her. "Do you understand? Someone needs to be calling the shots, and in this team, on this quest, that is me. That means I am responsible for everything that happens to this team, but if I tell you to do something, I need you to do it. I need you to trust me, or none of this will work. Do you understand?"

Annelise nodded. "Understood." Her voice came out in a hoarse whisper. She didn't fully understand. She didn't know how to trust them, even though she wanted to. But she did understand that he was angry she had not followed the plan to stay close to her teammates. She could see now that she had panicked and put them all in danger.

His eyes searched her face. He nodded back. "Good."

"Well," Michael stumbled back towards them, a goofy grin on his face and sweat beading on his brow. "That sucked!" He slung an arm around Annelise's shoulder that seemed half for camaraderie and half for stability. "Let's not do that again!"

"You okay, Michael?" Tristan asked.

"Yeah," Michael replied breezily. "But blackberries don't taste nearly as good coming up as they do going down,"

Annelise grimaced, imagining the flavor. "Gross."

"Gross indeed."

"Come on. We need to move," Tristan said.

"Yes, please!" Michael followed Tristan with unsteady steps. "I want to be as far away from that plane as possible! I've developed an aversion to oil spills of death." He raised a hand. "I vote we take a different route on the way back."

Tristan let out a weary chuckle. "Agreed." He led the way further north.

"You think the Dragon will give us a lift across it on the way back?" Michael slung his staff across his shoulders.

"We can ask her when we find her."

"Hey, guys," Annelise said before they got truly underway.

Tristan and Michael turned to her.

"Thank you for coming and rescuing me. And, I'm sorry I didn't listen. I panicked and wasn't thinking straight. I never meant to put you in more danger."

Michael clapped her on the shoulder. "We'll always have your back, Windstarter. Just…next time try to stick to the plan."

Annelise nodded.

They set out, but only five minutes later, they stopped again. Michael was stumbling every two steps, and he had vomited again. He needed rest to recover from the magical expenditure.

As soon as they sat down, he was dead to the world. Although spells performed with a staff did not drain one's energy as fast as the older blood magic, portal spells were still brutal. Portalling three people at once? Three times as brutal.

Annelise looked at Michael, asleep on the ground. She knew it was her fault that he was in this state. She knew she needed to do better. She might be bad at trusting, but that did not mean that the

Pendragons were untrustworthy. From now on, she would try to trust them—even if every bone in her body screamed against it—because Tristan was right. If they didn't work together, they would probably all end up dead.

Tristan sat watch, whittling on his makeshift staff. Annelise sat down next to him.

"What do you think she's like?" Annelise watched Tristan's pocket knife as it shaved scrolls of wood off the glorified stick.

He looked at her. "The Dragon? I think... I think she's powerful." He ran his knife against his staff again. "And she has a sense of humor."

Annelise chuckled. "What? Where did you get that?"

"My uncle used to tell us stories about the dragon, passed down from his father, who had quite the adventure with her." He gave his staff another scrape. "The stories always captured my imagination."

"What kind of stories?"

A smile tugged at Tristan's mouth. "Let's see if I can tell the story right." He put his carving down and spoke, his voice rising and falling in the lulling rhythmic pattern that all seasoned storytellers use.

"When my uncle's father— Michael's grandfather— was a boy, he decided he didn't want to go to school, or do chores, or share a room anymore, but wanted to go live in the mountains and live off the land. So he ran away from home and hiked high up into dragon territory. Things went okay for the first few days. He gathered berries to eat, built himself a simple shelter, and got his water from a mountain stream.

"Then it started to rain. It was a torrential downpour like he had never seen before. His shelter washed out. It was the middle of the night. He was drenched and freezing cold. So he started walking uphill to keep warm. He walked all through the night. Little did he know that as he was warming up, a mountain lion was stalking him."

Tristan leaned forward, his voice dropping to a hush, his tone laced with tension and anticipation. "It didn't take long for the hairs on the back of his neck to stand up on end. The body knows before the mind when danger is close. He kept looking back, hoping to catch a glimpse of what was stalking him. But the mountain lion was too crafty and blended into the forest around him. Only once did he catch a glimpse of the lion before it disappeared into the forest once again. He knew he had no chance against the mountain lion, but he also knew he was in dragon territory.

"He started calling out to the dragon. He hoped that the noise would either scare off the lion or bring the dragon. It shouldn't have worked. The dragon's territory was massive, stretching for miles and miles. But by some miracle, it did work.

"The dragon saw the mountain lion stalking the boy, scooped the boy up by his rucksack, and carried him high into the mountains to a cave up in the cliffside.

"'What are you doing out here all alone, mageling?' she asked him.

"So he told her that he had run away to live off the land because he no longer wanted to go to school or do chores, or share a room, or do anything else he had to do at home. He wanted to be free and live in the wilds.

"'Well,' the dragon said. 'There is no freer way of living than living like a dragon. And you are a Pendragon. I will adopt you and raise you to live the dragon lifestyle. And you will learn to eat wild food, and travel wild paths.'

"Naturally, Michael's grandfather thought that sounded pretty good. The dragon told him to rest up because he had been up all night, and he needed his rest. She would go hunt for some food for them.

"So he went to sleep. The dragon flew down the mountain until she found the search parties looking for the boy, whom they feared was in grave danger in the woods. She told them how she had found the boy and that he was safe. She also told them where they could find him, and she promised that by the time they reached the bottom of the cliffs, they would find him quite ready to come home."

"Oh no," Annelise chuckled with delight and anticipation. "What did she do to him?"

Tristan chuckled. "Well, for one, she fed him. She fed him in the manner that all dragons feed their young: By regurgitation."

Annelise wrinkled her nose. "Gross," she laughed.

"When Michael's grandfather asked if there was anything *else* to eat, some berries perhaps? The dragon told him that eating berries was not the dragon way. She did consent to roast the bit of meat at his request, but alas, she breathed her fire on it too hot, so now he had a rather burnt, half-digested piece of meat to eat. But who can say no when a dragon is glaring down at you to make sure you finish your supper like a good little drakeling?

"Well, it didn't take long for Michael's grandfather to be quite ready to be done living the wild dragon lifestyle. He asked to be let out of the cave, and the dragon was *so proud.*

"'It's always a big day for any drakeling when they take their first flight out of the nest.' She went on and on about how he shouldn't be scared, just to take a big jump and spread his wings, and let gravity do the rest. Michael's grandfather realized with horror that the dragon seemed to think he was going to *jump* from the cliff. He asked her instead if she could carry him to the ground, but she told him that he would never learn if he did not try himself. He tried to explain to her that he wasn't actually a dragon and that it would certainly be the death of him if he jumped, but his arguments fell on deaf ears.

"Eventually, he had to resort to attempting the dangerous and long climb down the cliff face with no rope or harness. All the while, the dragon was flying around him, telling him that flying down would really be the quicker option, that he would never learn if he never tried. Well, about halfway down the cliff, he slipped. Quick as a flash, the dragon snatched him out of the air and deposited him safely on the ground right as the rescue party was arriving.

"He was very happy to see them, and as much as the dragon *tried* to convince him to come back and live with her, he was quite resolute that his place was at home. That he had chores and schoolwork that urgently needed attention, and that he simply couldn't be parted from his brother any longer."

Tristan finished the story, his eyes twinkling.

Annelise chuckled, shaking her head. "I can't believe we're actually going to get to meet her. She's been lost for so long, I never really stopped to imagine what she might have been like. I only know what they teach in the history books. I don't think I've ever known anyone with a personal story about her, and I never imagined a dragon would have a sense of humor."

"I don't understand why someone would dream of sending her into exile like this," Tristan murmured. "She belongs in our world. She belongs with us. I cannot wait to return her to her rightful place."

They fell into silence.

"Was it Councilman Cawthorne who told you that story?" Annelise asked. She couldn't imagine his snooty voice telling bedtime stories.

Tristan chuckled. "No. This was Michael's father. Uncle Fitz isn't much of a storyteller."

"So, what is it like, having Councilman Cawthorne as your uncle? Is it weird being so closely related to the most influential mage on the planet?"

"Honestly, I don't think of him like that. But that's partly because he's not the only relative of mine who works in government. Councilman Jackson is also a relative, plus pretty much every Pendragon is on some level related to every other Pendragon."

"So what you're saying is that you're related to the majority of the council."

Tristan chuckled. "Pretty much. So to me, Uncle Fitz is just Uncle Fitz. I know he can be a bit snobby at times, sorry about that, by the way. He spends so much time with dusty old councilmen that he has lost all sense of politeness, especially after a day in council. But I owe so much to him."

"How so?"

"After my parents died, I went to stay with Michael's family, but it was Uncle Fitz who handled all the funeral planning, all the logistics, and managed my parents' estate well for years on top of all his own affairs. My parents owed the banks a fair bit of money when they died. He is the reason the house is still mine and in good condition. He managed it all so well that by the time I inherited the house, the debt was paid off, and the property and investments were making money."

"Wow. That's pretty amazing."

"I'm grateful to him every time I go home. So even though he sometimes drives me crazy, and uses my library liberally, I don't begrudge it to him."

"It's lucky that you had such people looking after you."

He nodded. "It is indeed. I wouldn't be where I am today without them. How about you? Do you have any extended family?"

"No. My dad left when I was young. I don't think any of my grandparents are still alive, and if I have any cousins, I don't know them."

Tristan made a small noise of sympathy. "So it was just you and your mother growing up?"

Annelise nodded.

"Are you still close?"

Annelise bit her cheek hard to keep the sudden rush of emotions that had ambushed her at bay. They were not close. Her mother was dead. But she did not want to talk about it. She took a moment to steady her voice. "No, we grew apart. She took it pretty hard when my dad left, and with her being sick and all, she just didn't have much time or energy for me. After that, I largely raised myself."

She glanced up at Tristan to see how much of her unsuppressed emotion he might have read on her face. His eyes were keen as he watched her face, but they filled with sympathy. "I'm sorry. That can't have made for an easy childhood."

Annelise shrugged. "I grew up fast in some ways. And in the end, I had other people who looked out for me."

"People like Jimmy?"

Annelise looked away. "Yeah. Jimmy was one of them." Thinking about Jimmy reminded her of how he had given her up. After all the time they had known each other...it stung. She turned her eyes back on Tristan, forcing the thought away. "And there was Professor Hale at the academy." Annelise forced some brightness into her voice. "He knew my mom from way back, and he kept an eye on me. He has given me a lot of good advice over the years."

"That's good."

She cocked her head. "Then again, he did sort of talk me into following through on this mission of yours, so I think that's a point against him. I think he's slipping."

Tristan chuckled. "Let's wait till we're done, and we will see if it was good advice or not."

Michael stirred. "What are we laughing about?" he murmured sleepily. His eyes were still shut, but he had rolled on his side to face them. Annelise couldn't help but smile.

"We're trying to decide whether Annelise's teacher gave good advice when he told her to follow through with this mission." Tristan grinned at Michael.

Michael smiled, his eyes still closed. "Mmm. That was definitely good advice. We would almost certainly be in prison if she hadn't joined us."

Annelise's eyes crinkled. "It's lucky for you, but was it good for me?"

"Hmm." Michael blinked one eye open. "We will have to wait and see."

Tristan rolled his eyes, but he still smiled. "That's what I said."

Now that Michael was awake, they started making their way forward again.

As they traveled onward, the trees seemed to brighten. Much like their clue marker, the sun poured through the canopy and fell dappled on the ground. They had not, however, come across the exact scene in their finding spell yet. Annelise hoped that they had not somehow passed it by during their portal jump, but they had not jumped far, so the probability of that was low. For now, the light was still too slanted, and the trees were not quite the same.

Michael fell in next to Annelise as they ducked their way under branches and stepped over rocks, roots, and ferns.

"So, how did you learn to wield blood magic?" Michael asked, holding back a branch so Annelise could pass by.

Annelise nodded her thanks. "My mom taught me the basics pretty early on. I guess it's a skill that's been preserved and passed down in our family for centuries. But after she got sick, I mostly taught myself. I knew the foundations and was able to learn a lot from books."

"What did she have, your mother?"

Annelise hesitated, chewing on the inside of her cheek. "She... she screwed up one of her blood spells really badly, and it caused magical hemorrhaging."

Michael winced. "That's rough."

"Well, it's a risk anyone casting blood magic takes. It's dangerous if you don't do it right," Annelise swatted a branch out of the way.

"Is she doing better now?"

Annelise stared into the trees. Her fingernails dug into her palms. "No."

"She's still sick?"

"No."

"Oh... I'm sorry."

Annelise swung her staff, swatting at a tuft of grass. "She died only two years before the treatment for magical hemorrhaging was developed. If she had only..." She stopped.

The past could not be changed. "If onlys" helped nobody. It was better to deal with reality than with wistful alternate timelines. She stared at the ground, blinking rapidly. She was not going to cry. She kicked a rock in her path that skittered down the gentle slope before them, bouncing off trunks and roots. She ran a hand over her face. She needed to get it together.

Michael gave her shoulder a squeeze. "Sometimes life gives us a rough hand. And sometimes the things that almost worked out are more painful than the ones where there was never a hope from the beginning."

Annelise gave a shaky sigh. "That's the thing. It's her own fault she's dead."

"Because of the spell she cast?"

"No. Because of all the spells she cast afterward."

"I don't understand."

"When a mage is suffering from magical hemorrhaging, accessing their magic only rips the wound open more."

"...that would be why the standard protocol is to abstain from any and all magic, no matter how big or small?" Michael supplied.

Annelise looked at him, baffled.

"They teach wardens the basic protocols for magical injuries," he explained.

"Well, you're correct. My mom's initial injury was not very serious. It made her sick, and she was in pain from time to time, but if she had simply followed the protocol, she would almost certainly have survived until the treatment and cure were found. She didn't need to die."

"So why didn't she?"

"After my dad left, I think she wanted to die. He was all that mattered to her. When he left, she got reckless, and I couldn't..." Annelise clenched her jaw. "She got what she wanted most, I guess."

"And after all that, you still decided to study and use blood magic?"

Annelise gave a rueful smile. "I guess a part of me wanted to prove to myself that it could be done safely. And once I started incorporating it into my art, I fell in love with it. There's something so pure, so primal about using it. It's the original method of spellcasting, and there is something beautiful about letting yourself be the conduit for the magic, instead of shunting it to a staff or some other object."

Michael glanced at her, his expression curious. "You paint a very different picture than most people do about it."

"That's because most people don't have a clue what they're talking about. They give opinions on things they have never experienced, influenced by the changeable tides of public positions." She took a breath. Her tone had gotten heated. "Sorry, I get a little worked up about this."

"We'll call it passionate." Michael grinned as he held another branch aside for her.

As the sun continued to slant through the sky, they started spreading out as they walked, so as to cover more ground and increase their chances of finding the next clue marker. Finding a particular patch of trees in a forest was like finding a needle in a pile of needles.

"Here!" Tristan called, his excitement ringing through the forest.

Annelise jogged towards the sound of his voice, Michael coming up beside her. Indeed, the sunlight poured in dappled splotches through the trees, just like they had seen in their vision. They were getting close!

With an excited grin, Tristan bounded forward, followed closely by Michael, while Annelise followed after. Not three steps further, she walked headlong into something solid. The force of the impact sent her stumbling back to the forest floor behind her with a grunt.

"Hey, guys?" she called, gingerly rubbing her nose and blinking through her watering eyes. The Pendragons turned and came back to where she was, concern written on their faces.

"You okay?" Tristan asked as he helped her up.

"I think so..." Annelise replied. "But I just ran into some sort of barrier. It wouldn't let me through." She walked forward again, this time holding her hand out in front of her. It connected with the invisible barrier. She pressed against it. It didn't budge.

Frowning, Tristan walked up beside her, held out his hand, and walked right past her, as though there was nothing there. Whatever the barrier was, it let him through while keeping Annelise out.

"Strange." Michael came up beside her. He, too, held out his hand, but couldn't seem to find the barrier that was keeping her out.

"It might be some sort of ward." He gripped his staff and tried to find it, but it seemed not to exist.

Annelise looked at the two of them pensively. "You two are cousins, right?" she asked, fishing a piece of obsidian she had found on the volcano out of her pocket. She struck it against another stone she had picked up and flaked a shard off the volcanic glass. It came away razor-sharp. She pricked a finger, and the tiniest drop of blood welled up. She held her hand out to the ward again.

There, she could feel it! She reached out with her magic, and the space between her and the Pendragons glowed a bright red, rippling through the air as it stretched from the forest floor up through the canopy and out of sight. Annelise's jaw dropped. It was a massive ward. Although she couldn't see it, she suspected that it formed an enormous dome over a vast section of the valley.

"What is that?" Tristan asked, his head tilted back, peering to where it stretched into the canopy.

"A blood ward," Annelise breathed. "A ward made with blood magic. It will only let blood relatives of the caster pass. But they are extremely taxing to create. Usually, they are only used to protect family vaults or other small spaces. To cast and maintain a barrier ward this large with blood magic... It must have been someone exceedingly powerful. Or they used a corrupted method to cast it..." She trailed off, trying to learn what she could from the ward.

Michael approached and reached out to try to feel it as well. Again, his hand passed right through it. "Can you dismantle it?" he asked.

Annelise considered the ward. "No. Blood wards are not as manipulatable as those made with runes and staves. I can observe it, but only the blood of the caster can dismantle it."

Tristan turned to Annelise. "How does one dismantle a blood ward?"

"I thought you two studied ward casting at the Academy?" she teased.

"They don't teach anything about blood wards."

"I'm not surprised." She removed her hand from the ward and let it return to its usual invisible state. "Usually, blood wards like these are sustained through gems containing the caster's blood. However, if we were to find this gem, we could dismantle the ward pretty easily. It's a simple ritual of destroying the gem inside the wards, and then pretty much anyone could take it down."

"My guess is that we're pretty close to the Dragon." There was only one way forward. She hated it, but it was the only way.

"You two go on ahead, and I can wait here. There's no way I'm getting through." She stepped back from the ward and crossed her arms, squashing the torrent of emotions within her. "I trust you to come back for me."

Tristan and Michael shared a look. They came back through the ward to her side. Tristan leaned against a tree while Michael took a seat on a nearby fallen log.

"Well, that's not going to do." Tristan slid his hands into his pockets.

Annelise frowned. "What's not going to do?"

"We can't leave you behind in this monster-infested forest." Tristan gestured at the trees around them. "We don't know how much farther it is to the dragon, and I'm not willing to risk something happening to you while you're here, alone. I'm responsible for what happens, remember?"

A shaky breath of relief escaped Annelise. "I mean, we can try going around, but usually wards create a fully enclosed space. We might waste days walking around this thing, just to find that it has no gaps or gates."

She pressed a hand against the ward again, proving its impenetrability. "I'm not getting through this thing. I'm guessing that the ward was primarily created to keep the dragon in. Which, by the way, throws another wrench into this mission. You might be able to find her, but you won't be able to get her through this. My guess is the ward was erected to serve as a cage. A very effective cage." She dropped her hand from the barrier and looked at Tristan. "How are we supposed to get her out?"

"I don't know," he replied.

They sat in silence for a bit, pondering the situation. Annelise waited for the inevitable conclusion that she was right and that they would have to leave her behind.

"Okay," Tristan said in a decisive tone. Annelise braced herself. "We might not be able to get the dragon out just yet, but we can meet her. Hopefully, we can get information on who locked her up here, and then we can pass that on to the authorities, and they can get whoever cast this spell to take it down."

Annelise nodded. "A reasonable plan. Though it doesn't have quite as much wow factor as riding out of the Subraek with the long lost Dragon in tow."

She peered through the trees. "Still, she can't be far now. One way or another, one of us will have to be alone. Either one of you waits with me, and the other goes on alone, or both of you go on together, and I wait here alone. More witnesses are more convincing, so it makes the most sense that you both go on. I'll be fine waiting over here."

"Maybe, then again, maybe not," Tristan said, "Either way, we work better together. We just need to figure out a way to get you past that ward."

Frustration welled up within Annelise. Why wouldn't they just get it over with and leave her behind? It was inevitable, so why drag this out?

"I don't think you understand. It's impossible to crack a blood ward. That's why they're used for sealing family vaults. Only family can get through." Annelise felt a knot forming in her throat. She had been so afraid of getting left behind at every turn of this misadventure, and now, when she needed them to leave her behind, they wouldn't. She wasn't sure if she should be relieved or dismayed at their steadfastness, but she was deeply moved by the gesture.

"What if we could make the ward recognize you as family?" Michael gave Tristan a questioning glance.

"You mean changing the parameters of the ward?" Annelise considered the suggestion. "I don't have any framework for achieving what you're suggesting. Even if it can be done, it would take us years to work out. I don't think it is possible."

Tristan and Michael fell into a wordless conversation where Michael gestured with his hand, tilted his head, and raised one eyebrow in an obvious question. Tristan nodded in agreement with whatever Michael was suggesting.

Michael turned to Annelise. "We wouldn't be changing the parameters of the ward, but changing your relationship to it. We could swear a blood pact with you, and the ward would then recognize you as family."

"What?" Annelise's brow furrowed in confusion. She had never heard of such a thing.

"It's a pact, where two people bind themselves in loyalty and trust to each other, granting each other any special rights or privileges associated with their name, title, inheritance, or family." Michael rattled off like he had memorized the definition out of a dictionary. Actually, he probably *had* memorized it out of a dictionary at some point with his *proper Pendragon education.*

"It's old battlefield loyalty, brotherhood magic." His tone was nonchalant, but his cheeks tinged pink as he spoke. "The magic will recognize you as part of my family, and it should let you through."

Annelise's jaw dropped. She looked for laughter on Michael's face, but his expression was earnest. Annelise was bewildered. It was absurd, and she kept waiting for the penny to drop, for his signature teasing smile to break across his face. But still, no trace of the joking or laughing expression made itself known on Michael's face.

"You're serious?" she asked.

"Yes."

"But what if it doesn't work?" She asked. "We don't know for sure that this would cause the ward to recognize me. It could all be for nothing."

"Your safety is not nothing," Tristan said. "Also, we are reasonably convinced it will work. It worked to get Aunt Tammy into the family vault, so why shouldn't it work to get you through this barrier?"

"How does it work?"

"It's Oath magic. One of the few instances where the words themselves are the channel for the magic."

"And I'm assuming you know how to perform this?"

Tristan smirked. "We're Pendragons. This is Bougie Pendragon Magic. We know how to do it."

Still, Annelise hesitated. "We're basically complete strangers. I'm a forger. I literally sell lies for a living. How on earth can you swear to trust me and mean it? I'm pretty sure you would have to mean it for a spell like this to work."

"I'm choosing to trust you," Michael said.

Annelise ran a hand through her hair. "But why? How? I'm not even so sure that I'm trustworthy."

"Because I must." Michael's expression was earnest. "I know what I am risking. But I would rather risk my wealth and reputation than your life. And I have glimpsed your noble side, Annelise Windstarter. It makes me optimistic that if you give yourself a chance, you will find that you can be just as trustworthy as you want to be."

Annelise considered his words, astonished. Nobody had ever displayed such trust in her. Trust in her ability? Sure, on occasion. But trust in her, as a person? Trust in her character?

"What if I let you down again like I did on the plains?"

Michael gave her a gentle smile. "Then I will be there for you, like I was on the plains."

Annelise's eyes burned. She turned away, blinking hard to clear them. She swallowed.

When it came down to it, Annelise realized she had every reason to trust him. In every instance where she had reluctantly been forced to rely on the Pendragons, they had not let her down.

They had not abandoned her in the vaults, but carried her dead weight with them. They had not left her behind on Wizard's Island, but waited for her. They did not leave her to her fate with the oily sea but they had risked life and limb to rescue her. And now, they refused to take the easy way out to find the dragon but were determined to move heaven and earth to bring her with them.

Even more surprisingly, she realized that she wanted to do the same for them. She wanted to be reliable, to have their backs. She wanted to be worthy of their trust.

Annelise turned back to Michael. "Okay, what do we have to do?"

Michael smiled brightly. "Excellent. First, I need you to break off another piece of that obsidian you have. If you have no objections, I will take the oath with you, and Tristan will stand as witness."

"Have you ever actually seen this done?" Annelise asked.

"A few times," Tristan replied.

Annelise flaked off a sizeable shard of obsidian for Michael to use, and another one for herself.

"Now what?" she asked.

"Follow my lead."

Michael made a shallow cut in his palm, which Annelise copied, schooling her face against the sting. A thin line of blood appeared, but the cut was barely more than a paper cut. He held his palm up toward Annelise, and Annelise stretched her hand out to place her palm against his. Michael caught her hand before she connected and drew it around his hand, placing them back to back. Now each of them was gazing at the other's palm.

As she observed his hand, the long, elegant fingers, and the lightly calloused points that ran across the top of his palm, Annelise decided that Michael had a very nice hand.

Beside them, Tristan started chanting a spell of witness. As he did, a ring of light circled the two hands pressed against each other.

Michael smiled at her and then spoke. "Annelise Windstarter, I swear kinship and loyalty to you in blood and in oath. What is mine is yours."

He then nodded to Annelise. "Michael Pendragon," she copied. "I swear kinship and loyalty to you in blood and in oath. What is mine is yours."

"I stand as witness," Tristan said. The light around their palms flared bright gold one last time and then faded.

As Annelise drew her hand back, she noticed that the cut on her palm had healed into a silver scar. She ran her finger over it. It was beautiful. She looked up at Michael, blinking back tears.

"It is the proof of our oath," Michael explained, showing her his own scar. She resisted the urge to run a finger along his scar as well. "Now, let us see if we can't get you through this blood ward." He took her hand and drew her forward. He passed through the ward, and as Annelise passed where the ward had been, she felt no resistance. It had worked!

"Excellent!" Tristan followed her through and clapped both her and Michael on the back. "Let's go find that dragon. We're practically on her doorstep, and I can hardly wait."

"You know what this means, though," Annelise said.

Tristan sighed. "Yes. It means that whoever put the dragon in here is a blood relative of ours."

"Who do you think it could be?"

Tristan swatted a low-hanging branch out of the way. "It would have to be someone old enough to have done it one hundred years ago."

"So, Grandparents? Great grandparents? Are any of your great-great-grandparents still alive?"

"Our Great-Great Grandmother Dee is still alive," Tristan said. "But are we sure that the culprit is still alive?"

Annelise pondered the situation. "I think either the original culprit is still alive, or they have a younger accomplice who has added their blood to the wards. Otherwise, the wards would have felt far more fragile than they did. But I can't imagine them finding anyone willing to be complicit in keeping the Dragon imprisoned."

"It would have to be a mutual relation of Michael and mine, which narrows things down a bit, but then, we are related to a lot of people."

"Is there any way to tell how distantly the ward allows people to be related before it no longer lets them through?"

"I don't know. If I had the gem that sustains the spell and some time to work, I might be able to figure it out, but I'm not sure."

"So it could be as broad as any Pendragon?"

"I'm afraid so. I think our best bet is to ask the Dragon who put her in here. Then, hopefully, we can find the culprit, get the gem, dismantle the ward, set the Dragon free, and bring the culprit to justice."

"Yes. It'll be a piece of cake." Michael didn't sound like he believed his own words.

"Let's just focus on the task at hand," Tristan said. "And hopefully we can give the Dragon some hope that her imprisonment here is almost over, that she hasn't been forgotten. That bit of good, we can at least do." He plowed forward into the trees, Michael hot on his heels, and Annelise following after.

Chapter 11: The Dragon

It was less than an hour later when they came to the glittering lake and knew they were very close. They walked along the shore for a while before the shore bent away, and they found themselves once again beneath the canopy of the trees. They came to an abrupt end of the tree line, and there they saw a large clearing that butted up against great cliffs, with a large cave gaping in its side. And there, in the middle of the cave, was…nothing.

There was no dragon. The three mages looked at each other with confusion. Where could she be?

"Should we go in to look?" Annelise asked.

"Yeah," Tristan said. "But carefully. Michael, stay behind us to guard our rear."

With Annelise and Tristan in the front and Michael behind them, they entered the cave. The great opening tunneled back through the rock. The walls of the cave were smooth, with striations running along the length of the tunnel. The floor was made of ropey stone, as though it had been liquid and roiling down the tunnel when it was frozen in time. The cave sloped down into the earth, and the occasional drip of water was heard as it trickled against the walls. The tunnel came to an abrupt end where the rock had collapsed. There was nothing more to find. The cave was empty, the Dragon gone.

"Maybe we're too early," Tristan said. "If the finding spell said she was going to be here, she will be here. I propose that we make camp nearby and get some rest. When she comes back, we can ask her who put her in here, and figure out how to release her."

It was agreed, so they made their way back out of the cave and found a suitable spot in the forest to set up camp.

Snagging their empty water bottles, Annelise made her way down to the lake to fill them with water. Halfway to the waterline, the hair on the back of Annelise's neck stood on end. There was something out there. And it was big. Her mind flitted to the dark creature from several nights ago, but the light around her was unchanged. No. This was something different.

She gripped her staff in her hand, trying to familiarize herself with its feel. She wished she had her real one. Now more than ever, the staff in her hand felt like nothing more than a piece of wood.

She strained her senses in hopes of detecting the other presence in these woods, but she couldn't pinpoint the source. At best, it was just a bear, or even better, the Dragon. At worst...

She used her staff to push through a patch of thicket.

She wanted to call out for Tristan and Michael, but she didn't want to alert the creature to her presence until she knew whether it was hostile or not.

Annelise stepped around the tree and almost walked into the Dragon. She gasped and sprang back. Her heart pounded. The sight of the Dragon took her breath away.

Green scales that glinted and blended in with the forest perfectly covered its body. Two glowing golden eyes peered at her from above a row of dagger-like teeth.

The rest of her body was obscured by the forest, but judging by how the size of her head was greater than all of Annelise combined, she must be massive. She was magnificent.

Annelise let out a sharp laugh and lowered her staff, her initial shock of coming face-to-face with a dragon subsiding. Though her knees still felt a little weak.

"What brings you out here, little mage?" The Dragon asked. Her voice was deep and rich, beautiful and mocking. Her head slithered close so that Annelise was directly face to eyeball with her.

"Hail, your Magnificence," Annelise said, overwhelmed by her presence. "You are... you are..." she drifted off, momentarily at a loss for words. She was vaguely aware that her legs were shaking beneath her. She prayed they wouldn't give out.

"Yes, I am, but I am not patient. Speak!" the Dragon snapped.

Annelise started. "We are here for you," she stammered.

"Who is this 'we'? What other traitors are with you?"

"I have two companions. They are not far. They are Pendragons, Your Fearsomeness. And... traitors?" she asked, confused. Annelise was so mesmerized by the sight of the creature, her beauty, and fearsomeness, she didn't register the signs broadcasting that it was about to strike.

The air left Annelise's lungs in a swoosh as the Dragon's massive tail appeared from the underbrush and struck her. For a moment, she was weightless, flying through the air, still entranced with the sight of the Dragon. The impact with the ground knocked some sense into her. Pain spiked through her ribs as she landed on her back with a sickening crunch. She groaned.

The Dragon roared. "You conspire with my jailer!" she cried, advancing on Annelise.

Annelise scrambled to her feet, grabbed her staff, and faced the Dragon. Realizing how futile it was to face a fire-breathing dragon with a burnable stick as defense, she opted for distance instead and backed away as fast as she could without falling.

The Dragon passed through a clearing, and Annelise was almost breath-taken all over again by the full magnificence of the creature.

An enormous pair of wings stretched out behind it, churning the air into a frenzy. Its body was covered in scales like emeralds which glistened in the beams of sunlight that filtered through the gaps in the trees, and each claw tapered into a sharp talon.

"No, that's not true!" Annelise cried, remembering the Dragon's words, and trying to reason with her.

It swung its tail at her again. Annelise dodged just in time, and the tail smashed into a tree with a resounding crash that rolled through the forest like thunder.

She heard Tristan calling her name, his voice muffled by the forest. He was close!

"Tristan!" she screamed, hoping he would hear her and find her. "Michael!" She just had to hold out until they arrived. Hopefully, the Dragon would listen to them. They were Pendragons after all.

The Dragon swiped her long talons at her. Annelise dodged the Dragon's claw, turned heel, and ran. Her breath burned in her lungs. Where were Tristan and Michael?

The Dragon's chest smoldered with fire, and Annelise leapt behind a very large tree just in time. Blazing dragon's breath seared the air around her. Her breath caught as the air around her wavered with the heat, and the tree behind her crackled with flames.

"Please!" she cried out, as the fire raged around her. "We're not here to hurt you!"

The inferno stopped, and Annelise started to peek around the smoldering tree in hope, when the trunk exploded in a cloud of embers and splinters. Annelise dove to the ground, narrowly avoiding being crushed by the Dragon's tail.

"I have heard these lies before!" the Dragon screamed, her voice full of rage and pain. Annelise scrambled away from her as the Dragon stalked towards her with startling speed.

A shout from across the clearing drew their attention. Tristan and Michael had arrived. They were shouting and brandishing their own staves. The Dragon turned on them, belching fire. Michael leapt between the Dragon and Tristan, throwing a shield before the two of them.

"Pendragons!" the Dragon bellowed. "How dare you betray me in this way. You would ally yourselves with the clanless cowards that chained me?" She belched fire in a blind rage, not seeming to care where it landed. All around them, trees erupted in flames.

The Dragon was going to set the forest on fire or get someone killed. *'And,'* Annelise amended in her mind, as the Dragon raked a claw through the air, mere inches from Michael's throat as he leapt out of the way of the lethal attack. The Dragon was going to set the forest on fire *and* get someone killed. She was not going to let that happen. They needed to restrain the Dragon and put out the flames. A plan formed in Annelise's mind. It was going to suck, but it was the best she could think of.

"I need time," she shouted from behind the tree. She couldn't see where the Pendragons were, but she heard Tristan shout back.

"Fine, but hurry."

She gripped her staff and ran into the clearing. Using her staff, she sketched ruins into the dirt. They weren't pretty, but they would do. Annelise jumped as the Dragon crashed into a tall tree only a few feet away from her, the explosion of sound reverberating through the forest.

What were Tristan and Michael doing? Whatever it was, it seemed to be making the Dragon more angry, but it was keeping her occupied.

Grabbing the broken piece of obsidian from her pocket, she found the sharpest edge and dug it into her poor, abused palm, and then repeated the action on her dominant hand. She winced as blood welled up from the cuts. She dropped to the ground, slammed her right hand against the ruins she had drawn into the dirt, reached her other hand up towards the sky, and started chanting. The magic flowed through her from the earth to the heavens.

The clear blue skies above them darkened with startling speed. With a low rumble, the skies opened and started pouring rain on the smoldering forest. The burning trees crackled and hissed as the rain doused the flames. Meanwhile, the trees nearest to the Dragon creaked and groaned as they stretched out their branches and roots, wrapping around the Dragon's claws, and stretching over her vast wings. They steadily interwove themselves into a cage, limiting the Dragon's movements. It was working.

The spell took over, catching her up in it like a wave. Annelise's magic flowed much more freely than she had ever experienced before. It was exhilarating. And terrifying. She was so used to straining to make her magic flow that she now worried she would overtax herself. But it was too late to rein it in. She was no longer controlling the magic; she was its servant. The world around her was performing the spell, and it was merely using her as a channel. She couldn't break away now, even if she wanted to. She had to see this through.

Annelise's head spun with the sheer power passing through her. Her blood mixed with the dirt as the magic poured through her, reaching into the trees around them and bending them to her design.

The Dragon swung her head around from where she had been snapping at Tristan, her pupils constricting as she caught sight of Annelise. With a great roar, the Dragon wrenched her tail from the roots, threatening to pin it down, and brought it crashing towards Annelise.

Tristan cried out her name in fear and warning, but she had no chance to react because she was still caught up in the spell. She couldn't break away. She mustn't break away.

The Dragon's tail knocked her up into the air, breaking her connection with the earth and with the spell. Annelise's eyes widened in horror as the magic stretched between her and the ground, whining as it pulled like a rubber band until finally, it snapped. The blinding blast of pure magic knocked the wind out of her lungs as it blew her across the clearing. Nearby trees splintered and toppled with earth-shattering crashes. The restraints dropped away from the Dragon. Annelise crashed into a tree, hitting her head. The world turned fuzzy, and her vision swam. She was vaguely aware of the Dragon bursting through the canopy and fleeing to the skies before she knew no more.

***

Michael sprinted to where he last saw Annelise, Tristan hot on his heels. The sight that confronted him when he saw her brought Michael up short. She was pale as death, blood pooling around her head. She lay unmoving on the ground. She couldn't be dead. They had promised her they would take care of her. His legs shook beneath him. He couldn't move, or he would collapse.

Tristan rushed forward to check her pulse. He looked up at Michael.

"She's alive," he sighed.

Michael sagged with relief, leaning on his staff for support. He stumbled forward, dropping to the ground beside her. He felt her skin; it was cold to the touch.

"This is bad." He had seen her spell get interrupted. A spell of that magnitude, and wielded through blood magic, for that to be interrupted...the magical backlash would be incredible. Annelise was alive... for now. But if she didn't get help soon...

"I know," Tristan replied.

"We need to go back. We don't know what kind of damage has been done to her." An urgency akin to panic had settled in Michael's stomach. They couldn't lose her. He wouldn't let that happen.

"We can't go back yet. If we go back now, we have nothing. We lose. We lose our freedom, and any chance of securing hers." Tristan nodded in the direction of the Dragon's cave. "We've come too far to turn back now, empty-handed."

"My priority is Annelise!" Michael shouted.

"And I'm trying to protect all of us." Tristan's voice was tight with frustration. "Look. Let's try the cave one more time. Maybe we can convince her that we are here to help. The time lost won't make much of a difference, and we could gain valuable information. Then we can get help for Annelise."

Michael looked at Tristan. His golden eyes were determined, and Michael realized that there was going to be no arguing with him. They had worked for years to come to this place, and he would not turn away now until they had a way forward. Besides, his plan was logical. It usually was. It was also usually frustrating.

"Fine." He thrust his staff into Tristan's hands. He reached down and cradled Annelise's limp form into his arms. "The sooner we get there, the sooner we can get Annelise help."

Tristan simply nodded and led the way.

They left the scene of destruction behind and returned to the cave. They found the scene exactly as they had seen in their finding spell. The Dragon was curled up in the mouth of the cave. Her eyes were closed. Michael did not believe that she was asleep. Judging from his body language, neither did Tristan.

They approached slowly, drawing to an abrupt halt when a low growl emanated from her belly. It caused the very air around them to vibrate.

"You must wish for death to come before me once again, Pendragons." The Dragon lifted her head. Her rich voice cut clear across the shoreline. "Leave now. Tend to your traitorous friend. I can see the magic bleeding from her system. She won't last long." Michael gripped Annelise in his arms a little tighter, the words striking fear into his heart. "Serves her right. But at least she had the decency to use her own strength to try to cage me. Her predecessor was not so considerate."

"What?" Michael asked, his face going pale. His mind refused to comprehend what the Dragon hinted at; it was so revolting.

"He used my blood!" she raged. Her throat glowed hot with her anger, and Michael took a step back, afraid that she might roast them where they stood.

"My own blood to trap me in this wasteland!" The Dragon turned her head and let loose a jet of fire over the lake. Even though it was not directed at them, Michael could feel the heat of her anger from where he stood.

"We came to set you free." Tristan stepped forward, raising his hands in a placating gesture.

"Is that why you brought her? How did you convince her to get you through the blood wards?" the Dragon spat. She was still angry, but no longer seemed ready to rain fire down on them.

"You think Annelise is the one who put you in this prison?" Michael asked.

"Not her," the Dragon said, dejected. "But she undoubtedly holds the key to my prison now. How else would you have gotten through the blood wards? And she is a powerful blood mage, just like her predecessor. Her conspiracy makes her just as guilty as the man who put me in here in the first place."

"Do you know who it was who put you in here?" Tristan asked.

"Ask her." She cast a disgusted look at Annelise, her throat rumbling with involuntary fire.

"Annelise did not get us through the blood wards," Michael said. "I got her through."

The Dragon's pupil constricted at his words, and her head stretched close until she was eye-to-eye with him. Michael couldn't look away from the burning golden eye that held him in her gaze.

She was unspeakably beautiful. Caught in her gaze, Michael could hardly think properly, let alone move.

"You?" The Dragon growled.

"Yes." Michael resisted the urge to take a step back. "It was Tristan and I who had no trouble passing through the blood ward, but Annelise couldn't pass. Whoever trapped you in here must be a relative of ours, not hers. I swore a pact with her to get Annelise through the wards. We came to set you free, but did not know about the wards before we came."

The Dragon's growl faded to a rumble. "You must care for her to swear such an oath."

Michael glanced down at Annelise's pale face. His heart clenched. He did care. As much as he wanted the Dragon free, he wanted to abandon the quest and get Annelise help. He couldn't stand to see either of them in pain.

"She risked much to help us set you free," Tristan said, stepping forward. "But now we need your help. What can you tell us about the man who trapped you here?"

"I can tell you that I am surprised you are related to that villain at all. You are both Pendragons. I can feel it humming in your magic. He was not." She growled. "Now go. I have no more information to give, and you, it seems, cannot help me. You might as well help your friend."

She turned her back on them and curled up, effectively ending their conversation.

Tristan stepped forward, wanting to ask more questions, but Michael stopped him. "Tristan," he pleaded. "We don't have time..."

Tristan looked back, his eyes darting to Annelise, and nodded. "You're right, let's go."

***

Annelise blinked her eyes, wincing as the bright light pierced her vision. She was immediately aware that her head was pounding, and the blinding light wasn't helping anything. She groaned, pressing a hand to her head. "What happened?" she asked.

"You tried to fight a dragon." Tristan's voice held a note of amazement as he spoke

"You almost won," Michael added.

"Almost." She grimaced. "Remind me never to try that again. Where is the Dragon now?"

"Sleeping in her cave, just like the finding spell showed," Tristan said.

"Were you able to talk to her?" Annelise asked.

"A bit. She thought you were working with the mage who had trapped her here. That's why she attacked."

"What did you find out about her captor?"

"Not much. But we know that he is not a Pendragon."

"And it must be someone who stood to gain something by trapping the Dragon in here," Michael reasoned.

"We also know that he's a blood mage," Annelise added, closing her eyes again to try to relieve her headache. "It would take an experienced blood mage to cast a spell of this magnitude."

"He used her blood." Michael's voice was hoarse as he spoke.

"What?" Her eyes snapped open.

"He used her blood to cast the ward. He used her strength instead of his own."

Annelise went pale. It was either from what was certainly a concussion or this new piece of information, but she felt like she was going to be sick. "That's pure evil. To use someone else's magic and strength to lock them up?"

"This is exactly why the laws against blood magic have gotten so much stricter." Tristan looked as pale as Annelise felt.

"We're going to find this person and bring them to justice." He paused. "How come she can't pass through the ward if the culprit used her blood to cast it?"

Annelise thought about it. "I think he tied the ward to his bloodline, but used her blood as the conduit. It's probably the same as when you use your staff to make a ward tailored to you, only less strong. The conduit is the staff, but you are the key... or at least part of it."

"Hmm." They fell silent for a moment, considering this new information.

"So," Annelise wanted to figure out who this traitor to all magic was. "We know the culprit is male, he's related to the two of you, he's NOT a Pendragon, he is a blood mage, and he got something out of this situation. Does that narrow it down at all?" Annelise asked.

Tristan sighed. "Some, but not much. There are many suspects to consider, though I don't know of any who are blood mages. We also have to consider that it's someone who had access to the Subraek, which, to my knowledge, limits the culprit to someone in government."

Annelise tried to sit up. They needed to find answers.

Michael helped her sit, his eyes flashing with concern as she swayed from the small movement. "Annelise, you need to see a healer. To have a spell like the one you were casting interrupted in that way... It can't be safe. Not to mention your head injury."

Annelise saw the concern in his eyes. She knew he was right. She had felt her magic rupture when the Dragon broke her connection to that spell. Even now, she could feel that something was off. Wrong. Much like one avoids prodding a tender wound, she dared not attempt to access her magic to ascertain the extent of the injury. At least not around Tristan and Michael. She didn't think they had time to fret about her condition right now. So, putting on her most nonchalant face, she waved his concern away.

"I'm fine." She got to her feet, only swaying a little bit.

Michael's face darkened. "You're not fine. You need help. And rest."

Annelise gave him her sweetest pleading look. "I do have a massive headache." She raised a hand behind her to gingerly touch the cut on her head. "But I think some water would help?"

He looked unconvinced but nodded and took the waterskins in his hands to fill them with fresh water. The water was cool and sweet, and Annelise did feel somewhat better after she had some.

They set out the way they came, straight back toward Wizard's Island. They decided to portal across the barren plain this time around. Michael had wanted to portal all the way back to Wizard Island, but that jump, carrying all three of them, would probably cause him permanent damage, and Tristan had put his foot down. They rested for a few hours once they were across so Michael could recover, then started walking again.

As they walked, the two Pendragons tossed around the names of relatives who they thought could potentially be the culprit, debated the possibilities, and moved on.

Could it be Councilman Jackson? Tristan was definitely related to him, but they weren't sure how Michael might be if he was at all. But since he had been the strongest supporter of locking the Dragon away during the integration, he was their best bet.

What about Councilman Cawthorne? But he had championed the campaign to restrict the use of blood magic. It seemed unlikely that he was secretly a blood mage using the most vile methods of casting himself.

Who else could possibly fit the profile who had access to the key one hundred years ago? They ran through any of their relatives that they knew about who were old enough to have committed the crime.

Great Grandma Dee was still alive, but she was a Pendragon, so she did not fit the profile.

Likewise, Michael's grandfather, the one who had been cared for as a child by the dragon, was still alive, but he was still a child when she disappeared. And on top of that, he, too, was a Pendragon.

They ran through other names, but as far as they knew, only Councilmen Jackson and Cawthorne seemed to come close to fitting.

Annelise listened to their debates. No one seemed a more likely suspect than any other, but something other than the pounding headache was nagging her in the back of her mind. She couldn't put a finger on it yet, but she felt that she was forgetting an important detail. But no matter how much she reached for it, it was always just out of her grasp.

Chapter 12: The Realization

They made camp for the night on the far side of the barren plain. They hoped to reach the Wizard Island portal the next day. The basalt stones had given way to patchy grass. With every ominous screech that ripped through the air, the three mages tensed, but so far, no creature had appeared to try and eat them. Tristan took the first watch, so Annelise curled up on a patch of grass. It wasn't until she was trying to clear her mind to fall asleep that she was struck by the image of her meeting with Councilman Cawthorne. He had been wearing a large red ruby... or maybe the key to the blood wards.

Could it be? It seemed preposterous.

"What about Councilman Cawthorne?" she blurted, needing Michael and Tristan to help her dismiss the ludicrous idea.

"Uncle Fitz?" Tristan asked, turning his head to look at her. "No, we've already discussed this. Besides, he's not a blood mage."

"That you know of. Most blood mages don't advertise."

Tristan stood up and started to pace. "But he has voted repeatedly to put tighter and tighter regulations on blood magic. He thinks that the potential for misuse is too high. I cannot believe that after all that, he would be a secret blood mage of the worst kind himself. Besides, he's been helping us with our investigation. He got us access to the minutes from the council meetings. Why would he do that if he's the one who locked her up in the first place?"

"I know," Annelise sat up and scooted back to face the other two, "But if you think about it, he is related to both of you. He is not a Pendragon, *and* the Dragon's disappearance cleared the way for the integration, allowing him to rise to his current position of power. Also..." She hesitated. "When we saw him, he had this big red ruby on. What if that's what he's using to sustain the blood wards? Gems are effective for sustaining blood wards, and a ward that size would need a massive gem. It just...seems to fit."

Tristan wheeled to face her. "He's a rich man. Of course he's wearing it! I'm sure that ruby has been in his family for generations. And even if it did contain a blood spell, how could you know that it was related to this ward and not some family vault?"

"I don't know for sure. It's just a theory," she ground out.

"Well, maybe you should give things a little more consideration before you start making baseless accusations against our one and only ally! Sure, it all looks so clear when you say it one way. But you're omitting all the other relevant details," Tristan snapped.

Annelise jumped to her feet. "But you have to admit that you're biased. You're so blinded by your reliance on Cawthorne that you refuse to consider the evidence staring you in the face," she shot back.

Tristan took a step in her direction. They were nearly nose to nose, but Annelise refused to back down.

"The only reason you think that is because you are incapable of seeing the value in human connection, and too *inexperienced* with it to know that you can be close to someone and still take facts into consideration!" Tristan shouted.

Annelise gaped at him. He might as well have hit her. She balled up her fists. "You'd rather protect your self-interests than free the dragon, and that's why we are going to end up dead or in jail!"

Tristan scoffed, his face red with anger. "If you had ever..." He stopped himself. She saw him struggle to rein in his anger for a moment, and then, "I need some air." He stomped off.

Annelise's heart was pounding, and she was breathing heavily.

"Annelise," Michael's voice was reproachful.

"What?" she snapped, her eyes turning to Michael and boring into his.

"You have to admit," Michael's voice was calm and thoughtful. "That the evidence you have is pretty circumstantial," he looked up at her from where he was still sitting in the dirt.

Annelise's eyes flashed with annoyance.

"I'm not saying you're wrong," he continued, "Just that we don't have enough evidence to act on yet." His eyes held no confrontation, just consideration, and she felt all the defensiveness drain out of her.

She groaned, almost annoyed that she was calming down. She didn't want to calm down. She wanted to win. But still... "I suppose you're right," she admitted, flopping onto the ground next to him. "But maybe there's a way to test my theory? To test Cawthorne and figure out where he stands?"

"How?" Michael asked.

She hugged her knees. "I'm not sure yet, but I'm sure we can come up with something."

"You know," Michael gave her a sideways look. "Tristan is pretty good at coming up with plans."

Annelise pulled at a bit of grass, tearing it into little tiny pieces. Now that she had calmed down a bit, she was feeling guilty about what she had said to him. Not so much about being biased, but about Tristan choosing himself over the dragon and all of them. She knew it wasn't fair. She knew she had said it because it was the most hurtful thing she could think of. She knew she needed to apologize.

"You think I can go talk to him?" she asked.

"If you can say nice things to him, I'm sure you can. If you plan to start another fight, which I wouldn't recommend in your current condition, then I would wait."

Annelise stood up, groaning and wincing as she did. "Don't worry. I'm not planning to get involved in any more fights tonight."

She wandered through the trees in the direction that Tristan had gone. She found him seated beneath a particularly large tree, his eyes closed, his breathing measured. She stopped.

Annelise's stomach was tied in knots. She was inexperienced in making apologies, at least sincere ones. What if she had permanently damaged their relationship? What if, in a few angry words, she had ruined things forever? What if he decided that she wasn't worth sticking around for? She wasn't sure she would blame him if he did. She wanted to puke. She slid her back down the trunk of the tree to sit next to him.

"I'm sorry about what I said," she said at last. "You know, about the self-interests, and getting us killed. I know it's not true, I was just angry. You didn't deserve that."

Tristan took another measured breath. "I forgive you." Another breath. "I'm sorry too. I shouldn't have attacked your valuing of interpersonal connection. I know that life has not been kind in that area for you, and it was unkind of me to throw that in your face."

Just the memory of his words made Annelise's eyes burn again. Her stomach coiled into a tight knot. She hated feeling this way. "I forgive you." She wanted to get back to a place where they were on good terms with each other. If he could forgive her, then she should be able to forgive him.

They sat in silence together for a while, neither one wanting to break the tenuous peace they had reached by bringing up the subject that had set them at each other's throats in the first place.

"What if..." Tristan started. "What if there is a way we can test your theory?"

Annelise nodded. "That's exactly what Michael and I were thinking. We find a way to test him, and," she raised her hands as if in surrender, "if he's not the guy, then he's not the guy."

"But it's probably best not to rule out anyone prematurely," Tristan finished.

"The question is how exactly to test Cawthorne to see if he's on our side or not. Michael said you were good at coming up with plans?"

Tristan tried to smother a yawn and gave her a rueful smile. "True. But not when I'm falling asleep. We can brainstorm tomorrow as we head back to the doorway. I'm sure our ideas will all be much better then."

Tristan stood up and helped Annelise to her feet. They walked back to the campsite, and Annelise flopped down onto her patch of dirt. She was bone tired, and she fell asleep as soon as her eyes closed.

***

They spent the next day's walk debating how to test Annelise's theory, exploring other potential suspects, and how to get Annelise the help she needed without getting her locked up.

At last, they settled on a test to determine if Councilman Cawthorne really wanted the dragon set free, or if all his help in the Pendragons' investigation was just for show. If he was not the culprit, he would help them. No respectable mage would obstruct their efforts to set her free. Annelise hoped she was wrong. Their way forward in this quest would be a lot smoother if they had Councilman Cawthorne firmly as their ally.

However, if he was the culprit, he would likely try to hamper their efforts, most likely by turning them in. The trap they set would test his loyalty. They just had to make sure they didn't set the trap and get caught in it themselves.

"There's no way that Uncle Fitz will betray us," Tristan said.

Annelise paused to catch her breath. "Honestly, I hope I'm wrong. I don't want to believe that the leader of our government would be so duplicitous. On the other hand, if it is him, then we are a lot closer to getting the dragon out than before. Either way, we need a contingency plan... just in case."

Tristan scowled a bit at the thought, but nodded. It was logical after all. Their plan involved letting the Councilman know that they had found the Dragon, and then letting him know exactly where they would be and when. If he wanted her to be free, he would help them and keep their location secret. If a dozen wardens happened to show up to the meet... it was most likely that he was trying to bury them, making him prime suspect number one.

They set to brainstorming some ideas for locations and escape routes from the meet. Through it all, Annelise tried to ignore the pounding headache that steadily increased in intensity. She also knew she was in rough shape, magically, but she hadn't had a moment alone to truly investigate.

Instead, she resolutely ignored both her magic and her headache and tried to focus on the debate and on putting one foot in front of the other. But as they started their long trek up the mountain, each step seemed to increase the pounding of her headache.

She almost cried when they reached the rim, and she remembered that they now had to make the trip back down into the caldera and through the water to Wizard Island. A concerned glance from Michael helped her bottle up her pain and frustration.

She refused to slow them down with her problems. They were depending on her, and she was determined not to let them down. She would deal with this herself.

The three of them slipped and slid their way down the caldera, and Michael cast a warming charm over them as they entered the icy waters. It was much more pleasant than the first time she swam in the lake. She slurped up some of the pure water and felt like her headache might even be lessening.

They reached Wizard Island as the sun started to hang low in the sky. Estimating that it was late enough that there would be no tourists left on the island, they traveled through the door, eager to leave the Subraek.

The birdsong was the first thing that struck Annelise. First, because it exacerbated her headache, and second, because she realized it had been entirely absent in the Subraek.

They set up camp as they didn't want to swim in the dark. They would wait until morning to get off the island. As the sun disappeared beyond the rim of the caldera, the temperature dropped sharply.

Annelise set about gathering the materials needed for a fire as Tristan went down to the lakeshore to try and catch some fish. She usually would light a fire with her staff, but she figured now was as good as any to try it the non-magical way.

An hour later, Annelise was still sitting in the dirt, rubbing two sticks together. She was getting nowhere. Her hands hurt and were starting to blister. Finally, she tossed the sticks aside in disgust.

"How do the sourceless do it?" she muttered.

"What, start a fire? I think they use matches," Michael said, coming up behind her.

"Whatever," she said. "Michael, would you care to do the honors?"

"Of course, Ms. Windstarter." Then, with far more flourish than was necessary, he waved his staff over the pile of firewood, and it erupted into flames.

"Thank you," She still felt the ire at her inability to do just about anything without her staff.

"You're very welcome," Michael replied in a sing-songy voice. He picked up their waterskins. "I'll go check on how Tristan is doing and fill these up." He disappeared down the darkened path.

Once he was gone, Annelise turned her attention to the issue she had been trying to ignore for the last two days. Her magic.

She closed her eyes and focused inward on the point where her magic bubbled up and pooled. Tentatively, she reached out, connecting with it to assess the damage. Annelise collapsed to the forest floor, sharp pain pouring through her. She withdrew her senses from her magic as though she had been burned. The after-echoes of the pain still washed over her in waves. Annelise stumbled over to a tree at the edge of their campsite and retched. There was little more than bile in her system, but her stomach continued to contract on itself until there was nothing left. Tears streaming down her face and her whole body shaking, she wiped the back of her hand across her mouth.

She would not be doing that again anytime soon. She dug her fingers into the dirt, trying to quell the fear within her. This was bad. An *'if she didn't get treatment soon, she would end up in the morgue'* kind of bad. She didn't think she would look too fetching in a toe tag.

She needed time. Time to figure out how to get the help she needed without becoming a burden to Michael and Tristan. They had been so good to her; they didn't deserve to have her dragging them down. Besides, the Dragon shouldn't be forced to stay locked in that blood cage a second longer than necessary.

She heard Michael's cheery whistling as he came back up the path, and she schooled her face into something that resembled carefree.

"Are you okay?" he asked as he approached.

"Yes," she lied. "Why?"

"You look a little pale."

Annelise shot him a weak smile. "I think I'm just a bit hungry. How's Tristan managing with the fish?"

"About as well as you were with the fire," he replied with a smirk. "I've helped him out. Never fear! I won't let you starve to death."

Michael spent a few hours that evening prepping flashbang potions with ingredients he gathered from the island as part of the escape for their plan the next day. Hopefully, they would not be necessary. But Annelise wasn't optimistic.

***

They left on the first boat the following morning, then caught a ride on a tour bus filled with tourists on their way up to Portland from the Lake.

They arrived in the city in the early evening. The sun was hanging low above the horizon and glittering off the Willamette River as the bus drove over one of the city's many bridges. They slipped off the bus, blending into the crowd. They walked a few blocks and stopped at a run down payphone.

Tristan picked up the phone and dialed the number. Annelise and Michael stood close by listening in.

"Hello?" Came the voice from the other side. Annelise could only just make out what it said.

"... It's me."

"Tristan? What are you doing? Where are you? You've got to come in. The wardens —"

"I can't do that, Uncle Fitz. I... I found her. I found the Dragon."

There was silence. Then, "Where?"

"In the Subraek. She's still trapped behind a blood ward. But we think we have a way to set her free. We just need some money and a little bit of time."

"So you stole the key to free the dragon. But she's behind a blood ward? Can you get her out?"

"Annelise is a blood mage. She can do things I've never seen before with blood magic. We just need some money to buy her some gems and other supplies, and she will be able to dismantle the blood ward and free the dragon. Then she will be able to tell the world herself who trapped her in there."

"Hmm. I saw the hole she blew in the government vaults. But, then... You don't know who did it? Who locked her up?"

"No. The dragon wasn't in a talking mood. The discussion turned...heated."

"Are you sure you can trust her? The girl? You know how I feel about blood mages. Also, did you know she was a con artist when you invited her to join your crusade?"

"Yes, Uncle, we knew. We trust her."

" Is Michael with you? Is he all right?"

"Yes, yes. He's right here."

"You should come in. Turn yourselves in to the Wardens, and I'm sure we can get this worked out."

"We can't stop until she's free. We were hoping you could help us with some supplies. Do you think you could get them to us?"

There was a pause. "Tristan, I fully support your cause, but I don't know if it's wise for me to get involved. Even being on the phone with you —" he stopped.

"Please, Uncle. We are so close."

Another pause. "What do you need?"

"We need about six thousand dollars to get the supplies we need and actually eat for a change. Then we can get back to the Subraek and free the dragon once and for all. We can be at the intersection of Park and Main in one hour —"

"Tristan..." the councilman interrupted.

"Yes, Uncle Fitz?"

The voice on the line hesitated. "Never mind. I'll have someone bring you what you need."

"Thank you, Uncle." Tristan hung up the phone.

"See?" He turned to Annelise. "He's willing to help."

Annelise bit her lip. Doubt creeping in. "I guess." She said. "But he seemed kind of reluctant to even be on the phone with you. Either way, we need that money. If it's not him, we will need a good way to lay low until we figure out who the real culprit is. We only have an hour before the meeting time. We had better get over there and scope the place out."

They headed to the appointed place of meeting. Standing in the shadowed archway of an old church, they peered around the corner, trying to see anything that might be out of place.

The clock ticked down. "Okay," Tristan turned to Michael and Annelise. "Michael, you stay back here. You'll be our getaway in case anything goes sideways. Annelise and I will go meet this guy."

"I still think Annelise should stay out of it. She's in no state to be getting into a fight." Michael reached a hand across Annelise, as if to shield her from Tristan's suggestion.

"Annelise can make her own decisions, thank you very much," she said, annoyance lacing her tone. "I appreciate you trying to protect me, but this is the best version of the plan. Tristan and I will do the meet. We can watch each other's backs, and you will be our ace in the hole. Besides," she flashed him a smile that she hoped looked confident, "we have the distractions you made us."

Michael dropped back to lean against the stone wall. "Fine."

"Have a portal ready, just in case," Annelise said.

"Goody," Michael snarked.

Just as the clock struck the one-hour mark, they saw a figure approach the park block. He was carrying a backpack in one hand.

Annelise followed Tristan out to meet him, her stomach contracting with nerves. She felt like she was being watched, but try as she might, she could not see anyone else around them.

"Tristan Pendragon and Annelise Windstarter?" He asked. Annelise shifted her weight and gripped the small potion vial in her pocket. She didn't think people usually exchanged names at these sorts of handoffs. The less you knew, the better. Still, if he had their money...

"Yes," Tristan said. "My uncle sent you?"

"Yes." The man shifted his weight. "Where is Michael Pendragon? I was told he would be with you."

"Michael is running a different errand."

The man seemed annoyed by this news but nodded nonetheless. He held the bag out to them, and Annelise took it in both hands. As soon as the bag left his hand, the man gripped his staff in both hands and pointed it at them.

"Freeze! You are under arrest."

Annelise's heart leapt into her throat as several portals sprang to life around them, revealing a dozen wardens. In the lead was Detective Poe. It was a trap.

Tristan and Annelise immediately turned back-to-back.

"Just come in quietly, and no one has to get hurt." Detective Poe was holding up her hands. They were, for the moment, empty of her staff, but the goodwill gesture lost some of its effectiveness since all the other wardens held their staves at the ready.

"I'm sure you have a good reason for doing what you're doing, and I'm willing to listen," Detective Poe continued. "Maybe I can even help, but I can't help you until you come in." Her expression seemed sincere. "Let's just talk about what you're doing and why." She still held her hands out in a gesture of peace.

Annelise was willing to believe that the Detective believed her own words. But they couldn't give up just yet.

Annelise took the vial from her pocket and threw it at the ground, shutting her eyes tight. A wall of light and sound exploded from the vial. The wardens recoiled, momentarily stunned, while Tristan and Annelise bolted past them to the alcove where Michael was waiting. As they ran, Tristan threw his vial to the ground as well, sending a second wave of light and sound rolling over the park block. They were only about halfway to Michael when the wardens recovered and started shooting spells in their direction.

Annelise hoped desperately that Michael had the portal ready. They dodged spells as they ran. The base of a tree next to her exploded in a confusion of wooden shrapnel. The tree swayed, creaked, and popped before tipping over. The leaves rustled as they sped through the air toward the ground, and then the tree crashed into the ground next to them, shaking the earth beneath their feet.

Annelise and Tristan now had to dodge branches while dodging spells. But once the tree was down, the mass of branches provided some cover from the spellfire behind them. When they got past the tree, Annelise could see the light from Michael's portal spell. He had already started to chant.

Annelise willed her legs to move faster. It wasn't going to be enough. Tristan grabbed her hand and pulled her forward. They made it inside the circle of light just as Michael finished his spell. The light flashed around them. When it died down, Michael sank to his knees, his face looking a bit pale.

"You're getting better at those," Tristan commented, as he and Annelise each grabbed one of his arms and pulled him to his feet.

"I really hate those," he shot back.

"And you wanted to portal halfway across the state with three people," Tristan snarked as they ran as quickly as they could while supporting Michael.

Michael gave him a hard stare.

"Sorry," Tristan said. "I shouldn't have said that."

Michael gave a curt nod in acceptance. He turned his attention to moving forward. The wardens would be on to their new location in a matter of minutes, and they needed to get away fast.

They slipped down several streets and then caught a streetcar. Once they had put enough distance between themselves and the wardens, they hopped off and made their way to the nearest motel.

The room was small and dingy, but it would do the trick. There were two large beds. The cousins would share one, and Annelise would take the other.

Michael promptly collapsed into one of the beds and fell asleep. Tristan sat in a chair, holding his head in his hands.

"You were right," he said. "Uncle Fitz betrayed us. I couldn't see it. I didn't want to see it. I'm sorry."

"I don't blame you for wanting to believe in your uncle."

"But why? Why would he do it? Why would he put us on the right path if he was the culprit? We would never have gotten as far as we did without him. Why egg us on only to turn on us?" He looked lost. His eyes were full of doubt and mistrust. "It doesn't make sense."

Annelise felt for him. Everything he thought he knew up until this point was coming down around him. He needed something to hold onto. She put a hand on his shoulder, both to steady herself and comfort him.

"I don't know. But I do know that we will get through this."

"He needs to pay for what he did to her," he ran a hand across his face. "How are we going to get the evidence we need? More than that, who is ever going to listen to us? By now, we have almost certainly been branded as criminals and terrorists. Who would believe our word against the most influential Councilman in government?"

"I can't believe I'm saying this, but we are going to have to trust someone," Annelise said.

"Trust doesn't seem to be working out too well for us at the moment." Tristan sounded broken.

Annelise gave his shoulder a squeeze. "First, we need to get some sleep. Tomorrow we are going to get that ruby to set her free, and then we are going to put your uncle in jail. And then," she slumped down to sit at the foot of her bed, "we will probably be going to jail too..."

There really didn't seem to be a way out of it now. They had no powerful ally. They were at the end of their rope. There was no escape. The only thing left to do was what was right.

Tristan nodded dejectedly. On the bed, Michael stirred.

"What's this about going to jail?" he said.

"We're most likely all going to jail," Tristan informed him.

Michael groaned and threw a hand over his face. "Can this wait until we've all had some sleep?"

"Yes," Tristan agreed. "In the morning, we will make a plan. Tonight we need to rest."

He turned out the light in the room and fell into the bed beside Michael. Annelise, too, was exhausted. After sleeping on the ground for several days, even the lumpy motel bed felt like a dream.

But Annelise couldn't sleep. Making sure that Tristan and Michael were out cold, she slipped out of her bed and padded into the bathroom, latching the door behind her. Biting her lip, she tentatively reached out to her magic once again, hoping that maybe it had gotten somewhat better on its own. Blinding pain assailed her, and she collapsed over the toilet and retched. She fought to steady her breathing as waves of pain washed over her. It was worse. She needed a healer, and she wasn't going to find one with the capacity to fix this issue while on the run.

She groaned and pressed her fevered forehead against the cool tile of the bathtub. How could she get the legal help they needed to put a councilman behind bars while getting the medical help she needed and keeping the Pendragons out of jail?

Slowly, a plan started to form. Maybe there was a way to get what she needed, while getting the Pendragons what they needed, all without burdening them.

The only problem was that it was going to suck.

Chapter 13: The New Plan

The **morning dawned** bright, but they were all so exhausted they slept through until mid-morning.

Annelise woke up first and went into the bathroom to wash her face, trying to shake the exhaustion from her bones. She had to steady herself against the wall as she went. It had been late when she had finally fallen asleep, the pain having subsided enough to drift off. In the meantime, she had worked out a solid outline of her plan.

Making her way back into the room, she saw that Michael and Tristan were starting to stir. She sat on her bed, trying to quiet her shaking hand.

Tristan sat up. "Are we ready to make a plan yet?" He seemed in better spirits this morning.

"Yes." Michael rubbed the sleep from his eyes with a groan. "I guess we should."

"So," Annelise said. "We need to get the Ruby off of Councilman Cawthorne. How are we going to do it?"

The Pendragons thought for a while, Michael staring down at the desk while Tristan gazed out the dusty window. They turned to look at each other at the same time. "Manny," they said in unison.

Annelise raised an eyebrow. They were like twins sometimes.

"Manny?" she asked.

Tristan nodded. "Yup!" He acted as though that would explain everything.

"Please explain."

"Uncle Fitz comes over to read every evening because he loves my library. He has done so ever since he managed my estate after the death of my parents, and before I was old enough to take it over. I'm sure that despite everything that has been going on, he has not stopped going to my house to read. Since we didn't involve Manny in our previous plans, and Manny will have been thoroughly questioned and cleared by now, he will be beyond suspicion," Tristan said.

"Now, Manny is an impeccable butler, but he is, after all, human. He has to make at least one mistake in his life, right? So if we can get him to spill Uncle Fitz's daily glass of wine on him as he's reading, he will have to change clothes. Manny can then get the ruby from him in the confusion and get it to us," he finished.

"The only question is if he will do it," Michael said.

"You don't think he'd help us?" Annelise asked.

"Oh, he would walk through fire for us," Tristan said emphatically. "But spill on a guest? That is asking a lot of him."

"But we can still ask," Michael said. "If he refuses, he might have an alternative solution."

"Once we have the ruby, how will we know that it's the real thing and not a fake?" Tristan asked.

Annelise tapped her finger on the worn desk. "I think I could teach you both enough blood magic to make that discernment. Your experiences with wards will be very useful. I just need to teach you to reach out along a new channel. I'll need some pins or something, though."

"How are you doing, by the way?" Michael asked, his eyes searching her face.

Annelise gave him her best, most brilliant smile. "I'm fine. My magic is pretty raw, so I shouldn't use it at the moment, but I'll be okay."

Michael's eyes narrowed, but he didn't press the matter.

"Okay. I'm going to get some food and other supplies," Michael said. "Tristan, you reach out to Manny and see what he can do for us. Annelise, you can do some lesson planning for when I get back and Tristan finishes." He walked out the door, and Tristan picked up the phone.

Deciding to follow Michael's advice, Annelise picked up a pen and the small complimentary pad of paper lying on the faded desk. She could tell her grip was weak, and as she made the first few notes, her hand shook. Giving up on the notes, she laid her pounding head down on the table and considered how on earth she could teach the basics of blood magic without using any of it herself.

Twenty minutes later, Michael had returned with food and a box of straight pins, and Annelise had her lesson plan in mind. Tristan recounted his conversation with Manny while they ate.

"He will do it," Tristan said. "He thinks he can successfully get the ruby away from Uncle Fitz, and wants one of us to be there to get it out of the house when he does."

"Excellent," Michael said. "We should all go. I don't like the idea of us separating."

"How are we planning on getting back to Canol Dinas?" Annelise asked. "I'm sure everyone is on the lookout for us, and since we turned up here in Portland and didn't get out, I'm sure they're on the lookout here as well."

"We're going to have to find a way to sneak onto a transporter pad," Michael said.

Annelise raised her eyebrows at the audacity of the plan. Security around those areas was tight, and there were so many people, any one of whom could recognize them from the Most Wanted list. But they couldn't afford the loss of time or the risk of discovery involved with taking a bus all the way back down to California.

"Why not a courthouse?" Tristan asked. "They have private transporter pads connected to other courthouses and the precincts for prisoner transfer. We could wait until they close, and then break in to use it."

Annelise stared at the two Pendragons. "You know, the last time we were going to use a law enforcement transporter pad, we almost got caught. I'm not feeling too hot about that right now. Let me reach out to some people and see if I can find us another way down to Canol Dinas, and we can save that as a plan B."

"Do you ever wonder if we're just not very good at being criminals?" Michael asked out of the blue.

Annelise looked at him, eyebrows raised. "How so?"

"Well, every plan of ours seems to have blown up in our face. Maybe we just suck at breaking the law."

Annelise smirked. "Anyone can break the law, Michael, it's not getting caught that's the trouble. And for the record, I'm *great* at breaking the law and not getting caught. I've done it for years. The secret is not biting off more than you can chew. You all tried to take on the wardens, the Subraek, and the Government on your first job. That's not a bite, that's trying to swallow the whole friggin cow."

Michael chuckled. "Well, when you put it that way…"

"Now," Annelise grabbed the box of straight pins. "I think it's time for our little lesson in blood magic. I want both of you to be capable of recognizing the ward source if possible."

Tristan leaned forward. "Sounds good. What should we do?"

"First, do some burpees, jumping jacks, push-ups, whatever. You need to get your blood flowing."

The Pendragons shared a look, then dropped to the floor, racing to see who could complete their burpees first. Michael won, panting and looking extremely pleased with himself. Tristan gave him a lighthearted shove.

Annelise wondered how their instructors on the warden service handled these two. "Now," She tried to regain their attention, "sit on the bed, and close your eyes. Put one hand on your heart, and concentrate on your heartbeat. Feel the blood pulsing not only through your heart, but through your palms, your throat, and temples." She let them sit that way for a while, tuning into their own circulatory system. "Now, feel your magic. Feel how it flows through you, using your blood as a conduit."

"Hmm." Tristan's eyes were closed, a faint frown of concentration pulled at his forehead. Michael had a faint smile on his face as he searched for his magic.

Annelise let them tune into the new realization for a moment. She then plucked two straight pins out of the box, handing one to each of them. "You must draw your own blood." She then took the small potion Michael had brewed for her out of her pocket and set it on the table in front of them.

"Reach out with your magic, through your blood, to feel the magic in the potion. Tristan, you go first."

Tristan pricked his finger, then reached out his hand and pressed his index finger against the vial. He concentrated. His face broke into a smile, and he withdrew. He nodded at her. He had felt the magic through his blood.

"Michael, now it's your turn."

Michael followed suit. Soon enough, he, too, had managed to feel the magic.

"Excellent! Your work with wards has helped you tune into the magic both in your body and around you. It will serve you well."

"So, how exactly does one use the ruby to dismantle the blood wards?" Tristan asked.

"Well, since maintaining a ward that large would probably kill the caster, it's safer, easier, and more sustainable to use a precious gem to contain the ward. You put up all the upfront power, and then you lock it into the gem to sustain it. To dismantle the ward, you simply would need to destroy the ruby within the bounds of the wards and then use blood magic to perform a simple dismantling spell. I will teach you that one next. It is not very taxing, and I think you both could manage it."

"That doesn't seem very safe. Wouldn't anyone be able to break through a blood ward then?"

"Keep in mind that normally they are used to secure small spaces, such as vaults. If you stored the gem in the vault it was protecting, it would be nearly impossible to breach. In this case, however, the councilman was trapping another sentient being against her will. If he left the ruby within the wards, the dragon would dismantle the wards herself. That is probably why he keeps it on himself at all times."

"Any chance we could destroy the ruby outside the blood wards?"

"Unlikely."

"Every lock must have a key?"

"Exactly." It was one of the fundamental laws of ward magic. "Outside of the wards, the ruby will be impossible to break. But once it passes through the wards, it reacts to the magic, becoming brittle, like glass."

"So we just need to take the ruby back into the Subraek, smash it, and dismantle the wards."

"Yup."

"And then we can get the dragon out, and she can testify against Uncle Fitz."

"Yup. It will be the biggest scandal of the century. He will go to jail for sure."

She spent the next hour teaching them the simple spell to dismantle the wards, and then made them stop. Blood magic was draining for the new learner, and she did not want them too exhausted to pull off the rest of their plan.

The Pendragons were under strict orders to rest and recover while Annelise sat by the phone, staring at it. She knew who would be most likely able to arrange discreet transportation, but she wasn't sure she could trust him.

Clenching her fist, she picked up the receiver and dialed a number. From there, she input an extension, followed by another extension, and a password.

"This is Jimmy, Cyber fixer extraordinaire. How can I help you today?"

"Jimmy, it's me."

There was a long pause. "Annelise?"

"Yeah."

"Wow. You're in some deep trouble. I'm pretty sure it's a record."

"Jimmy, I need your help."

"Ah." Another pause. "Look, Annelise. I know we've worked together for a long time, but I can't afford to get mixed up in whatever you're mixed up in. It's just too dangerous."

"Well, Jimmy, you're going to get mixed up in it. You know why? Because you're the one who got me mixed up in it, so now I'm getting you mixed up in it."

"What..."

"I *know* Jimmy." She couldn't keep the hurt at his betrayal out of her voice. "I know you sold me out to those wardens when they came knocking."

"Look, it was you or me. I had to choose me. But for what it's worth….Annelise, I'm sorry. I never wanted to get you hurt." He sounded sincere. It didn't help the knot she got in the pit of her stomach when she thought about what he had done.

Annelise clenched the receiver so tightly her knuckles turned white. "Look, I need a way to get from Portland to Canol Dinas. Something discrete and fast. Do you know of anyone who can do this?"

"Definitely," Jimmy replied, barely letting her finish her question. "At least, I think I do. Let me reach out and make sure."

"Thank you." She paused and glanced over to where the two Pendragons had nodded off after their blood magic lesson. Maybe she could come up with a better plan to get medical help than the one she had come up with last night? She held the receiver close to her mouth and said in a low voice, "Hey Jimmy, do you know any healers who can deal with magical wounds? Someone discreet?"

"I mean, I know one guy. You get yourself banged up?"

"Yeah. Kind of badly. Can you reach out to him? When we get to Canol Dinas, I'm going to need some help, asap."

"Yeah. Absolutely. Look, I'll get a message to you when I have all the details. You can call me again at this number then."

"Sounds good." She hung up the receiver and sat on her bed. Michael stirred as she moved across the room.

"Did your guy come through?" he asked.

"He's working on it. He will reach out when he has everything put together, and I will call him back then." Annelise sat on her bed. She was tired again. It was not yet noon. Perhaps she would lie down for a short rest. She laid her head on the pillow and closed her eyes.

She heard Michael shift. "How will he reach out?"

"No idea. But we will know it when we see it."

"Did you tell him where we are?"

"Huh?" She opened her eyes and frowned. "No," she closed her eyes again. "But he knows. He always knows." Her breathing evened out. Then, "Michael?"

"Yes?"

"Will you tell me when he reaches out? I think I need to rest."

"Of course."

Annelise woke up to the sound of knocking on the door. There was hurried shuffling as the Pendragons moved across the room. Annelise sat up, her heart racing, and her head immediately pounding. Michael took up a position behind the door and motioned for Annelise to get down. She slid off the bed and crouched in the space between the beds, scanning her surroundings for anything she might be able to use as a weapon. Tristan pulled the door open.

The voice she heard was not the one she expected. Peeking over the bedspread, Annelise could see a boy, early teens, with a plastic bag in his hand that looked like Chinese takeout. He handed it to Tristan and left with a smile. Tristan closed the door behind him.

"Did one of you order takeout?" Tristan asked, his voice laced with irritation.

Annelise stood up, her heart still pounding. "No. But I think I know who did." She grabbed the bag and opened it, going straight for a fortune cookie. Breaking it open, it read "Bon appétit. Call me."

She held up the fortune. "It's Jimmy. Lunch is on him."

"Are we sure we can trust Jimmy? He already sold you out to us. What's to keep him from doing it again?" Tristan asked.

Annelise looked up at Tristan. "Honestly? We simply don't have any other options." She passed him a pair of chopsticks and another pair to Michael. "Eat up. I'll give Jimmy a call." She sat down at the desk and picked up the phone. "How long was I out?"

"About an hour and a half. It's about 1 right now."

"Thanks," She dialed the number, extensions, and password.

"This is Jimmy, Cyber fixer extraordinaire."

"It's me."

"I know. I have a pilot for you."

"Excuse me?"

"You know. They fly airplanes? He can get you from Portland to Canol Dinas in under four hours."

"You're serious? We're actually going to fly? I didn't think anybody did that anymore."

"Well, this guy does. And he's discreet. All for the low, low price of four thousand dollars. Be at the Portland Airport by two thirty pm, Hangar D."

Annelise felt a thrill of excitement run through her. Who didn't occasionally think of what it would be like to fly like a bird? She had never flown before. "Thank you, Jimmy."

He paused. "Don't thank me yet," he warned, his tone full of bad news. "About that healer. He can't help you. He's on vacation in Jamaica."

 Annelise swore.

"Do you know of anyone else who might be able to help me?"

"I've looked. I asked around. I've made several dozen calls. I'm sorry, Annelise. There's no one else with the capacity to handle your case discreetly. I really tried."

Annelise nodded, her hands shaking. "I believe you," she choked out.

"Look, if you can wait two weeks, I'm sure he can see you first thing when he gets back."

Annelise stifled a sob. "I can't wait two weeks," she whispered, tears gathering in her eyes.

"Annelise..."

She shook her head, sniffing and blinking away the tears. "Don't worry about it. I'll figure something out. Thanks, Jimmy." She hung up the phone. She needed to get it together. She would figure something out. She had to.

"What's the news?" Tristan asked.

Annelise ran a hand across her face, schooling her features back to calm. She forced a smile and turned to face him. "We are getting to Canol Dinas in style. We're going to fly."

Tristan and Michael exchanged a glance of unbridled excitement.

"Awesome," Tristan said.

Michael glanced at her. "And the bad news?"

"It's unrelated. Don't worry. We're good to go."

Michael's face fell a bit, but he didn't push her. Instead, he held out a box of takeout to her. "You should eat."

Annelise picked at the food a bit, but between her pounding headache and some increasing dizziness, she didn't have much of an appetite.

By two fifteen, they had made their way to the Portland Airport. It consisted of a single runway that ran nearly parallel to the Columbia River. A couple of open bay hangars stored various aircraft with various numbers of propellers. Annelise even saw a jet airplane, which supposedly went much faster than the propeller planes and could fly much higher.

They found their way to Hangar D, where three propeller aircraft sat gleaming in the afternoon sun that streamed through the open bay doors.

"You must be my Portland to Canol Dinas crew," a voice called from the other end of the hangar.

Tristan turned to the sound of the voice. "You're…our pilot?"

"Sure am! Name's Vinni. "

Annelise saw Tristan and Michael share an uneasy glance.

Vinni looked to be no older than a teenager. He was tall and wiry: the look of someone who had just undergone a growth spurt. He had a mop of honey colored, wavy hair, and his eyes crinkled as he smiled.

He made his way over to the mages and stopped by one of the aircraft. "Looking forward to getting up into the air today with you. It's gonna be clear skies all the way, so that should help make for a smooth ride. We've also got a nice tailwind going on, so that will help speed us on our way."

"Vinni, how old are you?" Tristan asked.

"I'm seventeen. I'll be eighteen in November." He spoke with entirely too much confidence for someone so young.

"Have you been flying long?" Michael sounded like he was trying to be nonchalant, but it wasn't quite working.

"Only about three years, but I have an excellent track record."

Tristan gave Annelise an unimpressed look. "Really?" he murmured.

Annelise shrugged. "If Jimmy says he can do the job, he can do it. We don't have a lot of options."

"I still think we could have used the transporters—"

"And delivered ourselves right up to the police and courts for their convenience," Annelise shot back, her tone half-teasing, half serious.

Vinni spoke up, "By the way, do you have my money?"

Tristan held out the duffel bag that had most of their remaining money in it.

"Excellent!" Vinni's voice cracked as he spoke. "Honestly, most of this is going towards fuel for this trip. The rest is going towards paying off this beauty." He ran his hand along a white plane with a golden-edged Navy stripe. It had what looked like a pair of bulbous skis attached to the bottom. A pair of wheels protruded from each end of the skis.

"What's with the skis?" Annelise asked.

"Those are amphibious floats," Vinni explained. "They allow us to use both an asphalt runway or a water runway. We will be using both today, as Canol Dinas does not, in fact, have an airport. We will be landing on the river."

"Do you have the coordinates for where we will arrive?" Tristan asked. "I will want to pass this along to our transport in Canol Dinas."

"Sure thing!" He pulled out a notepad and scribbled some coordinates on it. He ripped off the top sheet and handed it to Tristan.

"Thanks." Tristan looked around. "Is there a phone I could use?"

Vinni pointed him in the right direction, and Tristan went in search of a phone, while Vinni made the final preparations for their flight.

"Won't the wardens be tracing any calls going to Tristan's butler?" she asked Michael.

Michael shrugged. "Sure. But they won't be tapping Manny's mother's phone. She never could figure out Tristan's name... Calls him Timothy. I believe Tristan has been capitalizing on this long-term error during our adventure here. Manny's mother tells him everything. She will let him know if young Timothy calls. Manny figures the rest out."

"I'm surprised that works."

"I guess we are about to find out for sure."

Tristan soon reappeared, and Vinny seemed to have finished all his preparations. Tristan took the front next to Vinni, and Annelise climbed into the back with Michael. She had one foot in the plane when a fierce wave of dizziness passed over her. She slipped and would have fallen, but Vinni, who was waiting to climb through the same door into the pilot seat, steadied her. "Careful," he warned.

She collapsed into the back seat, slumping against Michael. Slowly, her vision cleared to reveal Michael looking at her with concern.

"I'll be okay," she murmured.

"Annelise, please..."

She pushed herself into a more upright seating position and resolutely pulled her seatbelt around her. "I said I'll be okay," she snapped. She *had* to be okay.

Michael clenched his jaw and looked out the window. Annelise felt a pang of guilt. She didn't want him mad at her. Glancing around, she noticed that Tristan was giving her a searching look, his brow drawn in concern. She looked away.

Vinni handed out headsets and showed everyone where to plug them in, warning that once the engine started, they wouldn't be able to hear anything without them.

Annelise turned to Michael. "I shouldn't have snapped. I don't want to distract you or Tristan from the job. I will figure this— " she gestured at herself, "out in Canol Dinas. If you and Tristan can finish getting the Dragon out, then all our futures suddenly look much brighter...I hope." There was always the chance that the judicial system would not grant them leniency even if they freed the Dragon. Then again, there was also a chance, however small, that Annelise could disappear once the Dragon was free.

Any further conversation was cut off as the engine roared to life, and the deafening buzz of the propeller filled the cabin. Annelise pulled her headset over her ears, muffling the sound of the engine to a manageable hum.

She watched with fascination as Vinni maneuvered the plane out onto the runway. There were endless dials, blinking lights, switches, and levers. It all seemed very complicated. She gripped the seat beneath her as they accelerated down the runway. The nose of the plane tipped up, and the ground fell away beneath them. A wave of dizziness came over Annelise, and she wasn't sure if it was from the magical hemorrhaging or the flying. The buildings and cars and streets and trees shrank beneath them as they climbed up over the Columbia River. They banked hard to the left. Annelise closed her eyes, gripping her seat white-knuckled, every muscle tense. At last, they evened out, putting the river behind them and following the Willamette south.

She glanced at Michael, who was looking around him with amazement. He did not seem to mind the unsettling sensations of flying. Annelise could see that Tristan had a firm grip on his seat as well, but he, too, was looking around in amazement. She looked out the window. There were no clouds to impede their view. From this height, it hardly looked like they were moving at all. Slowly but surely, milestone after milestone passed beneath them, and Annelise started to relax into the experience. She only gripped the seat once in a while when a current of wind buffeted the small plane.

"There's absolutely nothing like flying," Vinni's voice came through the headsets in crisp, if clipped, quality. "It's pure freedom. From up here, not even the horizon can hold you back."

Tristan leaned forward to look up at the wispy clouds far above them. "I can see what you mean. It's unbelievable."

"So, they're saying you're terrorists," Vinni said in a conversational tone. The tension in the cabin shot up. All eyes were on Vinni. "You can't be surprised." He glanced at Tristan. "I watch the news. Your faces are all over it. They say you stole some sort of weapon?"

"It's not a weapon."

"So, my question is, why shouldn't I turn you in to the authorities?"

"Because we paid you not to?" Annelise offered.

Vinni grinned. "Thanks for the cash. But if you're planning on hurting people, I'm gonna have to make an executive decision to land next to the Canol Dinas Warden Precinct. You have until we get there to change my mind."

"Look, we're not going to hurt anyone. It's true that those who have tried to open the Subraek in the past did so because they wished to unleash monsters on the world. But that's not why we took the key. We did it because we discovered that the Dragon is trapped down there, and we want to set her free."

"The one who went missing just before the integration? I just learned about her in school."

Michael groaned and leaned his head against the seat in front of him. "We're all gonna die..." he whined.

"You really think she's down there?"

"We know she's down there," Tristan responded.

"How?"

"We saw her."

"So why don't you just let her out?"

"She's trapped by magic. We need to get the necessary materials to break the spell."

"Okay." Vinni paused, considering their words. "Do you have any proof?"

"Proof?"

"That you found the Dragon?"

The three mages exchanged a look. Even though the camera had burned up, it might have been good to try to bring something else back as proof.

Annelise spoke up. "We brought a camera, but it burned up due to magical overload. Then we and the Dragon ended up having a misunderstanding, and our conversation was cut short... It slipped our minds."

"Hmm. Not very convincing so far. You'll have to do better."

Michael sat up. "I could show you."

Vinni glanced over his shoulder at Michael. "How?"

"Magic. I can show you my memory of the dragon. But not while you're flying. The sharing of memories is a pretty all-encompassing sensory experience."

Vinni thought about it. "I won't wait until we get to Canol Dinas to see your proof." He turned to Tristan. "You can take the controls while your friend shows me his proof."

Tristan stilled, set his jaw, and then nodded. "Show me what to do."

Vinni showed him the main controls. "Just hold her there, and keep her steady." Tristan's hands were clenched around the controls. "Try to relax. Small adjustments are key. Air is a fluid, so it will take a moment for any corrections to catch up. Don't get impatient and overcorrect." He looked at Michael. "How long will this take?"

Michael shrugged. "A couple of minutes?"

Vinni gave Tristan a smile. "You'll be fine! It will be great. Just relax and enjoy the freedom of the skies."

He turned back to Michael. "What now?"

Michael reached forward and pressed his fingertips against Vinni's temples. "Close your eyes," he instructed. Both stilled as Michael revealed his memory to Vinni. Annelise glanced over at Tristan. His shoulders were rigid, and his grip on the controls was still tight, but not quite white-knuckled.

Annelise gripped her seat. "You doing okay, Tristan?"

"Uh-huh." His eyes darted between the front window and the attitude indicator. He didn't blink.

A current of wind buffeted the plane, causing a tremor to shudder through the aircraft and nudging the nose of the plane down a bit. Annelise stared wide-eyed as Tristan coaxed the plane back to level. Her stomach flip-flopped as the plane eased back into a settled course. Annelise released the breath that had caught in her throat. She closed her eyes, praying that Michael would hurry up.

Finally, Michael and Vinni opened their eyes.

"Whoa," Vinni said. "That was wild!" He looked around and, seeing that they were still flying, clapped Trisan on the shoulder. Tristan almost cracked. "Look at that! We're still alive! Well done. I'll take over now." Vinni took over control of the aircraft, and Tristan slumped in his seat, breathing somewhat heavily.

"First, I've got to say, having witnessed all that, Magic is epic. Almost as cool as flying. Second, that Dragon was perhaps the most incredible thing I've ever seen." The aircraft shuddered as it rumbled across another current of wind. "Except for you, my dear," he patted the console lovingly. "Can you imagine sharing the skies with a magnificent creature like that? You guys have got to help her."

"So you won't be handing us over to the authorities?"

Vinni paused. "I won't. But it sounds like you might want to consider reaching out to the authorities yourselves."

Annelise looked down. She *had* considered it. She was *still* considering it. She just didn't want to get Tristan and Michael tied up in it in case it went wrong.

Tristan glanced at Michael and Annelise, his gaze lingering on Annelise's pale face. "I've thought about it." He turned to face Vinni. Annelise looked up in surprise, but Tristan continued. "We just don't know who to trust. If we all end up in custody… What if they decide the risk isn't worth the reward? What if they're not who they seem? It's a risk I can't take."

Annelise looked out the window. He was right. They shouldn't all end up in custody. But she was starting to think that they really were going to need an ally. She only hoped she was making the right choice.

Vinni nodded. "I see your point." He adjusted the controls of the plane, tipping the nose down ever so slightly. "We're beginning our descent. We should be landing in about 30 minutes."

Another wave of dizziness washed over Annelise. The corners of her vision went gray. When the dizziness passed, she was slumped forward in her seat, and Michael was calling her name, his voice urgent. "Annelise!" He gave her shoulder a shake.

She lifted her head and blinked at him. "Sorry. I just got dizzy. I'm not sure I'm built for flying."

"Some people do react poorly to the changes in g-force." Vinni chimed in. "You must be pretty sensitive."

Annelise shook her head. "I'll be fine." She had to be.

As they approached Canol Dinas, Vinni made a couple of sharp turns, lining the aircraft up with the glittering river. The ground approached much slower than it had left during takeoff. Buildings, cars, and trees flitted beneath their wings as they glided over the city. Touchdown was a jarring affair. Water splashed up around them, and the entire airplane rattled as each bit of choppy water struck the bottom of the floats. Finally, they settled into the water, bobbing on the churn. After a moment, Vinni upped the power on the propeller again and navigated them to a dock on the river. As they approached, Vinni flung the door open and unbuckled his seatbelt, still navigating the plane. The plane slowed to a drifting float, and Vinni swung one leg out of the door, placing it on the pontoon. As they drifted parallel to the dock, he hopped out of the plane, grabbed a rope, and tied the plane to the dock.

He stuck his head back in the door with a grin. "Ladies and gentlemen, welcome to Canol Dinas." Annelise slid out of the seat, accepting Vinni's hand to steady her as she stepped from the pontoon onto the dock. The floating dock bobbed in the water, and Annelise couldn't wait to get back onto solid ground.

She stumbled as she headed up the dock. An arm wrapped around her, steadying her. It was Michael. He looked like he wanted to say something to her, then thought better of it and looked forward, his jaw clenched.

A short figure was standing at the top of the dock, trying his best to blend in with the shadows. "Jimmy?" Annelise asked, incredulous. Why was he here? The sight of him brought back a flood of emotions that Annelise did not want to deal with at the moment. She forced herself to focus on the here and now.

Jimmy cleared his throat. "I just wanted to make sure you made the trip okay." He looked her over. She was still leaning heavily on Michael. "You doing okay?"

"I'll figure it out," she murmured. Now was not the time to talk about that. She looked around them. "You came all the way out here, just to see if we made it okay?" She raised her eyebrows. "That's twice in one week, Jimmy. One might start to think you actually care." Her nails were biting into her palm.

Jimmy ran a hand over his bald head. "Annelise, I've known you since you were just a kid. I know I sold you out, and… Annelise, I'm sorry."

Annelise hesitated. The memory of his betrayal still sat like a stone in the pit of her stomach. His words did not change how she felt or the trouble she was in. And yet… she wished it did. Releasing a clenched hand, she put it on his shoulder and gave it a squeeze. It was enough for now. They would figure out the rest later.

Everyone tensed as sirens blared in the distance. "Jimmy," Annelise said, "where do the wardens think we are right now?"

Jimmy's eyes darted towards the source of the sound. "As far as I know, they've lost you completely."
They listened for a moment. The sirens seemed to be coming closer. "Then again, you never know." He looked at Vinni accusingly. "Someone might have spilled the beans."

Vinni raised his hands in denial. "I didn't tell anyone. Then again, there aren't a lot of planes that come to Canol Dinas. Maybe they got suspicious?"

"You won't tell them anything?"

He grinned and held up his hands in mock surrender. "What, me? I'm just a kid." He let his voice crack. "I don't know anything about what's on the news. I just thought I could do a good deed and help some poor travellers out while getting extra flight hours in. That way, I can get my commercial license as soon as I turn eighteen." He hesitated. "If they ask, you didn't pay me."

"We're not going to hang around long enough for them to ask," Tristan said. "Come on, we need to get moving."

"If you need anything else, let me know," Jimmy called after them as they left the dock parking lot. The sirens were definitely getting closer.

They hurried along the bustling riverfront park down to a corner where a black car was waiting for them. Tristan took the front passenger seat, while Annelise and Michael slipped into the back seat.

"Good evening," Manny's tone was professional, almost jovial. "It's good to see you all again. How are you doing, Sir?"

"All the better for seeing you, Manny. Let's drive."

"Very well," he pulled the car into traffic. As they disappeared down the road, Annelise looked out the back to see flashing lights pulling into the dock parking lot. As he drove, he handed Tristan a set of key cards. "I've taken the liberty of checking my mother into a local hotel, sir. Unfortunately, she won't be able to make it until the day after tomorrow. Here are the keys to your rooms."

"Thank you, Manny. What would we do without you?"

"Probably end up in prison, sir."

Tristan chuckled. "Quite right."

Chapter 14: The Betrayal

Annelise's heart pounded as they drove down the road. Her head was spinning. The corners of her vision were perpetually gray with static. And her magic...She was not okay.

She knew she needed medical attention, and she had one very bad plan to get it. But it meant that she would not be going with the Pendragons to get the ruby from Councilman Cawthorne. And her plan would impact Tristan and Michael's plans, so she owed it to them to share it with them.

She glanced at Michael. He met her gaze with concern. She took a breath to tell him everything, but the words died on her lips. What could she say? Her stomach clenched at the thought of saying the words that she knew she needed to be said. She gave Michael a small smile and shook her head.

She would tell him later.

They pulled into the hotel parking lot, and Manny led them up to the rooms. This hotel was much more pleasant than their dingy motel from earlier. The plush blue carpet of the hallways stood out against the cream colored walls. The rooms themselves were everything they could have hoped for. A soft bed with crisp white sheets, a large window over which Manny immediately pulled the curtains, two full bathrooms, a mini fridge, and a desk with a TV and a phone.

Manny placed a duffel bag onto one of the beds. "I raided a thrift store, as I thought you all might like a change of clothes... And a chance to wash up."

Annelise didn't want to imagine what they looked like. A swim in the frigid waters of Crater Lake did not count as a proper bath. "Manny, you're the best."

"Thank you. I do try."

She grabbed some clothes out of the bag and disappeared into the shower. She washed her hair, mindful of the cut on her head that was still healing.

A wave of dizziness washed over her, and Annelise was vaguely aware that she was sliding to sit down in the bathtub. After a few moments, her vision cleared. She knew she was not okay. She needed help. So why couldn't she bring herself to tell anyone?

Annelise wiped a hand over her face. She had to tell Michael and Tristan. And she had to do it soon.

She stepped out of the bathroom to find Tristan and Michael had already showered. They were watching the news and looked up at her as she entered the room. Her hands trembled. She took a breath to tell them, but the words stuck in her throat. Why couldn't she just say the words?

"I, um..." she started. She blinked back tears. Why was this so hard?

"Anelise, are you okay?" Michael asked with a tone that said he already knew the answer.

Annelise's expression crumpled. "No," she sobbed. "I'm not okay." Her whole body was shaking.

Michael closed the distance between them and wrapped her in a hug.

"I need... I need..."

"You need help?" Michael supplied.

Annelise nodded, trying to stifle the sobs. "I'm so sorry."

Tristan stood. "Don't be. I'm glad you told us. How bad is it?"

"Bad." Her voice was barely more than a whisper. "I'm sorry I didn't tell you sooner. I didn't want to burden you. You already have so much to worry about."

"You're not burdening us," Tristan insisted. "Remember, it's my job to make sure everyone is okay. We are going to find a way to get you help."

"I can take you to a healing center," Michael said.

Annelise pulled away from his hug. "No. If I go to a healing center, they will definitely turn me in. And if you're with me, you'll get arrested too. Our best bet for freeing the Dragon is for both of you to stay out of police custody for as long as possible."

"But you need help," he insisted.

"Yeah. I know. I, um... I have an idea for that." She held up her hands. "But if you have a better idea, I'm very open to suggestions. It's pretty sucky." She took a deep breath. "I think I need to turn myself in."

She waited for them to tell her that her plan was ludicrous — or that they had a much better plan. She was really hoping they would have a better plan. They did not.

Her heart sank but she continued. "You said Detective Poe was honest. And she mentioned being willing to listen. If we're going up against Councilman Cawthorne, we are going to need somebody on our side if anything else goes wrong, which, with our luck, it probably will. I think she's our best bet, and she can get me medical attention." She looked up. "Am I being crazy?"

Tristan sighed. "You're not being crazy." He sat back down on the bed. "I've been thinking that we need to let someone from law enforcement in on the situation, too. Whether that be Director Desmedt or Detective Poe. We need to let someone know what we found."

"So, what do you suggest?"

"I think that turning yourself in to Detective Poe is a good plan. It will get you the help you need, and it's a move that will garner her good will. She will be more likely to listen to what you have to say if you go in of your own accord."

"How... What is the best way to do that?" Annelise shifted her weight. "I've spent so long trying not to get caught, I haven't really thought through the best way to turn myself in."

Tristan gave a chuckle, but it lacked all mirth. "You'll want to call the hotline and ask to speak to Detective Poe."

"They'll probably push back on that request," Michael added.

Tristan nodded. "But if you tell them your name, they should connect you." He ran a hand through his hair. "Tell her you'll meet her at the Canol Dinas Precinct at," he checked his watch. "Eight o'clock."

Michael turned her to face him. "Make sure you tell them that you are in need of urgent medical and magical attention when you call. That way, they can have a qualified healer ready when you arrive. Getting better should be your first priority."

Annelise nodded, and immediately regretted it as her head spun. "Ask for Detective Poe, meet at the precinct at eight, ask for medical help. Got it." She pressed a hand against her forehead. The world went fuzzy. When it cleared, she was seated on a bed, and Tristan and Michael were looking at her with concern.

"Don't worry about me." She tried to smile. "You just make sure you get that ruby and get back to Crater Lake. What's your plan for that?"

Tristan looked unconvinced by her reassurance. "Once we have the ruby, Manny will drive with us to Crater Lake. As far as we know, they still don't know about the portal there."

Just then, Manny re-entered the rooms. The Pendragons shared a look.

"It looks like it's time for us to go." A frown pulled at Michael's forehead. "I hate to leave you like this."

"Just... let me know when you have the ruby, and then I will make the call. With any luck, me turning myself in will create enough commotion that you can slip out of the city unnoticed."

Michael nodded and turned to follow Tristan out the door.

"Wait," Annelise stood from the bed. She pulled Tristan and then Michael into a hug before they left. "Be safe."

Tristan released her from the hug. "You should call Professor Finchley. You might want legal counsel, and it would be good to have someone you can trust."

Annelise nodded. "Good idea."

Michael searched Annelise's face. "Tell me you're going to be okay." Annelise knew that if she asked, he would stay. But she couldn't do that to him.

She flashed him her best smile, but she knew it was shaky, and if she looked as pale as she felt, she knew she looked terrible. "Yup! I'll be just fine." She shooed them away. "Now get going. And don't forget what I taught you. Call me as soon as you have the ruby."

As soon as the two of them left the room, Annelise sank onto the bed, her vision blurring. Exhaustion overtook her, and she fell into a fitful sleep.

She jolted awake to the harsh ring of the hotel phone.

"Annelise?" It was Michael.

"Did you do it?"

"Yes. We got it."

"And was I right?"

"Yes. It's definitely holding a spell, and a big one at that. I think you were right."

A weight lifted off Annelise's shoulders. If she had been wrong about this, everything they had done would have been for nothing.

Now, Michael and Tristan had everything they needed to set the Dragon free.

"How... How is Tristan?"

"He's pretty shaken. I think a small part of him was holding out hope that it wouldn't be true... We'll get through this, though."

"Yes, you will." She looked around the hotel room. "I guess that's my cue. I'm gonna make the call."

"You can do this." He paused. "I've got to go, but I'll see you when we get back."

"Take care," she replied and hung up.

She picked up the off-white phone situated on the small table against the wall. Her hand hovered over the dial pad, hesitating. Was she really going to do this? Making a split-second decision, she dialed a different number. The phone rang on the other end.

The phone clicked slightly as it was picked up. "Professor Hale speaking,"

"Hi, Professor Hale," she replied, her voice shaking.

"Annelise?"

"Yeah."

"Are you okay?"

"... not really." Her voice caught in her throat, and tears were leaking down her face. "I don't... I wanted to hear your voice."

"Annelise, they're calling you terrorists."

Annelise shuddered. "Is that what you think I am?"

"Tell me that you had a good reason for doing what you did."

"We have a good reason. The most amazing reason. I believe that now more than ever. Now that I've seen her with my own eyes."

"Seen who?"

"The Dragon."

There was silence on the other end.

"We found her, and we are so close to getting her out. I know what I have to do to give us the best chance of success, but..." Her eyes burned as she choked on the words. "But I'm scared."

"What are you scared of?"

"What if I trust the wrong person, and everything we've done gets thrown away? I won't be able to fix it."

There was a moment of silence from the other end. Then, "That is a real risk. But I know you, Annelise. I'm sure you've thought this through from every angle. I trust your judgement. You should trust it, too. I think you'll find that some people are actually trustworthy." He sighed. "True trust always takes us past the point where we have control. It's always scary."

"Well, that sucks." Annelise groaned, the knot in her stomach growing. "This is going to suck no matter what I do."

"Then you might as well get on with it."

Annelise nodded into the phone. "Yeah. I guess you're right." A wave of nerves washed over her, causing her stomach to flip-flop.

"Annelise?"

"Yeah?"

"I'm proud of you," Professor Hale's voice was hoarse with emotion.

Annelise squeezed her eyes shut against the tears, but they forced their way out. She took a deep, shuddering breath.

"Thank you." Annelise glanced at the clock. If she was going to enact her plan, it would have to be now. "Professor, I've got to go."

"Good luck, Annelise."

She hung up the phone and immediately dialed the police hotline number before she lost her nerve.

The phone rang once and was then picked up.

"You've reached the warden hotline. Do you have information about the recent government vault break-in or the fugitive's whereabouts?" came the polite female voice from the other side.

"I would like to speak to Detective Poe," Annelise said.

"Detective Poe is very busy at the moment. Is there a message I can take for you?" the voice said in a businesslike manner.

"This is Annelise Windstarter. And I think Detective Poe will want to speak to me directly."

The stunned silence on the other side stretched on for a while. "One moment, please," the voice finally said.

Annelise waited while they connected her to Detective Poe.

"This is Detective Poe," came the voice.

"Hello, Detective, I'm Annelise."

"Are you ready to come in?"

"Yes."

"Wait... what? Really?"

The ghost of a smirk crossed Annelise's face. "Yes, Detective, I'm calling to arrange my surrender, but I'm willing to do so to you, and only you. I won't surrender to anyone else. You said you're willing to listen, and I hear you're an honest woman. I have some information you need to hear."

She could almost hear the detective sitting up straight in her chair.

"Of course. Meet me at the Canol Dinas precinct. Come unarmed. You'll have my word that no one will harm you."

"Thank you," She glanced at the clock. "I'll be there at 8:00 pm."

"We will be ready."

"Detective Poe?"

"Yes?"

"I'll be needing some medical and magical attention when I get there."

There was some shuffling on the other end. "Understood."

"Thank you."

Annelise hung up the phone and slumped back against the bed. It was the best plan she could think of. It would get her the medical attention she knew she needed. She could explain the situation to

Detective Poe and hopefully get Michael and Tristan the backup and support they needed. And they could get the Dragon free and put the Councilman in jail for his crimes, which everyone needed.

And maybe if she told the story right and with Detective Poe's help, Michael and Tristan could be exonerated... maybe. Annelise was definitely going to jail. It wasn't a great plan, but it was the best she had. It had to be good enough.

Sitting up, she picked up the phone once more. She flipped over the anti-tracing bracelet that she still wore. On the inside was the number she had written in ink before their adventure started, just in case. She dialed the number.

It rang and then, "Bombardier Offices, this is Robin Finchley speaking."

"Professor Finchley, it's me, Annelise."

There was a moment of silence. "Wow. You sure know how to bring me extravagant gifts, Annelise. This will be the biggest case of the century."

Annelise smiled weakly. "I don't know how much of a case it will be, but I do think I will need some legal counsel. Will you help me?"

"Of course, child. But I can't do that if you're on the run."

"I'm turning myself in at the Canol Dinas precinct. I have some information for the Detective, but if you can meet me there at 8:30pm, I would be forever grateful."

"Of course. I'll see you then." There was a click as the line went dead.

Annelise hung up the receiver and then stumbled out the door.

Twenty minutes later, Annelise was walking towards the precinct, her body trembling in part from anxiety and in part from her magical injury. Black spots swam across her vision. Her heart pounded, and her breath came in shallow gasps, which only made her vision blur more. As she walked, she could see several wardens near the front doors, armed and ready in case she decided to attack.

Annelise could have snorted at the notion. She didn't have enough oomph to produce an ounce of magic at the moment.

A few reporters were also present, keeping their distance, but speaking frantically into their cameras. She was sure she made a sorry sight.

Detective Poe was there, standing at the top of the stairs, waiting for her to arrive. As she started up the stairs, a dark spot clouded her vision, and her toe caught on a step. She stumbled forward, catching herself abruptly on all fours on the stairs. Her vision swam. She waited for it to clear.

She started when she felt a hand under her elbow. She looked up and saw the concerned face of Detective Poe.

"Come on, let's get you inside." Detective Poe supported her as she climbed the remaining stairs. When they got to the top, Annelise was obliged to hold out her wrists as Detective Poe snapped cuffs around them. Several bulbs flashed as the onlooking reporters worked to capture their next front-page headline.

Annelise shuddered as she felt her magic suppressed. It did nothing to help the spinning of her head. She was then led inside to an interrogation room where Detective Poe sat her down.

The detective went over to the door and poked her head out. "Hey, let's get that healer here ASAP. She's in pretty bad shape."

Annelise heard a set of footsteps hurrying off to fetch the healer. "Detective," her voice felt frustratingly weak. "I need to tell you about the Dragon."

Detective Poe's head snapped toward Annelise. "What about the Dragon?"

"We found her. She has been trapped in the Subraek all these years behind a blood ward. That's why we broke in. We need your help to break her out. We think councilman…" Her vision blurred, going almost completely black before it cleared again. "The councilman…" she tried again.

She must have zoned out for a moment because all of a sudden, there was a healer shining a light into her eyes. He performed several assessments, his eyes going a bit wider every time.

"She needs urgent magical attention," He turned to Detective Poe.

Annelise let out a hysterical giggle. "Tried to fight a Dragon with blood magic," she mumbled. What was she supposed to be doing again?

Detective Poe leaned in, taking Annelise's face in her hands. "Annelise, tell me what you need to set the Dragon free. You said you needed my help, why? What do you need?"

Annelise blinked at the Detective. "Yes, help us." Her head was getting heavy, and she could no longer hold it straight.

"Detective, this can't wait any longer," the healer insisted.

Detective Poe frowned but nodded. She stood up. "Tell me what you need."

Annelise stopped listening as the voices floated around her head. She no longer seemed to be able to make sense of what they were saying, let alone remember what she needed to tell them. It had seemed so important. Now the music of their words just danced around her head, sending off sparks of color that made her skin tingle.

***

When Annelise woke, it was not in a hospital bed like she had expected, but on the floor of a cold room with no light. Pain assailed her, and lights danced behind her eyes. The cuffs were off her wrists.

What had happened? Where was she?

Annelise groaned. She did not need to try to touch her magic to sense just how bad her situation had become. The pain was now constant.

Where was Detective Poe?

The door slammed open, sending shockwaves through her head, and a bright, pale light streamed in through the open door, blinding her. With the flick of a switch, the whole room was drenched in oppressive light. Piercing pain drilled through Annelise's temples. She groaned and shielded her eyes, trying to block out the light.

A hand grabbed her arm and dragged her up off the ground and out the door. There she was thrust into a too-bright room and into a chair.

"Annelise Windstarter," a familiar voice said, but it carried an unfamiliar tone. It was full of disdain.

Annelise blinked through the blinding light, trying to focus her blurry vision on the figure in the room. "Professor Finchley?" When did he get here? "Where am I? Where's Detective Poe? I need to talk to her."

"I wouldn't recommend that, Annelise. You're in a lot of trouble. It's best if you don't incriminate yourself." He pulled a chair up to the table. The metal chair screeched against the concrete floor, sending shockwaves of pain through Annelise's head.

"I need a healer."

"All in good time." Professor Finchley flipped through a file.

Annelise tried to focus on Professor Finchley's face, but her vision kept blurring. She couldn't make out his expression. "Professor, I really need a healer. Where was the healer from before?"

Professor Finchley dug around in his pocket and pulled out a little vial of potion. "Here." He handed it to her. "This should help until we can get you a private healer. Not one that will try to get answers out of you while you are unwell."

The potion was sweet, but it did nothing to help her pain. "Professor, I don't think it's working. I need to see a healer now."

"Tell me, Annelise, where are your co-conspirators now?" Professor Finchley asked. "Don't worry, anything you tell me is protected by attorney-client privilege."

"They are probably on their way back to Crater Lake by now to set the dragon free." With every word, Annelise's eyes widened more. Why had she said that? She hadn't meant to say any of that.

"Why didn't you set her free the first time you broke into the Subraek?"

"The dragon is trapped by a blood ward." Annelise brought a shaky hand up to her mouth. The words seemed to have left her lips before her mind had given them permission.

Professor Finchley leaned in close, gazing at her intently. "And how do you plan to get her through the blood ward?"

"Tristan and Michael stole…" Annelise took a breath. She didn't want to tell him this. Not yet. Not until their plan had succeeded. But the longer she waited, the more intently the words bubbled in her mouth. Finally, "They stole the ruby sustaining the blood ward from Councilman Cawthorne," the words burst out of her mouth. She looked down at the vial, which she now clenched between bloodless fingers.

"What did you give me?" she asked, horror blossoming in her chest.

"Truth serum." He turned back to the file.

Annelise blanched. She needed to get it out of her system. In a desperate attempt to purge the potion, Annelise reached out to her magic, hoping to induce vomiting. The pain brought her to her knees as she toppled out of the chair. Tears streamed down her face, but the potion refused to be regurgitated.

Annelise collapsed onto the floor, shaking as waves of pain washed over her. Her brow was drenched with sweat. Once again, the hand grabbed her under her arm and hauled her into the chair. Annelise did not have the strength to sit up straight. She braced herself on the table.

"Are you done being ridiculous?" Finchley asked, his voice a veneer of calm.

"Those were outlawed," Annelise gasped, wiping tears from her face. "Why are you doing this?"

"Special circumstances require special measures," Professor Finchley drawled, as he pulled her to her feet again. "It's time for you to testify." Annelise tried to understand his words and actions as he led her down a hallway and to a door. Just before they entered it, he pushed her against a wall. "You are to answer every question I ask and otherwise keep your mouth shut. Do you understand?"

Annelise pressed her lips shut, but her mouth seemed to move on its own accord. "Yes, I understand," she blurted. His instructions were the only thing that were clear at the moment. What was he playing at?

"Excellent. Let's go."

He pushed her through the door and into a chair in the center of the room. It was the High Council room. A singular chair had been placed in the center of the half circle table. Annelise was made to sit in the chair, her back to the stone Dragon's Seat.

On the raised platform were seven council members, dressed in their official emerald robes. This was not a civilian court. This was the panel that would determine her fate. There, in the center of the Panel, sat Councilman Cawthorne. Annelise paled. She knew she was done for.

Professor Finchley addressed the panel. "Ladies and gentlemen, esteemed council members, my client is prepared to make a full confession."

Annelise stared at Professor Finchley, her mind racing. She most certainly was *not* ready to make a full confession, but Councilman Cawthorn was nodding for Finchley to proceed.

Professor Finchley turned to Annelise. "State your name."

"Annelise Windstarter,"

"Did you break into the Government vaults to steal the key to the Subraek?"

"Yes."

"Were you aware before you broke into the Subraek that it is filled with all the most dangerous dark creatures and spirits that should never be allowed to reach our realm?"

"Yes."

"Are you aware that should such a dark creature make it into our realm, there would be countless deaths and widespread panic?"

"Yes."

"Are you aware that this would be disastrous for our relationship with the Sourceless?"

"Yes."

"Were you, or were you not, attempting to release a creature from the Subraek?"

Annelise's eyes were wide with alarm. "We were," her mouth said, in spite of her attempts to keep it shut. There were angry murmurs from the panel. Annelise felt panic rising in her chest. He was twisting her words so completely. How did the council members not see it? She wondered if they even knew about the Truth Potion.

"Did you manage to release a creature from the Subraek?"

"No."

"Small mercies. Other terrorists in the past have tried to access the Subraek to free the creatures, but none have managed. Tell me, did you enter the Subraek?"

"Yes."

"How? Which portal did you use?"

She did not want to answer. "The one on Wizard Island."

"There is no portal there." A younger councilman with sharp green eyes stood as he spoke, his tone incredulous.

Annelise said nothing. Since he had not asked her a question, she could not speak. How she wished she could speak!

Finchley barely acknowledged the comment but continued to interrogate Annelise. "Who were you working with?"

"Tristan Pendragon and Michael Pendragon."

"Tell me, did Michael and Tristan Pendragon plot to steal a ruby from Councilman Cawthorne's possession?"

"Yes— "

"I would like to ask the defendant a question, if I may, Mr. Finchley." Councilman Cawthorne rose to his feet. "I apologize for interrupting this... *enlightening* interrogation."

Professor Finchley's eyes blazed with irritation at the interruption, but he nodded graciously.

"Why did my nephews steal the ruby from me?" Councilman Cawthorne asked, his brow furrowed, and his eyes searching her face for any clue.

A small grin flashed over Professor Finchley's face. "Yes, Miss Windstarter. Why *exactly* did Tristan and Michael Pendragon steal a ruby from the esteemed Councilman?"

Exactly? "To break a blood ward," Annelise answered. Her eyes burned, but no tears spilled forth. How she wished she could say even a few words more! But Finchley seemed to know how to interrogate someone under the power of a truth serum, and so she could not. Councilman Cawthorne's eyes flitted to Professor Finchley, his brow furrowing even more. Annelise did not know what to make of his demeanor.

Professor Finchley pretended to be very disturbed by this. "You mean to tell me that after all this, Tristan and Michael Pendragon plan to go back into the Subraek and use the jewel to break down a ward that has kept a dangerous creature locked up, indeed that they are on their way to do so as we speak?"

"They are." A small tremble was all that her voice betrayed of the raging emotions and frustration that tore at her. If he would just ask her why, she could tell him. But his questions were too tight. She doubted this would fly in a normal court, but this was no normal court.

"Tell me, how did you manage to steal the key?" Professor Finchley asked.

The question surprised Annelise. "I did not steal the key."

"Who stole the key?"

"Tristan Pendragon."

"The investigators found this in its place," he pulled out her masterpiece forgery of a key. "A surprisingly convincing copy. Do you know who made it?"

"Yes,"

"Who made this?"

"I did."

"The new artwork for their gallery, I suppose," Councilman Cawthorne said, almost to himself.

Professor Finchley waved his hand over the key, revealing the runes she used for the perception ward. "It has a rather peculiar perception ward placed over it. Tell me, what kind of magic did you use to create it?"

"Blood magic."

There was a murmur from the panel. Councilman Cawthorne's brow furrowed, and his eyes narrowed. Once again, his gaze flitted over to Professor Finchley.

The younger councilman with sharp green eyes stood up. "Ladies and gentlemen, as much as it pains me to say it, I believe that Tristan and Michael Pendragon have been dabbling in both dangerous magic and ideology. There are many questions to be answered — about this ward and jewel, and about what we are to do with the perpetrators of this act of terrorism.

"But we can determine Miss Windstarter's fate at a later time when the immediate danger has been dealt with. Michael and Tristan Pendragon must be stopped at whatever cost. They have proved very slippery in the past in getting out of tight situations. We know where they are going, but we cannot afford to allow them to slip through our fingers again. I propose that our wardens be given full rein to do whatever they deem necessary to stop these radicals from achieving their objective."

A murmur rippled through the panel. Councilman Cawthorne made no obvious reaction.

"I agree with the councilman." One councilwoman with grey hair and a pointy nose said. "Michael and Tristan Pendragon should be stopped at all costs. I move to permit pursuers to use deadly force if necessary. Cawthorne, you should sit this one out. Nobody expects you to vote against your family."

Councilman Cawthorn pursed his lips but took his seat silently. Another council member seconded the motion. A short vote later, Tristan and Michael's fates were sealed.

It was all Annelise's fault.

Annelise was led out of the room.

As she went, she heard the grey-haired councilwoman speak again. "As head of the magical security enforcement committee, I am authorizing the use of a private security company to secure this key. I hardly expect the wardens to use the force necessary against one of their own. If they had, the key would have never left the vaults."

Annelise did not hear the conversation that ensued. She was led back down the hallway that had brought her to the Council Chamber. She was still under the effects of the truth serum and could not speak, but she could observe. As they walked by a large room full of wardens, she saw several dozen of them preparing themselves for the anticipated confrontation.

She spotted Detective Poe among them. Their eyes met. The detective looked stricken. Annelise's face went bloodless. She wanted to puke. These were the wardens who had been permitted to use deadly force if necessary. She had gone to Detective Poe for help, and had instead sent the Detective to execute her friends.

With a shove, the guard behind her pushed her forward, past the door, and led her back down the hall to her cell. She was thrust inside with a careless toss. She sank to the floor with a groan. The only mercy was that the light was gone, which was a small relief to her throbbing headache.

Her heart, however, was crushed.

She had betrayed her friends—betrayed those who had risked so much to keep her safe. Against her will, admittedly, but the result would be the same. They were all going to die, and the Dragon was never going to get free. All because she had trusted the wrong person.

She didn't understand why Professor Finchley had turned on her so completely. She had trusted him, and he had betrayed her. Why was Professor Finchley doing this?

She wished she could take back the words that had spilled out of her mouth at the trial, but she could not rewrite the past.

She had hoped that Detective Poe would help her, but she was wrong. Her magical wound was not healed. She would not last much longer. The thought of Tristan and Michael falling to some private security thugs was too much. Annelise broke down, weeping alone in her pitch-black cell.

Chapter 15: The Evidence

Annelise drifted in and out of consciousness. No one came to see her. Soon, there would be no need for the court to deliver a sentence. Soon, she would be dead. She was going to die alone in a hole.

At the start of her quest, no prospect could scare her more than her current predicament. Now, she was indifferent to it.

When she had enough lucidity, her mind flitted over the events of the last day. She worried for her friends. She felt as though she had failed—failed their mission, and failed her friends. She had trusted the wrong person, and Michael and Tristan would pay the price.

The thought of what might happen to her friends caused her to break down in tears again. She wished she could have helped them. They had been so good to her, and she did not want to lose them. She would give anything to see them safe again.

It was not long before her mind went fuzzy, and reality faded.

Annelise drifted into awareness again. Someone was shuffling around outside the door. The handle jangled, and the blinding, piercing light entered the room again. Annelise moaned in pain. She didn't have the strength to raise an arm to shield her face, but she managed to turn her head away from the too-bright lights.

"Miss Windstarter?" It was a woman's voice.

"Detective?" Annelise croaked, not sure if she was hearing things or not.

"Do you want to keep Robin Finchley as your lawyer?" The Detective's voice rang through the small room.

"No."

"I didn't think so. I'm taking you back into my custody." Detective Poe crouched next to her.

"Can you do that?" Annelise hated the hope that blossomed in her chest. She couldn't survive another disappointment.

"I'll ask for permission later. Come on, we've got to get you out of here."

"Blaire, we can't move her. She's in no state to go anywhere." The second voice was a male voice. Annelise squinted at him. She thought she recognized him as the healer, but she couldn't be sure. She hadn't seen enough of him to truly know his face.

"We can't leave her in here. I don't mean to take her far, just... far enough."

"Fine." His tone was clipped.

She felt arms wrap themselves under her as she was lifted off the ground. They walked into the burning lights, and the pain pushed Annelise over the edge again as her world tipped back into darkness.

The next time she woke, she was on a cot, in a dim room. A machine on wheels to her left monitored her vitals with soft beeps and blinking lights. A small stand to her right lay empty. The room was barren and white, and smelled like an office building.

She felt better than she had in days. Her cuffs were gone, and there was no one around. She sat up, and when her head didn't swim, she tried to get out of bed. Her legs promptly buckled beneath her.

"Whoa there," came a voice from her right. She hadn't seen anyone enter. It was a healer in a crisp white uniform. He had a square face, short-cut brown hair, and warm brown eyes.

He caught her by the elbow and eased her back into bed. "You shouldn't be up yet. You were suffering from massive magical hemorrhaging caused by an intense magical backlash. You're lucky you didn't die. You came quite close. Had you waited much longer…" he shook his head. "Now, we've stopped the hemorrhaging, but it will take you time to recover your strength both physically and magically. I'm giving you strict orders right now: no magic. Don't even reach for it. Not for at least the next 3 months. You could end up right back where you started if you do, or worse."

Detective Poe entered the room. "She awake?"

"She just woke up."

"How long have I been out?"

The healer flashed a small light in Annelise's eyes. "A couple of hours."

The detective pulled a chair to the side of her cot. "How did you manage to get yourself so beat up anyway?"

"I got interrupted while casting a spell."

The healer raised an eyebrow at his chart. "Must have been some spell. What were you doing, blood magic?" he snorted.

"Yeah, I was."

The healer's brow wrinkled in confusion at his paperwork, and then his eyes widened in surprise. "You're *very* lucky to be alive."

"Your spellwork is impressive. I saw what you did at the vault. I've never seen anything like it," the detective said.

Annelise turned to Detective Poe. "Desperate times called for desperate measures." She paused. "Where are my… where are Michael and Tristan?" She had been going to say friends, but the word stuck in her throat. "Are they…" She didn't dare finish the question.

"They are still at large." Detective Poe said. "I'm sorry that you were ever taken from my custody. When Finchley showed up and claimed to be your lawyer...it was out of my hands. But I haven't wasted the time. You need to come with me. If this really has anything to do with the Dragon, time is of the essence."

The healer put his hands on his hips. "Blaire, she's in no condition to be up and about."

The detective ignored the healer. "What do you think? Are you up to helping your friends?"

Annelise nodded. "I can do it. I have to do it."

"Excellent." She looped Annelise's arm over her shoulder to support her as she walked. With an exasperated sigh, the healer took her other arm in a similar fashion as they walked through the halls.

"I don't even know your name," she said to him.

He glanced at her. "I'm Evan,"

"Nice to meet you, Evan. Thank you for saving my life," she grinned at him.

A resigned smile flitted across his face. "My pleasure. Please don't screw it up."

They made their way through various hallways and into an elevator. There, Annelise slumped against the wall, breathing hard. Her hands felt clammy, and her forehead had a sheen of cold sweat. Her legs were shaking.

"Where are we going?" she asked.

"To get help," Detective Poe said. Help was good.

The elevator dinged as they reached their destination. Up here, all the offices seemed to be made of glass. The rooms with the greatest transparency probably held the most secrets, Annelise mused to herself.

The detective and Healer Evan helped her down the hallway and into the one room that had the curtains drawn. Several people were already gathered. She recognized Councilmen Jackson, Sayer, and Trewson from the High Council broadcasts.

Jackson and Trewson were older members of the council. Councilman Jackson had a long, crooked nose and tufty white hair that grew in a ring around the crown of his head. Councilman Trewson, on the other hand, had neatly cropped hair and a few streaks of dark gray still graced his head and his beard. Councilman Sayer, meanwhile, was more middle-aged, with only a few streaks of grey coloring his temples.

The room also held a couple of people she didn't know.

"Annelise, you probably recognize the councilmen already, and this is my boss, Director Desmedt," she gestured to a middle-aged man with pointy features, a businesslike face, and glasses, "and my lieutenant, Tim Haled." Haled had shockingly blonde hair that was almost white, cut short and swept straight back from his face, with electric blue eyes. They each nodded as they were introduced. "Now, Annelise, tell them what you told me."

Annelise looked at the men in the room. "We found the Dragon."

Councilman Trewson stood up from his chair, going pale, and Officer Haled covered his mouth, tears of joy gathering in his eyes.

"Where?" Councilman Jackson asked.

"In the Subraek. That is what we went there to find. She's trapped there behind a blood ward."

"Can you prove it?"

"I could show you my memory of her."

"No, you can't." Healer Evan gave Annelise a stern look. "Miss Windstarter is on strict magic restriction until she heals."

"Then Michael or Tristan could show you if you can bring them back alive."

"Memories can be faked. Do you have anything tangible?" Councilman Sayer spoke up.

Annelise held her head in her hands. "We tried to bring something to take pictures, but the Subraek fried the electronics. And our interaction with the Dragon was...volatile. After one hundred years of being imprisoned, she has every reason to be suspicious. We think... We thought Cawthorne was the one who put her there. At the very least, it looks like he might have helped."

"The recorded testimony we saw painted a very different picture." Councilman Jackson narrowed his eyes at her. "Why did you mention none of this during your interrogation?"

"I was given a truth serum. I could only answer the questions Professor Finchley asked me, and nothing else."

The director stepped forward. "That is a very serious accusation. In fact, you have made several serious accusations. Do you have any proof for any of them?"

Annelise held up her empty hands. "I have nothing tangible. Only circumstantial."

"We do have the recording from the phone call between Tristan Pendragon and Councilman Cawthorne from yesterday." Detective Poe offered. "At the very least, it lends credence to their claim that the Dragon was their objective."

Annelise's eyes snapped to Detective Poe. "You were listening in?"

"Yes. It's how we knew where to find you. The Councilman was less than pleased to have us listening in on his phones, but I was reluctant to let his position earn him special treatment."

Annelise's mind spun. Had the Councilman not betrayed them after all? Perhaps he had no choice with the wardens listening in. But... he had the ruby. And the ruby had a blood ward. Nothing made sense.

She pushed her questions away for now. "I know of a way to prove everything to you... If Tristan and Michael are kept safe."

Director Desmedt crossed his arms. "The high council has dispatched some private security men to take down Tristan and

Michael Pendragon. At Detective Poe's request, I managed to get a team of my own wardens sent as well, for extra security. Good men and women. I trust them. They will bring the Pendragons back alive if at all possible."

"Thank you." A dangerous hope started to blossom in Annelise's chest.

"Here's what I want to know," Lieutenant Haled said, "Why did you all decide to break into the Vaults and steal the key? If Tristan and Michael had brought their theories through the proper channels, a lot of this could have been avoided. Finding the dragon is a top priority, even after all these years."

Annelise glanced at Councilman Jackson. "They assumed that since the council members were the only ones with access to the Subraek, the culprit might be a Council member. Then, they continued to hit walls in their investigation and thought that if they kept prodding, whoever was behind her disappearance might move her. So they opted to go dark."

"What evidence led you to believe that Councilman Cawthorne was behind this?" Councilman Jackson asked.

"Both Tristan and Michael could pass through the blood ward, trapping the Dragon unhindered, which indicates that they are related to whoever cast it. It would take a massive jewel to sustain a blood ward of the size which currently imprisons the Dragon. The Councilman wears just such a jewel. Finally, the Dragon mentioned that the caster was not a Pendragon. Once again, Councilman Cawthorne fits the criteria." She paused. "I don't deny that those points alone make for a weak case; however, I spoke to Michael after they had acquired the ruby. It does indeed contain a blood ward. And so, the case seems ever more concrete."

"What part does Mr. Finchley have to play in all of this?" Director Desmedt asked.

"I don't know. His actions are a mystery to me. I thought... I don't know what I thought, but I didn't expect this."

"Professor Finchley may not be what he seems." Councilman Trewson's voice shook as he spoke.

"Is he involved?" Director Desmedt asked.

"I... I don't know. I certainly hope not. I just..." Councilman Trewson took a steadying breath, adjusting his necktie. "We will need to see how things play out to gain more information. I do not have anything to offer at this time."

"How big is this blood ward?" Detective Poe asked.

"The size of at least ten city blocks. I've never seen anything like it. The only reason he survived the casting is that he used the dragon's blood to do it."

Director Desmedt's eyes widened, and he swore. "You know this for sure?"

"That's what the Dragon said, at least."

"And you have this ruby?"

"Tristan and Michael Pendragon do, yes. I haven't had a chance to look at it myself, but Michael said that it definitely was sustaining some sort of spell."

"And they still have the key to the Subraek?"

"Yes. They are heading for the entrance at Crater Lake to try to free her."

Councilman Trewson leapt to his feet. "But there is no entrance to the Subraek at Crater Lake." It sounded more like a plea than a statement.

Annelise turned to him. He did not look well. He was gripping the edge of a desk as though it were the only thing keeping him from falling over.

"I assure you, there is an entrance on Wizard Island. I have been through it myself."

Councilman Trewson sank into his chair, looking as though he might pass out.

"Are you well, councilman?" Detective Poe asked.

Councilman Trewson nodded weakly. "Yes, yes. It's all just... so shocking." Councilman Trewson wasn't a very good liar, but they didn't have time to figure out what was eating at him right now.

Councilman Jackson turned to Detective Poe. "Do you believe Miss Windstarter? About the investigation and her theories? Do you think it holds up?" His voice was gravelly.

"I do. I have spent a lot of time in the last week poring over the Pendragons' notes as they looked into the Dragon case, and the evidence that she might be down there is compelling. But there is one clear way to prove their theory true once and for all."

"How?"

Detective Poe put her hands on her hips. "We do what no official has done in over a hundred years, and go take a look. Council Members have the authority to open the Subraek. If there is even a chance that the story is true, it warrants investigation." The council members exchanged a look but said nothing. Councilman Trewson was nodding and wiped a shaky hand across his brow.

Just then, Director Desmedt's phone rang. He picked it up and exchanged a few staccato words with the speaker on the other side. He hung up.

"Michael and Tristan Pendragon have been found," he announced.

Annelise stared at him, her heart thudding in her throat. "Are they okay?" she croaked.

The director nodded at her. "They are being brought in."

Annelise sagged against Healer Evan in relief. Her vision blurred with tears as the knot of tension in her stomach eased just a bit.

"I suggest we go meet them." Director Desmedt started walking towards the doors. "I want to prevent any shenanigans if even half of what Miss Windstarter said is true."

They made their way back down the elevators to the ground floor. A long lobby lined with windows formed the official enterance to the magical law enforcement headquarters building. A help desk stood against the back wall. The windows were all black, only reflecting the golden lights from inside the building as the sun outside had long since set. They reached the ground floor just as the wardens were portalling in via the transit pad. The transporter pad flashed a bright blue, and then the light faded to reveal Michael, Tristan, and Manny all cuffed and surrounded by guards.

Tristan sported a gash on the right side of his forehead that was dripping blood down his face. Michael looked dejected and was cradling a broken arm as best he could in his cuffs, but they were alive. Manny had a split lip, but seemed more concerned with the welfare of his friends than himself. Annelise made to move toward them but was held back by Officer Haled.

Detective Poe stepped forward. "Tristan Pendragon, we meet again."

"Detective," Tristan said in a businesslike manner, as though he wasn't in magic-suppressing cuffs.

"Michael." She gave him a curt nod. He responded with a cheeky smile that didn't reach his eyes and a little bow.

"And you are?" She turned to Manny.

"Manley Sutton, ma'am." He gave an elegant bow of his head.

"Ah, yes. You're Tristan Pendragon's employee."

"Indeed. I'm his butler, ma'am."

Detective Poe tried to suppress a smile. "Indeed."

"Michael," Annelise said, trying to convey all her regret in the two syllables. She felt it was her fault they were caught—her fault they were injured. Michael glanced at her briefly, but anything they might have said was interrupted when Detective Poe spoke again.

"Did we find the key and the ruby?" She addressed the wardens.

One of the wardens stepped forward. "Yes, detective. But the Councilman's private security insisted on holding on to them." He nodded in the direction of one of the guards.

Detective Poe stepped forward almost cheerfully, holding out two tamper-proof evidence bags. "Thank you for holding on to them, but as they are part of an ongoing investigation, I need you to turn them over to evidence."

The guard looked at her, a sceptical look on his face. "Councilman Cawthorne wanted them turned over to him alone. He was concerned about them falling into unsafe hands. And judging by these two wardens, he wasn't wrong to be concerned."

"Quite right," said Detective Poe. "But you can trust me. I am acting on behalf of the Director of Magical Law Enforcement and several council members."

The guard still hesitated.

"Come on, man, just give her the evidence." Councilman Jackson snapped.

With a curt nod, the guard handed the items over to the detective. The precinct doors blew open, and Councilman Cawthorne, Professor Finchley, and the sharp, green-eyed councilman from her trial strode through the precinct doors.

"I see you brought the terrorists in." The green-eyed councilman gave Tristan and Michael a dirty look as he approached.

"Yes, sir," one of the council guards said. "We found them just where Miss Windstarter said they would be."

Shame washed over Annelise, and she stared at the ground, tears blurring her vision. What must they think of her?

"Well done." Cawthorne turned to Detective Poe. "Thank you for recovering my stolen property." He reached for the evidence bag.

Detective Poe pulled the bag back out of his reach. "I'm afraid I cannot turn this over just yet, Councilman. It is part of an ongoing investigation. When we have finished, you will have it back."

"What ongoing investigation?" The green-eyed councilman asked, narrowing his eyes at her. "You have the culprits right here. You have Miss Windstarter's confession." He pointed at Annelise. "You have more than enough evidence to lock them all away forever."

Annelise didn't dare look to see the betrayal on Michael and Tristan's faces. She knew she had a lot to explain to them.

"Councilman Verdre is right." Professor Finchley said. "You have an airtight case against these three, even without the ruby. Let the Councilman have his property back."

"Perhaps," said the detective. "But there is a cold case that has not yet been solved. And I believe that these artifacts may in fact play a vital role in resolving it."

The green-eyed councilman stepped forward. "What cold case?"

"The missing Dragon," Councilman Jackson said. "Apparently, she's been locked away in the Subraek this whole time. We were on our way to see for ourselves if the stories they've been telling are true. Why don't you join us?"

"You don't have the authority to open the Subraek," Professor Finchley said.

"But I do." Councilman Cawthorne's tone was cold as ice. "I very much want to see."

Annelise looked at him, stunned. Had those words truly come out of his mouth? Had they been wrong all along? She glanced at Detective Poe, who flashed her a look of concern but revealed no more of her thoughts at this unexpected turn of events. Tristan and Michael were staring at their uncle too hard to pay any attention to her.

"Is it safe?" Councilman Verdre's brow was drawn in concern.

Director Desmedt gestured at the assembled wardens, private security guards, and councilmen. "I believe there are enough of us to mitigate most dangers. And we can keep it short. In this case, the reward is worth a little risk."

"Lead the way." Councilman Cawthorne motioned to the transport pad. "Mr. Finchley, why don't you join us?" The professor looked like he might object, but the councilman cut him off with a smooth "I insist." He nodded at a couple of the wardens, who fell into line next to the professor, ensuring that he joined them.

Annelise was led to the transporter pad. Bright golden heatless flames danced on the ground, forming various runes in a circle. It was beautiful. There were too many of them to transport all at once, so they went in groups. Annelise stepped into the circle with Lieutenant Haled, Director Desmedt, Manny, Councilman Trewson, and Councilman Verdre. Councilman Verdre placed his staff in the center, his green eyes glittering in the golden firelight. The flames around them burst with a dazzling light. There was a flash of heat, and then they were in a different room. The flames were once again small dancing lights glittering over their feet.

They appeared in a room with austere halls and a vaulted ceiling. The walls looked like they were all made of pale marble, and glowing orbs of magical lamps gave off light everywhere, twinkling like fairies. This felt like the government building.

They took an elevator down several floors and came to a room large enough to fit her entire house several times over inside it. One of the walls was made out of stone. Every inch of it was carved with Draconic runes laid out in concentric and intersecting circles. The opposite wall seemed to glow softly with yet unformed magic.

Annelise came to a stop just next to Michael. Tristan was on his other side.

"You okay?" she whispered. Her heart clenched as Michael winced when his arm was jostled. It was because of her that they were captured and injured. "Mostly. I lost my staff."

Guilt swirled within her. That, too, was her fault. "I'm sorry." She choked back a sob.

He looked at her, his expression questioning, but they didn't get to exchange more words.

"What you are looking at is the only manipulatable portal into the Subraek." Councilman Jackson's gravelly voice cut through their conversation. His years as an orator were evident as he explained the magical marvel before them. "We can open the portal anywhere we need to. So, where exactly are we to find this blood ward and dragon?" he asked. "If the three of you can prove that you have been telling the truth, you might just avoid the charge of terrorism."

Tristan and Michael shared a look, and Tristan gave the coordinates for both the cave to the dragon and their best approximation of the ward's border.

Councilmen Cawthorne, Jackson, and Trewson worked together to input the coordinates for the cave on the great stone wall of concentric and overlapping circles. They tapped various runes carved into the stone, which lit up with a pale blue light. Annelise grabbed Michael's good arm. His hands were cuffed, but he squeezed her hand against his side under his upper arm, giving her a reassuring glance.

With a turn of the key, the stone wall glowed a familiar blue and then faded. Nothing happened. It seemed they could not connect to a location within the blood ward.

They tried again, this time putting in the coordinates that led to the edge of the blood ward. Once again, the stone wall glowed a brilliant blue. Annelise squinted as the wall of unformed magic on the other side of the hall blazed with light, before melting away, revealing trees and a too-sharp morning sun.

Instead of being transported into the Subraek, they had brought the Subraek to them. On the far end of the room, the stone floor ended, and the Subraek began.

And no birds sang in the Subraek.

Chapter 16: The Sacrifice

Detective Poe looked over to the captives. "Does this look right to you?" she asked.

"Yes," Michael replied. He made eye contact with Annelise. "This is where the blood ward starts." And where they had made their blood pact to each other.

Annelise bit her lip hard to force back a sob. What if he felt that she had betrayed him? She knew it was because of her that he was hurt. "I'm so sorry," she whispered, leaning into him, her eyes burning.

"Sorry for what?" came the soft reply.

"There is indeed a ward!" Detective Poe called out, drawing their attention. She was standing a few paces past the place where the chamber ended, and the Subraek began. She pressed a hand against the ward's invisible surface. It did not budge. She pulled the ruby out of her pocket and turned to Tristan and Michael.

"This is madness!" Professor Finchley shouted. "You don't know what is on the other side of that ward. You are trusting the word of three criminals and risking the release of the most dangerous creatures known to man onto an unsuspecting population." He turned on the councilmembers. "You should all lose your seats on the council for this foolishness."

He looked back at the wardens. "Are there none among you who are willing to stand up to these members of government who have clearly lost their senses? Put an end to this madness! Will you not risk your position to uphold the oaths you swore, oaths to defend and protect the people?"

Some of the wardens hesitated. Annelise did not blame them for their uncertainty. At this moment, even she wasn't sure who was trustworthy and who was false.

Detective Poe considered his words. "Their tale has proven accurate so far. I am willing to believe them just a little farther," She turned to Tristan. "Can you break the ward?"

"If that ruby is what sustains it, yes," he said.

She motioned him forward.

"Stop!" Professor Finchley extracted his staff and leveled it at Tristan. Tristan stopped in his tracks. "I will not let you set a monster loose on the world, because you were too blind to see the truth."

Some of the wardens nodded at his words and drew staves as well, drawing back to flank Professor Finchley. The guard holding onto Michael drew back to fall in line as well, dragging Michael with him.

"It's not worth the risk," one of the wardens said. "I want the Dragon back as much as the next, but we don't know what is locked behind that ward. If we're wrong, we would be complicit in all the deaths that follow, and it will destroy our relationship with the sourceless. I cannot stand by and let this happen. Professor Finchley has been a faithful mentor and teacher for years. I see no reason to cast aside his wisdom now."

Haled, Desmedt, Poe, and the warden who had been holding Tristan each extracted their staves as well, holding them at the ready.

The council members drew back, ready to put up shields, but Councilman Cawthorne stepped forward, addressing the wardens who had sided with Professor Finchley.

"I understand your concerns, and I sympathize with your loyalty. Professor Finchley was once my professor, too. But you should also know that it was Professor Finchley who gifted me with that ruby many years ago when my bill for the integration passed. If the Dragon is in there, he has every reason to want to keep that fact hidden, and he's using you to do it."

Annelise's mind spun with this new information. The ruby was given to him by Finchley? Could it be that he had not known what it was? She glanced over at Tristan and Michael. Tristan's jaw was hanging open, and his brow was drawn in confusion. Michael was squinting at Councilman Cawthorne as though he was trying to piece together this new information.

"With all due respect, Councilman, I still don't think it's worth the risk. The Dragon isn't here, and we cannot risk keeping this portal open any longer," the warden said.

"And if the Dragon is in there, we cannot risk letting the opportunity to set her free pass us by," Tristan exclaimed, his voice laced with desperation.

Lieutenant Haled pushed Annelise back toward the safety of the council members. Neither side seemed willing to back down. Annelise felt a stab of sympathy for the wardens who had sided with Finchley. If only the Dragon would show herself...

There was a moment of tension as they waited to see who would strike first. Finchley sent a bolt of magic flying at Poe, and the room erupted in battle.

Annelise hit the deck as the first spells went flying. Tristan, too, had to duck for cover. Michael was trying to squirm from his guard's grip, but the guard held him tight and used him as a human shield. Michael threw his head back, striking his guard in the face with his hard head. The guard was momentarily stunned. Seeing an opening, Tristan tackled the guard to the ground. The guard, not expecting this attack, toppled with a heavy thud, and the two Pendragons were locked in a grappling contest with the guard.

Annelise started crawling for the protection of the trees in the Subraek. She yelped and covered her head as a stray spell struck near where she was lying, sending broken bits of stone flooring skittering her way. Another spell struck mere inches from where she lay, pressed into the ground. When it happened a third time, she searched for the source.

Finchley, in the midst of his battle with Detective Poe, shot venomous glances in her direction, often followed by targeted spells. He was a master spellcaster, and even the adept and powerful detective Poe struggled to hold her own against the older mage.

Annelise pushed herself off the floor and sprinted for the cover of the trees. She ducked behind one trunk just as the ground behind her erupted with a crack and a burst of heat as Finchley leveled another spell at her.

From the relative safety of the trees, Annelise peeked around the trunk to see what was happening. She saw Director Desmedt take one of Finchley's wardens out with a sharp spell that splintered his shield and staff. Haled took a stray spell to the shoulder and crumpled to the ground, his face white as a sheet.

Councilman Cawthorne looked like he was trying to make his way over to his nephews, but a warden blocked his way. He was hopelessly outmatched against the trained battlecaster and was not making any headway.

Councilmen Jackson and Trewson had taken shelter to one side of the room, casting shield spells to protect them, while councilman Sayer fired the occasional spell over the top of the shield at any of the guards he felt he could safely hit.

Councilman Verdre was cut off from the rest of the council members. He was keeping Manny close by, ensuring that no stray spells struck the sourceless butler.

Detective Poe was fighting Finchley with her signature crisp, ferocious style. But that wasn't what drew Annelise's eyes. What drew her eyes was the forgotten ruby lying in the evidence bag on the floor, not far from her. She looked back at the battle and saw that Finchley's eyes were burning into her.

He sent several spells her way, and she ducked back behind the tree. Wood splintered around her, sending dust and shrapnel flying. She had to get that ruby and destroy it!

Identifying a new shelter closer to her objective, Annelise threw herself out from behind the trunk and booked it to the next copse of trees. Spells impacted around her. Her limbs felt like jelly as she ran, and her mouth was dry with fear, but she was strengthened momentarily with adrenaline.

She nearly collapsed behind the trees and took a moment to regain her breath. She looked around the edge of her shelter. One more mad dash, and she could have the ruby.

She ducked out from behind the trees and sprinted with all her strength. She glanced to her right in the direction of the battle and saw a spell hurtling right towards her. The spell was burning through the air, shooting off sparks and embers as it went. The air around it vibrated with the heat and low rumble of a blasting spell.

It crackled with magic in a way that made Annelise's hair stand on end. She allowed her shaking legs to buckle beneath her and slid on her knees underneath the smoldering spell, close enough to smell the burning metallic scent as it whizzed mere inches above her face and exploded against a tree to her left, disintegrating it in a shower of leaves and mulch.

Her momentum carried her within reaching distance of the ruby. She grabbed it and scrambled back to the safety of the trees, this time on the other side of the barrier.

The sounds of the battle behind her intensified. Her heart chilled when she heard Tristan shouting Michael's name. With shaking hands, she ripped the evidence bag open. The ruby went flying some feet away, and Annelise dove to the ground for it, grasping it in her hand.

The room went silent. "If you destroy that jewel, Michael dies," Finchley called across the room at her.

Annelise looked up. Finchley was holding Michael by his black curly hair, forcing his head back, and exposing his throat to the knife he held in his other hand. The arm that Michael had been cradling before now looked badly deformed, as though it had been rebroken.

Annelise stilled. Then, the ruby still clutched in her right hand, she tucked a stone lying on the ground into her left hand.

Finchley saw the slight movement and pressed the knife tighter against Michael's throat. "Do not doubt my resolve, Miss Windstarter. I would do anything to protect this world from the horrors in the Subraek. Even take the life of one of my favorite students."

Annelise's eyes locked with Michael's. His were resolved and unafraid, but Annelise was terrified.

"Do it, Annelise," Michael shouted, but was silenced by Finchley with a sharp blow to his ribs that turned the end of his call into a cry of pain.

Annelise's hands shook. She didn't know what to do. The more she looked at Michael, the more she realized that she couldn't stand the thought of Finchley hurting him. Annelise had kept people out for so long; now she remembered the pain that friendship threatened. Inasmuch as Finchley held her friend under his knife, he held her heart. The harder he pressed his knife to Michael's throat, the more he crushed her hope. She couldn't do this on her own. Not anymore.

"Don't force me to hurt him." Finchley let go of Michael's hair and grabbed his broken arm, twisting the palm up towards him. Michael screamed in pain, but Finchley simply scoffed at what he saw there. He dropped the palm in disgust.

"After all, you are bound by a word pact to each other," Finchley said. "You wouldn't bring harm to Michael, would you? You wouldn't betray him that way. Not again."

Annelise recoiled, almost dropping her stone. She could not betray Michael. But what would be the bigger betrayal? Following his wishes, even though he might die, or denying his wishes in the hopes that he might live.

Desperately, she looked around for any source of help. Tristan was on the ground, pinned by the guard he had tackled earlier and the one whose staff had been destroyed. His face was desperate, tears streamed down his face, but he couldn't move.

Manny was crouched on the ground, his eyes locked on Tristan. He took advantage of the distraction to move closer to where Tristan was being held, undetected.

Annelise's eyes flicked across the battlefield until they met Detective Poe's. Her gray eyes were calm and resolute. Annelise latched onto that confidence. The detective's eyes flicked down to the ruby in her hand and then back up to Annelise's. She then gave a slight, imperceptible nod.

Annelise stared at her, her heart beating in her chest. She knew Detective Poe would not let Finchley kill Michael without a fight. The only question was whether it would be enough. As she stared into the detective's eyes, Annelise realized that she had no choice but to depend on Detective Poe to save Michael.

Her stomach lurched, and her hands became clammy as she tightened her grip on the rock and the ruby. She looked at Michael one last time. He was cradling his broken arm with his good one. His beautiful eyes were awash with pain, but despite the knife still at his throat, they held strength and resolve. They urged her onward. She could not fail him. She would not fail him.

She looked away, dropping her eyes to the ruby. She lifted the rock and brought it crashing down on the gem. The ruby shattered into tiny shards. The entire ward rippled with blood-red light, crackling as it became fragile as glass. The din of battle resumed, and Annelise looked up, searching desperately for Michael, half afraid of what she might find.

He was scooting away from the battle on his back, cradling his abused arm against his chest, his face ashen. Finchley was locked in a fierce physical battle with Detective Poe, knife versus staff. Poe's superior training and greater reach soon overpowered him. With a swift strike of her staff, she knocked the knife from his hand and sent it clattering across the stone floor and then through the trees of the Subraek.

It fell at Annelise's feet. She looked down at the blade, and then up again at the battle raging.

Desmedt was fighting one of Finchley's guards, who was using surprisingly brutal spells. Haled was still unconscious on the ground, and the last warden was clutching his side and had taken shelter with the council members, who had put up shields to protect them from stray fire. One of Finchley's guards was relentlessly battering their shields with spell after spell, ordering them to close the portal, and she could see the council members, unused to combat, shaking under the pressure.

Finchley and Poe were now locked in a fierce spell battle, with Poe standing between Finchley and Michael. Finchley was sending spells out wildly, taking no care as to where they went. His spells blazed with light and crackled as they went. Everywhere they landed, trees burst into splinters and stone shattered like glass. The air around his spells rippled with heat. Annelise had never seen spells loaded with such power from any mage before.

Tristan was on the far side of the room, struggling against one of the guards who had him pinned to the ground. Manny had apparently tackled the other guard and was locked in a grappling contest with him. He screamed as his arm was twisted into an unnatural position, and Annelise felt more than heard the sickening crunch as his shoulder was dislocated. Michael, too, was separated from her position and the wards by the errant spells hurled across the room by Finchley and his guards.

Her eyes flitted to where Haled still lay motionless on the floor.

She needed to end this now before someone else got hurt...or killed. She looked around. There was nobody else close enough to do what had to be done. She remembered what Healer Evan had said, and she knew she wouldn't survive this spell, but there was no one else. She pressed her back against a tree, steadying herself. How ironic that after so many years of being angry at her mother for choosing to use magic despite knowing it was breaking her, she would meet her end in the same way? The same way, but for very different reasons. She only hoped that Michael and Tristan would forgive her someday.

She scooped up the knife from where it sat at her feet and ran to where the ward was still flickering and crackling.

She pulled the knife through her closed hand, not feeling how deep it cut this time. It didn't matter anyway. She heard Michael screaming her name. The pain in his voice hurt more than the pain in her hand. She forced herself to ignore it.

She threw herself towards the ward, but something slammed into her from the side, sending her sprawling before she reached it.

She scrambled to her feet, ready to fight whatever had run into her, and found herself once again face to face with the Dragon.

The Dragon said nothing but just gazed at her with her burning golden eyes. Behind her, the sounds of battle diminished. Only Finchley fought now.

Councilman Trewson was shouting at Finchley, tears pouring down his face. Annelise could not understand what he was saying.

In a smooth motion, the Dragon drew one sharp talon across her own claw. Rich golden blood welled up from the wound, and she pressed it against the ward. With a single word, it shattered like glass and, like glass, came crashing down around them. Annelise pressed herself against a tree and covered her head, wincing as stray pieces struck her hands and her head.

By the time the sound of falling glass quieted, the sounds of battle had also stopped. Annelise peered around the tree. Finchley was subdued. Desmedt was pinning him to the ground and wrestling cuffs onto his wrists. The other guards had seemingly stopped fighting when they saw that there was indeed a dragon and not some monster.

Detective Poe approached Annelise and touched her elbow. Anneliese started, her eyes snapping to the detective's.

"Come on." Detective Poe tugged on Annelise's arm. "Let's go. It's not safe to leave the portal open for too long."

Annelise let herself be drawn across the threshold of the portal. Her whole body trembled, and her hand bled profusely through her clenched fist. Her other hand still held the knife.

With a sweep of her wings, the Dragon soared across the threshold between the Chamber and the Subraek. The room shuddered as she landed with a thud. Once everyone was safely across the threshold, the key was withdrawn. Blue light gleamed, and the trees of the Subraek disappeared once again behind the wall of unformed magic.

Annelise stumbled over to where Michael was lying, propped up by Tristan, and collapsed to the ground.

"Are you okay?" she asked, her eyes raking over Michael's pale face, his broken arm, the thin line on his throat where Finchley had applied too much pressure with his knife, and the various other scrapes, bruises, and singes he was sporting. He wouldn't look at her.

"I'll be okay," he said, his voice clipped. "You?"

Her strength was fading fast, and the stone floor was looking more and more like a soft feather bed. "I think I'll sleep for a week, and then probably be okay."

She closed her eyes and laid her head against the cool stone floor. His voice told her that he was angry with her about something. She had a million guesses as to what it might be. Maybe he blamed her for giving up their position to the council? For costing him his staff? She knew it wasn't her fault, but she still felt responsible. She wanted to work it out with him, but she did not have the energy to discuss it with him now.

"Tristan?"

"I'll recover." His tone was grim. He was... disappointed?

Annelise's brow furrowed above her closed eyes. This was their moment of triumph. Somehow, it didn't feel much like one.

But the Dragon was free at last. Speaking of...

A fierce snarl echoed through the hall, and Annelise pried her eyes open once again.

The Dragon had her eyes fixed on Finchley, a grinding growl emanating from her throat, as the fire in her belly flared. Annelise could feel the temperature in the whole room rise from where she was lying on the cold ground.

Detective Poe stepped between the Dragon and Finchley, holding her hands out in a placating gesture.

"Your Mightiness," she said, "I understand that you are angry and want justice. We *will* bring to justice any who were involved in your imprisonment, and you will have a hand in it. But please, if you shed his blood here, your story will be overshadowed with confusion and revenge. Let us try him in front of the courts and the people, and you will have justice. Will you trust us with that?"

The Dragon flicked her eyes over to where Finchley stood, his face defiant and haughty. The growling increased, and she opened her mouth and roared, her hot breath rippling the air around him. His face paled, and fear finally flashed through his eyes, but she did not release her fire on him.

"Very well," she said. "I suppose it will be fitting for him to languish in a cage for years to come, with nothing but rats to feast on." She turned to the detective. "I will let you hold your trial. But know that I will have justice, one way or another."

Detective Poe bowed deeply. After all, who can truly argue with a dragon?

Councilman Trewson stepped forward, falling to his knees, tears streaming down his face. "I beg your forgiveness, your Thunderousness. Years ago, Finchley coerced me into giving him access to the Subraek key. He said it was for research. When you vanished, it never occurred to me he might be behind it. I believed all the entrances were secured. Only today did I realize my grave error. I am so sorry." Through his confession, his eyes never left the floor.

The Dragon snarled at his words, and fire sparked in her belly. She took in a great breath, and Annelise's eyes widened. Detective Poe, likewise, was alarmed and stepped in front of the Councilman and threw up a shield spell. The Dragon unleashed a mighty roar. It thundered around the chamber, but it held no fire. Councilman Trewson looked ready to faint.

"Leave my sight," the Dragon spat. Councilman Trewson scurried out of the room, his knees knocking together as he went.

The Dragon turned to where the two Pendragons and Annelise were huddled together. Her golden eyes gleamed. "I misjudged you." Some of her ire still rang through her voice. "You have my thanks."

The three of them nodded, too exhausted and battered to do anything more.

The Dragon's massive head hovered mere feet above them. "My gift to you." She opened her maw blew her hot breath over the three of them.

Annelise's brow crinkled in confusion.

Tristan hesitated, then put his hand over his heart. "Um… Thank you." He managed to look sincere. Michael looked ready to faint. Annelise wasn't sure if he had even registered what was happening.

None of them understood what kind of gift that was, but none of them were willing to offend the Dragon. That warm breath could quickly become a burning inferno.

Annelise was just wondering how on earth they were going to get the Dragon into the elevator and out the front doors when the Dragon started drawing a great circle sealed with a rune on the stone floor with her tail.

"You're leaving?" Annelise asked.

"For now," the Dragon said. "I refuse to be closed in a moment more. But don't worry, I'll be back. I'm going to testify for a long time against that vermin." She snapped her jaws in Finchley's direction. In a flash of golden light, the Dragon was gone, and the room felt hollow.

Annelise stared at the spot where the Dragon had disappeared. "I'm so confused."

The Dragon was free, and it was Finchley who had done it. He had separated himself from the jewel by giving it to Councilman Cawthorne and gained access to the Subraek by coercing and lying to Councilman Trewson. He had gotten away with it for years because nobody knew about the Wizard Island entrance.

The question was: Why had he done it in the first place?

Chapter 17: The Consequence

Once the Dragon had left, Director Desmet led Finchley away. Finchley's eyes burned into Annelise as he was led past her.

"You're pathetic, Annelise," he spat. "As long as that Dragon is around, you'll always be a second-class citizen; cast aside for a better option. Better you had left her where you found her."

Annelise stared back at him, too exhausted to feel one way or another about it all. The adrenaline was draining from her system, and her insides felt like they were turning into jello.

She laid her head against the cool stone ground once again, letting it soothe her pounding head. Detective Poe sent Councilman Sayer out to fetch medical help while she and the other warden took the staves from the guards who had stood by Finchley. They gave them up peaceably. There would be a lot of inquiries and further investigations before they could return to work.

Detective Poe knelt by Haled's side. He was still unconscious and pale, but she breathed a sigh of relief when she checked his pulse. He was still alive.

Councilman Cawthorne was kneeling by Manny, who was clutching his dislocated shoulder.

"Manny," Tristan called to him.

Manny looked over. "Yes, Tristan?" his voice was strained with pain.

"You're getting a raise."

Manny simply nodded, a weak smile tugging at the corners of his mouth despite his pain. "Quite right, sir."

Several minutes later, a small army of healers streamed through the elevator doors. Evan was among them. He made a beeline for Annelise, while others tended to Haled, Tristan, Michael, and Manny.

Councilman Cawthorne, seeing that Manny was well looked after, stood up and made his way to his nephews.

Tristan looked up at him. "I'm sorry that I thought the worst of you. I never wanted to believe it. I'm glad it wasn't you in the end."

Councilman Cawthorne put a hand on Tristan's shoulder and knelt next to him. He placed his other hand over his chest, right in the spot where his ruby used to hang. "I'm here for you, and I always will be."

Evan started running a field scan on Annelise, little dots of magical light floating above her. The world and the lights seemed to spin around Annelise. She looked up at Evan's face, which was poorly concealing his displeasure. "Is it safe to pass out now?" she asked, feeling dazed.

Evan's expression softened a bit. "Yeah." he grasped her hand. "You're safe."

✳✳✳

Annelise found herself lying on a crisp white bed, surrounded by pale curtains. She was once again connected to a beeping monitor. Her hand, which she last remembered had been bleeding profusely, was completely healed. As she sat up, her wrist jangled. She looked down. She was cuffed to the bed. It was not a magical cuff, but a regular sourceless cuff.

The curtain swung aside, and Evan appeared. "This time, you're not going anywhere," he said smugly, his brown eyes glittering in satisfaction as he pushed her back into a lying position. "You're going to stay here and rest until I'm content that you're well enough to be up and about."

Annelise smiled faintly. "Great," she snarked. "My prison sentence has already begun."

"Your prison sentence will seem like freedom compared to the next couple of weeks, Missy." He raised a dark eyebrow at her. His warm brown eyes brooked no argument.

"How are Michael and Tristan?" she asked.

"They are recovering as well. Tristan is about ready to be released into the warden's custody, and Michael's arm is healing nicely. He should be out by the end of the week."

"I need to talk to them."

"I'm afraid I cannot allow that," Evan said.

"Please. It's important,"

Evan crossed his arms. "What is so important that you need to discuss with your co-conspirators?"

Annelise tried to sit up again, but was stopped by a firm hand from Evan. "I need to apologize to them. I didn't get the chance earlier. I need to heal our relationship. Surely you can understand?"

Evan eyed her critically for a moment. "I do not have the authority to let you speak to them," he said finally. "But I will bring it up with the people who do."

Annelise nodded. "Thank you."

Two days later, Detective Poe entered her tiny white beeping prison. Annelise bolted up in her hospital bed.

"I hear you want to speak with the Pendragons."

"Yes, please."

Detective Poe regarded her for a moment and then nodded crisply. "Very well. But you will be monitored the entire time. If I even think you're planning more shenanigans... You will regret it."

Annelise nodded emphatically. "Of course. Thank you. How is your deputy, by the way?" she asked. "Haled, was it?"

The detective's expression softened. "He is healing. It will take time, but he will recover. Thank you for asking."

Shortly after, Annelise was led to a small lounge with two guards at the door. The far side of the lounge had three large windows. On the right side of the room was a small kitchenette. Chairs were clustered throughout the room in groups of three or four. Tristan and Michael sat in chairs, already speaking as Annelise entered. Their magic was bound with cuffs, but the cuffs were unlinked, allowing them the use of their hands for the moment. They looked much better than the last time Annelise had seen them. They stood up as she entered the room.

Annelise hurried forward and threw her arms around both of them.

"I'm sorry." The words tumbled out of her mouth as a wave of remorse and affection washed over her. "I'm so sorry."

Michael stilled and pulled back from the hug. "What exactly are you sorry about?" he asked, his face a veneer of calm.

Annelise bit down on her lip to distract herself from the knot in her throat. "I told the council everything. But you have to believe me, I didn't mean to do it. Professor Finchley—he drugged me with a truth serum. I almost got you killed."

Michael took her face in his hands and looked her square in the eyes. "We're not mad at you for telling the council."

"None of us predicted that Finchley was dirty, or I would have never suggested you go to him." Tristan clenched his jaw. "I'm sorry I did. It's not your fault."

She looked down. "But now you've been caught, same as me," she looked at Michael, "and you lost your staff... I was hoping to save you from going to jail, but—"

"Just be aware that I am listening," Detective Poe's voice rang out from across the room. She was perched on the kitchenette counter, her back leaning against the window side wall. Her left leg was propped up on the counter, while her right leg dangled off the edge, swinging lightly. Annelise had almost forgotten she was there. "If you plan to incriminate yourself at all, just do it knowingly." A small smile pulled at her mouth.

"Thank you," Annelise said a bit awkwardly. "I would have thought you would jump at the chance to get more evidence."

"Nah…I like you guys. I'm rooting for you." Detective Poe swung her dangling leg lazily. She looked relaxed as a cat on a windowsill. "But I will not hesitate to bring any crimes I do hear and record," she waved a small recorder at them, "before the courts."

Tristan nodded curtly at her. "Thanks."

Annelise looked up at Michael. "So… you're not angry with me?"

Michael released a shaky breath. "Annelise." he stared at the wall behind her. "I'm very angry with you." His voice trembled with emotion as he spoke.

Annelise's stomach dropped. "Look. I'm sorry I put you in danger. If there was anything I could have done to avoid it, I would have—" she broke off when Michael gave a sharp, harsh laugh.

Tristan shook his head ruefully at Michael. "I told you she wouldn't have a clue."

Annelise stepped back, clenching her fists, her remorse turning to irritation. "Okay…" Now she felt frustrated and hurt. "Why, exactly, are you angry with me, then? If I'm so clueless?"

Michael fixed his golden eyes on her, burning with the full anger he was feeling. "I'm angry at you because you were going to lower the blood wards yourself. It would have killed you. I'm angry because you almost killed yourself."

Annelise gaped. "But the Dragon— "

"The Dragon saved your life!" His voice was barely under control.

Now Annelise was angry. "I'm sorry… what? No! You don't get to be angry at me for being willing to die for this cause, when moments before you begged me to destroy the ruby even though you had a knife to your throat!"

She gave his shoulder a shove. "Did you ever think about that? What *that* put me through? If not for Detective Poe here, *you* would be dead. And what's worse, it would have been *my* fault! I would bear the responsibility of that for the rest of my life. So what makes you so special that you get to be angry at me when you did the exact same thing to me?" She stepped close to him, every inch of her shaking with ire.

"I just am," Michael snapped, not backing down or away. They were almost nose to nose.

"Why?" Annelise asked, raising her voice.

"Because!" he shouted.

"Because what?!" Annelise shouted back, just about ready to punch him in his pretty face.

"Because you're my friend, damn it!"

Annelise's jaw dropped, her breath catching. He said it like it was the easiest thing in the world. She supposed she should be happy, but she was still too angry at the moment.

"And did you ever consider for a moment," she seethed, her voice shaking. "That you're my friend too? I destroyed that ruby because you asked me to. Because I respect you. Because I trust you," she held up her oath-scarred hand. "Because I swore loyalty to you. And all the while, I was convinced that I was killing you. Do you have any idea how hard that was?" Her voice broke off into barely more than a whisper. Tears welled up in her eyes as the grief, fear, and despair from that moment echoed back to her.

Michael's face softened from anger to compassion and remorse. He reached out and drew her into a hug again.

Annelise did not return the hug.

"I'm sorry." His voice hitched. "I was only thinking of my own pain."

Annelise sniffed, blinking back tears as she nodded into his shoulder. The tension and anger slowly drained from her as well. She wrapped her arms around him.

"I'm sorry too. I didn't want to cause you grief. I just didn't see any other option."

Michael held her tight. "I understand," he pulled away from the hug. "And I forgive you."

"What about me?" Tristan asked, his tone light. "Do I get an apology?"

Annelise smiled a watery smile and turned to give him a hug, too. "I'm sorry if I scared you. I know you felt the burden of responsibility for our safety on this job. I know I didn't make things easy for you."

Tristan wrapped his arms around her. "I forgive you. How about we make a new agreement?" He pulled away. "No more trying to die, for either of you."

Annelise let out an involuntary, harsh laugh. She smiled, her eyes watery. "Sure. I'll agree to that." She wiped her eyes. "Thank you."

Tristan cocked his head. "For what?"

Annelise blinked rapidly. "For everything. For forcing me to realize that I didn't have to do everything on my own. I don't think I would have figured it out without you."

Michael wrapped her in another hug. "You've taught me something too, you know." He did not let go of her. "I thought I had to make a mark on the world for my life to matter, but I've seen you grow and change along our adventure. To have made some small contribution towards that growth... that is as meaningful a mark as any grand gesture."

Annelise laughed and pulled back from the hug. "You could start a camp for cons. You blackmail them into joining, and take them on the craziest crime spree of their life, so that in the end they learn the true meaning of friendship."

Michael waved her idea away. "Nah. Not just anyone is worthy of our adventures. You, Annelise Windstarter, are singular." He glanced over to where Detective Poe was sitting. "And maybe less talk about crime sprees while we're being recorded," he whispered, a smile pulling at the corners of his mouth.

Annelise ducked her head and giggled. "Ooops."

"I'm proud of us." Tristan sank into one of the chairs. "We actually brought the Dragon home. Most people had given up hope of it ever happening. Whatever happens from here on out, they can't take that away from us."

They sat in companionable silence. Annelise did feel proud of what they had accomplished. It was the first time in a long time that she had felt true, untarnished pride. She grinned. As much as she had resisted it at the start, she was beyond grateful for the Pendragons coming into her life.

"So," Annelise said. "Have you figured out how you were able to get through the wards? I didn't realize you were related to Finchley."

Tristan chuckled. "We didn't either, but we've done some digging, and we think we have figured it out."

"Do you remember that portrait of our great-grandmother?" Michael asked.

"Yes, you said her name was Dee?"

"Well, her full name is Chickadee Finchley."

Annelise raised her eyebrows.

"I know," Tristan said. "Her father really leaned into the bird motif. Anyway, apparently, Professor Robin Finchley is her half-brother from an affair that her father, our great-great-grandfather, had in his youth before he married into the Pendragon family. Finchley is, apparently, our great-great-half-uncle."

"So that is how you managed to get through the wards."

"Yup. It's a wild world."

Tristan turned to Detective Poe. "Here's what I want to know."

The detective turned to him, her head cocked in curiosity.

"Who told the Council about our plan to steal the key? We thought we had kept that top secret."

Detective Poe's expression darkened. "Professor Finchley. He must have pieced together enough of your investigation to suspect that you might try."

"But we only consulted him on the art forgeries."

"You forget that he knows just about everybody. We got nothing out of him, but in talking to everyone who passed him information, we discovered that he got word about you making inquiries into the Subraek as a possible location for the Dragon. After your official channels were shut down, he must have figured you might try to go rogue, so he alerted the Council to the danger. The rest, you know."

"Yup," Annelise said with more cheer than she felt. "We got to meet you." She looked down at her empty hands and frowned. "And then you broke my staff, and I had one of the worst days of my life." It had been a couple of weeks since the detective had destroyed her staff, and still her hands felt bereft without it.

Detective Poe grimaced. "I can't say I'm sorry I did it, but I'm sorry it had to happen. I can't make any promises, but with everything that has happened, there is a good chance that you will be permitted to grow new staves when you get out of prison."

Annelise flopped into a chair. "If we get out of prison."

Detective Poe graciously gave them several more minutes before ordering everyone back to their rooms.

"Thank you, Detective," Annelise said as Detective Poe walked her back to her room.

"Call me Blaire," the detective said, smiling.

"Thank you, Blaire," Annelise corrected.

She settled herself back in her bed, and the familiar cuff clicked around her wrist. "Now, I have a question for you," Detective Blaire Poe said. She grabbed a backpack off the ground and pulled an evidence bag out of it. She tossed it to Annelise. "Did you have these made?" The evidence bag contained a new set of Identification Documents.

There was a state ID, a Passport, a birth certificate, and a stamp with a new magical sigil—for official magical document work.

The only problem was that they were terrible. There was no way that these would ever hold up to scrutiny. Ink was smudged in multiple places, and the colors in the passport were way off. The birth certificate looked like it had been printed on a regular home printer. And the sigil was obviously a Pendragon family sigil with some very minor tweaks. A child could have spotted these as forgeries.

Annelise gaped at the disasters on her lap. "Why that little..." she trailed off, not sure she could find a word quite insulting enough to fit. To think she had paid triple for this. He clearly had taken her money and intended to leave her hanging. All along, her backup plan of running away with her new identity had been an illusion. She looked up at Detective Poe, feeling vindictive. "Blaire, how would you like to know *exactly* who made these awful fake ID papers?"

Detective Poe smiled and pulled out a notepad. "I thought you'd never ask." Once she had all the information, she packed up her stuff. "Now I trust that you'll be good and rest?"

Annelise nodded, exhausted from the rollercoaster of emotions she had gone through. Soon after she laid down, she drifted off to sleep.

***

Michael and Tristan were released into warden custody the next day. Annelise was released a week later. She was assigned a lawyer and questioned about everything she knew. She didn't see any point in holding anything back. The fact that she had broken into the Subraek was irrefutable, and that alone carried a life sentence. She just wanted to ensure that the truth would shine through and that Finchley got his own fair share of justice, too.

Three days of questioning later, she didn't think there was anything about this case that she knew that they didn't. Her lawyer, Mr. Kent, was sitting next to her. The prosecuting attorney had requested an audience. The door swung open, and Detective Blaire Poe entered the room, joined by Councilmen Cawthorne and Jackson, as well as a dark-haired woman in a smart suit, whom she had never met before.

The woman stepped forward, placing a dark briefcase on the table. "Miss Windstarter, I'm Clarissa Jones. I'm the prosecuting attorney."

Annelise nodded at her. "Hello."

The attorney eyed her for a moment. "You and your comrades have been very forthcoming about your crimes." She pulled some papers out of her briefcase. "And considering the circumstances, and reasons behind your actions, and the positive outcome of those actions, the council and the state would like to offer you a plea deal."

Annelise gave a slow nod. "I'm listening." She refused to let herself hope for much.

"Testify against Finchley, and plead guilty to your crimes, saving the courts and the state a long and somewhat embarrassing trial, and we will give you two years."

Annelise's jaw dropped. "I'm sorry." She was sure she heard wrong. "Did you say two years?"

The attorney nodded.

"And by that, you mean two years? Not two hundred or two thousand?"

"Two years, Miss Windstarter."

Annelise looked at her lawyer in amazement. He was smiling at her, but turned to the attorney. "One year."

The attorney chuckled. "This is not a scarf we are haggling over, Mr. Kent. Two years is the minimum if she pleads guilty."

"I need a moment to confer with my client," Mr. Kent said.

Everyone but Annelise and her lawyer left the room.

"What do you think?" Annelise asked.

"I think you should take it. The chance of you getting convicted on even one of your counts is very high, and the penalty for any of your crimes would normally be more than two years. This is a good deal. Take it."

"Okay. Two years," she laughed. "You can tell them I'll take it."

He left the room to tell them her decision.

Blaire came back into the room when she heard the news, smiling. "I told you I was rooting for you."

"Hey, Blaire, did Michael and Tristan get deals as well?" she asked. "I'd feel guilty if I got off so lightly, and they didn't."

Blaire gave a light, frustrated smile. "They got deals too."

Annelise grew concerned. She frowned. "Was it a terrible deal? Are they in for like fifteen years, or —"

"One year."

"What?"

"The state offered them each one year," Blaire said, her disapproval leaking into her tone.

'Ah." Annelise processed the information. "Well, they are Pendragons. And they're wardens." The disparity was bitter on her tongue. "I suppose it was never going to be fair."

"No. Not fair at all," Blaire agreed. "To give them credit, they both individually refused to accept it until they knew that we were working on one for you as well."

Annelise swallowed. "Well, two years is still amazing. With any luck, it will go fast." She chuckled, a thought striking her,

"Technically, since Michael and I swore the blood pact, I'm entitled to the privileges of a Pendragon too. I just don't have the dragon eyes to prove it. You think we can convince them?"

Blaire grinned. "I doubt it, but you're welcome to try."

***

The day the Dragon came to testify against ex-Professor Finchley was an exciting day in court. Such a sight had not been seen in centuries. Reporters from the magical community and the sourceless community swarmed outside the courthouse to catch their shot of the Dragon.

She arrived by air, landing on the stone steps of the courthouse in a flurry of wind and with a great thud that shook the ground. Luckily, this courthouse was old. It had been specially chosen because the halls had been designed large enough to fit a dragon. There had been a day when a Dragon in court was not so unusual.

Her great form filled the courthouse, and her clear voice rang out, heard by all. Her testimony was moving as she described just how Finchley had lured her into the Subraek under false pretenses of recovering a precious dragon egg. Her wings twitched in agitation as she described how he had then used shameful methods of blood magic to cast the ward, trapping the Dragon at her own expense. Annelise burned with anger against her old professor as the Dragon described what happened to her in excruciating detail. What he had done was an affront to all magic.

A week later, ex-Professor Finchley was convicted on all charges and sentenced to life in prison. Annelise had already started her prison sentence, so when she was finished giving her own testimony, she was shuttled back to her small, barren prison cell.

***

"Windstarter, you have a visitor," Todd said, walking up to her cell door. He was a squat man with a round face and a goatee who managed this section of the prison.

Annelise stood up and approached the cell door. The magical restraints flew off their hook by the door and locked themselves around her wrists. The cell door clacked as the buzzer rang, signaling that it was unlocked.

"Do you know who it is?" Annelise asked, curiosity piquing.

"I didn't ask," Todd replied. Of course, he didn't. The man had about as much curiosity as a tree stump.

He led her down various hallways to the visitors' room. There, sitting at a table with a steaming pot of tea and two teacups, was Professor Hale. Annelise laughed a full-bellied laugh at the sight.

"Let it never be said that I don't keep my word," Professor Hale chuckled, holding a cup out to her. Annelise took the cup and settled into the seat across from him. The warm scent of black tea wafted up to meet her.

"So." Professor Hale leaned back in his chair. "What are your plans now?"

"My plans? For when? I'm pretty much booked for the next two years," she said with a wry grin.

Professor Hale chuckled. "I mean, for when you get out. I think it could be a great opportunity to turn over a new leaf. Perhaps get into a line of work less likely to end with you back in here."

Annelise thought about it.

"I'm not sure. Maybe I could try selling my art? My original art," she clarified. "But I know very little about marketing original art."

"Well, you've got two years to figure it out. I think that your best chance of success when you get out is to have a solid plan, and I'd like to help."

They spent the next twenty minutes brainstorming possible avenues. By the time Todd returned to collect her, Annelise had quite the homework assignment to complete, which involved research into several different career possibilities.

"Time to go, Windstarter," Todd said when Annelise tarried at the table. Annelise suppressed her disappointment and stood up while Professor Hale collected the tea things.

"Thank you for visiting."

"It's always a pleasure to see my favorite student. I'll see you again soon," he said. "And I expect that homework to be done when I do." He chuckled at his own joke and was shown through the doors that led out of the prison.

Annelise let herself be led back to her cell. As the door clanged shut behind her, the magical cuffs dropped off and hung themselves by the door, awaiting their next use. In their cells, Mages were permitted to have access to their magic, but not to the means of channeling it.

For Annelise, that mattered little. Her staff was gone, and she had only just received a clean bill of health from the healers. She reached out tentatively to connect with her magic. She half braced herself for blinding pain, but instead found it humming like normal, near her heart.

She smiled and stood up, pacing in her cell. She walked over to the small sink situated in the corner, looked at her reflection and smiled.

She was kind of happy.

It was hard to believe because everything she had ever been afraid of had come to pass, but she had survived. In just under two years, she would be free, and she had friends waiting for her when she got out.

As the joy flowed through her, Annelise's eyes flashed golden in the mirror. She jumped back, startled. *What was that?*

She searched her reflection again for any trace of what she had just experienced, but they were back to their ordinary blue.

Perhaps it had been a trick of the light, she mused, and went to lie down on her cot.

She did not know that Tristan had recently started coughing up fireballs, or that Michael's skin would sometimes turn tough and scaly before returning to normal.

But that is a story for another day.

The end...

If you enjoyed this book, please consider leaving a positive review wherever you bought it. Leaving reviews helps your fellow readers find the books they will love, and it helps indie writers like me continue to do the work they love.

If you want to stay in the loop for future books, you can find me on instagram @kverbruggen_writes.

Aknowledgements

To Adrienne, Ryan, Kinhly, and Lindsay: Thank you so much for being my the first readers of this story. Your support, insight, and encouragement mean more than you know.

To my family, thank you for your support over the years. You made this possible.

And especially to Esther, for being my writing buddy, accountability, constant source of encouragement, and my common sense: this book would not be what it is without you.

Soli Deo Gloria